ROCKY MOUNTAIN FUGITIVE

BY
ANN VOSS PETERSON

AND

RAWHIDE RANGER

BY
RITA HERRON

MILLS
BOON

ROCKY MOUNTAIN
FUGITIVE
BY
RITA HERRON

AND

RAWHIDE
RANGER
BY
RITA HERRON

ROCKY MOUNTAIN FUGITIVE

BY
ANN VOSS PETERSON

All the characters in this book have no existence outside the imagination of the author, and have no relation whatsoever to anyone bearing the same name or names. They are not even distantly inspired by any individual known or unknown to the author, and all the incidents are pure invention.

First published in Great Britain 2011
by Mills & Boon, an imprint of Harlequin (UK) Limited,
Eton House, 18-24 Paradise Road, Richmond, Surrey TW9 1SR

© Ann Voss Peterson 2010

ISBN: 978 0 263 88542 2

46-0811

Harlequin (UK) policy is to use papers that are natural, renewable and recyclable products and made from wood grown in sustainable forests. The logging and manufacturing processes conform to the legal environmental regulations of the country of origin.

Printed and bound in Spain
by Blackprint CPI, Barcelona

Ever since she was a little girl making her own books out of construction paper, **Ann Voss Peterson** wanted to write. So when it came time to choose a major at the University of Wisconsin, creative writing was her only choice. Of course, writing wasn't a *practical* choice—one needs to earn a living. So Ann found jobs ranging from proofreading legal transcripts, to working with quarter horses, to washing windows.

But no matter how she earned her paycheck, she continued to write the type of stories that captured her heart and imagination—romantic suspense. Ann lives near Madison, Wisconsin, with her husband, her two young sons, her border collie and her quarter horse mare. Ann loves to hear from readers. E-mail her at ann@annvosspeterson.com or visit her website at www.annvosspeterson.com.

To Michael Voss and Ty McBride. Thanks for
showing me a whole different side of Wyoming!

Chapter One

No one was supposed to be up this high in the mountains. Not in the first week of June, too early in the tourist season for most recreational climbers. Not with a cold wind ushering in dark clouds from the northwest.

Hands steady on the belaying rope, Eric Lander dared a glance away from his climbing partner, Randy Trask, ten feet below him, and focused beyond the lodgepole pine stabbing the open Wyoming sky. Sure enough, the stirring of movement he'd seen in his peripheral vision was accurate. Two men. Heading their way. At this point, they were not much bigger than dots against the sparse grass and sagebrush of the slope below. But he recognized the trademark brown coats of the county sheriff's department.

"Ready to climb," Randy called.

Eric bit back his nearly automatic response. He wasn't ready for Randy to start his climb. Not yet. There was something wrong here, something he could sense riding the wind as clear as the coming storm. And as a wilderness guide, he'd learned to listen to his instincts. "Friends of yours?"

Randy secured his hold, then squinted over the tops

of the trees. His eyes flared wide. The reaction took only a split second, like the shifting of light caused by cloud wisps blowing past the sun. But the tension riding on the air increased threefold.

In light of Randy's recent history, Eric could guess the reason. "Are you in some kind of trouble?"

"It's not like that."

"Then what is it like?"

"It's just something a guy told me about."

"Let me guess. Your cell mate?"

Randy glanced away and shifted his feet on the rock shelf.

Eric had taken Randy climbing before Eric's wilderness guide business started its season with the hope of helping his old friend start a new life. He should have known better. "Damn it, Randy. You promised your sister you'd stay clean." As angry as he was with Randy, he couldn't bring himself to say Sarah's name out loud. He couldn't afford to think too much about her, either.

"I haven't done anything."

"Then why are they here?"

"I'll tell you about it later. After we get to the top of this rock face. Ready to climb."

Eric glanced back to the men. They were closer now. And they were definitely sheriff's deputies. One pointed up at them. The other was carrying a rifle.

Eric shook his head. "I don't like the look of this. We'd better rappel down."

"I can't do that."

"Then I will. See what's going on."

"You can't, either. We need to get out of here. Now." Something trembled behind Randy's words.

Something that made the back of Eric's neck prickle. "What's going on, Randy? What have you gotten us into?"

Randy blew a stream of air through tight lips. "Listen, I'm sorry. I'm into a guy for a lot of money. I thought this might be my chance to wipe the slate clean."

"What are you talking about?"

"An opportunity."

"An opportunity that you heard about from your cell mate?"

"It sounded easy. I didn't believe Bracco when he said the sheriff would be watching me. That they'd know as soon as I made a move. It seemed like something from a movie. Or one of his paranoid delusions."

Eric shook his head. Delusions? Sounded like Randy was having some delusions of his own. If they were higher on the mountain, he might be able to pass the whole thing off as altitude sickness. Yet as much as Eric wanted to explain away the deputies' presence and his old friend's fear, he couldn't shrug off the pressure assaulting the back of his neck. He needed to get control of this situation. "Rappel down to the slope, and we'll circle through the crevasse." He had to be crazy, suggesting they run away from lawmen. But the deputies hadn't made contact yet. And he needed to buy some time, figure out what was going on. As soon as he could compile a few facts, he'd lead Randy into the sheriff's department himself.

"No. We need to keep going up to Saddle Horn Ridge."

"Why?"

"Bracco said there was something big at the campsite up there. I don't know what. I just wanted to check it out. An easy trip. Just in case he was telling the truth, you know?"

Because he owed someone money. No doubt resulting from the failure of some other "get rich quick and easy" arrangement like this one. "This isn't looking quite so easy."

"Like I said, I didn't believe his rambling about the sheriff making whoever knew about it into a marked man or whatever."

Marked man? Eric glanced down at the deputies. They were close to the rock face, now, nothing separating them but a couple of toothpick-straight pines and fifty feet of vertical rock. "So that's what this climb is about? We're on some sort of damned treasure hunt? A treasure hunt for something *obviously* illegal?"

"I guess."

I guess? As if he had no role in them being here? As if he hadn't begged Eric to guide him to the ridge? As if he hadn't lied? Again?

There were plenty of times Eric wanted to wring Randy's neck. So many that he'd learned to keep his distance from his old climbing buddy in the months leading up to his fraud arrest and subsequent stint in jail. But Randy had promised to turn over a new leaf, and Eric had wanted to believe him. For his friends' sake… and for Sarah's. "I can't believe you would—"

The crack of gunfire split the air.

Randy slammed into the rock as if shoved. His eyes widened, staring at Eric.

"Randy!"

"Get to the top." Randy flattened his body to the rock. A spot bloomed on his T-shirt, darker than the black cotton.

Eric didn't know what he was seeing, what he had seen. These were lawmen. They hadn't identified themselves. They hadn't said a single word. They'd just opened fire. This couldn't be happening. "Are you hit?" The words left his lips before he knew he'd spoken them. He didn't have to ask. He knew the answer.

Randy gritted his teeth. He leaned chest to rock, the fingers of one hand gripping a handhold, the other wrapped around his middle, as if trying to stop the spreading stain. "Get out of here. Go to the top. Find…"

Eric shook his head. He couldn't care less about some stolen money or drugs or whatever the hell was up there. He should have climbed down to the shelf Randy was on as soon as they saw the men. At least then he'd have a shot at reaching him, helping him. Now that Randy was hit, he didn't dare loose his grip on the belay. "Move toward me. Behind the trees." At least if Randy wasn't out in the open, the deputy wouldn't have such an easy shot. Maybe then Eric could get a hold of him, help him…where?

Down below, the deputy raised the rifle to his shoulder again.

"Randy! Move! Now!" Eric's voice rasped his throat. Begging. Pleading. Thinking of nothing but helping Randy, he surged forward, but his backline anchored him to the cliff. He couldn't breathe. His hands were sweaty, shaking. He took up all slack on the rope, resisting the urge to pull Randy to him. All that would do was knock him off balance, then they would really be in trouble. "Come on, man. You can do it. I got you on belay."

Randy shook his head and remained rooted to his spot. He made a noise deep in his throat, something between a growl and a sob. "Didn't mean for this… really, Eric…didn't believe…"

A second rifle shot shattered the air.

Randy's body jolted stiffly. He slung back in his climbing harness and sagged off the shelf's edge.

The rope yanked hard against the belay device. Eric locked it off and braced himself against the pull of his friend's weight. This couldn't be happening. "God, no. Randy."

His friend dangled ten feet below. His full weight bore down on the rope, the belaying device and Eric's break hand all that was between Randy and a fifty-foot fall onto scree at the bottom of the slope.

At least Randy was now behind the treetops. The deputy no longer had an open shot. Not that it mattered, if Randy was already dead.

Another crack split the air. Rock exploded. Something hit the crown of his head with the force of a hard kick.

He staggered, trying to lean toward rock and not plunge off the narrow shelf. His head whirled. His ears rang. Had he been hit?

He raised his hand to his head. Blood soaked his hair and dripped down his neck, hot and sticky. A scrape, not a hole. He'd only gotten nicked, probably by a chunk of rock. He'd survive.

Randy might not be so lucky.

He had to reach his friend. He had to get him out of here. Off the mountain, to town, to a hospital.

But how?

He would have to figure that out later. First he had to reach Randy. He tied off the belay rope and released his backline with shaking fingers.

In his peripheral vision, he saw the second deputy raise his pistol. If he stayed here another second, he'd be no help to Randy or himself. He'd be dead.

Praying his anchor in the rock would hold under

their weight, he grabbed the rope and stepped off the ledge.

The pistol cracked below.

Eric braced himself for the cut of the bullet. It missed, pinging off the rock face above. He lowered himself down the rope, palms sweaty on nylon.

When he reached Randy, he knew his friend was already dead. He could feel it, sense it. Securing a hold on the rock, he checked Randy's pulse to be sure. His skin was warm, but no throb beat against Eric's touch. He checked the other side of his throat, moving his fingers several times. Praying he'd detect something. Anything. But he felt nothing at all.

Shouts rose from the men below.

Eric's breath shuddered deep in his chest. He couldn't help Randy. Not anymore. Now he could only help himself. He had to think. He had to get out of here or he would share the same fate as his friend.

A marked man.

The words blared in the back of Eric's mind. By trying to find whatever it was up on Saddle Horn Ridge, had Randy marked himself for death? Had he marked everyone he was close to? Eric? Layton, the foreman at the ranch?

Sarah?

Eric scanned the rock face. He had to get out of here, like Randy said, but he wasn't climbing to Saddle Horn Ridge. He had to get to the ranch. He had to make sure Sarah was all right.

And he had to do it now.

Chapter Two

Sarah was leaning down from her gelding's back to lock the yearlings in the corral when Radar started barking. Straightening in the saddle, she focused on the SUV pulling up the long gravel drive. It swung past the house and headed for the barn, finally coming to a stop on the other side of the fence. A lone man dismounted from the vehicle and strode toward her.

The brim of his silver belly hat shaded his eyes, but Sarah had no trouble recognizing Sheriff Danny Gillette. The last time she'd seen him was months before, at her brother's trial. He was bald as a baby pig under that cowboy hat, and his voice held the growl of a man who'd smoked his way through life. She could still recite his brutal condemnation of her brother.

"That'll do, Radar," she called to the dog. He stopped barking, but remained alert, his white-tipped tail waving like a flag in the constant basin wind.

The sheriff rested one boot on the lower rail of the fence and skimmed his gaze over corral, barns and rough pastureland beyond. The place was quiet, vacant. Her foreman, Layton, and two ranch hands had taken a herd of steers to graze land she'd leased from the Bureau of

Land Management and wouldn't be back for hours. But as much as she wanted to tell herself the sheriff was here to talk to Keith or Glenn about a drunken brawl at the nearby Full Throttle saloon, she doubted that was the case.

Sarah let out a shaky breath and rolled her shoulders back, trying to loosen the cramp bearing down on the back of her neck. Not even twenty-four hours since Randy had gotten out of jail, and the sheriff was already paying a call. She sure as hell hoped he meant it only as a warning. Randy promised he'd stay clean if she let him stay at the ranch while he got his feet under him. He'd better have kept his word.

She resisted the urge to cup her hand over her middle. In her fourth month, she was just starting to show, but the urge to cover her belly every time she felt nervous or defensive had started before she'd even admitted to herself that she was pregnant. Somehow her body had known before her brain. She rubbed her palm on her thigh.

Better get this over with.

Bringing a leg to her gelding's side, she pushed him into a lope. When they reached the far side of the corral, she lifted her rein hand and brought her mount to a stop with just a touch of slide. "Can I help you, Sheriff?"

"Miss Trask," he said with a nod of his head. He pulled a package of smokes from his shirt pocket and tapped it on the heel of an upturned hand. "We need to have a little talk about your brother."

ERIC SPOTTED THE SHERIFF'S SUV as soon as he crested the hill. The half-dozen horses milling behind the corral fence kicked up dust, dulling the SUV's white gleam, but even though he was too far away to make out the sheriff department's emblem on the door, Eric knew who the vehicle belonged to.

It hadn't been easy making it down off the mountain while avoiding the armed deputies. Fortunately he knew the peaks in this area better than he knew his own heart. If he hadn't, he never would have been able to work his way into the crevasse to the north of the rock face where Randy died. He never would have been able to make his way down, past the slope where the deputies scoured the mountain through their rifle scopes. He wouldn't have been able to reach the guide cabin at the base of the mountain and retrieve his truck.

He had gotten away unseen, all right. But it had taken him too long.

He scanned the corrals and outbuildings. Sarah's pickup sat in front of the house. But other than the horses in the corral, he could see no movement. The Buckrail only employed a foreman and three hands, but every time Eric had visited, the place had been bustling. Now it looked vacant. The big stock trailer was nowhere to be seen.

Where was Sarah?

Eric forced back the urge to push the pedal to the floor and race down the remaining half mile to the ranch. Rushing in like some sort of damn knight would only get him killed, and probably Sarah, too. He had to be smart about his next move. He had to think.

He raised his hand to his throbbing head.

Pulling the truck off the dirt road, he bounced over rough ground to a rock outcropping. He parked out of sight on the far side.

He'd regretted not taking a weapon with him on the climb with Randy. He wouldn't make that mistake this time. He twisted in his seat.

The rack in the back window of the cab was empty, the locking mechanism broken. His hunting rifle was gone.

Damn, damn, damn. He hadn't thought to look when he'd reached his truck. He'd just wanted to get out of there as quickly as possible. But he had a good idea of who had taken it. The deputies who'd shot Randy. And he had a bad feeling his rifle was the weapon they'd used.

He gripped the wheel in front of him. He couldn't think about the implications of that. Not now. The only thing he could afford to focus on was Sarah. He had to make sure she was okay.

He climbed out of the truck, strode to the back and opened the tailgate. There had to be something inside he could use for a weapon. He focused on the tire iron clamped down under the spare. It would have to do.

He released the spare and grabbed the tire iron. Testing the heft in his hand, he circled the red rock and set off in a steady run. He'd approach the house and barns from an angle, instead of straight on. He didn't have much on his side. He needed surprise.

He set off for the house first. Tufts of rough grass and sagebrush dotted the rocky soil. Still, after the mountain terrain, the short trek was easy. He reached the back of the house without seeing a soul. He didn't have to peer in the darkened windows to know no one was there. No one seemed to be anywhere. Not even the bark of her Border collie, Radar, broke the stillness.

He needed to check the barn.

Negotiating the maze of wood rail fence, he crossed

corrals and circled loafing sheds until he reached the two-story barn. Flies buzzed in his ears. One landed on his forehead. He brushed it away, his hand coming back sticky with drying blood. At least the gush had slowed, but pain still throbbed through his skull.

Pushing the pain away, he wiped his hand on his jeans, climbed the fence and dropped into the corral closest to the barn.

There were few horses in the corrals, and most looked too young to work cattle. Three of the horses gathered around him, nickering and nudging him with their noses. Others pawed the ground and chased one another, jockeying for the best positions in front of the feeders.

The sun was already hovering just above the peaks to the west, its feeble glow quickly being overtaken by the leading edge of storm clouds. Sarah was adamant about her livestock being fed on time. She was never late.

Dust rose into the air thick as fog and whirled in the wind. In front of the barn door, Eric caught a glimpse of black-and-white fur.

Sarah's dog wouldn't be far from his mistress. She had to be in the barn. But the fact that Radar wasn't inside with her had him worried.

He raced across the corral, horses swirling around him. He couldn't afford to think too hard about what might have already happened to Sarah. He had to stay alert. He was used to testing himself against rock, snow and rough mountain terrain, not a living adversary. Certainly not armed lawmen. He needed to be ready.

Radar spun away from the door and stared at him, one ear pricked.

Eric froze. He knew the dog, but he hadn't been

around for months now. The last thing he needed was for Radar to start barking, tipping off whomever was inside.

Eric raised a hand. Tilting his palm downward, he lowered his hand, gesturing for the dog to lie down the way he'd seen Sarah do countless times.

Radar crouched to the ground. Still watching, he stayed silent.

Blowing a breath through tense lips, Eric scaled the final fence and crept to the barn. The center part of the structure rose to two stories. Each side only contained one, the roofs slanting over stall areas. He stepped to the center door. The deep hum of a male voice came from inside. An inch of space gaped between the sliding door's two halves. The barn was dark inside. If Eric stood directly in front of the door, or even peered inside, he would block the feeble light. From inside, his presence would be as obvious as if he'd rang a damn doorbell.

He tried to hear over the loud beat of his pulse.

"Where was he headed?"

Eric recognized the low, graveled voice of the sheriff himself.

"What was your brother looking for?"

"I don't know. He went climbing. That's all he told me."

A jumble of emotion spun through Eric's mind and settled like an ache in his chest. He'd tried to drive Sarah's strong contralto from his memory. He hadn't succeeded. But hearing it again, under these circumstances…it was all he could do to keep from throwing the barn door open and rushing in to protect her.

In light of the way things had ended between them, she'd probably find that ironic.

"Who has your brother talked to since he was released?"

"I don't know. No one, I guess. He's only got home last night. Did he do something? What is this about?"

"I'm not messing around here, Miss Trask. Eric Lander. You. Who else?"

"I want to talk to a lawyer. I have the right to see a lawyer."

"Listen," the sheriff said, his voice getting quiet, controlled in a way that made Eric's pulse spike. "You have the right to tell me what I want to know, or I'll have to assume you're in this as deep as your brother."

Eric stepped away from the door. He couldn't stand here and listen any longer. He'd been slow to act to help Randy. Slow to figure out what kind of danger the two of them were in. Slow to believe the deputies were not there to uphold the law. He wasn't going to make the same mistake again. He needed to find a way inside. He needed some kind of strategy. Some way to take control of the situation before the sheriff could draw his gun. Before he could hurt Sarah.

Think.

He knew the barn's layout. Hell, he'd helped Sarah feed enough times in their few months together that he should be able to move around the ranch in the dark.

Think.

He pictured the inside of the barn in his mind's eye. The place was small, only a half-dozen stalls, a wash stall and a good sized tack-and-feed room. Judging from the closeness of the sheriff's voice, he and Sarah were in the main barn area, not closed off in the tack room. That meant Eric should be able to see them from one of the windows above.

As long as he could get up on the roof without giving himself away.

He circled to the flank of the barn, climbing over fences and dodging demanding horses. Reaching a spot where the roof slanted low, in back of the barn, he focused on the windows used to let natural light into the structure and shoved the tire iron in the back waistband of his jeans. The metal was cold against his skin. Bracing. Its chill sharpened his focus and resolve. He eyed the wood siding. Freshly painted a rich brown, it held few spots to get finger holds, let alone a spot for a toe.

Good thing Eric didn't need much.

Fitting his fingers into the ridges between the planks, he pulled himself up the siding and grasped the edge of the roof. He pulled himself onto the shingles and scrambled up to the windows under the upper eaves. The windows were locked. Holding his breath, he jimmied the pane up and down and prayed the sheriff wouldn't hear. The lock popped open. He slid the glass wide and listened for movement from inside the barn.

Below in the corral, horses snorted and whinnied. A cloud of dust plumed on the crest of the hill. Another vehicle heading this way…another sheriff's department SUV.

A wave of dizziness swept over him. Clamping down on the inside of his lower lip, he concentrated on opening the door without losing his balance. He couldn't let himself think about all the things that could go wrong. If he wanted to get Sarah out of this mess, he had to focus.

He pushed his head through the open window and looked down into the barn aisle. The scent of wood shavings and manure stuck thick in his throat and tickled his nose.

"Horse accidents are funny things," the sheriff's voice

boomed from below. "They can happen at any time. To anyone. Even people who work with horses every day."

"I can't come up with answers I don't have."

Sarah's voice sounded forceful, but there was a sharp tinge to it Eric knew came from fear. He leaned farther into the barn to get a better angle.

The sheriff stood almost directly below. He reached up to a peg holding a collection of old horseshoes. He grasped one and shook it up and down as if testing its heft. "Something unexpected can happen, spook the horse, and…"

Sarah pressed against the wall of the wash stall. She was a slender woman, all sinew and muscle developed by back-breaking ranch work. But the woman he was looking at was softer than he remembered. More vulnerable. Her hands were behind her back, and when she moved, Eric could see a set of handcuffs bound her to a metal rail.

"No threat. I'm stating fact." Sheriff Gillette slapped the steel shoe against his palm.

Eric didn't know what he'd missed while climbing to the loft, but he sure as hell wasn't going to let this go any further. He pulled the tire iron from the back of his jeans.

The sheriff looked up. He reached for his gun.

Chapter Three

Sarah leaned back on the wash stall wall and lashed out with a foot. She connected with the sheriff's ankle, the force shuddering through her boot and up her leg.

A shot exploded in her ears.

A body landed on the sheriff, knocking him to the ground. A body…oh, God…Eric.

For a moment, she couldn't think. She couldn't breathe.

Eric shoved a forearm under the sheriff's jaw, bending his head back. He grabbed the sheriff's gun hand and slammed it against the floor. The gun skittered across the ground. He picked it up, and held it on the sheriff. The side of his face was covered with dried blood. "Get up."

Sarah's legs wobbled, weak with relief.

The sheriff struggled to a sitting position, holding his hand to the side of his head. His hat lay in the dust several feet away. "You don't want to do this, son."

"No. You're right. I want to just kill you and take the handcuff key off your dead body. Unless that's what you want, too, you'd better get the hell up."

The sheriff struggled to his feet. "What you're doing here is against the law."

"Oh, you mean like gunning down a man in cold blood? Or preparing to beat on a shackled woman with a damn horseshoe? Those kinds of against the law?"

The sheriff squinted. "You're Lander."

"Keys," Eric ordered.

Gillette pulled a key ring from his pocket, and Eric snatched it from his fingers.

Eric unlocked one of Sarah's wrists and handed her the keys. Once she freed herself, he motioned to the sheriff. She slipped the shackles around one fat wrist and slipped the cuff around the steel bars of a nearby stall before securing his second.

She rubbed her sore arms. She couldn't make sense of any of this. First the sheriff. Now Eric's sudden appearance. He was supposed to be climbing with Randy.

Barking erupted outside.

Sarah's mind raced. Someone was here. Layton? Keith and Glenn?

The sheriff glanced over his shoulder and smirked. "Looks like my backup is here. Sure you don't want to rethink this?"

"Backup?"

"That's right. You might as well give yourselves up right now. It'll go easier on you."

Ignoring Gillette, Eric grabbed her arm. "Hurry." He pulled her toward the barn's back door, and they slipped into the corral. Yearlings gathered around them, looking for dinner. Something raced around the side of the barn, a black-and-white streak.

"Radar."

He headed straight for her. Flying through the air the last few feet, he bounced off her thigh with his front paws and started back the other way, as if he was playing a game.

He was telling her something, that someone was here. "Radar." The dog's head snapped around at her serious tone. He bounced back to her side.

Eric pulled her through the gathering horses. "We have to get out of here."

"What is happening? Where is—"

"We'll talk later."

Men's voices rose from the front of the barn.

"Who's here?"

"Deputies. And they aren't here to help."

He wasn't making sense. None of this was making any sense. She bit back the questions crowding at the tip of her tongue. "Where do we go?"

"My truck is up by the rocks, but I don't think we can get there. Not without being spotted." He spun back to the corral. "Are any of these horses broke to ride?"

She scanned the group of yearlings, stopping on the only older mare in the bunch. "She is." She led Eric to the mare, Radar following at their heels.

Grabbing a handful of mane, she raised a foot. Eric grabbed her lower leg and boosted her onto the mare's back. He swung open the gate leading to the pasture.

"Stop. They're back here."

Sarah's throat closed. At first she almost did as he said. Almost dismounted right there and gave herself up. He was a deputy, wasn't he? She was no criminal. He had to be there to help, didn't he?

Unlike the sheriff?

She didn't have to think too hard to remember the threat in the sheriff's eyes, the brutal tone in his voice, the way he lifted the horseshoe implying he'd use it on her.

"Sarah." Eric held up an arm, about to swing his leg up.

She looked down at him. Eric was no criminal, either.

She was more sure of that than anything. They had to get out of here. She grabbed his arm, and he vaulted into place behind her. She laid her heel into the mare's side and they broke into a full bore gallop.

THEY'D RACED ALL THE way to the creek before Eric dared take a breath. The mare slowed as she approached the water, breaking to a jog before splashing into the shallow current. Sarah's dog plunged in behind.

"Follow the river bed," Eric said.

Sarah directed the horse upstream. Her dark hair whipped in the wind, lashing against his face. "You think they'll track us?"

"Can't be too careful." He was still shaken from the moment he looked down the barrel of the sheriff's gun, the split second before Sarah's kick made his shot go wide. "You saved my life back there."

"I have a feeling you might have saved mine, too." She turned her head to the side, letting her words drift back to him more easily. From this angle he could see the sweep of her eyelashes and the curve of her cheek through her dark cascade of hair. "Are you going to tell me what's going on?"

"I'd like to, but I don't really know myself."

"Where's Randy?"

He swallowed into a dry throat. He didn't have the words to tell her. And neither of them had the time. "We need to get moving. I'll explain things once we put more distance behind us."

"Where are we going?"

Now that was a damn good question. Obviously they couldn't call 911. "Our best bet is to get ourselves across the county line. Get out of Gillette's jurisdiction."

"This is ridiculous. All of this. This is a nightmare. There must be some kind of mistake."

"That's what I've been telling myself. Only problem is, the nightmare just keeps going, whether we take control or not. I've opted to take control."

Her chest rose and fell in a deep breath. Finally she nodded. "So we head for the county line."

The Big Horn Basin was a huge plain rimmed with mountains on all sides. County lines fell along mountain ranges and across open territory. He eyed the mountains to the west. "How long will it take if we go to the east?

"Maybe a couple of days by horse."

That sounded about right. And with a storm hovering over the mountains bringing rain and maybe even snow, it would take longer if they chose to go to the west. "Any better ideas?"

"Layton lives closer."

The thought of pulling someone else into this web Randy had tangled them in made Eric feel sick to his stomach. "I don't know…"

"He's been the Buckrail's foreman since before my parents left. He was more of a father to me than my own dad. We can trust him."

"That's not my worry."

"What is?"

He tried to swallow, but his throat wouldn't cooperate. He didn't even have to close his eyes to see the way Randy jolted when he took the first bullet. No warning. No way out.

"Eric? I need to know what's going on, and I need to know now."

He shook his head. Not now. Not until he could look

her straight in the eye. Not until she had time to let the tragic news sink in. Not until she had time to cry.

A sound tickled the horizon, rising over the splash and babble of the stream. Radar froze and pricked his ears.

"Stop the horse."

"Whoa." Sarah shifted back, her hips settling against Eric's thighs. The mare stopped in the stream and lowered her head for a drink.

A growl vibrated low in Radar's chest.

Eric strained to hear over the babbling water. It took a second for the sound to register, but once it did, he knew the danger was far from over and their escape far from assured. "Bloodhounds."

Sarah tilted her head. "You're sure?"

"I wish I could say no. How the hell did they get them to the ranch so quickly?"

"What do we do?"

"Keep moving upstream, for one."

Sarah clucked, and the mare lifted her head. She broke into a trot, water splashing around them.

Eric held on to Sarah, a hand on either side of her waist. He didn't know much about scent-tracking dogs, but he'd heard they could do remarkable things. He was far from sure that a trot upstream would keep the animals from picking up their trail on the other side of the water. Not unless there was something else to draw their attention.

They continued for another mile, maybe two. The barking grew louder, clearer. One dog. Probably no more. The sound drew out into a half bark, half howl.

The animal had picked up a scent.

Sarah turned her head to the side. "Eric?"

Even though he couldn't see her expression, he could

feel the alarm in her muscles, hear it in her voice. Not that he didn't have enough of his own. "We need to give the dog something else to track."

"Something else? What?"

"Will Radar go back to the ranch if you order him to?" He wasn't sure the dog would follow Radar instead of them, but it might be worth a shot.

She glanced down at the black-and-white Border collie prancing in the stream as if thrilled to be on this grand adventure. "I doubt it. He's never good about leaving me. He'd probably just double back as soon as he got out of my sight."

One idea down. He only had one more. And it wasn't his first choice by a long shot. "How far to Layton's house?"

She glanced around as if taking stock of the landscape. Though with few discernable features nearby other than hills and sagebrush, he wasn't sure what she was seeing. "Seven miles. Maybe eight."

He nodded. Not bad for country where it often took a half hour or more of driving through uninhabited wilderness to get anywhere.

"He should be home by the time we get there."

Better if he wasn't. That way they could use his phone, borrow supplies or even a vehicle from him and yet manage not to drag him into this mess. "Do you think we can make it that far on foot?"

"Not before nightfall."

He glanced at the last glow of sun beyond the shadow of distant mountains. In this case, darkness would help them. With cloud cover and no sunlight, they might not be able to move very quickly, but neither would their pursuers.

"I can find the way after dark."

Of course she could. She had grown up on this land, and worked it every day of her life. She knew it better than he knew anything, even the mountains. "What do you think of sending the mare back to the ranch?"

"You're thinking the tracking dog will keep following her and not us?"

"Something like that."

"She's getting tired anyway. She'll probably be glad to be rid of us. And she'll be glad to be back at the barn before nightfall."

At least they had a plan, although the thought of being out in the middle of this vast open country on foot made him more than uneasy. He was used to the vertical wilderness. All this horizontal space made him feel small. And vulnerable.

He slipped off the horse's back. The water came to his knees, gurgling and swirling, cold as death. His hiking boots filled with water. His legs ached to the bone. He helped Sarah dismount.

"Okay, girl. Go back home." She smacked the horse on the rear and the mare trotted through the stream and up the bank. Once she hit dry land, she broke into a gallop and disappeared in the direction of the barn.

Sarah turned back to face Eric. Tears sparkled in her eyes and spiked her lashes, but her cheeks remained dry, as if she was fighting for composure. "I need to know what happened, Eric."

"We need to make some time. My legs are already going numb."

She started trudging upstream. "He was supposed to be climbing with you."

He opened his mouth, then closed it. Emotion bombarded him. How on earth could he find the words?

She didn't look at him. Instead she wrapped both arms around her stomach and kept moving forward. "Please. I need to know."

"He didn't mean for anything to happen. He just…" A sob lodged in Eric's throat. He pushed it back, but if he opened his mouth again, he knew he wouldn't be able to keep the emotion in check. He could feel Sarah watching him.

"Randy's dead, isn't he?"

Somehow Eric managed to nod.

"How?" Her voice was quiet, barely a whisper, as if it had taken every ounce of strength in her to say the word.

Eric fixed his gaze on a clump of big sage about ten feet away from the creek's bank. As long as he focused on that clump and on trudging forward in the cold water, he might be able to get the words out. "He was shot in order to keep him from reaching Saddle Horn Ridge."

"By the sheriff?"

"By two deputies."

He could hear Sarah gasping for breath. She was crying. He could feel her sobs in his own chest, taking over. He could almost smell her tears. He wanted to say soothing words. To touch her. To take her in his arms. Something. But he doubted his touch would be welcome. Besides, one move toward her and he feared he'd crumble.

They kept walking. Finally she swiped at her eyes and cheeks. "Why?"

"I'm not sure."

"What do you *think* was the reason? Take a flying guess." The pitch of her voice rose. The mix of anger and fear and need ate away at him like acid.

He pulled a breath into tight lungs. He had to find a way to explain it. At least the small part he knew. He owed her that much.

Still careful not to look at her, he told her about the cell mate named Bracco. The mystery Randy was searching for at the top of Saddle Horn Ridge.

"What's up there?"

"Randy didn't know."

"But no doubt he thought it would be an easy score."

"He owes someone money."

Sarah nodded as if that was all he needed to say.

Worry over Randy had been what drew him and Sarah together in the first place. After her brother's fraud conviction, she'd needed to talk to someone who knew him, someone who cared. As an old climbing buddy who'd spent more than a few worried thoughts on Randy Trask, Eric had fit the bill. As they'd spent time together, it had ceased being about Randy. It had been strong and passionate and all-consuming. And finally it had grown to the point where it had ceased being possible. At least for Eric.

Eric shook his head. It had taken Randy's death to throw them back together again. Even worse, Randy's newest scheme had almost gotten them both killed.

And it was far from over.

He stared out at the twilight glow on the horizon and kept plunging on. He couldn't think about Randy. He couldn't think about what he and Sarah had almost had. Not now. Now he needed all his concentration. He had to focus on one thing—getting Sarah to her foreman's house, where they could call for help. Because if he couldn't do that, none of the rest mattered.

They trudged through the stream bed, water splashing to their knees, rocks slippery under their feet. Radar followed behind. The baying stopped. Shadows lengthened and darkness crept over the land. Finally Eric dared to step out on dry land. He reached out a hand to help Sarah over the rocks and tangle of vegetation.

She didn't accept his offer. Once on solid ground, she faced him. "Eric."

He willed himself to look at her. Pink rimmed her eyes. Dust and tears streaked her face. But the way she raised her chin and met his gaze made him dread what was coming next. "What?"

"I want to hire you."

He frowned. Not what he expected. Not at all. "Hire me?"

"I'm going up to Saddle Horn Ridge, and I want you to be my guide."

Chapter Four

For a moment, Eric looked like he was about to clap a hand over Sarah's mouth and demand she take back what she'd said. "Weren't you listening?"

She'd listened. And what she'd heard had her trembling more violently than she had after escaping Sheriff Gillette. But feeling shaken and scared didn't change the facts. And fear didn't erase what she needed to do. "I'm going up to Saddle Horn Ridge. I'm going to find out what this is all about."

He turned away from her and trudged over the rocky shore and through Russian olive, grass and sagebrush, grown large and thick from the nearby water source.

Sarah set off after him. Radar trotted beside, glancing from her to Eric like a child caught in the middle of his parents' argument.

Parents.

Sarah fought the urge to clutch an arm over her abdomen. She couldn't think of that right now. She had enough to deal with in the present. Enough to absorb. Right now all she could focus on was what had happened to Randy and how she and Eric could escape the same fate.

"I've climbed before. I'm in shape." She resisted the urge to look down at the slight bulge in her belly. If this had happened a month ago, she didn't know where she would have gotten the energy. The fatigue of early pregnancy had come as a shock. While she'd been ready for the nausea, that bone-deep weariness had nearly flattened her. But her stamina had started to return in the past two weeks. And although she felt drained from the ebb of adrenaline after their escape from the sheriff, she was infinitely more capable than she had been in the first three months of her pregnancy. "I do physical work every day. A little hiking and climbing isn't going to kill me."

"Hiking and climbing? I'm more concerned about flying bullets."

"The bullets are just as likely to fly if we run away as they are if we try to find out what's going on."

He looked to the side, as if absorbed in contemplating a tangle of sagebrush.

"There's something up there, Eric."

"Of course there's something. Something that got your brother killed. Something that could get you killed, too."

"Whatever it is, the sheriff already thinks I know about it. And you…you were there when Randy…" Her throat felt thick. She swallowed and blinked back the mist assaulting her eyes. Her lower lids ached, swollen from squeezing out a seemingly endless flood of tears. She still couldn't believe this was happening. That it had happened. That they were on the run from a sheriff who wanted to harm them. That her big brother had gone out on a hiking trip and now he was dead. "They know you saw everything."

"Which is why I'm not taking you to the ridge. It's too dangerous."

"But if we could find what this is all about, maybe we could use it."

"Use it for what?"

"I don't know." Right now what she wanted most was to have Randy back. And no matter what they found on that ridge, that would never be. "To stop the sheriff. To let us return to our lives."

"To make Randy's killers pay?"

"What's wrong with that?"

"Nothing. It's what I want, too. But rushing into the same situation that got your brother killed is not the way to do it."

"Then what is?"

"Getting to Layton's house. Calling for help."

"Who do we call? Not the county 911."

"There are other law enforcement agencies. We call one of them. State police. Even the FBI."

"And what if they don't believe us? We can't run for the rest of our lives."

"It's better than not having a rest of our lives."

She shook her head. She wasn't sure of that. Ranching was the only life she'd ever wanted. The open sky. The freedom she felt on the back of a horse. The strength that came with hard work and autonomy and knowing the land. She didn't even want to think of a life on the run.

And Eric. He liked to control things, be in charge. He would gladly be responsible for the world, as long as he had a say. Being on the run, always reacting, never in control…it would kill him. He would never choose that, not if he were choosing for himself. "If you were in this alone, you'd go up on that ridge. You'd find out what this is about."

He slowed his stride and glanced back at her. For the first time since she'd brought up the idea of going to the ridge, the hard line of his mouth softened. "But I'm not in this alone." His voice sounded soft, too. Tender.

She pulled her gaze away and stared out at the dark forms of rock and sagebrush, growing more sparse the farther they traveled from water. She wanted to turn back time. Go back before Randy was killed, before he'd decided to take his damn hiking trip. Before everything had gotten so terribly broken.

She knew she was being ridiculous, but she couldn't help it. Just as she couldn't stop the yearning to give in to the softness in Eric's voice. To open herself to him. To pretend trusting him to be there for her was a luxury she could afford.

She watched him out of the corner of her eye. Even in the dimming twilight, she could see the taut muscles along his jaw, the light stubble, just a shade darker than his sandy brown hair. He still looked like the same Eric, so much that even now she wanted to reach out and skim her fingers along his cheek.

She'd wondered if Eric had noticed the change in her body as they galloped bareback away from the ranch, his hands around her waist. At one time his heat pressed against her back would have reduced her to a puddle of need. This time, all she could think about was whether he felt the bulge in her tummy. The solid life growing there.

Did he suspect?

If things were different, she would have been thrilled to tell him. If they were still together. If he hadn't left.

She could still kick herself. The moment she'd uttered the damn *M* word, she'd wished she could bite it back. It had been a generic reference. Nothing about the two of them getting married. Just a fantasy of a wedding in the little basin behind the ranch house she'd had as a starry-eyed teen. But as soon as the comment had left her lips, she'd seen the look on his face.

She'd gotten too comfortable. Too trusting. She'd forgotten to be careful and had just said what was on her mind. At least he'd waited until the next day to break it off.

Radar looked up at her, searching for a way to help. Her dog would stick with her no matter what. Do what she wanted. Follow her anywhere. Men weren't quite that easy.

She swallowed into an aching throat. That was all in the past. Dead and done. But focusing on the mistakes she'd made with Eric was easier than thinking too hard about what had happened to Randy or what the future might bring. "If you don't want to guide me up there, Eric, I can always go alone."

He wiped a hand over his face. "You could, but you won't. We'll call the state police, the attorney general, the FBI. Report all that's happened. They can take care of whatever is on that ridge *and* the sheriff at the same time."

Sarah pressed her lips together, her steps slowing, stopping. Fatigue bore down on her shoulders and made her legs heavy. A moment ago, she thought she had the energy to take on anything. Gillette. Eric. The climb to Saddle Horn Ridge. Now she wasn't so sure.

She cupped her hand over her abdomen. She had to think for more than herself. Her life wasn't the only one she was risking. And as much as she wanted to tell Eric he was wrong about what she would or wouldn't do, if there was a safer way out, she needed to take it. "Fine. We'll call."

"It's the right decision, Sarah." Eric glanced down at her arm. His brows dipped in a frown.

She let her arm fall to her side and resumed walking. Feeling him watching her, she could only hope he was trying to figure out her change of heart and not mulling over what her protective gesture might mean.

ERIC DIDN'T HAVE TO ask if Sarah had been serious about climbing to Saddle Horn Ridge on her own. He recognized that jut of her chin, those thrown-back shoulders, that look in her eye as if she was daring anyone to get in her way. She'd do it. And he couldn't have stopped her if she hadn't changed her mind. He was both relieved and surprised she'd seen things his way.

And a little suspicious.

They trudged toward the light that marked Layton's place twinkling in the distance. The silvery sheen of sagebrush dotted the path in front of them like bumpers in an old barroom pinball game. Eric could sense wildlife around him, and prayed one of them didn't step on a rattler yet to descend into his hole for the night. He watched Radar for warning of anything his own senses didn't pick up.

But mostly he stole glances at Sarah.

He'd thought she looked different the moment he saw her in the barn. Softer. More curvy. Even now he wanted to reach out and touch her, pull her into his arms.

He shook his head. As attractive as he found her, he'd made his decision three months ago. And he knew not letting the connection between them get out of hand was the right one, even now. Sarah couldn't be part of his life, and he certainly wasn't up to being part of hers. The emotions tangling inside him were proof of that. It seemed every moment around her was a struggle to keep his head on straight. The scent of her skin. The sound of her voice. The way she made him feel alive just by glancing his way.

He brought his focus back to the mountains. This was going to be tougher than he'd thought. Not that he'd ever imagined being around Sarah and not touching her would be easy. That was precisely why he'd left after dating for only five months. If he didn't get out then, he wasn't getting out.

And he was worried about the consequences for both of them.

The wind picked up from the west and carried rain with it. The downpour was hard and short-lived, like most in the area. They kept walking through it following the light they could no longer see. By the time the storm blew over, they were soaked to the skin. The strong scent of wet sage permeated the night air.

Sarah walked with both arms wrapped tightly around her body. Her hair curled, cupping wet around cheekbones, jaw and collarbone. Her chin trembled with an endless shiver.

"You okay?" He wished he had a jacket to put around her shoulders. As it was, he was starting to shiver, too.

"Fine."

He doubted that. But at least he could get her to Layton's. The foreman would take care of her. Get her clothes dry. Lend them a phone. It would all be over soon.

Layton's place was less than impressive. A small trailer nestled at the foot of a flat-topped hill referred to as a bench. At least the bench offered some shelter from the wicked basin winds. To the rear of the trailer sat a nice-sized horse barn flanked on one side by a corral fenced in lodgepole pine rails. As far as Eric knew, Layton's horses were kept at the Buckrail. But all horse people he'd ever met invested far more in their horse operation than their own homes. Layton Adams seemed to fit that mold to a *T.*

"Looks like no one's home."

Earlier he'd been surprised Layton wasn't at the ranch. If the foreman and the other hands had been, the sheriff would never have been able to nearly get away with hurting Sarah. "Where is he?"

"He and the other hands took a herd of steers to the BLM. I knew they'd be late getting back, but he should have been home by now."

Eric nodded. The BLM was a shorthand way of describing the vast amount of acreage in Wyoming controlled by the federal government's Bureau of Land Management. Sarah must have leased some of the land to graze her cattle. "Maybe he got detained."

Sarah snapped around to stare at him. "You think the sheriff might do something to Layton?"

"I'm sure he's okay." Truth was, he didn't know. And judging from the way Sarah looked at him, she took his assurances for what they were worth. Not much.

He gestured to the trailer. "Is there any way we can get in? Use his phone?"

"I don't have a key, if that's what you mean. And I doubt he would stash one outside. Not after what happened to his daughter. He's been pretty paranoid about things like locking doors ever since."

"His daughter?" As long as Eric had known Layton, he was a man alone. No wife. No family. He lived for his work and the only emotional attachment he seemed to have to anyone was his devotion to Sarah. "I didn't know Layton had a family."

"His daughter was murdered."

"Murdered?"

"It happened years ago. Layton's daughter was shot at a friend's slumber party. An ex-boyfriend of one of the girls. It was the stuff of legends at my school. Only difference was, I knew one of the families."

"Man. That had to be tough."

"He and his wife split a few months later. That's when he came to work at the Buckrail."

Eric wiped a hand over his face. It explained a lot about Layton. The man had no sense of humor and little personality. Life had obviously kicked it out of him.

But as bad as he felt for the Buckrail's foreman, all the sympathy in the world didn't earn them the use of a phone. "Is there some other way in?"

"You mean break in?"

"You got a better idea?"

Sarah frowned at the tiny trailer. "If you lift me up to a window, maybe I can jimmy the lock."

They wound through Layton's sorry excuse for a lawn, shadows making the sage look as big as hedges. When they reached the trailer, Eric clasped his hands and lowered them, ready to boost Sarah up to the window like he'd boosted her onto the bay mare's back.

A click and scrape came from somewhere behind his head. The sound of a rifle chambering a round. "What the hell do you think you're doing?"

Chapter Five

"Layton." Sarah turned and wobbled on one foot, her other cradled in Eric's hands. "It's okay, Layton. It's me."

She could barely see her foreman's frown in the darkness. He held a long gun at the ready, its barrel pointing square in the center of Eric's back. At her feet, Radar scooted in close, trying to catch Layton's attention. His wagging tail wiggled his whole body.

"Sarah." Layton glanced at her but didn't lower the weapon. "Thank God you're okay."

"I'm glad you're here. Some bad things are happening. We need to use your phone."

Layton's bushy gray brows dipped. His narrowed eyes drilled into Eric's back. "Bad things. Yeah, I heard."

Eric released her foot. He started to straighten.

"Don't move, son."

Sarah stepped toward him. "Layton—"

"Careful, Sarah. I don't think you know what this man here has done."

"Done?" She scrambled to make sense of what he was saying. Eric had done nothing…unless Layton was talking about how he'd ambushed the sheriff to save her. "Did you see Sheriff Gillette at the Buckrail?"

"'Course I did. Had to put up the horses and park the rig, didn't I?"

"I don't know what he told you, but…"

"He told me all I needed to hear. The law is looking for this man."

Eric raised his hands to the level of his ears and stood straight. "Maybe I can—"

"You shut your mouth, boy."

Sarah gasped. For a moment, she thought Layton was going to pull the trigger. She held her breath.

"I ain't listening to anything you have to say, after what you did. You move again, and you won't be alive to say another word."

Sarah tried to angle her body between Layton and Eric. She had to convince her foreman to lower the rifle. She had to make him understand. "Eric only did what he did to save me."

Layton stared at her, brows arched. "Did what he did? For you? I don't think you know what's gone down today, Sarah."

"The sheriff. He was asking me questions. He threatened me. He was going to hurt me, Layton. Eric stopped him."

He shook his head. "What I'm talking about don't have much to do with the sheriff. It's Randy, Sarah. He's dead."

Even though Sarah had spent the last hours dwelling on her brother's loss, hearing Layton say the words out loud jolted through her as if she was experiencing them for the first time. She swallowed and willed herself not to begin crying anew. "I know."

"There's more. More that you don't know."

Her head felt light, like it was spinning. She needed

to ask, to find out what else had happened. But she couldn't manage to squeeze the words past her lips.

"It's him, Sarah." Layton tipped the brim of his Stetson at Eric. "He's the one who did it. He killed your brother in cold blood."

"No. No. Listen, Layton—"

"I'll listen. Long as you need me to. First I got to call the sheriff."

"No, please. Wait. Just for a second. You don't understand."

"I think I'm understanding everything just fine. He's wanted for murder. Your brother's murder. There's a statewide manhunt."

A manhunt. For a fugitive. Sarah felt dizzy. So much for convincing other law enforcement agencies to help. The sheriff had beaten them to it. But maybe she could convince Layton to at least give Eric a chance to get away while he could. "Please, Layton. For me."

Layton paused. His breath fogged the air before dissipating into the night.

"Talk to me. Inside. Alone." She glanced at Eric. She could tell by his wary expression, he was worried about letting her out of his sight. Despite herself, a warm flutter centered in her chest. She pulled in a sharp breath of cold night air. "It will just take a minute. Then you can do what you need to do."

Layton focused on Eric and frowned. "He's not going anywhere."

"He won't." She exchanged looks with Eric, willing him to see she was giving him a chance to flee.

Layton shook his head slowly. "I ain't taking the chance that he'll run off." He motioned for Eric to walk toward the trailer door with a wave of his rifle.

"What are you going to do?"

He eyed a lariat that was laying on the steps leading to the door, as if he'd dropped it when he'd seen them approaching his home. "I'm going to make sure he doesn't sneak away before our talk is over."

"This isn't necessary, Layton. I'm not going to run off and leave Sarah here."

She tried not to think about how he'd done exactly that just three months ago, but some bitter remnant inside her couldn't help taking note. It figured that when his leaving finally made sense, Eric resisted the urge. "Please, Layton. He won't leave."

Layton dropped his gaze to the ground. "Take off your boots. Socks, too."

Eric glanced at Sarah, then knelt and did as Layton ordered. He tucked the socks into his boots and stood barefoot on the rocky ground.

"Bring those along, will you, Sarah?" Layton asked, his stare not wavering from Eric. "I'll be keeping an eye on you, Lander. You wander out of the light here, and you're game during hunting season, as far as I'm concerned. Understand?"

"Understand." Eric met Sarah's eyes and he mouthed, *Be careful.*

Sarah focused on Layton. She'd known him most of her life. Layton was like a second father to her. No, more than that. He was far more attentive and caring than her own father had ever been. Layton wouldn't hurt her. He wouldn't turn her over to the sheriff. He couldn't.

Unease fluttered over her skin like the cold wind. She followed him into the trailer, carrying Eric's hiking boots in her hand. Once the screen door slammed behind her, she set the boots on the floor and faced Layton.

The foreman closed the solid door and stepped to the living room window. Watching Eric outside, he lowered the rifle, pointing the barrel at the floor, and slipped his finger out of the trigger guard. "That man killed your brother, Sarah."

"That's what the sheriff told you?"

"Not just him. It's been all over the news. Like I said, there's a statewide manhunt. We have to call the sheriff. Report that he's here."

"Eric didn't kill Randy."

"I figured you'd say that."

"He didn't."

"Were you there?"

"No."

He let out a breath. "Then you don't really know what happened."

"Neither do you."

"The sheriff does. They have forensics people. They found his hunting rifle."

"Eric's?"

"That's what Sheriff Gillette said. They think it's the murder weapon, Sarah."

"No. It can't be. Or at least Eric wasn't the one who fired it."

"They found his truck at the ranch. Towed it away for testing. It had blood in it."

"His head was bleeding. Eric didn't kill Randy." Sarah had to find a way to make Layton listen. He didn't understand. How could he? He hadn't seen the sheriff's desperation when he didn't get the answers he expected. He didn't know what the man was willing to do to her.

What he'd almost done. "It's the sheriff, Layton. Two of his deputies shot Randy. The sheriff himself threatened to hit me."

Layton focused his full attention on her. "He...what did he do?"

"He handcuffed me and asked me questions about Randy. Where he was going. What I knew." She held up her hands to show him the bruises on her wrists, starting to purple.

"And what did you tell him?"

"That I didn't know anything. I mean, I knew he was climbing with Eric. That's all he told me. But Sheriff Gillette didn't believe me."

"Did he hurt you?"

"No. No. Eric got there first. But if he hadn't jumped Gillette, I don't know what would have happened."

Layton stared out the window. Although he focused on Eric, who was standing unmoving within the circle of light glowing from above the door, his thoughts seemed far away.

Maybe she was reaching him. "If Eric's rifle was used to shoot Randy, then someone else was firing it. One of the deputies."

Layton rubbed his chin between fingers and thumb. "You really believe him?"

"I do."

"You believed him last winter."

Sarah's cheeks heated. She'd thought she'd found something with Eric. Something that would grow. Something that would last. She had been wrong. Although she'd never told Layton exactly how she felt about Eric, it didn't surprise her that he knew. He had to have seen it, in her happiness when she and Eric were together and in her devastation after Eric had broken it off. "I know I was wrong then. But I'm not wrong now. Eric is not a murderer."

"If he's as innocent as you say, he should turn himself in."

She didn't want to argue with him. Not when she knew she couldn't win. Layton trusted the law. The system had delivered justice when his daughter was killed all those years ago. It was no surprise he wanted to trust it now. "That's up to Eric."

He shook his head. "Maybe so. But if you're with him, you're in danger. The sheriff will think you're part of Lander's plan. That you're working with him or something."

"I am working with him. I'm working to find the truth."

"I don't want you hurt, Sarah. You're my family… like my own daughter."

An ache hollowed out at the base of her throat. It was true. Since Layton had lost his daughter, he'd adopted Sarah in every way that mattered. He'd watched over her, cared for her, been there for her, while her parents were too wound up in their war with one another to give much thought to their children. Sometimes she couldn't help but feeling that Layton's attention had saved her from following Randy's self-destructive path. "I know. I feel the same way about you."

"Then do as I say. Let the sheriff take Lander. Let the law sort things out. You can stay here with me. I'll protect you."

That had always been the bottom line for Layton. Protecting her. But he hadn't seen the sheriff's face, his desperation, his refusal to let anything stand in his way.

Layton was a good man, but he didn't have any special kind of pull in the county. As the owner of a decent-sized cattle operation, she had more political muscle than he did. If the sheriff continued to come after her, as he'd already started, a man like Layton couldn't stop him, no matter what the foreman wanted to believe.

And she didn't believe for one second that the law would sort anything out. The sheriff couldn't have Eric and her testifying in court. He would never let things go that far. "I can't do that, Layton. I can't sit by and let you turn Eric over to the sheriff."

The older man looked at her. His fence-straight frame seemed to droop in front of her eyes. "Don't throw your life away on someone like him."

"The sheriff is framing Eric, Layton. He might even have him killed. Just like he and his men killed Randy."

The foreman shook his head. "I know you loved your brother, but he chose the type of life he wanted. He hung out with a rough crowd. Scum. Keith and Glenn saw his truck down to the Full Throttle the very afternoon he got out of jail. You hang out with people like that, you become one of 'em, Sarah. Any one of those friends of Randy's might have killed him at any time."

She could feel the tears again, that pressure, that sting. He wasn't listening. "But Eric saw—"

"That's just it. Eric saw. You don't know what reasons he might have to lie. The sheriff and deputies shooting people down? That's pretty hard to believe."

"You didn't see the sheriff the way I did. He's convinced I know whatever it is Randy was looking for. He's not just going to let me walk away, even if I am not with Eric."

"Do you know what he's looking for?"

"No. And neither does Eric."

Layton looked down at the floor. He stroked the stock of his rifle with his thumb.

Did he believe her? She'd like to think so, but she couldn't tell. "We need to find out what's going on. We need to learn the truth."

"Seems like the truth is staring you in the face, but you don't want to see it."

She was sure it did seem that way to him. She shook her head.

"You stay with him and you're putting yourself in danger, Sarah."

"I might be in danger, but it's not coming from Eric."

"You're sure of that?"

"I'm sure."

Her stomach tightened, making her feel sick. She had to think of something to convince him. Her and the ranch were all Layton really cared about. Maybe that was the key. "I'll make you a deal."

He tilted his head and looked at her out of the corner of his eye.

"If you don't call the sheriff, if you forget Eric was here, I'll stay here with you."

"You're asking a lot, Sarah."

"Please, Layton. The sheriff is corrupt. I'm afraid if he catches Eric, he'll kill him."

He shook his head. "Sheriff Gillette believes in justice. He's a lawman to his bones."

Despite his obvious doubts, Layton would never believe the sheriff was a murderer. He had no reason to distrust the law and every reason to distrust Eric. She doubted anything she said could make him change his mind. But maybe she didn't have to. "All he needs is time to find out what's going on. Time to discover why Randy died. Listen to me. Please, Layton."

He stared over the top of her head and out the window. Finally he gave a hesitant nod. "I'll always listen to you. I just don't agree that letting a murderer go is a good idea."

"Whether he finds something at the place where Randy was headed or not, he'll turn himself in, just not to Sheriff Gillette."

Layton watched her under bushy brows. "And you can promise me that?"

"Yes." She wasn't sure how Eric would feel about her promise. But he'd have to understand she was struggling to do the best she could…and she had to pray it was the right thing.

Layton tilted his head to the side, a gesture that usually showed he was softening.

"So you won't call the sheriff?"

"I have to report Lander was here, Sarah. It's against the law to keep something like that to myself."

"But you'll wait a bit? Give him a chance to find out why Randy was killed?"

He let out a groan and shook his head. "God help me."

Sarah's whole body felt spongy with relief. She'd hoped she could explain the situation to Layton, make him understand, but she'd had her doubts. And while she wouldn't be surprised if he called the sheriff first thing in the morning, at least Eric would have a head start.

Unfortunately that wasn't all he needed. "I hate to ask you for more, Layton, but…"

"What is it?"

"Can Eric borrow some supplies and equipment?"

A chuckle rumbled low in his chest. He shook his head, not in a way that indicated he was turning her down, but in an "I can't believe you'd ask" sort of way.

"You can tell the sheriff he stole it."

"What does he need?"

"Water, food, climbing gear."

"Fine."

"And the ATV?"

"That belongs to the ranch, and you know it. Where I'm sitting, he's going to have to ask *you* if he wants to borrow that."

"Thank you, Layton. Thank you so much." She reached up to him and he gathered her into a hug.

The warm scent of pipe smoke and fresh air made her throat clench. And for a moment she felt like she was a little girl once more, with Layton always there to watch out for her. Always there to make things right.

Too bad this time the problem was far too big for him to make it go away.

ERIC SORTED THROUGH ROPES, harnesses and assortment of carabiners and other equipment Layton stored in the barn. Jamming the gear into a pack alongside protein bars, water and a small first-aid kit, he tried to push the myriad of what-ifs to the back of his mind. He'd cleaned the cut on his head, even if it did still throb like a son of a bitch. Now that he had transportation, food, water and most of the equipment he needed, he was in good shape to make the trek to Saddle Horn Ridge. That didn't mean he was eager to leave Sarah behind.

The ranch foreman had promised to keep their secret

and keep Sarah safe, but Eric still felt uneasy about the whole thing. He never could read Layton. The foreman was good at keeping his feelings squirreled away, at least those other than contempt for Eric. But though Sarah trusted him, Eric didn't.

Sarah stuck her head into the tack room. Their clothes had been dried, and she was wearing an oversized coat provided by Layton. Her black-and-white shadow padded into the barn and laid down at her feet. "The ATV is gassed up and ready."

So this was goodbye. He felt a little shaky in the pit of his stomach. "You're sure Layton isn't phoning the sheriff as we speak, so he can head me off at the ridge?"

"He promised."

"And you believe him."

"He's never let me down before."

"Good to know."

"Eric?"

A little jolt shimmered up his spine at her tone. "What is it?"

"I…" She pressed her lips together as if trying to keep words from slipping past. She raised her hand to touch him, then let it fall to her side. "Good luck is all."

He reached out a hand and skimmed it down her arm. What he wouldn't give to be able to pull her into his arms right now. Take her in a kiss. Show her all the things he couldn't let himself feel, couldn't let himself want. He blew out a breath and pushed his clamoring feelings down. "Thanks."

The tack room door flew open. Layton pushed inside. His gray hair was tousled, as if he'd been running agitated hands through it. His eyes gaped wide with alarm. "You got to get out of here. Now."

Sarah stared at him, blood draining from her face and forcing her lips taut. "The sheriff?"

"He's on his way."

Eric finished shoving the equipment into the pack and yanked the zipper home. "How did he know we're here?"

"A neighbor? A hunch? I don't know. But he just called me. Started asking questions." Layton motioned for them to move, scooping the air with his hands.

A neighbor? Layton didn't have any neighbors, not for miles. Of course it probably didn't take a big guess for the sheriff to figure Sarah would go to the closest place she could for help. Layton's. Not that the reason mattered. The only thing important now was getting the hell out of here. He was grateful Layton tipped him off. "What did you tell him?"

"That I didn't know what he was talking about, but I don't think he believed me. And Sarah?"

She looked up at the older man.

"What you said before about the sheriff? It's true. He isn't just after Lander. He wants you, too. You'll have to go with Lander after all."

Sarah nodded, that determined set returning to her jaw.

Eric stifled a protest. As much as leaving Sarah bothered him, having her go with him to the ridge was not what he would choose. "It's too risky."

Layton gave him a sideways glance. "Believe me, it's not my choice. I don't want her near you."

Sarah nailed him with a determined glare. "The sheriff's on his way. I'm going."

Eric hesitated, then forced a nod. He couldn't very well leave her here. Not with the sheriff bearing down on her. No matter what happened, he had to make sure she was safe.

Shoving extra climbing equipment into the back-pack, he glanced down at Radar. The dog had been lying flat out on his side a moment ago, but now he crouched, staring at Sarah as if waiting for a command so he could fly into action and fix everything the humans were upset about.

Eric didn't want to say anything. Sarah had lost so much in the past hours. Randy. Her belief in the law. Every shred of security she'd known. He knew that to her, giving up Radar would feel like the ultimate blow. But there was nothing he could do. "What about your dog?"

Sarah sucked in a breath. She ran her fingers over the black-and-white head.

Layton rested a comforting hand on her shoulder. "Can't take a dog on an ATV."

She nodded and swiped at her cheeks with the back of one hand. It didn't work. Tears wound down her cheeks, reflecting the barn light in mirrored rivulets. "Will you take him?"

"You know I will."

She parted her lips to speak, then covered them with a hand as if holding back a sob.

Layton rubbed a hand over her shoulder. "I'll stall the sheriff as long as I can."

"Thank you, Layton." Sarah reached up and hugged him.

When she released him, he shooed them out the door. "Hurry."

Layton grabbed the backpack and helped Sarah slip it on her shoulders while Eric climbed on the all-terrain vehicle. He started it up, the engine buzzing loudly in the night. Sarah climbed on behind.

The foreman raised a hand in a wave as they sped away, his eyes glistening in the yard light.

Chapter Six

Each jolt of the ATV over rock and sage shuddered up Eric's spine and throbbed through his head, as if the very landscape was beating on him. The engine roared loud in the quiet night. At least it had stopped raining. With any luck, the snow wouldn't be too deep, at least not at lower elevations like Saddle Horn Ridge. But although the calendar said early June, spring had yet to arrive in many parts of the mountains.

He focused on the wrap of Sarah's arms around his waist, the warmth of her thighs pressing to the back of his. Even though the rain was long since over, the night air was downright cold as it rushed past. He could feel her shiver as she pressed against him. At least she now had a coat, thanks to Layton.

Obviously the foreman shared Eric's need to protect her. The urge never made sense. She was the strongest woman he'd ever known. She took care of others, animal and human alike. She never seemed to need anyone.

Of course, the jumble of feelings that overwhelmed him whenever he was around Sarah never made a lot of sense. In the rest of his life, he was controlled, logical.

But as soon as he saw the way she tilted her chin, heard her voice or touched her skin, he lost all reason. All he could think of was her.

He had to keep his mind clear if he wanted to get out of this mess.

They reached the mountains just as the first evidence of dawn started glowing from the east. As the light grew, driving became easier. The ATV could carry them farther up the mountain than his truck had allowed, cutting hours off the trip he and Randy had taken on foot. Good thing. After a night of no sleep and a lifetime's worth of trauma, the only thing keeping either of them going was adrenaline. And who knew how long that could last?

The ATV bucked at every bump. The pitch grew steeper. Eric settled into a switchback trail nearby guest ranches used to take tourists through the area on horseback. They wove back and forth up the side of the slope, until the pitch grew too steep and the trail circled back. Stopping the ATV behind a jut of rock, Eric switched off the engine. "We're going to have to go the rest of the way on foot."

Sarah nodded and released his waist. She swung a leg over the seat and dismounted.

Cool air fanned over his back where her warmth had been. For a moment, he wanted nothing more than to have her back on the seat behind him, arms circling his waist.

Stupid.

He climbed off the ATV. His hands still vibrated from the feel of the handlebars. His ears buzzed with silence, now that the roar of the engine was gone. He focused on Sarah. Her skin was the color of aspen bark. Dark circles cupped under chocolate eyes that glistened with fatigue. She was far more exhausted than he'd even guessed. "Take a few minutes and sit down."

"I'm fine." She raised her chin in that way he'd once thought was sexy.

Now it struck him as nothing but stubborn. "You look like you're about to keel over."

She nodded her head toward the east. The glow of sunlight pinked the horizon. "The sun is going to be up any second. We don't have time to sit down."

She was right. As much as she needed to rest, they couldn't afford the delay. It had taken them a good long time to make it to the base of Saddle Horn Ridge. Pickups traveling paved roads would make it here a lot faster, although they'd have to cover more miles and couldn't drive as far up the mountainside. Unfortunately that small time advantage would be eaten up by the detour Eric planned to take. They needed every second they could get. "We'll keep going then. But I'll carry the pack."

She shrugged the backpack off her shoulders and handed it to him.

The pack was heavy in his hand, weighed down with harnesses and ropes, water and food. He slung it onto his back. "Let's go."

He stepped off the switchback trail and started picking his way over sage and around rock. Most of mountain climbing was a matter of walking uphill. It didn't involve ropes or vertical rock faces. It was about hiking, pure and simple. But that didn't mean it was the same thing as following a trail. Eric scanned the terrain ahead, aware of every rock and crevasse and ripple of the wind. Off-trail hiking was about being present, being aware. Of the surroundings, of animals, of the weather, of the capabilities of one's own body. It was about being awake in the present and being able to guess the future. And guiding meant he was responsible for Sarah as well.

The sun warmed their backs as it rose in the sky, beating down strong, even though the mountains still boasted a good amount of snow along their peaks. They worked their way through vegetation raging from the ever-present sage to tall stands of lodgepole pine and subalpine fir. The roar of a waterfall hung in the thinning air, though the creek itself was over a mile away.

Finally Saddle Horn Ridge loomed above them, stretching between two peaks. The ridge wasn't a common tourist destination, but the few guides working the area knew it was there. Most of the area itself was flat and sheltered from sometimes brutal mountain winds, an ideal spot for camping. On one side, a rock formation rose. A shifted slab of rock capped the top of the formation, giving it the appearance of the horn on a western saddle.

On one end of the long ridge, a vertical rock face rose nearly to the ridge itself. Made of hard, volcanic rock, like the rest of the Absaroka Range, this was one of the best and least known climbing areas north of the Tetons. It was also the cliff he and Randy had been scaling when the deputies had opened fire.

Eric turned away from the stretch of rock and started through a long stand of lodgepole pine.

"Where are you going?"

"We'll circle to the other end of the ridge. Most of the terrain is hikable on that side."

"Won't that take a lot longer?" She tilted her face to the east, no doubt checking the position of the sun.

"A little. But it's easier. Multipitch climbs can be slow, tough going."

"You don't think I can do it."

Under normal circumstances, he might let her. She was pretty advanced. If she was in practice, she could probably handle it. They'd done some climbing together last September before the snow hit. Before he realized how important to him she was becoming. But circumstances were different now. "It's not a simple climb. We've both been through a lot in the past few hours."

"I told you, I'm fine. I can make it."

He hadn't believed her then, and he didn't believe her now. But her obvious fatigue wasn't the only reason he wanted to avoid this stretch. Just the sight of that rock face made a shudder travel through him and his head ache to high heaven. "We'll go through the pass and up the other side. It won't take much longer."

"But it will take longer. Do you really think we can afford that extra time?"

He didn't know. He was surprised they hadn't heard vehicles yet. Or helicopters. But to lead Sarah up that face? "We'll move fast. A climb like that is too dangerous."

"And letting the sheriff catch up to us isn't?"

"I'm not going to let you get caught on that face…."

She narrowed her eyes.

He pulled in a breath and gritted his teeth. He'd said too much. Way more than he should have. "Let's move. Now."

"This is the spot, isn't it?" She turned away from him and peered up at the rock face.

He started walking, heading for the pass.

"It's the spot where Randy…"

He slowed his steps. The pain in her words hollowed out a pit below his rib cage. He turned to face her and reached out a hand. "Come on. We'll follow the pass. It will be better."

"Where? Where did it happen?"

"Sarah, come on."

"Tell me. Please."

With that last whispered word, he felt the walls inside him crumble. A torrent of pain and regret filled his throat.

PRESSURE BUILT AROUND the edges of Sarah's eyes and stung through her sinuses. "Please, Eric. I have to know." She'd never understood the need of survivors to mark the spot where a loved one died. Every time she passed a cross on the side of the highway or flowers woven into a chain-link fence, she'd felt uneasy, as if she was witnessing a very personal pain, something that should be shielded from the public.

She understood now.

She needed to know exactly where Randy had taken his last breath. She needed to mark the spot, if only in her mind, in order to make any of it feel real.

He watched her for what had to be a full minute. "About three quarters of the way up. See the shelf of rock?"

She followed the direction of his pointing finger. "Near the top of those trees?"

"Yes."

She saw it. What looked like a smear of something brown on the stone. A trick of the noon sun…or her brother's blood? She couldn't tell.

Shivers fanned out over her skin. Her chest heaved in a barely controlled sob. She half expected him to still be there. Hanging in his climbing harness. Or lying in the short slope of scree at the bottom of the rock face. But she knew he wouldn't be. He would be at the morgue, his body dissected, his wounds used as evidence to frame Eric for his murder. "Was he in pain?"

"No…no." His voice hitched.

She could tell by his hesitation that wasn't entirely true.

She closed her eyes, trying to block the tears. Randy was gone. Murdered on this spot. And now nothing was left but to find out why. And make sure the same fate didn't fall on Eric or her…or their unborn child.

Nausea swirled in the pit of her stomach. She hadn't suffered morning sickness for a couple of weeks now, but it seemed a touch had caught up to her in the stress of the past hours. Maybe it had nothing to do with the baby. Maybe it was seeing the spot where Randy died. Or leaving Radar behind with Layton. Or maybe the confusion of all that had happened.

"Sarah. Is there something…"

She took a deep breath and braced herself before turning back to Eric.

His eyes focused on her belly.

She hadn't realized she was shielding her middle with her forearm. But she could tell by the expression on his face he had. And along with probably the dozen other signals she'd subconsciously given, he had a guess as to what the protective gesture meant.

Her throat went dry. "I was going to tell you."

"You're pregnant." He brought his eyes up to her face. For a long time, he just watched her. Struggling to make sense of her words, searching for words of his own, she didn't know. But just as she was about to break the silence, he nodded. "It's mine."

His voice sounded dead, void of emotion, and somehow that bothered her more than the anger and betrayal she'd imagined he'd feel in all the times she'd played this scenario out in her imagination. "Yes. The baby is yours."

"How far along?"

"Four months. I found out shortly after we…after you…"

"Left."

"Yes."

"Why didn't you tell me then? Call me?"

"I was going to. Really I was…but…"

"But what?"

She'd made excuses to herself for months. She didn't want to try to make them now. Not when she knew the reason she hadn't told him. "I was afraid."

"Of what? You had to know I'd marry you."

She flinched and took a step backward. Of course, she knew. It was the right thing to do. And Eric would never walk away from doing the right thing.

And that was exactly what she feared most.

SARAH STARED AT ERIC as if he'd just said exactly the wrong thing. Slowly, she shook her head. "You don't want to get married."

Eric couldn't disagree. "It wasn't in my plans. But some things are more important than plans." He closed his eyes. Dizziness swept over him in a sudden, stomach-wrenching bout of vertigo. He pulled in a breath and beat back the sensation. He wasn't a man who ran out on his responsibilities. Ever. If he wasn't sure he could come through, he didn't take it on in the first place. He approached things in a controlled way, a logical way. Reason instead of emotion. He just had to get used to the idea and the weak, shaky feeling in the pit of his stomach would go away.

Wouldn't it?

"I'm not going to marry you, Eric."

He opened his eyes and stared at Sarah. He couldn't have heard her right. "What?"

"I don't want to marry you."

He shook his head. "But you're pregnant."

"And people have babies without getting married all the time. Really, it's fine."

How could she say that? "No. It's not fine. I'm tired of you saying everything is fine." If there was anything he knew about any of what he'd had sprung on him the past two days, it was that absolutely nothing was fine.

"A couple of months ago, you told me you didn't even want to date anymore. Now you have a pressing desire to marry me?"

"Things have changed."

"Nothing's changed."

"How do you figure that?"

"You just think marrying me is something you have to do. Your duty or whatever. Well, I'm telling you it isn't."

His duty. That was how he felt, she was right. But that didn't mean she could absolve him of it. "I *want* to do it."

She tilted her chin down and looked up at him. "Well, I don't."

He looked away. He couldn't blame her. He knew when he'd broken things off she'd assumed he didn't care about her. And for the ease of the breakup, he'd let her believe that. He'd told himself the truth was far too complicated. Compared to the mess they were in now, it was amazingly simple. Not that it mattered. Not anymore. "So where does that leave us?"

"Same place as before. We find whatever it is that's up on that ridge and we use it to try to get our lives back."

Their lives. He knew she meant their separate lives. But to him, that was no longer an option.

"They're here."

He followed her gaze to where the white dot of an SUV bounced over rutted gravel road, slowly making its way to the head of the switchback trail.

SARAH KNEW ERIC DIDN'T want to get married. Hell, he probably knew it, too. But that split second when she told him she wouldn't consider wedlock, the look of rejection on his face felt good.

She wasn't sure if that officially made her a horrible person, but…whatever.

She shook her head and found her next foothold. As satisfying as revenge felt, her reason for turning him down went a lot deeper. As much as she wanted to go back to the way things were before Eric left, before Randy died, before her life totally fell apart, when he'd asked her to marry him, the feeling that he was merely doing his duty hit her like a kick to the gut. No, more like a void. An emptiness that could never be filled. There was no use pretending things might have worked out between them if she'd played things differently, said different words, batted her eyes just so. There was no more pretending at all.

The bottom line was that Eric didn't love her. If he had, he never would have walked away. And she wasn't going to marry someone without love.

Period.

Now all that was left was the task ahead. Finding whatever had gotten Randy killed and using it to clear their names.

She shoved all other thoughts from her mind and concentrated on fitting her fingers into a jam-crack in the short rock face at the top of the ridge that Eric hadn't been able to avoid letting her climb.

Last summer, Eric had said she was a natural climber. She was patient, and she relied on her legs to make the climb, using her hands only for balance. That might have been the case back then. Today she felt clumsy and hurried and her arms ached with exertion. And every time her tummy rubbed against the rock, all she could think of was the danger to her baby if she fell.

Concentrate.

She placed her boot on a block. Keeping her heels low, she took weight onto the foot and pushed herself up. Eric took up the slack in the belaying rope. She pulled herself to the top of the ridge and shifted her weight to her elbows.

"You got it." Eric's voice sounded in her ears, right above her head. "Now just bring your foot up, and you're home free."

Home free. She knew it was merely a saying, but she couldn't help the hitch in her stomach all the same. She might be home free as far as this climb went. But the situation they were in stretched in front of them like the most rugged of mountain ranges. And even if they could get through all the obstacles before them, she might never be home free again.

She raised her foot to the ledge and thrust her body up onto the top of the ridge. For a second, she just lay there, her muscles quivering under her skin. Then she pulled herself into a sitting position.

Saddle Horn Ridge.

All around her mountains rose above them, jutting their snow-topped peaks into the sky. Rock and stretches of lodgepole pine seemed to go on forever. "Beautiful."

"It is." Eric quickly looked away from her and out at the gully cutting below the other side of the ridge.

She watched him for a second, like he'd been watching her. Now that he knew about the baby, now that they'd gotten the marriage discussion out of the way, they seemed as awkward as strangers. "Do you see anyone?"

A light swirl of wind blew past her ears and swept away his answer, but she could read from his body language that he hadn't. She scanned the area with her own eyes. No sign of human life other than them. But then, Eric had led them on such a winding path up to the ridge, she was no longer sure in which direction to look.

She scooped in a long breath. "Now what?"

"Now we look around."

He moved to the far edge of the ridge, where the rock rose in a column and formed a shape some explorer must have thought looked like a saddle horn. He peered down, not moving except for the light breeze rifling his hair.

She thrust herself up from her resting place. "If the sheriff was worried about Randy finding money or drugs, why didn't he just come up here and take it himself?"

"Maybe he tried."

Something in the tone of his voice stopped Sarah as effectively as if he'd grabbed her. Pulse thumping, she willed her wobbly legs to carry her along the rocky ridge toward the base of the saddle horn.

The area was wider than it seemed, flat, but on all sides the plunge was straight down. And even though she logically knew she was in no danger, she couldn't shake the feeling that the wind could push her off her perch at any moment and toss her to the rock below, even though there was surprisingly little wind. "What is it?"

"Not what we thought." He pointed to a fissure in the rock.

Deep in the shadows, she could see light tan against dark. Something with a trunk, with arms… "A person?"

"A body. And judging from the shape he's in, he might have been stuck in that crevasse a good long while."

Chapter Seven

"Randy was looking for a dead body?"

Eric felt as shaken by the discovery as Sarah sounded. "He was looking for something valuable enough to pay off his debt."

"So what makes this guy valuable?"

Shielding his eyes from the sun, he tried to get a better look. What he wouldn't give for a pair of binoculars. "Maybe there's something valuable on the body."

"Like money or drugs. But what would he be doing with money or drugs out here? And how did he die? Fall?"

"Good questions." And ones he couldn't answer. "I'm going to rappel down. Take a look."

Sarah inched closer to the edge and craned her neck. Swaying a little, she clamped her hand to her stomach.

"Are you okay?"

"Just a little dizzy."

"Heights do that to some people."

"I climbed up all right."

"Not the same as rappelling down."

"I guess not." She took a deep breath, as if she could push the vertigo down with willpower alone.

"You don't have to do it. I'll go alone. You stay up here and watch for the sheriff's men."

She nodded, as if eager to jump at the chance to sit this one out.

She had to be tired. Even though she was in great shape, and they'd avoided the worst of the climbs, scaling rock worked different muscles than ranch work. Add that to a sleepless night and extreme stress and anyone would be dragging. He couldn't even begin to imagine adding the strain of being pregnant.

Pregnant. He still couldn't wrap his mind around the fact that he and Sarah were going to have a baby. He felt excited about the idea on some level, but jangled and confused at the same time. And not just about the baby. Seeing Sarah again, being near her, made him feel like a broken compass with no sense of north.

He needed distance. A chance to think things over logically, approach the whole thing with a clear mind.

But in order to get control of that situation, he needed to get out of this one first.

Using a tape sling, he set up an anchor around a solid rock formation. He ran a coil of rope through a carabiner, forming a pulley. After formulating a plan and giving Sarah a quick lesson in threading the rope through a descender, he started down the side of the cliff. It took mere seconds to rappel down the thirty-foot drop. As soon as his feet hit the narrow shelf of rock on the edge of the crevasse, a thick sweet smell touched his senses.

Apparently the body hadn't been here as long as he'd thought. He crouched down to take a look at the dead man.

From the top of the ridge, all he'd seen was the clothing. A shearling coat sun-bleached and ratty from the elements. A pair of Wranglers. Cowboy boots. And at first that was all he could see. Wedged about four feet down into the crevasse, the body was angled head down. Eric focused on the boots. Great for riding, but not something a hiker or climber would wear—he thought of Sarah's footwear—not by choice, anyway. But the popularity of Wrangler jeans and shearling coats in this part of the country meant the rest told him little about who this man was and how he had ended up here.

Or what of value he might have.

He bridged the narrow crack, one foot on either side, and settled in as low as he could get. Reaching down, he patted the coat pockets. Empty. He grasped the bottom hem and yanked it up, exposing a stained shirt. There was little left of the guy except clothing and bones, but a strong wave of odor still wafted up at him and tainted the air around him. His stomach bucked for a moment, then calmed. He breathed through his mouth and prodded further. All the man's pockets were empty. Not even a wallet.

A leather belt loosely circled the man's waist. Judging from the circumference, it had likely propped up a good-sized belly, back when their mystery man was alive. An ornate belt buckle fastened the ends of the tooled leather.

Eric grabbed a small flashlight from his pack and focused its beam on the buckle. Exposure to the elements had tarnished the silver to a dull gray, but Eric could still make out the inscription among the curlycues surrounding a man on a bucking horse—*Cody Nite Rodeo Bareback Champion, 1978.*

He skimmed the beam up the torso. What he'd thought was the man's head when looking down from the ridge above was really his shoulder. The crevasse cut deep into rock, narrowing on its way down to blackness. One arm reached down, but he could see nothing below, no bag or pack or anything that could be considered valuable. Below the shoulder, the skull wedged between rock, only a small tuft of gray hair clung to shriveled skin and bone.

Eric ran the questions the sheriff had asked Sarah through his mind. Even if Gillette knew the area to look, he would have only been able to see the body from directly above the crevasse. And even if he'd known exactly where it was, it would have been difficult to move a body wedged deep like this.

"Who in the hell are you, Mr. Rodeo Champion? And why are you so valuable?"

Of course, dental records or DNA could tell them who he was. Not that he nor Sarah could waltz into the Wyoming crime lab with a sample. Even a private lab would ask too many questions, provided they asked questions at all and didn't merely call the police.

And in light of what Layton had told them, they couldn't rely on police to do anything but arrest them and ship them back to Sheriff Gillette.

He moved the light beam over the skull, stopping on a spot at the back of the head.

Wait.

Throat dry, Eric adjusted his position and leaned as far into the crevasse as he dared. He scanned the skull again, raking the beam slowly over hair and bone. There it was. A hole marked the cranium like a perfect dark circle, just an inch or so behind the ear.

He pulled in a breath of foul air. There wasn't any treasure at all at the end of this treasure hunt. The deputies hadn't been hiding a stash of money or drugs. They'd been trying to cover up a murder.

The rope around Eric's waist jolted.

Sarah's signal. He looked up. The men must be getting close. Too close. He needed to get back up to the top of that ridge and he needed to do it now. He reached for the rodeo belt buckle, unhooked it and gave it a hard pull. The leather started slipping through the denim loops, then caught. He tugged harder.

No good. It held fast.

Twisting the buckle upside down, he fumbled for the snaps holding leather to silver. He popped one snap, then the other. Slipping buckle free of belt and body, he stuffed it into his pack.

The rope tugged again, more frantic. He needed to hurry. The thought of Sarah up on the ridge alone, frightened, facing down men with guns… He spun around. His foot skidded beneath him. He struggled for balance, grasped at rock for a hold. No good.

He plunged into the crevasse up to his waist. Damn.

The body's skull pressed against his thigh. The scent of decay coated the back of his throat. A wave of revulsion shuddered through him before he could take control.

Calm. Logical. Pull yourself out and get the hell up to that ridge.

He placed his palms on the edge of the crevasse. His forearms were already over the ledge, in a position where he could push himself over the rock instead of pull. He'd mantled more times than he could remember. Performing the move next to a dead body didn't change anything.

He pushed down with his hands and slung his left foot up onto the narrow ledge. Scooping in a breath through his mouth, he pushed upward.

His right foot didn't budge.

He tried again, giving it every ounce of strength he could muster. No good. His foot wouldn't move. A cold sweat blanketed him, thick as the odor of decay.

He was as stuck in the crevasse as the dead man.

SARAH TUGGED ON THE ROPE for a third time. What was taking Eric so long? The men had crested the point and had now disappeared behind a stand of lodgepole pine. She wasn't sure how long it would take for him to make the climb back up to the ridge and then for them to make their escape, but time seemed to be tightening at an alarming rate.

"Sarah."

She leaned over the edge.

Eric seemed to be standing in the crevasse next to the body. He hadn't moved, even though she'd warned him three times.

The beat of her pulse drowned out the whistle of wind in the rocks above.

Eric scooped the air with one arm.

At first she didn't understand what he was trying to tell her. The second time he made the gesture, his meaning dawned.

He was telling her she'd have to come down to him. He was asking her to rappel down the sheer drop of rock.

A tremor seized low in her stomach. She looked back in the direction of the men. Eric must have figured out that he didn't have time to make the climb and then make their escape. Something had delayed him. Something was wrong.

She pulled in a breath of too thin air. She'd rappelled down a rock face before. She was the same person. She could do it again. But somehow every risk seemed to be bigger now, every possible danger more dire.

She glanced back at the path one more time. She couldn't see the men. Not yet. But they were coming. And they would be armed. If she wanted to think about danger, that was the direction from which it would come.

She grasped the rope Eric had used. Still threaded through the pulley he'd set up, the rope was now loose on Eric's end. He'd detached it from his harness, freed it for her. Hands shaking, she threaded it through the big circle of the descender. She looped it around the small end and clipped the device to her harness the way Eric had shown her.

So far, so good.

After checking the ropes, she stepped to the edge. Eric's instructions rang in her ears. She had to trust her equipment, take her time. Breathe.

She leaned back and dug her heels into the rock. Her front hand shook, fingers aching. She forced her grip to loosen. Her right hand, resting along her thigh, was controlling the rope. She had to remember that. If she moved it to the side, the rope would slide through the descender. If she held it behind her back, the rope would stop.

She inched down the cliff, forcing herself to keep her eyes down, on the rock under her feet and the cliff below, and not on the ridge above. She leaned back, but not too far. She had to hurry, but not too much. Finally she could see the rock flatten into a narrow ledge.

"You got it," Eric's voice sounded from behind her.

One of the most welcome sounds she'd ever heard. She let the rope slide through her hands. Her feet rested on horizontal rock.

His hands steadied her hips. "Don't step back. Stay right where you are."

For a moment, she was content not to move. She just stood there, soaking in the solid feel of his touch. The smell of decay and tension and relief made her stomach swirl. She looked up at the cliff she'd just descended, half expecting to see men peering down at them, gun barrels leveled at their heads, although she knew they weren't that close. "They're on their way. I spotted them on the point, just where you said to look."

"We have a problem."

She turned around on the narrow ledge. He was standing waist-deep in a crevasse, just as it had seemed from above. And beside him, the body they'd spotted from above wedged a few feet deeper. She suppressed a shudder.

"My boot is jammed."

She looked down, following his leg to where it was swallowed by shadow cast by the narrowing slash in the rock. "Can you get it off?"

"I can't bend down to get it unlaced. The crevasse is too tight. I need your help." He pulled a knife from his belt and handed it to her. Blade tucked neatly into handle, the knife still looked brutal, the blade big enough to hack down a small tree. The olive drab handle looked military-serious. "The laces. Can you reach them? Cut them with this?"

"Not unless I stand on my head."

"Okay, then."

She eyed the crevasse, the body lodged beside Eric. The thought of diving headfirst into that confining space made sweat bloom damp on her skin. "I wasn't serious."

"I was. I'm not going to get out of here any other way."

She wiped her palms on her jeans and took the knife. "I hope I don't get sick."

His eyebrows turned down.

"Don't worry about it. I can do it. Just wanted to warn you."

"You sure?"

"Believe me, I'm used to it. I'm sure it will bother you more than it bothers me." She turned to face him on the ledge. He was so close to her. "As long as you can pull me back up."

He nodded, but he didn't have to. She knew he could. Eric was one of the strongest men she'd ever known. Rock climbing honed some brutal muscle tissue.

"You might want to breathe through your mouth."

Sarah tried not to look at the body. She scooped in a deep breath through tight lips. Leaning forward, she lowered her head in an awkward half headstand, half squat.

Eric's hands closed around her waist and he lifted her into the air. She stretched her arms out in front of her, the knife clutched in one fist.

He lowered her into the crevasse, her body sliding down his. Darkness closed around her. The odor of decay wrapped around her like a wet fog. She kept her eyes on Eric's boot, trying not to think too much about the skull just inches away.

The opening narrowed. Her face grew hot, blood rushing to her head. The weight of her stomach pressed into her throat. The urge to break out of here, scramble for light, for air, clawed inside her.

She had to hurry.

Locating a lace with one hand, she slipped the blade

under and drew it upward. She jiggled the knife until the lace gave. She cut another, then clawed the rest loose with her fingers and pulled at the boot's tongue. She folded the knife and tapped Eric's leg.

He started to lift her upward. She hadn't yet emerged from the crevasse when she heard the first crack of gunfire reverberate off stone.

Chapter Eight

Nothing could get adrenaline pumping like a bullet screaming past a person's head.

Eric's arms shook as he lifted Sarah out of the crevasse. She wasn't that heavy. Not heavy at all, really. But slam after slam of adrenaline over the past hours was taking its toll.

His heart hammered against his ribs. This couldn't be happening again. Images flashed through his mind. The sick jolt of Randy's body. The animal look in his eyes. They way he slumped off the ridge and hung limp in his harness.

Think. He had to get Sarah out of here. He'd failed Randy. He wouldn't fail her.

Sarah and his child.

Setting her on the edge, he yanked his foot free from the boot and hefted himself up beside her.

Crack. A plume of dust exploded from rock.

A choked sound came from Sarah's throat.

Grabbing her hand, he flattened himself against the base of the cliff. She did the same. At this angle, even a few feet made a difference. Rock and the occasional straggly sage obscured them from above. It would be tough for the men on the ridge to pull off an accurate shot at this angle. Until they decided to rappel down the rock face as he and Sarah had. Or circle around the gentler slope to the other side of the ridge.

Or split up and try both.

Eric swallowed into a dust-dry throat. That's what he would do, if he were the hunter instead of the prey. It was the logical move. Come at them from both sides. Get into position before making his presence known.

Sarah pulled his hand, leading him back around the ridge the way they'd come. "Hurry. If they're up there, maybe we can reach the ATV before—"

"They'll be coming from both directions. We'll run right into them."

She stared at him a moment, processing his words or deciding whether or not to trust him, he wasn't sure. "So where do we go?" She searched his eyes, waiting for his answer.

Eric scanned the mountains that rose all around them. To someone who hadn't spent the hours in these mountains that he had, the formations of rock, slopes of pine and peaks dusted with snow looked interchangeable. All beautiful, but one much like the other. For him, each mountain's shape and features felt as distinctive as human faces. And these particular faces were all well loved.

"That way." He pointed to the other side of the crevasse. The slope stretched bare and open for fifty yards then plunged into a stand of lodgepole pine.

But first, he needed to make things a little tougher for their pursuers and easier for themselves.

He grabbed the rope and gave it a good pull. It slid through the carabiner above and pooled at the base of the cliff. He coiled it as quickly as his hands would move. Taking the rope was time-consuming, he knew. But with the route he was planning to take, two ropes would be important. Hell, they'd be the difference between one of them making it or both.

Slipping the coil over his shoulder, he grabbed Sarah's hand once more. He nodded to the open landscape in front of them and the stand of lodgepole pine beyond. "We'll need to cross this stretch quickly. Once we get into cover, we'll be in good shape. But until then…we need to move fast. Keep down and stay with me. You think you're up to it?"

Holding her hand to her belly, she set her jaw and nodded. "Just tell me what to do." Her voice trembled, but there was a determination underneath it, a confidence in him he thought he'd never hear from her again. And despite the fact that he had little idea how he was going to get them out of this mess, her confidence that he'd find a way made him want to believe it, too. "On three, run."

"One."

Sarah gripped Eric's hand for all she was worth. She couldn't let herself think about what they were about to do. She just had to feel, trust.

"Two."

She mimicked Eric's posture, knees bent, muscles coiled like springs. Time stretched forever, slow and painful. Finally he opened his lips a third time.

"Three."

They sprang over the crevasse and into the open, racing for the stand of pine. Her boots skidded on rock and tripped over prickly pear, but she kept her legs under her, kept them moving, kept hold of Eric's hand.

A crack echoed off stone. Another.

They plunged into the forest's edge. From the ridge the trees had appeared closer together. Dense. Now she could see how sparse the forest really was. Some pines ravaged by past fires were bare as matchsticks thrust into the sky. Others had needles, but were too young to provide cover.

They kept moving. Sarah's breath panted raw in her throat. She tried to make herself breathe deeply, sucking in all the oxygen she could with each breath, but still her lungs craved more.

Eric picked and dodged around rocks and through brush. Finally the forest grew darker, the understory more sparse until only a bed of dead needles cushioned the rocky soil beneath their feet.

Instead of stopping, Eric ran on. No longer a mad dash, but a steady jog. Sarah gamely kept up. The gunshots coming from the top of the ridge echoed in her ears. They were too close. Too real. Those moments before Eric had led her to shelter had scared her as she'd never been scared before, and every cell in her body seemed to still be shaking from it.

Her breathing settled into a steady rhythm. In and out. In and out. Blood hummed through her arms and legs. Hair stuck to her face and neck, sweat slicking her skin.

They ran on, through forest then open space. They hiked over ridges and rappeled down steep slopes. By the time Sarah made it down the cliff near the waterfall, she was starting to feel like a pro. Either that or she was just so exhausted she was becoming delusional.

Her side stung with each breath as if a knife had been jabbed between her ribs. She swallowed into a dust-dry throat. "I have to stop. Just for a second."

Eric paused as if listening for the sound of pursuit. Finally he nodded and led her to the side of the stream. He handed her one of the water bottles Layton had provided and slugged back the other himself. Once they were empty, he refilled them from the stream, slipped them back into the pack and propped a hip on the slope of a felled log.

Even though the sharp pain in her lungs had lessened, Sarah's whole body still ached, and she knew if she sat for long each of those overtaxed muscles would stiffen, making things worse.

But a few minutes would be nice.

The sound of water washing over stone lulled her like the mellow tones of New Age music. She breathed in the fresh tang of pine and plopped her elbows on her knees. "Did you find anything? You know, on the body?" They had been in such a hurry to escape the gunfire, she hadn't had a chance to ask until now.

"You mean like something on him that would carry stolen money or drugs? No."

She leaned forehead to hands. She'd hung everything on the hope they'd find something on the ridge. Something to explain why Randy was killed. Something to help them get out of this mess. "Then the hike up to Saddle Horn Ridge…it was all for nothing?"

"I wouldn't say that."

"We almost got killed, and we know nothing more now than we did before we climbed to the ridge."

He scanned the rough landscape around them, always on guard. "We know several things."

"Like what?" At the moment, she couldn't think of one.

"We know there's a body."

Yes, they knew that, all right. The rotting flesh, the sickening smell…she suppressed a shiver. "So? If he didn't have anything Randy could have thought was valuable enough to pay back his debt, we have no proof he's part of this at all. He might just be a hiker who fell."

"He was no hiker."

"How do you know?"

"First, he was wearing the wrong boots." He glanced down at the cowboy boots on her feet. "You know from experience that wouldn't be the first choice for a hike."

She couldn't disagree. She studied the confident line of his mouth. "I get the feeling there's more?"

"He was murdered."

The word sent a jolt of energy through her she didn't know she still possessed. "How do you know?"

"There was a bullet hole in the back of his skull. And…" He hefted the backpack up on the log beside him, unzipped it and pulled something out. He handed her a silver belt buckle.

"This is from the body?" She held it by the edges, balancing it between two fingers, not sure she wanted to touch it.

He pointed to the lettering surrounding the bucking horse. *Cody Nite Rodeo.* "We learn the name of the bareback champion in 1978, we identify our murder victim."

She turned the buckle over in her fingers. Maybe things weren't so hopeless. Maybe they could still find a way out. Thanks to Eric. "And from there, we find out why he was killed."

Eric nodded. "And who killed him."

"You're thinking the sheriff did it?"

He shrugged a shoulder. "At the very least, he's trying to cover it up."

"So this whole thing…it's not about stolen money or drugs at all?"

"Maybe not." He gestured to the buckle in her hands. "Is there a list of the cowboys who've won awards like this? Something that goes back to 1978?"

"Pro rodeo results are listed on the PRCA Web site. But this is a year-end award for the Cody Nite Rodeo. I doubt there's a list online. Especially one that goes back to 1978." She searched her memory. She wasn't certain, but…

"What is it?"

"Back when I was barrel racing and Randy had just started riding bulls, I remember one place had the champions listed on the back of the grandstand. Like an honor role of sorts. I always dreamed of my name being up there someday."

"You think it was Cody?"

"I don't know, but Layton used to take Randy and me to the Cody rodeo pretty often."

"Then let's go to Cody."

"How? Walk? That should only take…forever."

"If we had to travel by road the whole way, that might be true. But as the crow flies…we aren't as far from Cody as you think."

Sarah scanned the topography. She'd gotten so turned around on their hike up to Saddle Horn Ridge and even more confused in their escape. "Where are we, exactly?"

He pointed to a narrow pass between two peaks. "Cody is that way, maybe thirty miles."

She looked down at his stocking foot. The bottom of

his thick sock had worn away in spots, and the rusty color of dried blood colored the tattered edges. "Still a long way to walk."

"I'm betting we can find a ride." One corner of his mouth turned up.

She wanted to return the smile. Eric seemed as if he had thought the whole thing through, as if he had it all figured out. But while it felt good to have him with her, to be able to rely on him, to not have to handle everything herself, she knew things weren't so simple and clear-cut. And for all Eric's crooked smiles and confidence, she had the feeling he sensed that, too.

Chapter Nine

Although the brief stop for rest and water had helped, by the time they'd descended into the foothills, Sarah's bones ached with a fatigue from which she couldn't imagine recovering. Of course, Eric had it worse, traveling with only one boot. He hadn't said a word on the long hike down the mountain, but she'd been aware of his limp, which was growing more pronounced by the hour.

If they were where Eric said, they should find ranches and green hay fields flanking the river ahead. Civilization compared to the land they'd just crossed. Maybe there they could find the ride Eric had so cockily promised.

She sure hoped so, because she didn't know how he was going to manage to walk much farther.

The first ranch they came to seemed locked up tight. No sign of life stirred in the house. The small barn, corral and fields were vacant, and the garage didn't have so much as a bicycle inside. "Must be a summer place," Eric said.

Sarah nodded. The beginning of June was summer in most places, but not necessarily here in the mountains. And even though the countryside was enjoying a nice growth spurt before the July sun dried the landscape to a dull brown, summer vacation and tourist season didn't really get cooking in this area until nearby Yellowstone opened its gates in a few weeks.

They moved on to the next ranch. Instead of hay fields, cattle dotted the valley. "Now we're talking," Eric said. "They must have some kind of vehicle."

"You're thinking of stealing a car?"

He nodded.

"Do you know how to do that?"

"I'm hoping I can figure it out."

She hoped so, too. And that the ranch didn't have dogs keeping watch. And that the rancher didn't have a gun. It seemed they were hanging a lot on hope. "There has to be a better way."

"You come up with one, I'm all ears."

They circled the house and crouched behind a clump of big sage. From this angle, they had a clear view of the barn and other outbuildings. And in the middle of the gravel drive, a truck idled, hitched to a four-horse stock style trailer.

"I told you we'd find a ride. He even left the keys in and the engine running."

Movement stirred in the barn's open doorway.

"Wait." Sarah grabbed Eric's arm as if to stop him, even though he hadn't moved.

A dog trotted out, tail held high. Behind him, a man emerged leading a saddled horse. Lead rope loose in his hand, he stepped up into the trailer. The horse followed, horseshoes thunking on steel, as willing as if he was walking into his stall in the barn.

After a moment, the man jumped down from the back of the trailer. He closed the back gate and headed for the house, dog on his heels.

Clean Wranglers. Bright, striped button-down shirt. Perfectly shaped hat and a nice pair of boots. No cowboy dressed that well for day-to-day work. And although the saddle on the horse's back was no silver-encrusted monstrosity you sometimes saw in pleasure horse shows, it was as clean and spruced up as the man who would sit in it.

She glanced at the sun, hovering over the mountains, poised to take a plunge. "You wanted to go to Cody? To the rodeo grounds?"

A smile turned both corners of Eric's lips. Two days worth of stubble shaded his chin. Evening sun slanted low through the sagebrush and sparkled in his green eyes. "I could kiss you."

A jitter lodged beneath her ribs.

"I mean, it's a good idea." He focused on the trailer.

She nodded. She knew that's what he meant. But somewhere dangerous inside her, she wanted it to be more.

LIKE EVERY PLACE IN Wyoming, it took much too long to drive to Cody, even though it was the closest town. Exhaust from the old truck swirled in the wind. Sarah's hair lashed against her cheeks. And the trailer's jolting motion actually made her grateful she hadn't eaten in a good number of hours. Even though they were sheltered behind a solid kick board rimming the lower half of the trailer, the wind felt more like a gale in October than a spring night in early June. By the time they reached town, it seemed Sarah couldn't do a thing to smooth the tangle on top of her head other than shave it off and start fresh.

The truck turned left and followed the light flow of traffic on the west strip, the road leading to the Buffalo Bill Dam and Yellowstone National Park. Sunset sparkled on the Shoshone River as the sun slipped behind the mountains. Hotels on the strip boasted few cars in their lots, the early tourist season trickle just a warm-up for the flood of people who would flock to enjoy the parks and a slice of the west come July.

The rodeo grounds loomed on the right, lights blazing. Tonight was rodeo night, as was every summer night in Cody. Even though she hadn't attended in years, some of her ranch hands… "Oh, no."

Eric's head whipped around. "What?"

"Keith and Glenn." She couldn't believe she hadn't thought of them. She only wished she was more aware of their plans. "They've been competing in team roping. They might be here tonight."

The truck turned in to the exhibitors' entrance and circled to the back of the arena.

Eric leveled a calm gaze. "If they see you, are they the types who will turn you in?"

She didn't have to think too hard about Glenn Freemont. "Glenn is. Between his fascination with crime novels and cop shows on television, I suspect a career in law enforcement is his secret dream."

"And Keith?"

Keith Sherwood was another story. "Keith would probably prefer to shoot us himself." She supposed she should feel lucky that he didn't carry his assault rifle to rodeos, although she was sure he'd have an assortment of rifles in the rack in his truck along with a handgun or two.

"No loyalty, eh?"

"Glenn hasn't worked for me long. And I imagine Keith believes you killed Randy. He might even believe I was there, too, at this point." They had no clue how large the news story about the murder and subsequent manhunt had grown in the past day. Maybe the entire state would be gunning for them. And here they were, riding smack into the middle of a crowd of people, any one of whom could identify them, call the police, or worse. "This was a bad idea."

"It'll be fine. We'll be in and out before anyone sees us. We'll just have to avoid the competitors."

"Not such an easy thing to do when we're driving right into the middle of them."

They entered the gate and bumped through a rutted lot between trucks, horse trailers and motor homes. Sarah peered through the slats in the back gate and focused on the small grandstand above the bucking chutes, a place called the Buzzard's Roost. Below were the stock pens. The scent of manure and the warm tang of horse sweat surrounded her like a favorite blanket. She took a deep, bracing breath. The trailer's jolts slowed as the truck circled.

Now came the tough part. Getting out of the trailer unseen. "Ready?"

Eric nodded. He rose to his feet, careful to stay tight to the side of the trailer in case anyone was behind them.

Sarah focused on his bloody sock. Another problem she'd forgotten about. "You might be a little noticeable walking around with only one boot."

"I have an idea." He motioned for her to move to the back gate. Once she took her spot, he placed his hands around her waist.

His touch felt familiar, comforting, but also disconcerting. Her body seemed to sway toward him on its own, leaning against the pressure of his hands, molding to his touch.

Stop it.

She focused on the slowing trailer, scouted for stray riders warming up their mounts behind the trailer parking area. If anyone spotted them jumping from the trailer, they would be sure to ask questions. Questions she and Eric could never answer.

"As soon as your feet hit the ground, make for that rig over there." He extended a finger, indicating a motor home with a four-horse slant hitched to the back. "There shouldn't be anyone there. I just saw them leave."

"Okay. Ready." Sarah tensed. The trailer bumped, jolted and stopped.

Eric lifted her as if she weighed nothing. She grasped the trailer gate and swung her legs over. She hit the ground knees bent and running. The force shuddered through her bones.

She reached the other rig before the driver opened his pickup's door. Eric was right behind her, limping as fast as his feet would move. They opened the trailer dressing room and ducked inside.

A dog's bark sounded from outside. A whistle split the air.

"Just in time." Sarah panted.

Eric checked out the tiny window in the dressing room's door. "All clear. No one seems to have noticed except the dog."

Sarah struggled to catch her breath. The rodeo had to be close to starting time. Likely most of the competitors had already drifted closer to the arena.

She glanced around the cramped and darkened space, the typical dressing room, tight and full of a jumbled form of organization that made sense only to the people to whom it belonged. She breathed in the warm fragrance of leather, mixed with Eric's distinctive scent.

He stepped to the side, his body pressing against her. "I found boot boxes. Yeah, these should do." He let out a soft grunt as he pulled one on.

She shifted to the side to give them both room. "How does it fit?"

"A little big on my good foot. But the other foot is so swollen, it's perfect."

"How about your head? I can still see some blood in your hair."

He added a black felt cowboy hat she found stuck in a corner and he was ready to go. "Don't you need something?"

"I'm fine," she said, although she didn't feel very fine at all. She glanced around the space. "Doesn't look like there's a woman that goes with this rig."

"Maybe we'll spot something on the way out."

She hated stealing peoples gear like this, especially since there was no way they could get it back to the poor guy when they were done. But it couldn't be helped. She didn't know how much cash Eric was carrying, but she didn't have a dime on her. When she'd gone out to do chores two evenings ago, she didn't exactly expect to need her wallet.

By the time they emerged from the dressing room, the man who'd acted as their unknowing chauffeur was nowhere to be seen. His dog barked from the rolled-down window of the pickup. Eric slung the backpack onto one shoulder. It didn't go with the outfit, but that couldn't be helped. They didn't exactly have a place to stash it. They strode through the exhibitors' area as if they belonged there.

A man in a silver belly Stetson and button-down shirt stood at the gate leading to the arena. "How the hell are we going to get around him?"

The sound of hooves trotting through gravel crunched behind them. Sarah glanced at Eric. "Slow down, I have an idea."

A tiny boy bounced past them on the back of a towering quarter horse, well over sixteen hands. Sarah plastered a proud-parent smile on her face and followed the boy through the gate as if he belonged to her.

The man in the hat gave the kid a grin, then focused on Sarah and Eric. "Good luck," he called.

"Thanks!" Sarah said.

Eric gave the guy a friendly tip of the hat. As soon as they cleared the gate, he turned to Sarah. "Pretty slick."

She couldn't help turning a genuine smile on him. In the past day and a half, she'd had to lean on Eric more than she had leaned on anyone since she was a child. It felt good to have a venue where she could put her expertise to use. And it felt better than she wanted to acknowledge to have Eric notice. "I'm glad he didn't know the boy. That would have been dicey."

"You'd have come up with something."

She'd like to think so, but she wasn't so sure. Her mind felt as fuzzy as her muscles were tired. Along with the fatigue, she couldn't shake the constant sense that tears were pressing at the corners of her eyes and longing poised to uncurl in her chest—emotion waiting for the slightest excuse to push to the surface. She normally went by what her gut told her, but fighting through all she had in addition to having Eric again at her side was overwhelming. She prayed she could hold it all together.

And that they wouldn't run in to Keith or Glenn or someone else who would know who they were.

Finding the track that circled the opposite end of the arena from where the competitors congregated, they headed for the grandstand. They fell into the light stream of foot traffic behind a young family. Sarah plastered a smile to her face and tried to look like she was here to enjoy a fun night at the rodeo instead of hoping to identify a murder victim.

In front of her, a toddler girl looked over her daddy's shoulder and gave her a smile. Wrapping her little arms around his neck, she whispered something in his ear, and he laughed. Her older brother held both mom and dad's hands. Picking up his legs, he swung between them like they were human monkey bars.

Sarah's throat felt thick, her chest painfully empty. What she wouldn't have given for a happy family scene like that when she was a child. Her parents rarely took them to the rodeo, only Layton had bothered to do that. Even when one of them did trailer her barrel horse to the grounds, usually their mom, she seemed distant, more inclined to hang out with adults than help her daughter or cheer for her son to stay on his steer for the required eight seconds.

The worst part was that Sarah had always vowed her kids would have it different. That their rodeo experiences would be all about family. A mom and a dad…together. A mom and a dad who loved each other. She'd always wished she could give her own children those moments she'd never had. Precious moments the family in front of them probably took for granted.

She blinked back the mist of tears and gave the little

girl a wave as the family split off to take a seat in the stands and she and Eric continued on the same path.

In the concession area behind the grandstand, people milled around, buying raffle tickets to win a bedroom set handcrafted out of knotty pine. The crowd seemed bigger than the parking lot suggested. The scent of popcorn teased the air, making Sarah's stomach growl. She looked up at the back of the grandstand.

Plain, white walls greeted her, broken only by a few sponsors signs.

Her stomach dropped. "It's not here. The list of champions."

From the arena, the announcer boomed his introductions. Boots shuffled in the stands above them. Flags flapped in the wind as riders paraded them around the arena at a lope.

"There are seats on the other side," Eric said. "Maybe it's there."

Sarah thought of the small section of grandstand overlooking the bucking chutes, where cowboys mounted horses and bulls, and shook her head. "I got a glimpse of The Buzzard's Roost when we pulled in. It wasn't there either. I must be remembering the wall of champions from a different rodeo grounds. I have so many memories of this place, I guess I just assumed…"

Eric rubbed a hand over her back. "It's okay. We'll find his name another way."

His touch felt good, as it had in the trailer. Too good. She wanted to lean in to him. Let him hold her. Fill her up. She felt too weak to stand on her own a moment longer.

She shook her head and beat back the threat of tears. She supposed it was natural to have this reaction. Between the hormones and lack of sleep and losing her brother, it probably wasn't surprising that she was now losing her mind. "We came here for nothing."

"Pardon, but don't I know you?" a man's voice called from behind her.

Sarah's heart stuttered in her chest.

Chapter Ten

Eric's pulse thrummed in his ears, drowning out the first strains of the national anthem. He glanced at the front gate. A good fifty feet lay between them and the parking lot. If this guy recognized them, they'd have to make a dash for it. Gathering himself, he turned toward the voice.

An older man stood grinning at Sarah, his face as round as the brim of the hat on his head. He raised a hand and stroked the corners of a nearly white mustache. "Didn't you used to do some barrel racing around here a few years ago?"

Sarah glanced at Eric with wide eyes, then returned her focus to the man. Pink crept up her throat and touched her cheeks. She opened her mouth, as if to answer, then closed it without saying a word.

Eric thrust his had toward the man. "I'm Joe. So you've been involved with the rodeo here for a while?" He'd learned a while ago that if you wanted to distract someone, get them talking about themselves. It worked every time.

The man enveloped his hand and gave it a firm shake. "They call me Smithy. Been coming here since I was a boy up in Powell."

"Then you're just the man we want to talk to, Smithy." He knew it was risky, sticking around any longer than they had to. The guy's memory could come back at any moment. And if he remembered Sarah's name, he might just tie her to the story he'd heard about in the news. But without the list of champions, they were without answers…answers Smithy just might be able to provide.

He had to take the risk.

Eric pulled the belt buckle from the pack. "We came upon this out on the BLM. Wanted to return it to its owner. Problem is, we don't know the name of the man who won it."

The man took the buckle and held it out as far as he could reach. Hard muscle roped forearms spotted with age. "Bareback bronc riding?"

"1978." Eric supplied.

"Long time ago."

Sarah gave him a smile, this time looking more sweet than scared out of her wits. "Are there records of who won back then?"

"Of course."

"Where could we find something like that?" Her voice was still a little shaky, but curious. She'd obviously recovered from the shock and was playing along nicely. As if they'd planned this course of action all along.

She never ceased to amaze him.

The man stroked his mustache once again, then trailed lower to rub his chin between fingers and thumb. "1978…I think I can tell you who won this. But if you want to check—"

"Really? Who?" Sarah jumped in a little too quickly.

Smithy narrowed his eyes on her as if once again trying to remember where he'd seen her before.

"We just need to get back to our children." Eric motioned to the stands. The lie had slipped out so easily, and it suddenly struck him that in just a few months, it wouldn't be a lie any longer. "You understand."

Smithy smiled. "Rodeo's fun for a family." He motioned to the arena and began telling them about an upcoming event where children in the audience tried to capture a ribbon from a calf's tail and win prizes.

Eric didn't hear a word.

A family. That's what he and Sarah and the baby could be. His throat constricted. He kept his focus on Smithy, smiling and nodding at the older man's story, careful not to look in Sarah's direction, careful to keep control of the emotion bubbling inside.

He'd never wanted a family. Never considered it. He told himself he liked his life as it was. Clear-cut and logical. Always in control. Being around Sarah was never that. He always felt like he was over his head, scaling a cliff solo with no harness. Just a slip away from a disastrous fall.

But right now, listening to Smithy, thinking about a life with her, a family with her…

"So if you'd like me to look up the winner of that buckle to be official…"

Eric forced his mind back to the conversation at hand. Before he had time to think about any of that, he needed to make sure Sarah was safe. And the way to do that was to get some answers.

"Do you know who it belongs to? Off the top of your head?" he prompted. "We don't need anything official."

Smithy handed the buckle back to Eric. "Larry Hodgeson's the one you're looking for."

"You're sure?" The man had come up with the name so easily, Eric was almost afraid to believe him.

"Sure, I'm sure. He beat me out for that buckle. I can still feel that last ride on rainy days." He rubbed his hip to illustrate. "A man don't forget something like that."

"Thank you so much." This was turning out better than Eric had dreamed. "Do you know where he lives?"

"Cheyenne. At least last I heard, that's where he was. Worked for the state down there, I believe."

Eric almost groaned. The capital of Wyoming, Cheyenne was in the opposite corner of the state from Cody. He didn't relish the thought of that drive. Of course, driving wasn't even possible unless they located some wheels.

"You want to return that buckle, you can give it to me. I'll give it to his wife. She lives here in Cody."

"His wife?" Sarah echoed.

"Ex-wife, I should have said. After they divorced a little while back, Joy moved home. She's got family here, you know. She can probably make sure it gets back to him."

"If you don't mind, we'd like to return the buckle to Joy ourselves. I'd love to meet her." Sarah gave the man a smile that could charm just about any man out of anything. "Do you know where we can find her?" she asked.

Once again the man studied her with narrowed eyes. "I ain't in the habit of giving out ladies' addresses to strangers."

"Maybe she would meet us somewhere?" Eric asked. It was up to Eric to get the man's attention away from Sarah and focused on him. Smithy obviously still felt he should know her, and judging from his expressions every time she spoke, he wasn't about to give up until her remembered her name.

Sarah shifted her boots on the gravel under her feet. "If you think she's too busy, that's all right."

"Too busy?" The man shook his head so hard his jowls flapped. "Joy would welcome a social call. Let me ask her. What section are you and the kids sitting in?"

"What section?" Sarah glanced at Eric.

To the man, it probably looked like she just couldn't recall. Eric knew she was feeling the same jolt at being caught in a lie that rattled through his own stomach. But there was more implied in the man's comment than a question they couldn't answer. He grasped her hand and gave it a reassuring squeeze. "Is Joy Hodgeson here at the rodeo?" he asked.

"She don't miss a night. She's up in the announcer's booth. Acts as kind of a secretary up there, keeping track of the entrants and such." He pointed to the announcer's booth across the arena in the top of the Buzzard's Roost. "One of the reasons she moved back, I think. They have a grand rodeo in Cheyenne, but it ain't Cody."

Sarah nodded. "Good memories. I can appreciate that. I'd love to meet her. Is there any way we can pop in to talk to her? It'll only take a second, and I've always wanted to see what everything looks like from up there."

Those narrowed eyes again. "I knew you were from around here."

Eric sucked in a breath. He groped for a distraction. Something he could say. A question he could ask. A way to take back control of the situation. This time, he came up empty.

"You know how people say they never forget a face? That's me. At least my wife swears it." He looked at her as if waiting for her to fess up.

This time, Sarah gave him a relaxed smile that should have had her up for some kind of acting award. "I ran the barrels when I was a teenager. I have a lot of good memories of this place as well. I'd love to talk to Mrs. Hodgeson."

"Can I tell her your name?"

There it was. Eric hoped she could come up with something. Because even if Mr. Never-forget-a-face didn't recognize them from photos on TV, he might have heard their names enough over the past two days that it all would click into place.

"Mary Ann Johnston was my maiden name. I didn't win much, so I doubt you'd remember. I sure had a good time, though." Emotion infused her voice—too much real feeling for anyone to fake.

Eric almost did a double take.

"Mary Ann…Mary Ann…you've grown up a lot, young lady. And here I was thinking you looked like that Trask girl. Well, follow me, Joe and Mary Ann." He started walking back around the track that curved the arena's edge, motioning them to follow with a wave of his arm.

Sarah glanced at Eric, relief plain on her face.

Eric seconded that feeling. He didn't know how she'd come up with the name, but it had worked. He'd been caught flat-footed that time, and she'd pulled it out. The feeling that someone had his back, so to speak, that if he faltered she'd step in, was a new experience, one he didn't entirely know how to process.

Eric and Sarah followed the man up a steel staircase

and onto a walkway. A day and a half had passed since Randy had been shot, but it seemed like they'd been on the run without sleep for a week. The setting sun glowed orange off the Absarokas to the west, its reflection making the Shoshone River look as if it were on fire. Below, horses, steers and bulls milled in steel-pipe pens, waiting for their turn in the arena. The announcer's voice boomed out the name of the first bareback rider on the program, and a roar went up from the crowd.

They had one more person to talk to. One more role to play, and hopefully they'd get the answers they needed. He just prayed at least one of them was still sharp enough to get the job done.

JOY HODGESON WASN'T anything like what Sarah had imagined. Shockingly white hair cropped short and stylish and dressed in Wranglers and a form-fitting western shirt with hot pink piping, the woman looked far younger than she had to be. And her energy...the way she was flying around, organizing entry forms, and feeding them to the announcer, made Sarah feel even more tired than she already was.

After making introductions, Smithy stepped to the side of the narrow staircase outside the booth's door. "Go on in. There's not enough room in there for me, too. Besides, that place gives me claustrophobia *and* vertigo. It's like a damn tree house without the tree."

Eric motioned for Sarah to go first and the two of them crammed in to the little room. The place smelled of new paint and cigarettes. Smithy closed the door behind them. The announcer didn't even turn around, his ball cap pulled down to his brows, his attention glued to the action in the arena below.

"So what brings you two up to see me?" Joy managed to beam them a friendly smile at the same time as she organized entry forms for the next event and handed them to the announcer. Down in the arena, a man dressed as a ragged clown launched into a comedy routine.

"We have something you might want to take a look at." Eric pulled out the belt buckle and handed it to the woman.

She stared at the tarnished silver and ran a fingertip over its gold lettering.

"Smithy said it might have belonged to your husband?" Sarah prodded.

"Yep. It's Larry's. Where did you get it?"

Sarah glanced at Eric, but she didn't have to look to him to know the last thing either one of them wanted to do was give Joy a truthful answer to that question. "We found it out on the BLM."

"Careless fool." She handed it back to Eric. "It's nice of you to return it, don't get me wrong. I just…I've put that part of my life behind me. If you give me your name and number, I'll have him call you if he ever comes looking for it."

"When was the last time you saw your husband?"

"Oh, I threw him out over two years ago."

Sarah didn't have to spend much time counting the months to know the body in the crevasse probably hadn't been there that long. She was no forensics expert, but she'd assume the bones would be clean and the smell gone after that amount of time in the elements. And the smell had definitely not been gone. "Smithy said you moved back to Cody not long ago. That you used to live in Cheyenne."

The woman bobbed her head as she laid out the

entrants on the table in front of the announcer. The man focused on his job, still not taking the time to spare them so much as a glance.

"I love Cheyenne, don't get me wrong. But I only moved there because of Larry's job. Cody is my home."

"Where does Larry work?" Eric managed to make the question sound natural, as if they were merely having a casual conversation.

She waved her hands in front of her as if erasing words from the air. "He doesn't work there anymore. Not long after our divorce, he up and quit his job. Here he just had to stay in Cheyenne instead of moving back with me, and yet he didn't even wait to take advantage of the incentives for early retirement." She shook her head and clucked her tongue as if the illogic of it still bothered her.

"What did he do for a living?" Sarah asked.

"Oh, he worked for the state. In the crime lab."

"The crime lab?" She exchanged a look with Eric. "What did he do there?"

"He looked at fingerprints. It was a good job. But sometimes I wish I'd never encouraged him to go back to school. I wish we'd stayed right here and worked my folks' ranch."

Sarah tilted her head. "Why is that? It seems like a pretty good job."

"It was. Not great money, but steady, good hours and health insurance. But that was before all those shows started on TV. You know, *CSI* and the like."

Now Sarah wasn't following her at all. "What about *CSI?*"

"Nothing against the show, but Larry started thinking he was one of those TV stars or something. He started talking with a writer. Having lunch." She made air quotes with her fingers around the word *lunch*. "Getting a bit of a swelled head, I think. That's when I left. He didn't even try to talk me out of it. Probably had visions of dating some television star in a low-cut blouse."

A knock sounded on the door. Joy scootched past them and opened the door a crack. A man pushed a file of entries into Joy's hand.

Eric pulled the brim of his hat down to shield his features and Sarah turned her face to the side. She gazed over the announcer's shoulder, pretending to be studying a skit that two clowns—or bullfighters, as they liked to be called—performed to kill time while the announcer and Joy and all the people running things behind the scenes readied the next event's entries. Best to be safe. There was always a chance whomever was at the door was more of a news hound than either Joy or Smithy.

The door thunked closed, and Sarah let out a heavy breath of relief.

Joy wedged herself through the tight space once again. "I got the breakaway roping here next, Billy."

"All right." The announcer turned, hand reaching for the file. He looked up at Eric…and froze.

Sarah's blood froze with him.

Seemingly in slow motion, he reached for the microphone. He turned on the switch and leaned his lips close. *"Security. I need security. Up here in the announcer's booth. Hurry."*

Chapter Eleven

Eric grabbed Sarah's arm, but he didn't need to. She was already moving, throwing open the door, racing down the steel steps. They reached the main walkway and dashed past a concession stand. Their feet thundered on the steel grating.

Two men in Stetsons rounded the corner. Shoulder to shoulder, they nearly blocked the stairs.

Sarah slammed to a stop, Eric almost running in to her from behind. She whirled around, looked up at him, the whites of her eyes bright in the arena lights.

He had to get her out of here. He had to think.

The men started up the steps in unison, a wall of cowboy they couldn't get around. Eric spun in the other direction. A man came at them from that direction, too. Striding out from the seats of The Buzzard's Roost. Another entered the walkway behind him.

Eric had to do something *now*.

He grabbed the rail and looked over the edge. A maze of steel fence shown in the dimness, ten or fifteen feet below, chutes that returned bucking horses and bulls to the holding pens. He grabbed Sarah's arm. "Over the edge."

She nodded, no hesitation. Grabbing the rail, she swung a leg over the edge and jumped.

Eric followed. He hit the ground behind her. The impact sent a stab of pain through his foot and a shudder through his body. But the ground was soft, stirred up by hooves and padded with manure.

"Eric!" On her feet already, Sarah was moving for the gate. He struggled to his feet and followed.

Voices clamored behind them. The tramping of feet rumbled down the stairs.

Sarah half climbed, half vaulted one pipe gate, then another. She slipped over the last of the gates designed to funnel the bucking stock and disappeared into a holding pen.

Eric followed her path. Each time he jumped a gate and landed, his foot screamed. By the third one, his foot was numb.

Fine by him.

He raced across the churned-up ground of the pen. A loud snort sounded to his right. He glanced in the direction of the sound. A huge gray bull stared back.

Damn.

"Over here. Just run for it."

He made for the sound of Sarah's voice. Behind him, he could hear the animal. The beat of his hooves. The snort of his breath. He braced himself for goring horns.

Sarah stood near the fence. She flapped something in her hands, something…

The bull raced straight for her.

"No." Eric veered to the side.

"Keep running! Jump the fence!" she yelled.

Her coat. That's what she held. She waved it like she thought she was some damn Spanish bullfighter. As the bull drew close, she tossed it. It fluttered in the air. He stabbed into it with his horns and dashed it to the ground.

Sarah jumped for the fence. Ten feet down, Eric did, too. They clambered over. When their feet hit the ground on the other side, they raced for the back gate.

Men's voices jangled behind them. Asking questions. Yelling directions. Someone shouted he'd called police.

Eric pushed his legs to move faster. When they'd arrived, a man in a cowboy hat had been watching the gate. No one was there now. Eric could only guess that he'd responded to the call for security. That he was one of the men pursuing them now.

Eric grasped the chain looped around the gate's latch. He yanked it open and he and Sarah slipped through. He veered to the left, racing past the trailers and motor homes.

Sarah motioned to the jumble of rigs. "We—"

"Too obvious." No way they could stow away aboard a random trailer now. Not with men combing the grounds for them, men who would be out of the stands and smack on their trail at any moment. It was the first place they'd look. "The river."

They ran across the flat area as fast as they could, gravel shifting and scattering under their feet like marbles. The gravel ended and the ground grew rough. When they hit the spot where it started sloping down to the river, Eric dove for the dirt, pulling Sarah with him.

Behind them, shouting came closer, rising over the sound of the river's rushing water. Eric scooped in breath after breath, trying to satisfy his hungry lungs. The faint odor of sulfur in the water hung in the back of this throat. "We'll follow the river bed to the highway. We have to get out of here before the police arrive."

Cheeks pink from their escape, Sarah nodded. Her eyes glowed with determination. Her dark hair swirled around her in the wind. She looked so alive and vibrant, his chest hurt.

He had to get her out of this mess. He had to find someplace safe. He looked at the rushing water. "Ready?"

Sarah nodded. "I'm right behind you."

He jammed the black hat low to cover as much of his hair as he could and half crawled, half stumbled down the bank to the water, keeping his body as low to the ground as he could. Rock bit into his hands, his knees. He kept moving, Sarah right behind him.

Above the roar of the water and thunder of his pulse, voices rose in the night air. Somewhere a siren screamed.

They had no time to lose.

SARAH COULDN'T REMEMBER ever being so cold.

They followed the river until it flanked the highway. Most of the way, they were able to stay on the shore. But in some spots, the bank rose almost vertically from the water. Then, they had to plunge into the frigid river. Deeper than the stream that crossed through her ranch, the Shoshone's current tumbled and swirled around them, fast and relentless. And even though she was soaked and scared and drained of any energy she had left, she was grateful to make it to the highway alive and not in the custody of police.

They followed West Yellowstone Avenue, and turned toward downtown. They needed to find a car or a place to hide, and the other direction only promised the reservoir and a road that dead-ended at the closed gates of Yellowstone. But still, walking into civilization made Sarah nervous.

She tried not to look behind her. Tried not to focus on the red and blue lights pulsing from the rodeo grounds. There wasn't a lot of foot traffic in this stretch of Cody, making it hard to blend in. So they stayed off the highway, moving through ditches and along parking lots.

Eric reached out a hand to help her up a steep ditch and to a more level cluster of driveways leading to restaurants and motels, busy on a Saturday night. "You're trembling. Cold?"

She nodded. But that wasn't the half of it. The cold, the fear, the ebbing adrenaline…her list went on. But try as she might, she couldn't stop shaking. It wasn't within her grasp. Not any longer. The best she could do was stumble forward and pray Eric was in better shape.

He rubbed a hand over her back as they walked. "So if you were a tourist, where would you want to stay?"

She glanced at him out of the corner of her eye.

"Come on. Price is no object." He gave her a smile that seemed a little tired and forced, but she had to admit it was better than she could have done.

She could at least put in what effort she could muster. "The Irma," she said, suggesting the famous hotel Buffalo Bill Cody named for his daughter.

"A sucker for history, eh?"

"You bet."

A police car sped past, lights flashing red and blue.

Sarah sucked in a breath and tried her best to keep focused straight ahead, to look like she didn't have a care in the world, not that she remembered what that felt like anymore.

"What would you have for dinner?"

She forced her mind back to Eric's game. "A steak,

of course. Baked potato with sour cream. A salad, ranch dressing." Her stomach growled, right on cue.

"Steak, huh? Who would have guessed? I suppose a beef rancher is required to say that."

"Hey, it's real food, that's what Layton always likes to say. How about you? You're not going to choose seafood or quiche or something, are you?"

He didn't answer. His steps slowed.

"What is it?"

"Not sure."

They cleared the strip mall and walked to the next drive. A small restaurant sat off on its own at the back of the parking lot, a sign in front proclaiming it had the best steaks in town. The building was cute but older, built of rough-hewn logs and sporting a green roof that made Sarah think of kids' Lincoln Logs. But unlike the restaurants they'd passed earlier, the lot in front was vacant and no lights shone from the interior.

Eric pointed to a sign on the front door announcing the restaurant was temporarily closed for renovation. "I can't promise a room at the Irma, but I might be able to get you that steak."

ERIC CARRIED A BUCKET of fried chicken the workers must have had left over from lunch and plopped it on the table. He added two dinner plates and linen napkins he'd found in the waiter's aisle.

"You promised me steak," she said, lighting a candle with a wooden match. Gentle light flickered over the booth.

Covered with thick upholstered padding and wide enough for sleeping, the booths were the first thing Eric had spotted after they broke in through a window that was fortunately not alarmed. In addition, the pantry and walk-in freezer still held a stock of staples and the plumbing in the kitchen worked like a dream. They would even have coffee in the morning.

Eric set down two tall glasses of water and slid into the opposite bench. "Have I ever told you that you're awfully picky?"

"Funny, I've always thought I wasn't picky enough." She tilted her head to the side and gave him a smile.

For a moment, he felt like they'd turned back time. That he'd never walked away from her. That no one had been killed. That the police and sheriff and half the state of Wyoming weren't looking for them now. That all he had to concentrate on was how good being around her made him feel. To accept it. To soak it in.

It was a nice fantasy.

For a long while, all they did was eat and drink, not wasting even a moment on talk. By the time they came up for air, the bucket of chicken was empty and piles of bones lay on the plates.

Sarah tilted the bucket toward her and picked crumbs of greasy breading from the bottom. "Hope the workers bring a lunch tomorrow. This 'being fugitives' stuff has turned us into criminals."

"We could always leave them some cash to pay for it."

"How much cash do you have?"

"Under fifty dollars. Forty-eight to be exact."

Her smile faded. Clearly she understood there was no way they could get more. Not without the law tracking them down. "I guess they'll just have to deal with it."

Eric was sorry he'd brought it up. For a moment,

they'd had a little reprieve, food, relative safety…they'd been able to forget a little. He was sorry his comment had brought them crashing back to earth. "Ready for dessert?" The lightness in his voice sounded forced, even to his own ears.

She arched her brows. "Dessert?"

Eric thrust himself up from the booth and strode into the bar area. Even in the dim light, he could make out boxes lining the wall. What he wouldn't give for a stiff shot of whiskey. But since Sarah couldn't drink because of her pregnancy, he skipped over the booze boxes and found a different kind of treat. Twisting open the jar's cap, he carried it back to the table and set it in front of Sarah.

"Maraschino cherries?" A chuckle escaped from her throat. "I haven't had these since I was a kid with a love for hot fudge sundaes."

"I'm afraid that's the only part of the sundae I can manage." Although he'd found some staples like sealed, premeasured bags of coffee that were still stored in back, steak and ice cream and other perishables were harder to find in a restaurant closed for renovation.

She plucked out a cherry by the stem and took it between her teeth. Tearing it from the stem, she closed her eyes as if it was the most decadent of treats. She opened her eyes. "Aren't you going to have one?"

"Maybe I'll just watch."

Her laugh sounded deep and rich and intimate, and he realized it had been a long time since he'd heard it. "Feeling better?" he asked.

"Trying. I think my mind needed food."

He was sure she needed sleep, too. Probably more than they could afford to take. But if she was like him, her mind churning these questions would make sleep unlikely. At least until they decided what they were going to do next. "At least we came up with a name for our murdered man."

The candle's flicker caused shadows to shift across Sarah's face. "I kept finding myself wanting to tell Joy her husband was dead. It's sad that she thinks he grew too arrogant to talk to her."

"There are a lot of things that are sad about this mess." He'd lost count.

"A lot that's confusing, too. I can't figure out why on earth a sheriff would want to kill a fingerprint analyst."

Eric felt relieved to focus on the mystery at hand. Mistakes and motives of other people were a lot easier to examine than his own. "Because Hodgeson wouldn't give him the result he wanted?"

"But his wife said he was retired. Has been for a while. So he wouldn't be working on any pending cases. Maybe it was personal?"

He tilted his head to the side, considering. Could a sheriff in Norris County and a state crime lab analyst in Cheyenne have a personal connection? It was possible. Of course, knowing as little as they knew, a lot of things were possible. "Or Larry Hodgeson found evidence in an old case, something Sheriff Gillette wants buried."

"What kind of evidence? Fingerprints they hadn't noticed before?"

He shrugged a shoulder. "I'm just grasping at straws. But we'll find out."

"How?"

It was a good question. They'd gotten a break in finding this restaurant tonight. They needed another.

"Tomorrow we check out junkyards, car lots, whatever. See if we can find a vehicle that runs."

"Steal one, you mean."

There was nothing he could do about that. "I doubt forty-eight bucks will buy one."

"And then?"

"We need to find out more about Larry Hodgeson. If we know who he was, what he worked on, maybe we can come up with why someone would want him dead."

She nodded. "But how do we do that? That's what I can't figure out. We can't very well drive down to Cheyenne and waltz into the crime lab. Seems a bit bold."

He gave her a teasing grin. "You've got to admit, Sheriff Gillette wouldn't expect it."

"Right," she said, tone dry as the Bighorn Basin in August.

"Actually I was thinking of newspapers."

Sarah nodded. "The writer. Joy said he was talking to a writer."

"Exactly."

"We can search for news stories mentioning him online. The library has computers we can use."

"Still risky." He still felt shaken by their close call at the rodeo grounds. Even now the police could be tracking them down. Closing in on the restaurant under the cover of darkness.

He watched Sarah pop another cherry into her mouth. Whenever he looked at her, touched her, heard the sound of her voice, a need to protect her welled up inside him like a snow-melt flood.

He'd always felt too much for her, and the past two days, those feelings had grown tenfold. The threat of something going wrong, her getting hurt, something happening to the baby…all of it was hard to take. And the hardest thing to accept was that he had so little control over what happened next. From the moment Randy had been shot and the sheriff had shown up at Sarah's ranch, he had been scrambling to react, to keep disaster from crashing down on them and sweeping them away. So far, he'd barely been half a step ahead.

"What is it?" Sarah leaned forward, hands splayed on the table in front of her.

He forced himself to take a deep breath. "Nothing. I just…the risk can't be helped. But we'll find a library in some other town. They'll have their eyes out for us here in Cody." He looked down at her hands.

Her fingers were trembling. She folded her hands together. "Okay."

For all their attempts at lightness and conversation, they were both exhausted. It was amazing they were still holding it together as well as they were. "We'll find answers, Sarah. I promise."

"That's a promise you might not be able to keep."

Maybe not. But at least he could try. He could give it everything he had.

He fitted his hands over hers and gave them a gentle squeeze. Her fingers felt so fine in his big mitt, so delicate. Yet he'd seen her use those hands to rope cattle and string fence right along with the men who worked for her. She was strong. But even strong people had vulnerabilities. Even strong people needed to be able to rely on someone.

A tremble centered deep in his chest. Had he been afraid of being that someone? Was that why he left just as things between them were getting serious? Was that what caused the jumble of emotion inside him whenever she was near?

He wasn't sure. But there was one thing he did know. Now that Sarah was in danger, now that they had a baby on the way, he no longer had the right to opt out. Scared, confused, none of that mattered. He had to be that someone Sarah could rely on. And he couldn't let anything get in the way.

Chapter Twelve

Sarah soaked in the feel of Eric's hands sheltering hers and watched the candle's flicker play across his face. Over the months since he'd told her he couldn't see her anymore, the months the life they'd created was growing inside her, she'd longed for moments like this. His eyes looking at her as if she was the most fascinating thing he'd ever seen. His skin touching hers. His voice washing over her, full of feeling he didn't often show. She wanted to believe all of it was real. Lasting. Not merely the by-product of their situation.

Unfortunately, she was far too pragmatic for that. "I have to know something. Something kind of off-topic."

His brows lowered. "Yeah?"

Pressure squeezed at the base of her throat and hollowed out her chest. It was one thing feeling this insecurity about Eric, wondering about him deep in the back of her mind. It was another to broach the subject out loud. But after their trek through the mountains, the way her body wanted to sway into him at every touch, the way she longed for him to fold her into his arms, the need she had to kiss him…she had to know the truth. "Why did you leave? Three months ago, why did you walk away?"

He tilted his head, shadows sinking around his eyes, making them unreadable. "I used to think I knew the answer to that."

"I remember what you told me. Every single word. That a man who climbed mountains for a living couldn't commit to a serious relationship. That you were doing it for me, to protect me from future heartbreak. It just never made a lot of sense to me. It seemed like an excuse."

He rolled his lips inward, pausing before he spoke. "I suppose it was."

She leaned against the back of the bench. She felt empty, exhausted. Too tired to speak. Too tired to think. As if the fatigue she'd been struggling to hold off had swamped her. "I wish you hadn't bothered with excuses. I wish you had just told me the truth outright. It would have been easier for me that way."

His brows dipped low. He shook his head a little from side to side. "What do you think the truth is?"

It seemed obvious. "That you didn't care for me enough. Not enough to stay, to have a future."

"That's not it."

"Then what is it?"

"I'm just…I'm not good at this kind of thing. I'm just not—"

"Give me a break." She wished at that moment she hadn't brought any of it up. "The last thing I want is more excuses."

"What do you want?"

"The truth."

"The truth." He stared at the cherry jar, as if convinced the truth was hiding between the little artificially red orbs. "I'm not sure what the truth is, but I can tell you how I felt. How I feel even now."

Inwardly, she braced herself. "So tell me."

"I had this sense that something was bound to go wrong. That I was losing control. Just this general sense of dread."

"Dread? Of what?"

He shook his head. "I'm not sure. It was like…it was like the way I felt after my father died."

She remembered the story, at least the facts. He'd died in a car accident when Eric was fourteen. One day he'd climbed off the school bus to find police officers in the living room and his mother sobbing. But while Eric had told her the facts, he'd never talked about the emotions he'd gone through. Eric had rarely talked about emotions at all. But she knew him, the things he liked. The things he couldn't stand. She remembered. "You felt out of control?"

He let out a heavy sigh. "My mom cried herself to sleep every night. I heard her through the walls. And there was more. She took pills. Drank. I watched her self-destruct right in front of me, like the grief was grinding down what was left of her."

"That must have been horrible." She ached for him, for the boy he'd been. She ached for his mother, a woman she'd never met.

"One moment my life was secure and logical, the next…it was like everything I knew had been blown away."

She'd like to say she understood, that she knew the feeling. But the truth was, except for the ranch land itself and perhaps Layton, her life had been anything but secure and logical. Her parents' marriage, the worries about what Randy would do next…all of that seemed subject to a cruel whim.

Of course, maybe that just made her better at adapting. "So you were worried about things changing? And that's why you left?"

"Change? No." Muscles drew tight around his mouth, his forehead. He looked as if he was in pain. As if the dread he talked about in the past was here. Rooted in her.

"Then what is it?"

"The feelings. The lack of control. I just…it scared me."

It seemed ludicrous. Here was this big, strong man, a man who scaled mountains, and he was talking about being afraid. "What scared you? Me?"

"No, me." He held up a hand. "I know it sounds stupid. Right now, I can hardly believe I let those words out of my mouth. But it's the truth. When I met you, I wasn't looking to get married. You're right about that. I wasn't expecting to feel as much for you as I did. It just all seemed too fast. Crazy."

"Out of control."

"Yeah. I needed to get away and think. I could never really think when I was around you." He rubbed his forehead with thumb and forefinger. "I still can't."

That, she understood. The fire between them had burned fast and furious from the beginning. The difference was, she could never manage to pull herself away. She never wanted to. "And now that you've been away? Now that you've had a chance to think?"

"I've asked you to marry me."

"Because I'm pregnant."

"Not just that." He leaned forward on his elbows and took her hands, one in each of his own. "I won't leave you again, Sarah. I can promise you that. I will never again let you down."

Tears misted Sarah's eyes, turning the dim dining room into a mosaic of shadow and light. She didn't know how she could possibly have more tears to cry, but here they were.

Three months ago, she'd yearned to hear those words from Eric. That commitment. That promise. Now she wasn't sure what to think. But there was one thing she no longer had questions about. "I know you'll come through for me, Eric."

The ridges lining his forehead seemed to smooth in the flickering light.

She had the sudden urge to kiss him. To lean in and take his face in her hands. To fit her lips to his mouth. To taste him and hold him and never let him go.

She clamped her bottom lip between her teeth.

He drew in a breath and focused on a spot above her head. When he returned his gaze to hers, his eyes glistened. "I hope you reconsider my offer. Once you've had a chance to think about it, I mean. Once all this is finished."

She looked away from him and concentrated on the candle's flame. "Our baby will be lucky to have you for a father." She wanted to see his expression, but didn't dare meet his eyes. One look and she could change her mind. One kiss and she'd be a goner. She had to hold fast.

He shifted on the bench. "But?"

"But you don't love me."

"You don't know how I feel."

"Neither do you." She brought her eyes to his despite the risk. She saw something there. Affection, certainly. Caring. Always desire. But love? She didn't know what that would look like.

He reached across the table and took her hand back into his. "What if I told you I think I'm falling?"

She shook her head.

"What do I need to do? Make me understand. What do you want?"

"I—I want you to be different."

"Different?"

"Stupid, huh?" She let out a stab of laughter. It echoed through the room, stiff and inappropriate.

He didn't say anything. He obviously didn't know what to say.

She couldn't blame him. But the fact was, he didn't need to speak. She did. He just needed to listen. "I won't have an empty marriage like my parents did. I want a man who loves me. I've always promised myself that, and I won't give it up. Even for you."

"I don't want you to give that up."

"No?"

"I just want you to give me a chance."

She pressed her fingers to closed eyelids until color exploded in plumes and swirls. She wanted to. She wanted him. Enough to make excuses of her own, rationalizations just to be with him, to believe he loved her like she deserved. Like she needed. And that he always would.

"I'm sorry, Eric." She shook her head. "I can't do that."

ERIC JOLTED OFF THE bench. For a moment, he didn't know where he was. Dark shapes loomed to either side. The odor of paint and newly laid tile hung in the air. Outside, a truck roared past. His heart pounded against his ribs. He gasped air as if he'd been running for his life in his dreams.

Was that what had awakened him? A dream?

He knew instinctively he'd been asleep for only a few

hours, and those hours had been anything but restful. All he remembered was the feeling of chaos, of searching for Sarah, of finding her. Then they were climbing without harnesses or ropes or anchors. She started falling, and he grasped her hand. But she refused to grasp his other hand, and he couldn't hold on. Couldn't save her. Her hand slipped from his, and she was gone.

It didn't take a psychiatrist to interpret that one.

His mind adjusted along with his eyes. Darkness still cloaked the dining room, sunrise just starting to pink the sky through windows facing east. A rustle of movement came from the next booth.

"Sarah?" he whispered.

"Yeah?"

"Did you hear something?"

"I…I don't know. What was it?"

He levered himself off the bench and onto his feet. He wasn't sure. It didn't make sense for construction crews to be here so early, did it? And on a Sunday? "A rattle, maybe. Like someone opening the lock."

Sarah climbed out of her booth as well. "Front or back?"

He tried to recreate the sound in his memory. "I'm not sure, but I'm betting back." He grabbed the backpack from where he left it after refilling the water bottles. He strained to hear more, the creak of a door, a footstep.

A clatter rose from the kitchen.

Eric gestured to Sarah with a tilt of his head. He set off for the back dining room, trying to keep his footsteps as quiet as possible on the tile. He could hear Sarah follow behind, running on her toes. He didn't want to jump to conclusions about who might be in a closed restaurant this early. It could simply be a manager. An owner. Someone working on the renovations. If the police had tracked them down, they would have stormed the place last night, wouldn't they?

Not that it mattered. If whoever was here found them, their first move would be to call the police, and it wouldn't take a brain surgeon to figure out the woman and man who were camped out in the dining room of a closed restaurant probably weren't your average tourists.

"You sure it's in here?"

Behind him, Sarah jumped at the male voice echoing from the waiter's station outside the kitchen.

Eric grabbed her arm and ducked behind the back dining room's open door.

Two young men dressed in jeans, boots and hats swaggered between tables. The way they were dressed probably ruled out construction workers, and they didn't look nearly old enough to own or run a place like this. If Eric had to guess, he'd put them at barely out of high school. They passed the doorway and headed toward the bar.

Eric pushed up from the wall just as the tinkling sound of a giggle followed in the boys' wake.

He flattened back into the shadow. Sarah did the same. Seconds seemed to stretch longer than minutes before two girls walked past, heels clacking unsteadily on tile. They didn't spare as much as a glance in Eric and Sarah's direction.

Eric let a relieved breath stream through his lips.

The foursome crowded behind the bar where Eric had pilfered the bottle of cocktail cherries the night before. "Is there any beer?" a male voice said.

"Beer? Ain't you had enough beer? We got some good whiskey here. Look at this."

"Can you make Sex on the Beach?" one of the girls asked.

Now was their chance. Eric nodded to Sarah, and they made their way to the fire exit at the back of the dining room. Bracing himself for an alarm, Eric pushed the door open.

No sound but the predawn tweet of birds met his ears.

The two of them rushed outside. The cool morning air felt like a slap to hot cheeks. Eric stopped dead in his tracks and stared.

A gray SUV that should have been junked long ago sat outside the kitchen entrance, no doubt waiting while its driver and his friends stole some liquor so they could continue their party.

And the engine was still running.

"SARAH? I FOUND SOMETHING. You're not going to believe this."

The tension in Eric's voice zinged along Sarah's nerves and curled in her chest like a spring. They'd only had one free computer at the tiny library, so she'd let Eric take the Google honors, pulling a chair up next to him to see what he turned up. Unfortunately the morning light streaming through the front window was making the print on the screen fade into oblivion.

She shifted on her chair, perching on the edge of one hip and leaning forward. From here, she could smell Eric's shampoo and the soap they'd picked up at an area Wal-Mart. They'd used some of their money to buy new shirts, too, and cheap jackets, although they didn't have enough for new jeans. They'd showered at a camp-ground, and Eric had even shaved. Between that and a box of hair dye that changed his hair from sandy to dark, he looked like a different man. But although she'd considered cutting her own hair, she'd settled on plaiting it into a thick braid, a move that always accentuated the tiny bit of her ancestry that was Native American.

What she failed to pick up was a pair of sunglasses. She squinted against the glare, trying to see the newspaper story on his screen. "Where?"

He pointed to a spot midway through the article. "Woman killed in a car accident eight years ago. Driver left the scene. He was caught by matching fingerprints in the stolen car to prints police had on file. The woman's name was Marion Strub."

She leaned toward him a little more, sensing a punch line coming.

"Her maiden name was Gillette." He turned and looked at her, the glow from the screen making his green eyes look electric against his new dark hair.

"The sheriff's sister?"

"That's right." He looked back to the screen. "Sister of Norris County Sheriff Daniel Gillette."

So his sister had been killed in an accident. She hadn't remembered that. Of course, eight years ago, she hadn't had a lot of reason to think about Sheriff Danny Gillette. She hadn't even voted for him. "And Larry Hodgeson? Is there some connection with the fingerprints?"

"That's how I found the story. Hodgeson matched the prints and testified in the drunk driver's trial."

She searched her mind, trying to come up with a reason that could lead to the sheriff wanting Hodgeson dead. She knew she felt a sharp need for the men who killed Randy to pay for what they'd done. Maybe Gillette felt that way, too. "And the driver got off?"

"Nope. He had a long history of driving drunk, and he was slam-dunked by the fingerprints. He got fifteen years. He's still in the state pen in Rawlins."

"Then how—" She caught the glare of the librarian at the circulation desk across the room. She hadn't spoken above a whisper, but apparently, even that was too loud. She gave the woman a sheepish smile and mouthed *I'm sorry,* then brought her finger to her lips, warning Eric. The last thing they needed was to draw attention. She'd almost blown it. She lowered her voice until she could barely hear it herself. "How does that explain anything?

"It doesn't. But at least we have a connection between them."

There had to be something more. Hodgeson worked a lot of criminal cases. Surely there had to be more fingerprints from cases in Norris County that went to the state crime lab for analysis. Something.

"Got another hit on Hodgeson. But this trial didn't take place in Norris County."

"What is it about?"

He held up a hand as he read the story.

She squinted, straining to make out the words through the glare. She wished she could stand and lean over Eric's shoulder, but that might make her more noteworthy to the librarian. She didn't dare risk it. Besides, being that close to Eric, smelling his scent, moving her face next to his…bad idea.

Eric glanced up at her. "It's a drug case. Methamphetamine. Police found a trailer home that was being used as a meth lab. A guy named Walter Burne owned the land and the double-wide, but his prints didn't end up matching the prints inside. The jury decided that added up to reasonable doubt."

"And Hodgeson analyzed the fingerprints?"

"Yeah. But there's no connection to Gillette. Not that I can see here." He grabbed for the mouse, and clicked back to the search window.

Something shifted in Sarah's memory. "Wait."

Eric paused.

"Go back to that last story."

He did as she asked.

"What was the guy's name?"

"Walter Burne. You know it?"

She did, didn't she? "Is it spelled with an *e* on the end?"

"Yeah."

"There's a guy named Burne at the Full Throttle. Spells his name with an *e*. I don't know his first name."

"You're drinking at biker bars now?"

"It's not a biker bar, really. Not anymore. But it's still a rough place. Maybe rougher than it used to be. The guy named Burne is the new owner."

Eric shook his head and stared at her as if she were speaking a language he couldn't understand. "Biker bar, rough bar, what are you doing hanging around at a place like that at all?"

"I wasn't. Randy was. It was the first place he went when he got out of jail. Keith saw him there, was worried he was up to no good. And he said he'd also seen Randy with this Burne guy back before his arrest." She hadn't taken Keith's warnings very seriously. The kid had an ax to grind with just about anyone, it seemed. She merely told him she'd talk to Randy about it. And she had meant to the next day…after he returned from Saddle Horn Ridge.

Eric tented his fingers in front of his lips. "Maybe Gillette's not the connection. Randy is."

Sarah nodded, regret stinging her eyes. She blinked back moisture in time to see the librarian abandon the circulation desk and start walking their way.

Chapter Thirteen

"She might just be going to warn us to keep it down." Sarah's whisper quavered.

She might be right, but Eric wasn't about to count on it. He noted the name of the reporter who wrote the article was the same as the last one and clicked the mouse, bringing the computer back to the blank search screen. "I'll talk to her. Get up and head for the bathroom. Take the back exit like we planned."

"Not without you."

"It's not like she can physically stop me from leaving. I'll meet you at the SUV. Go."

Sarah pushed out of her chair and walked for the hall that housed the restrooms…and the back exit door.

They'd known a trip to the library was risky. Although he didn't yet know what to make of what they'd found, he hoped the risk was worth it. Better yet, he hoped they were wrong about the librarian's motives.

He looked up at the woman and smiled.

She smiled back as she approached, laugh lines creasing tanned skin. A short-sleeved blouse showed muscular arms. Probably in her fifties, she looked less like the stereotypical librarian and more like an outdoors enthusiast.

"I apologize if we were too loud. We're on our way out."

"That's not why I came over."

"Oh?"

"You just look so familiar to me. I was wondering if I know you from somewhere."

Yes, probably from those news reports you've watched. He forced a laugh. "That always happens to me. You're the third person who's said that this week. My wife says I have a generic face."

She laughed and pushed curly hair back from her cheek. "Sorry to bother you."

Eric let out a breath as she walked away. When she reached her spot at the circulation desk, she turned back to take another look.

He had to get out of here.

He pushed to his feet and casually walked to the restroom. At least he hoped it looked casual. He felt like his nerves were jumping out of his skin. When he reached the hall, he bolted past the marked doors and went straight for the red exit sign.

Sarah sat in the passenger seat of the SUV. Eric slid behind the wheel and started the engine just as the library door opened and the librarian stuck her head out the door.

Great. He pressed the gas and drove. Not too fast. Nothing to see here.

"That was close," Sarah said as they turned on to the highway. "What did she say?"

"She thought she recognized me."

"Did she figure out why?"

"Don't know. But even if she didn't just take down

our license plate, we're going to have to come up with a new ride. Driving a stolen truck is pushing our luck." Too bad. Eric liked the feeling of control having a vehicle once again gave him. Of course he knew it was an illusion. He didn't really have control of anything. But the act of researching connections, uncovering pieces of the truth, as small as they were, at least made him *feel* like he was getting somewhere. Taking charge of something. Fighting back.

Taking steps to protect Sarah and the baby.

"Maybe we can find something to drive at the Full Throttle."

He glanced at Sarah out of the corner of his eye. "Conviction or not, Burne seems to be a meth dealer. There's no telling what Randy got himself into with someone like that. You sure you want to go there?"

"I don't see how we have a lot of choice. If we can't get help from law enforcement, maybe it's time to try the other side of the equation."

He nodded in agreement, but he didn't like the desperate tone in her voice.

SARAH SQUINTED THROUGH thick smoke at the half-dozen or so men spending a Sunday afternoon drinking in the hazy dimness of the Full Throttle. Two wore cowboy hats. Most sported prison tattoos. None of them looked friendly. She'd dealt with hard-edged men her entire life, but she was glad Eric was with her all the same.

She and Eric stepped to the bar. The place smelled of stale smoke, stale beer and sanitizer, probably stale as well. A bartender zeroed in on them. Face overwhelmed by a handlebar mustache he must have started growing when they were in style in the early 1900s, he slapped a bar towel down and leaned forward on meaty palms. "What can I get ya?" He ran an assessing gaze over Sarah.

She ignored whatever demeaning message he was trying to send. "Are you Walter Burne?"

The man chuckled. "Do I look like Burne?"

"I don't know. What does Burne look like?"

"Not like me. Now what are you drinking?"

"Did you know Randy Trask?"

He gave a disgusted roll of his eyes. "You sure as hell ask a lot of questions."

"Did you know him?"

"Maybe. Who are you?"

"I'm his sister."

She could feel Eric tense up.

She knew it was dangerous, letting anyone know who she was. She wasn't sure if her name and photo were being broadcast alongside Eric's, but she wouldn't be surprised. Layton was pretty adamant that the sheriff wanted her just as much. He never would have encouraged her to run otherwise. But as nervous as she was about identifying herself, she had little choice. She doubted she'd get anywhere with this guy by playing coy games. Besides, she'd bet the patrons of the Full Throttle wanted a visit from the sheriff about as much as she did. She needed to take a chance.

"The rancher lady." A smile curved beneath all the hair, teasing, knowing, cruel. "Well, Randy ain't here. But then, you probably know that."

A man down the bar stood and moved several stools closer. "Why are you looking for Randy? He's dead."

"We're not looking for Randy," Eric said. "We're looking for people who knew him."

"Ahh." The newcomer to the conversation chuckled deep in his skinny chest, the sound infused with the rattle of someone who was a long-time smoker. He perched on the edge of the stool. His leg bounced, as if he was itching to move. "I might have known him."

Even though he was sitting, Sarah could tell he was close to Eric's height. But where Eric was fit and built with more than his share of muscle, this guy was narrow as a wire. And judging from his jumpy demeanor, she'd say a live wire at that.

The kind of nervous energy that might have come from dipping in to the drugs he produced? "Are you Burne?"

"Me? Ha! You've got to be out of your mind."

"Who are you?"

"Name's Jerry."

"Sarah." She held out her hand and they shook. His palm was moist, and Sarah fought the urge to wipe her hand on her jeans. "Were you here when Randy came in the other day?"

"What, after he got out?"

"Yes."

"Maybe. Don't remember."

"Well, have you heard what he stopped in here about?"

"Having a drink isn't a good reason for stopping in a bar?" the bartender boomed. He leveled a look on them, a clear hint they should order if they intended to stay.

"Give us a Sprite and a tapper." Eric threw a ten on the bar.

Sarah turned back to the guy on the next bar stool. "Was there any other reason Randy came in here? Something *besides* having a drink?"

"Don't know whatcha mean." He folded arms that were little more than flesh stretched over bone across his chest. Tattoos marked his pale skin with thick black lines. Not the most delicate work Sarah had seen by a long shot. They looked as if they were done with makeshift equipment and an untalented hand.

"Looks like you've done some time yourself." Eric gestured to the tats Sarah had noticed. "What can you tell us about a guy named Bracco?"

"Bracco?" The guy glanced around the bar as if his overabundance of energy had deteriorated into paranoia. "Never heard of him."

"He was Randy's cell mate," Eric supplied.

"How would I know Randy's cellie? It's not like I was in at the same time." He drew himself up and pushed out his bony chest. "Besides, Randy was just in county. I've done real time."

"Something to be proud of, no doubt." Sarah did her best not to roll her eyes as the bartender had at her. But as ridiculous as this guy's pride over his record was, maybe she could use it to her advantage. "I think you know him. I think you're scared."

He pulled in his chin like a surprised turtle. He shifted his weight backward and the bar stool creaked under him. "Scared? Why would I be scared of Bracco? He's dead."

Eric narrowed his eyes. "You sure about that?"

"Offed himself in his cell. Happened before Christmas."

Sarah added this piece to the puzzle in her mind. If Bracco told Randy something was on Saddle Horn Ridge, he must have done it when her brother was first sentenced.

"What makes you think it was suicide?" asked Eric.

"That's what the papers said."

"And you don't find that a little strange?"

"I guess. Hardened guys usually don't off themselves like that, if that's what you're getting at."

That had been exactly what Eric was getting at. It wasn't a suicide. Sarah looked up at him. The sheriff must have killed Bracco, too. Only before he died, he told Randy there was something up on Saddle Horn Ridge. Something valuable worth finding. Was it possible?

She lowered a hip to the bar stool next to Jerry. The question was, how did Bracco know Larry Hodgeson's body was on that ridge? "What was Bracco arrested for?"

Jerry spun back and forth on the stool, as if it was beyond him to sit still. "How the hell should I know? Some damn thing."

"You said he was a hardened guy, that he'd been in before."

"So?"

The bartender set her soda and Eric's beer on the bar. He reached out for the money.

"So what was he in for?" she asked.

Jerry waved his hand in front of his face, as if clearing the air of the bad smell her question brought with it. "Don't they have records you can look up? I've talked with you people so much, my throat is getting parched." He eyed the drinks sitting on the bar.

Eric nodded to bartender and motioned to their skinny, pale friend. "Whatever he wants."

The bartender leveled a bored look on their companion. "What'll it be, Jer?"

"Your best whiskey. A double. And a beer to chase it."

Eric fished out his wallet and threw the last of their cash on the bar.

A chill moved over Sarah's skin. So that was it. They could no longer pay their way. Couldn't buy a drink or a sandwich or a clean shirt. They were forced to be criminals all the way, now.

The bartender plunked Jerry's double shot and beer on the bar, and the skinny man took a long drink of whiskey. He set the highball glass down and reached for the beer.

Eric slid the glass out of Jerry's reach. "First, Bracco."

Jerry let out a wheezy sigh. "Rumor has it, he took care of problems for a price."

"Problems?" Sarah asked. "What kind of problems?"

Eric kept his hand on Jerry's beer. "By problems, you mean he killed people for money?"

"Killed people, cleaned up messes, whatever needed to be done. Can I have my beer back?" He reached out, and Eric slid the beer into his palm.

Sarah's mind raced. So was that how this Bracco knew where to find Larry Hodgeson's body? He'd pulled the trigger? Had the sheriff hired him to do his dirty work?

"Do you know a man named Larry Hodgeson?" Eric continued.

Jerry met his question with a blank stare. He took a chug of beer.

"He worked in the state crime lab. He analyzed fingerprints," Sarah supplied.

A light seemed to come on behind those jittery eyes.

She leaned forward. "You know him?"

"Nah. Not me." Jerry laughed, his lips pulling back to expose teeth that smelled as bad as they looked. "But Burne does. Don't ya, Burne?"

Sarah followed Jerry's gaze.

At first she thought he was looking at one of the two men standing at the back of the bar wearing cowboy hats. A man who from this distance looked very much like her ranch hand, Keith Sherwood. Then a man standing next to a pool table barely ten feet away turned around slowly.

A black leather duster fell to his knees. He stepped toward them, expensive lizard boots clunking on wood plank floor.

He skimmed his gaze down her body, but instead of the leer she got from the bartender, his expression was cold, clinical, like a rancher sizing up a steer. His black shirt was opened at the collar. Tattoos circled his throat, the ink forming intricate patterns of twisted barbed wire. "So you're Sarah Trask."

It wasn't a question, and she didn't answer.

"Glad to finally meet you. Randy often bragged about that big, profitable ranch of yours. Said you have a good business sense. Make smart decisions. Something he obviously never inherited."

The bad feeling that had been niggling at the back of Sarah's neck became a full bore bite. She hadn't liked the fact that Randy knew this guy before she'd met him. Now she liked the idea even less.

Eric stepped around her stool so he was standing by her side. "You know Larry Hodgeson?"

"Never met the man."

Yeah, right. "He was a fingerprint analyst for the Wyoming crime lab," Sarah said. "He testified at your trial."

He brought his focus back to her. His eyes gleamed cold, emotionless, brutal. As if he could kill her right now, without a second thought. Like swatting a fly. "I said I never met the man. Not that I was never in the same room with him."

Sarah set her chin. "Then why did Jerry say you did?"

"Jerry?" He threw a dismissive glance the skinny man's way. "He's a meth head. Look at him. He don't know what's going on in his own mind half the time."

Jerry sat back on the stool and clasped his hands in his lap. Where most people twiddled their thumbs, he twiddled all fingers at once. "Okay, yeah, my bad. He doesn't really know him. The guy just—"

"Shut…up."

"The guy just…" Sarah repeated, leaning toward the jittery beanpole of a man. "What did Hodgeson *just* do?"

"Listen, Sarah Trask." Burne's voice held an edge like a knife. "I don't want to talk about Larry Hodgeson."

"Hodgeson's dead. Murdered," Eric said.

Burne kept his eyes riveted on her. "So? I sure didn't do it. The guy saved my ass."

He had a point. Hadn't the online article said that Hodgeson's testimony had caused the jury to acquit Burne? It didn't make sense for him to be involved in the fingerprint analyst's death. So where did that leave them? She couldn't believe Burne and Hodgeson and Sheriff Gillette and Randy were all tied together by co-incidence. It had to add up somehow.

"Like I said, I don't want to talk about the CSI guy. I'd much rather have a chat about your brother."

Sarah's pulse picked up its pace. "What about him?"

"He owed me. And with him dead, looks like you're the one who's going to have to pay."

ERIC STRAIGHTENED HIS shoulders and stepped in front of Sarah, fully blocking her from Burne. When he'd heard Randy was involved with a guy like this, he'd been furious. And now Burne thought he could pull Sarah further into this mess? Guess again. "Randy's debts died with him."

The scumbag finally looked at him. "Not from where I'm standing." The man's hand hovered at his waist. His long leather duster reached to his knees, covering the holster Eric bet was underneath.

He couldn't win this argument, especially not once guns were drawn. And although the prospect of walking away sent a pain shooting through his head like an ice pick to the eye, he had to remember that Sarah was the important one in all of this.

He had to get her out of here.

"Sarah doesn't know anything about what her brother was into. She can't help you."

"Well, someone is going to give me back my money. If it isn't her, who's it going to be? You?"

Sarah's fingers closed around his bicep. "How much did he owe?"

Burne leaned his face inches from Eric's and grinned. "See? No need for bluster, friend. The lady believes in paying her debts."

It was all Eric could do not to push his fingertips into the guy's eyes. He didn't know what Sarah had in mind, but if she thought this debt was a small thing she could take care of like a bar tab, he had a feeling she was going to be unpleasantly surprised.

"How much?" Sarah repeated.

"Twenty thousand."

Sarah gasped. "Twenty… Why?"

"He screwed up. Lost the money I fronted him for a sporting goods shop he wanted to open."

"Sporting goods shop, my ass," Eric growled under his breath. He hadn't heard anything about a sporting goods shop. More likely the money was meant for expanding Burne's current business, making drugs. And knowing Randy, he'd probably blown the money. Bet it in Vegas or on football games, sure that he was going to win big, have enough to set up Burne's new meth lab and pocket the profits himself.

Sarah's eyes glistened. She looked like she was about to cry. "Randy told you he could get that much money?"

"The day he got out."

It all added up. Randy on the cliff…explaining he didn't think Bracco's warnings of danger were real… swearing the only reason he'd risked it was he owed a guy a lot of money. And apparently that guy was Burne. "How did he say he was going to get it?"

"Told me he heard about an opportunity while in county. Told me he just had to take a little hike and he'd have the money, just like that."

A little hike led by his sucker of a friend. "So that's why Randy stopped by the night he got out of jail?"

"He knew I'd be looking for him, so he came looking for me first. I like a man who shows initiative. I like a man who pays better." He motioned to Jerry and the skinny man slipped off his bar stool and stepped toward the door. Sliding into the vacated spot, Burne leaned toward Sarah and rested a hand on the bar, blocking the path in front of her. "But since sister Sarah is going to take care of that now, I guess I have no cause to curse his damned memory. So where's the money?"

"I don't have it."

"Wrong answer."

Eric's heart slammed against his ribs as if fighting

to get free. Burne was a violent man, an unpredictable man. Eric could tell by the way he moved, the cold deadness in his eyes. He had to come up with a way to get Sarah away from him. "She can get it."

"Good. I'll go with you." He glanced in Eric's direction, then returned his focus to Sarah. "Just the two of us."

"There's no way in hell that's happening." Eric balled his hands into fists. He wouldn't let the meth dealer take her. There wasn't a chance.

The man gave him a smug glance. His hand moved under his duster. "Really?"

Sarah shook her head. "You can't come with me. Not unless you want to catch the sheriff's attention. He's watching my ranch. I don't even know if I can get into my house without being seen."

"Ah, yes. The two of you are wanted for your brother's murder, aren't you? All the more reason for you to pay up now. I've already waited for my money long enough. I'm not planning to wait twenty to life. So I suggest you find a way. Now." He pushed the duster back with one hand, flashing a semiautomatic handgun strapped to his hip, buckle of the holster popped open, ready to draw. Just as quickly, the duster settled back over the gun.

The move was fast, fluid, even casual, as if showing the gun was an absentminded accident. Eric knew it was anything but. It was a threat, pure and simple. If Sarah didn't get the money, she was dead.

Footsteps scuffled outside the room. Jerry stood in the doorway looking like he was about to climb out of his skin. "They're here."

Burne raised black brows. "Who?"

"Sheriff's deputies. Flashing lights. They're pulling into the parking lot right now."

Chapter Fourteen

In a flash of movement, Burne grabbed Sarah by the braid and pulled her head back, cradling her against his chest like a lover.

Eric surged forward. He wasn't going to let Burne hurt her. Damn it, he wasn't going to let the scumbag *touch* her.

An arm came from behind him, a knife blade flashing inches from his face. "I wouldn't do that." The bartender's beer-tainted breath fanned his face.

Eric's mind stuttered. He hadn't seen the guy move out from behind the bar. He'd been caught flat-footed, unprepared.

Burne pressed his cheek against Sarah's. "Have my money by noon tomorrow, all twenty grand, or the sheriff will be the least of your problems. Understand?"

She glared at him.

"Understand?"

"Yes."

"You'll get a call telling you where to meet. You'd better answer." He shoved something into her hand, released her hair and pushed her away.

Sarah stumbled against a bar stool, clutching a cell phone in her fist. She scrambled to regain her balance.

Eric tried to move toward her, but the bartender's hand clamped down hard on his shoulder. The blade pressed cold just below his ear.

"Get out of here," Burne said. "Through the back. The last thing I need is for you to be arrested before I get paid. Go."

The knife pulled back. The arm released Eric. He focused on Burne, that smug face, those brutal eyes. When he'd grabbed Sarah he'd awakened something primal in Eric. The urge to rip a man's tattooed throat with his bare hands. But as much as he wanted to stuff those threats back from where they'd come, he needed to get Sarah out of there more. He needed to protect her from Burne, all right, but he couldn't forget the sheriff.

He grabbed Sarah's hand. They dodged the pool table and raced for the back door. The men in cowboy hats he'd noticed standing in the back of the bar were gone. Cleared out. Before Jerry had yelled his warning or after, Eric didn't know.

They reached the door and Eric pulled it open. As soon as they pushed out into the clear basin wind, Eric could hear the bark of male voices coming from the front of the building. A white SUV sat in the gravel drive, blocking all vehicles from leaving. Sheriff's deputies stood among the vehicles in the lot.

So much for dumping their stolen SUV. And inside the SUV was the backpack with the belt buckle inside. Damn.

"We have to go on foot." Before the words were out of his mouth, they were racing across the gravel and into land dotted with sagebrush and dry tufts of grass. A quarry gaped behind the bar like a wound, the land gashed and marred by heavy machinery. Reaching the pounded dirt road, they followed it, running for all they were worth.

With every stride, Eric prayed Burne was serious about wanting his money, serious enough to stall the sheriff until they got away. Relying on the man who'd just threatened Sarah to save them tasted as acidic as bile in the back of Eric's throat. But at this point, he'd take any help they could get.

Sarah pointed to a flat-topped hill on the other side of the gaping quarry pit. "Everything beyond that bench is BLM land. It backs up to the ranch." She panted each word, the rhythm of her strides slowing.

The ranch. Reaching the far side of the mine, Eric pulled Sarah behind a pile of gravel. There, sheltered from the view of the men back at the tavern, he slowed to a walk, giving Sarah a chance to catch her breath. They needed a plan. "How far is the ranch?"

"Not far. Probably less than two miles."

"You have other vehicles there, right? Another ATV?"

She nodded. Leaning forward, she braced her hands on her knees. "You think they won't be watching it?"

"Not if they're tied up at the bar." He knew it was risky, but he'd managed to sneak into the ranch undetected once before. And Sarah knew the land better than anyone. "Where are your hands? Layton?"

"Should be out on the BLM, checking the cattle. They would have taken the horses, though, not the ATV. Layton's preference."

"Good."

"Say we manage to get the ATV and get out without being seen, where do we go from there?"

"Not sure. We'll figure it out. But in the meantime, I know a place. A friend's cabin. No one will be there until about a week before the parks open. We can stay there." It had been the place he'd thought about at the beginning. A place where they could hole up. See no one. A place where he could keep Sarah safe until they sorted out this mess and decided what to do next.

The hike to the ranch didn't take long by Wyoming standards. They ran most of the way, a steady jog. The sun was just settling low in the sky when they crossed the fence line and started through the east pasture. By the time the house and outbuildings came into view, twilight still glowed over the mountains to the west.

"God, it seems so long ago…I used to feel so safe here. I wonder if I ever will again."

The ache in Sarah's voice settled into Eric's bones. She had told him about her feelings for the ranch before. Said it was her rock. The only thing she could rely on between her parents' turmoil and the problems Randy stirred up everywhere he went.

Now she'd lost the ranch, too.

He wanted nothing more than to get it back for her. Maybe it was possible. He had to believe it was. But possible or not, clearing their names was still a long way off and would require more than a few miracles. The best he could do right now was to get his hands on that ATV and use it to get her someplace safe for the night. "Come on."

The place felt as vacant as it had when he'd rescued her from the sheriff. Not a body around. No movement but the horses in the corral. And this time—thankfully—no sign of the sheriff's SUV.

With any luck, he'd be tied up with Burne and his criminal drinking buddies for a good long while.

Sarah led the way to a freestanding garage on the

other side of the house. She twisted the manual garage door's handle and Eric helped her slide the door up on its overhead tracks.

They stared at the back bumper of a blue pickup.

Eric didn't recognize the truck. He glanced at Sarah. "Yours?"

"No. I think—"

"You move, you're dead."

Eric turned. The barrel of a rifle was leveled straight at Sarah's forehead.

"GLENN." SARAH'S FIRST URGE was to hug her ranch hand. Her second was that although he wasn't the sheriff, that didn't mean they were home free. "What are you doing here?"

"God, Sarah. I almost shot you." He tilted his hat back from his forehead and lowered his gun from his shoulder, but he didn't avert the barrel, as if he wasn't quite sure what he should do.

"Glenn, listen. This whole thing you've heard about Randy's death. It's not true."

"I know you didn't have nothing to do with killing Randy."

"You know?" She'd expected him to say a lot of things, mostly reciting platitudes about justice and doing the right thing. She'd never expected this.

Glenn glanced at Eric. "Layton thinks it was all him."

"Eric didn't do it, either, Glenn."

He pressed his lips together, making his cheeks bulge on either side of his mouth. Everything about Glenn was square, from his boxy legs to his shoulders to the shape of his head. And nothing was more square than his attitude toward the law.

Sarah had to find a way to convince him. "Layton is wrong. It was the sheriff and two of his men who killed Randy. They were trying to cover up another murder, and Randy got too close."

Glenn pointed the barrel at the ground and rubbed his sweaty forehead. "I wondered what the hell was going on."

"What?" Eric stepped forward. "Do you know something about the sheriff?"

Glenn looked from Eric back to Sarah. His square shoulders slumped a little, as if it was taking a lot out of him to face what he was about to tell them. "I heard Sheriff Gillette talking to Keith. Said something about getting justice."

"Getting justice? For what?"

"I don't know. Every damn thing."

Sarah didn't know what to think. Here she thought Glenn was the law-and-order guy. The man who loved cop shows and novels. The man who wanted to be a cop and would do anything to help someone like the sheriff, if he believed his cause was just. She always thought Keith was built more along the lines of a vigilante. The perfect recruit for a homegrown militia group, maybe, but a man who chafed at government and had no patience for law. "How did Keith react?"

"He has the kid all fired up. It's all Keith can talk about. People getting what they deserve and what all."

She pictured the cowboy hat at the back of the smokey bar. The shaggy blond hair and rangy face underneath. She glanced at Eric. "I thought I saw him at the Full Throttle just now."

"The cowboy hat at the back."

She nodded.

"Don't surprise me. He left the ranch around lunchtime and didn't come back. He ain't been anywhere he's supposed to lately."

Sarah straightened. Things were starting to add up, and she didn't like where they were going. "There were other times he left work? When?"

Glenn adjusted his hat with one hand. "Man, I don't know."

She did. "The day Randy was killed?"

He narrowed his eyes and stared at the garage wall, as if counting back in his mind. "Was that the day we took the herd out to the BLM?"

Sarah nodded. She had a feeling she might know what was coming. A bad feeling. She braced herself.

"Yeah, he disappeared that day."

"When?"

"After we loaded up. Didn't even say where he was going. Layton went out to look for him, but never found him. I had to unload the cattle alone."

She glanced at Eric, trying to read if he was thinking the same thing. Then she brought her focus back to Glenn. "Has Keith said anything else to you?"

"Like what?"

"I don't know, anything about Randy or a place called Saddle Horn Ridge?"

"He talked about Randy. How he saw him at the Full Throttle talking to some drug dealer."

Sarah nodded. "He told me that, too."

"How about a man named Larry Hodgeson?" Eric asked. "Has Keith mentioned him?"

Glenn started to shake his head, then paused.

"Think of something?" Sarah fought the urge to lean toward him and grab his shoulders, shake him into re-membering whatever it was that made him pause.

"Yeah. Hodgeson. He was in the news a while back, wasn't he?"

"He has been. Did Keith mention him?"

"Yeah. Last summer he was all mad. Said this Hodgeson took a payoff to let some drug dealer go, and now he was going to make things even worse. Keith said people like this Hodgeson were what was wrong with law enforcement. Is Hodgeson a cop or something?" Glenn's eyebrows pinched together, as if he wasn't sure he wanted the answer.

"No."

Glenn let out a shaky breath.

Sarah's mind whirled with Glenn's words. *Make things even worse?* Hodgeson no longer worked for the crime lab. He hadn't for years. How could Hodgeson make things worse?

"We'd better get out of here, Sarah." Eric's voice cut through her thoughts. "Where's the ATV?"

She pointed to the other side of the garage.

"Tell you what," Glenn said. "Why don't you take my truck?"

She scanned his face. He seemed sincere. Like he wanted to help. But if she couldn't trust one of her hands, could she really afford to trust the other?

"Things are strange around here," Glenn said. "Real strange. I don't know what to think, but I don't think you'd kill your brother. And I don't want to see you pay for something you'd never do."

She nodded. She hadn't thought anything bad about Glenn Freemont in the time he'd worked for her. Not until this mess. But he really was a good guy. And he really did seem to care about her. It felt good to know she'd been right about someone. That everyone she knew wasn't harboring some secret that would come back to hurt her. "Thanks, Glenn." She gave him a hug, and he slipped the truck's keys into her hand.

Eric wheeled the ATV to the mouth of the garage. "Let's take this, too. It'll give us some flexibility."

After Glenn helped Eric heave the vehicle into the pickup bed, she passed the keys to Eric and climbed into the passenger seat. A second later, they were speeding out of the gravel driveway and down the road. For a moment, she just stared out the window at the landscape rolling by, trying to absorb how little she knew about some people in her life. Randy. Now Keith. "Do you think Keith is in on this thing with the sheriff, whatever it is?"

"Could be. Or Glenn is."

"Glenn?" She shook her head. She must not have heard him right. "Why Glenn?"

"Think about it. The only thing we know about Keith Sherwood is what Glenn told us."

"And that he was at the Full Throttle."

"Which means nothing. From the sound of it, he hangs out there all the time."

"True."

"And being out at the Full Throttle ties Keith to Burne more than the sheriff. Either that or he just has a simple drinking problem."

"Good point. But none of that suggests Glenn has anything to hide. He helped us. Gave us his truck."

Eric nodded. "His truck, which is equipped with a GPS."

Sarah gasped and held her hands against her chest. Again she'd been so trusting. So blind. That Glenn had been offering his truck for a reason, to trap them, had never occurred to her. "You think the sheriff is using it to track us?"

"Not anymore. I turned the damn thing off."

Chapter Fifteen

Eric didn't want to take a chance.

They took Glenn's truck as far as the campground outside Norris. There, they left it among a dozen vehicles belonging to early summer tourists and hiked the rest of the way to his guide friend's cabin on foot.

The cabin wasn't exactly rustic, more like a tiny house on the outside of town than a real cabin. But the neighbors were few and far between, no one in the area nosed into others' business, and most important of all, he knew where to find the key.

Throughout the entire trek, all Eric could think about was their close call at the Full Throttle. How little control of the situation he'd had. How he'd almost lost Sarah for good. Add that to what had happened with Glenn Freemont, and he was reeling.

He needed to put an end to this. And he would do whatever it took.

He found the cabin's key hidden in its usual place under a flap of loose siding, opened the door and ushered Sarah inside.

The cabin was tiny, only one real room. One end of it formed a small kitchen, the other a living area with a full sized bed in one corner and a television in the other. Definitely a bachelor pad. A bathroom the size of a closet was tucked against the wall.

The place smelled dusty, the air dead. At least out here the weather was so dry they didn't have to worry about mustiness and mildew. But it wasn't exactly homey. "Dev probably hasn't been here for a while. We'll have to keep our eyes out for scorpions and black widows."

She nodded, unfazed. "It's nice."

"I don't know about that, but it's safe. At least for a while."

She gave him a sad smile. "These days 'safe' is the same as nice to me."

He knew the feeling.

Sarah strolled deeper into the cabin. He followed her in time to see her lower herself to the bed and let out an exhausted sigh. For a second, he had the urge to sit beside her, to take her in his arms, to lay her down and show her how much he wanted to take care of her. How much he had changed.

"There's only one bed," she said.

Warmth fanned out over his skin. He'd like to think that by the tone in her voice, she was thinking the same thing. But he'd probably be fooling himself. Last night in the restaurant, she'd told him she couldn't take a chance on him. He doubted anything had changed. At least not with her.

He was a different story.

With every minute Eric was with her, he grew more sure she was what he wanted. Her and the baby. Maybe the turmoil he felt just wasn't that big of a deal to him in light of the crazy turn their lives had taken, a simple matter of perspective. Maybe moments where he could glimpse what it would be like to lose her had made him want to hold her that much more. Maybe the thought of the baby—of a family—was responsible for his change of heart, but he didn't think so.

The maelstrom of emotion that came with caring about her, of maybe even falling in love with her, made him feel as if he was climbing without the safety of a belay, but it also made him feel more alive than ever before. And like climbing, dangerous or not, he wanted more.

God help him, he wanted everything.

"What about this money Burne says I need to pay?" Sarah's voice didn't sound inviting this time. It sounded shaken. Scared. She held the cell phone Burne had given her, turning it over and over in her fingers. "How am I ever going to come up with it with the sheriff watching? I can't exactly walk into a bank."

Eric shoved his thoughts to the back of his mind. It wasn't the time for fantasy. Even if by some miracle Sarah decided to give him another chance, he couldn't take it until she was safe. Until this was over.

His stomach clenched at the thought of the dead-eyed meth dealer, the way he'd threatened Sarah. The way he'd touched her, pulling her head back by her braid. The way Eric had had to just stand there and watch with a knife to his throat. But as much as he'd like to take care of that guy, they couldn't get distracted. Having all law enforcement in the state of Wyoming after them made a single drug dealer seem insignificant. They had to solve the more pressing problems first. "Burne is the least of our troubles."

"Do you think Randy was selling drugs? Or making them? Do you think that's why he was in debt?" Her voice dipped to just above a whisper, as if she didn't want anyone to hear, even though there was no one around but them.

Maybe she just didn't want to hear her own questions and the answers that likely went with them. He couldn't blame her one bit.

Eric lowered himself to the mattress next to her. Just a few seconds ago, he was thinking about rolling around on the bed together. He still wanted that, but now he needed more. To comfort her. Reassure her. Make everything all right, something he knew he could never fully do.

Randy had brought Sarah a lot of worry and pain. To think he'd stooped to depths so vile in his quest for easy money was hard to reconcile with the brother she loved. Something like that was hard enough for Eric to swallow about the man he'd thought of as his friend. "Was he selling drugs? I don't know. Maybe we'll never know for sure."

"Maybe…or maybe that's what this whole thing is about. Burne, Randy, Larry Hodgeson, the sheriff— maybe they're all involved in drugs or profiting from drug money."

He considered this. "It's possible. Only it didn't seem like Burne was very eager to see the sheriff this afternoon."

Sarah looked down at the phone clasped in her hands. "Burne wants his money before the sheriff gets ahold of us. That could change things."

"Money can change a lot of things." He thought of Hodgeson, of the fingerprint evidence in the case against Burne. "Maybe Hodgeson was bought. Maybe the sheriff was, too. But that doesn't tell us why Gillette would want Hodgeson dead or want to cover up the murder."

"And it doesn't explain Burne, either. Even if someone found out he paid Hodgeson off, he can't be tried on the drug charge again, can he?"

"I suppose he could face bribery charges, if they can prove it."

"Would he kill for that? I don't know. But if not, neither the sheriff nor Burne had a reason to kill Hodgeson." She sounded as bereft as when he sat down.

Some comfort he was. Of course, he doubted anything but answers would provide comfort for Sarah. "They didn't have a reason that we have found. Not yet, anyway."

She raised her eyes to his. "So how do we find it?"

He thought of the library, the detail in the articles he'd read about Hodgeson. He glanced at the phone in her hand. "We call the reporter who wrote about those cases. Dennis Prohaska."

"You think that's the writer Joy was talking about? The one she said was giving her husband a big head?"

"I don't know. But if he isn't, he might know who is." He pushed himself up from the bed and crossed the room. He opened one cabinet near the phone, then another. Sure enough, there was a big fat telephone book. He called the number for the *Wyoming Tribune-Eagle*. Although they wouldn't give him the reporter's phone number, they promised to pass along the message.

"It's urgent," Eric said. "It has to do with the manhunt for that murderer. If he'd like an exclusive interview, I can arrange it. Tell him to call back at this number right away."

Prohaska called back within the hour. They had eaten some canned chili and turned on the television while they waited, and Eric stepped into the kitchen so he could focus on the call. Sarah stayed in the living area, watching him. "Thank you for calling," Eric said. "I have a few questions."

"I usually ask the questions." His voice was brusque over the phone, in a hurry. "I thought you had information about the manhunt for Eric Lander."

"Bear with me, will you?" He took a deep breath and held Sarah's gaze. "What can you tell me about Larry Hodgeson? He's a fingerprint analyst with the state crime lab."

Silence.

At first Eric thought the reporter had hung up on him. Then the soft whoosh of an expelled breath shuddered over the line. "Why are you asking about Hodgeson?" His voice was measured, interested, whatever he'd been in a hurry about forgotten.

"You know the man?"

"Of course I know him. I've covered Wyoming criminal trials for years."

"When is the last time you heard from him?"

"He's retired. I haven't heard anything from him in almost a year."

Almost a year. "So you had contact with him after his retirement?" He met Sarah's big brown eyes.

"I really need to know who this is. What does this have to do with the manhunt?"

Now it was Eric's turn to be silent. Apparently his questions about Hodgeson had struck some kind of chord with the reporter. "Why are you so protective of Hodgeson?"

"Not protective. Curious. Hodgeson was a special project of mine."

A special project? Eric's mind raced, trying to figure out what that could mean.

"Who is this? Can I meet you, face-to-face?"

"Not possible." Maybe Eric could get the reporter to give him what he needed if he came at it from another angle. "What about Walter Burne? What can you tell me about him?"

"He was arrested for producing and selling methamphetamine a good five, six years ago. He was acquitted."

"And Larry Hodgeson worked on that case," Eric said.

"Pick a place. I'll meet you there."

"Why are you so eager to meet?"

The reporter paused. "Okay. I'll level with you. I'm writing a book."

A book. Of course. Being the subject of a book might give anyone a big head. "About Larry Hodgeson?"

"About the Wyoming criminal justice system. But yes, partially about Larry Hodgeson. At least it used to be, before I lost contact with him. So your questions piqued my interest."

The story seemed legitimate. Still, meeting in person was risky.

"This is Eric Lander, isn't it?"

Eric bit the inside of his bottom lip. He hadn't wanted Prohaska to know who he was, but when it came right down to it, his identity probably didn't change anything.

"I won't call the law."

"How do I know that?"

"I want the story, not an arrest. You have my word."

"You're going to have to do better than that." If there was anything Eric had learned while going through this mess, it was that taking people at their word was a fool's move.

"What if I tell you that Hodgeson's disappearance wasn't random? That something happened to him, and I might know what?"

Eric pushed up from the counter and paced across the kitchen half of the room.

"Meet me. Choose a place. I'll drive through the night if I need to. The worst that could happen is it'll be a waste of your time."

No, that wasn't the worst. Eric stopped and focused on Sarah. He thought she would be hanging on his every word, trying to use them like clues to figure out the other side of the conversation. But she stood with her back to him, her attention fully absorbed by the television, both arms cradling her abdomen as if trying to protect their baby.

She must be watching news of the manhunt. Or maybe something went down at the Full Throttle.

Their close call in the tavern still trilled along his nerves. He could have lost her. Either to a drug dealer or the sheriff. He had to get some answers. Whatever the risk, it couldn't be greater than what they already faced. He had to end this craziness now. "Be in Thermopolis by noon. I'll call you and tell you where we'll meet. Give me the number for your cell."

He did. As soon as he uttered the last digit, Eric hung up.

SARAH HEARD ERIC HANG up the phone, but she didn't take her eyes from the television. Her body alternated between a hot and cold sweat. It was all she could do to take in the images on the screen. She cupped her arm over her abdomen and willed herself to stay standing.

"Sarah?" Eric strode into the room. He glanced from her to the television.

The news coverage was live, a breaking story. The headline on the bottom of screen read Murderous Fugitives Strike Again. The camera panned over wood corral fencing, a modest house, a barn she had redesigned and remodeled herself. A still image flashed on the screen. Eric's face. Hers. And then another. The face of a man she'd just seen, just talked to, just given a hug.

The smiling face of Glenn Freemont.

She didn't know anything anymore. She'd gone from being suspicious of Glenn to grateful to him and back to suspicious. And now…

She'd watched the images once already. One after another, ending with Glenn. She'd heard the newscaster's words. The story of how Glenn's body was found at her ranch, shot with his own rifle.

Now a new clip flickered on the screen. The sheriff stood in her driveway. Behind him, county vehicles crowded around the barn. Yellow crime scene tape barred the doorway, flapping in the wind. He adjusted his silver belly Stetson lower on his bald forehead. "We have a strong lead. Just as in the Randy Trask murder, we believe the perpetrators are Eric Lander and his accomplice, Sarah Trask."

Sarah's shock turned to numbness. She didn't know what to think. She didn't know what to feel. It was as if her entire life and everything she knew had been picked up by a tornado and flung into a million pieces.

"Sarah." Eric's voice was tender, solid.

She could feel his hand hovering near her arm, wanting to touch her but holding back. "It was only a few days ago that I was so excited Randy was home." Her voice sounded raspy, like it belonged to someone else, someone barely hanging on. "I thought he had a chance to turn his life around. I thought I could see the future stretching ahead."

"I know. I know."

"And now Glenn." A sob shuddered from her chest and clogged in her throat. Glenn was dead. He'd tried to help them, and now he was dead.

"It's not our fault. You know that, right?"

She knew it. She did. The sheriff or one of his men had pulled the trigger, not her, not Eric. But that didn't mean they hadn't played a role. "If he hadn't given us his truck, he'd still be alive. He'd be going home to his wife."

Tears swamped her eyes, reducing the TV screen to glowing smeary color. She could feel the moisture on her cheeks, but she didn't wipe her eyes. She needed to feel this, not deny it, not duck from it. That was the only way the horror could ever be washed away.

Eric stepped up behind her. He wrapped his arms around hers, around her belly. His chest warmed her back. "I'm so sorry, Sarah. For Randy. For Glenn. For everything that's happened."

"It's not your fault, either."

"I know. But I'm sorry everything has happened the way it has all the same."

His words flowed over her like soothing balm on a burn. She knew she shouldn't lean in to him, but her body wouldn't listen. His chest felt so solid. Like something she could depend on. His arms strong around her.

She knew she was rationalizing, brushing all her

concerns about their relationship aside because she needed him right now. But she couldn't help it. She wanted to be sure of something. She wanted to be certain to her bones. And while she might not be sure of Eric's feelings, she did know hers. She loved him. Pure and simple. She had for a long time. She'd just tried not to admit it.

But right now she needed to feel it, whether he returned those feelings or not. She needed to lose herself.

She turned in his arms. Tilting her head back, she looked up at him. She couldn't ask, couldn't speak. She just had to trust he would know what she wanted. What she needed.

He moved a hand up her side to her face. With tender fingers, he skimmed over her forehead, along her cheekbone, brushing away a strand of hair that had escaped her braid. His touch moved lower, cupping her jaw. He tilted her head back and brought his mouth to hers.

She'd craved the touch of his lips for months, yearned for his taste. She opened to him. Wanting to lose herself in him. Urging him deeper.

His arm drew tight around the small of her back, and she pressed against his length. She threaded one leg around his. She knew how his bare skin would feel against hers. She knew the sounds he'd make nuzzling her breasts, the stubble on his chin rasping tender skin. She'd run those feelings over in her thoughts for months. In her dreams. And she never thought she'd get to experience them again.

"Sarah." His voice was little more than a whisper, but it rumbled through her chest. "I want you to know—"

"Shh." She pressed her lips hard against his. She didn't have a clue what he wanted to say, but she didn't want to hear it. She didn't want to know anything more than what she felt right this minute. What she knew deep in her own heart. "I want you. That's all. I just want you. Is that okay?" She brought her lips to his again.

He nodded without breaking the kiss. Trailing his hand down her neck, he encircled her with both arms, pulling her tight, no space between them.

Yes. This was what she needed. To be held. To be loved. To love him back. Even if it was only for tonight.

Heat raced over her and swept her along. He peppered kisses over her face, her neck, her collarbone. She explored his mouth, remembering. She breathed him in, the scent of his skin making her sigh deep inside.

Skimming her hands up his sides, she pulled up the hem of his shirt and slipped her palms against ridged muscle and warm skin. She'd always loved the feel of his body, and she wanted more. She wanted all of him. She slipped her fingertips under the waistband of his jeans.

He pulled back from her. Cool air surrounded her and for a second she thought he was going to push her away. She opened her eyes in time to see him pull his shirt over his head, not taking time to mess with the buttons, and toss it on the bed.

Shadows cupped around smooth muscle. He unzipped his jeans and shucked them down his legs. Wearing nothing but a pair of briefs, he reached for her. But instead of pulling her back into his arms, he lifted her T-shirt and skimmed it over her head.

She shivered, yet she was anything but cold. Arching her back, she reached behind and unhooked her bra. Her breasts had become heavier just in the four months since she'd gotten pregnant, the nipples larger. She let the bra slide down her arms.

Eric's hands replaced the cups. He took her lips again, kissing and massaging. Slowly, he moved her to the bed. Gently, he lowered her to the mattress. She lay on her back, and he leaned over her.

His kisses grew more demanding, and Sarah answered with demands of her own. All she could sense was how much she wanted him. All she could think about was the taste of his body, the scent of him that had always driven her wild, made her forget everything and just feel.

Feel how much she wanted him. Feel how deeply she loved him. That was all that mattered. Wipe everything else away.

He laced his fingers in hers and brought her hands above her head. He moved his kisses lower, down her throat, over her collarbone. His tongue circled a sensitive nipple.

The sensation took her breath away. He flicked and kissed and sucked, then moved to the other, lavishing, taking his time.

She thought she'd go mad with want.

By the time he released her hands and littered kisses to her jeans, she wanted nothing more than to be naked. To see him naked. To feel him inside her.

He unbuckled her jeans with deft fingers. Lifting her hips off the bed, he stripped off both jeans and panties and brought his lips to her belly.

As he kissed the slight bulge of baby, tears swamped her eyes. She blinked them back, wanting to see him, to smile at him, but it was no good. She cried as he moved his lips lower, shudders of pleasure already seizing her. And when he worked his way back up her body and kissed away her tears, she thought her heart would burst.

Chapter Sixteen

Gooseberry Badlands were carved into the floor of the Big Horn Basin. Years of erosion had eaten away soft rock, leaving red, yellow and tan layered spires and canyons twenty-five feet deep. Many of the rock towers were topped by wider caps of harder rock called hoodoos, looking to Sarah a little like the formation on top of Saddle Horn Ridge. From one of the high spots among the hoodoos, the sole highway could be seen for miles stretching in either direction. A parking lot rested at the top of a circular foot trail weaving through the badlands.

Sarah and Eric had slept later than they'd planned. Tearing herself from Eric's warm arms had been one of the hardest things she'd ever done, and even now she wished she could curl up, skin to skin, and just pretend the rest of the world didn't exist.

"What are you thinking about?"

She hadn't even been aware that Eric was watching her. Suddenly she felt insecure. Exposed. Even her cheeks heated, and she hadn't blushed in years. "Last night. This morning. How I wished we were still in bed."

He moved up behind her, circling his arms around her and pulling her against his chest as he had last night before things had heated up. "I love how you think. In fact, I love everything about you, Sarah."

His words were so close to the ones she longed to hear, longed to believe, that at first she thought she must be imagining it. Dreaming it.

She reached her arms above her head and rested her hands on his shoulders. The wind whipped off the basin, buffeting against them and whistling through rock formations.

He pulled her tight. "Just think of it all being over and us living back at your ranch— you, me and the baby. Our little family."

That image brought a smile to her face. She could almost see it. Almost feel it was true. "You're looking forward to being a dad?"

"The more this seems real, the more excited I get."

Something wobbled deep in Sarah's chest. She'd always thought Eric would make a great dad. But somehow she'd never envisioned him being excited about their baby, eager for it to be born.

Had her dad been like that when her mom was pregnant with Randy?

She didn't know where the question had come from, but once it popped into her mind, she couldn't shake it. She also couldn't give it an answer.

The wobble turned to a gnawing void, something hungry, something that couldn't quite be filled. She fitted her bottom tight to Eric's groin, yearning to feel him, but layers of denim kept them separate. She wanted to strip off her clothes, for him to plunge into her, fill her like he had last night, so she could feel the same way, close and intimate and loved.

So she could finally be sure.

She shook her head and dropped her hands to her sides. Oh, sure, they could get it on right here with Prohaska on his way and maybe the entire sheriff's department behind him. What was wrong with her? This need of hers was out of place, stupid, insecure. But try as she might, she couldn't let it go.

"What's wrong, Sarah?"

"Nothing…I don't know."

He pulled her back against his chest. "It's all going to work out."

She soaked in his warmth, tried to draw it into herself, make it hers, keep it from ever going away. "I can't do this."

He turned her in his arms, eyes searching her face. "This?"

"You and me."

"Listen, soon we'll find the truth. This will all be over. And the two of us, we can take our time, let things settle in and grow naturally."

Was that the problem? Things happening too fast? God knew their romance had bloomed quickly last summer and fall. And in the past few days since they'd been reunited and were suddenly running for their lives, she'd totally lost perspective. Could she get it back after this was over? Could she then look into his eyes and *know* that he loved her?

Could she then be *sure?*

"I…" Craning her neck, she turned and looked up at him. She drank in the swirl of color in his irises, green flecked with brown. He was excited about the baby. Felt it was his duty to be a good dad. But did he really love her enough? Did it even matter as long as she couldn't make herself believe? "I'm afraid."

"It's going to be okay. We can see the highway from here, both directions." He pointed at the gray ribbon, still void of cars. "No one can sneak up on us. If Prohaska brings the sheriff along, we'll know about it in plenty of time to get away on the ATV."

She hadn't been talking about their meeting with the reporter, but she didn't know how to tell him what she really meant. That as wonderful as making love with him was and as many times as he told her he loved her, she was afraid she'd never really know if he'd come back for her or the baby.

There was really no way *to* know.

ERIC ANGLED HIS HAND to his forehead to block the midday sun's glare. He wasn't sure what had happened just now. One moment he thought he and Sarah were closer than they'd ever been. The next, she seemed gone. She was standing here physically, her butt nestled against him and driving him wild, but something was different. She'd grown distant. Closed off. The very pressure in the air had changed.

He wasn't sure how to take it.

His whole life he'd relied on logic, reason, preparation and hard work to see him through. And it had worked. It had protected him from the chaos. It didn't make for an exciting life—instead his was measured and safe. But that was fine by him. He could get his excitement scaling a challenging rock face or viewing a waterfall human eyes might never have seen before. It suited him fine.

The past days, though, everything had changed. Each time he thought he had things under control, each time he thought he was relying on logic, he'd been wrong.

But feelings…they were all he could be sure of any-more. Namely his feelings for Sarah. When he'd told her he loved everything about her, he wasn't lying.

Wind whistled through the rock formations above them, every few seconds gusting nearly as loud as a freight train. She pointed to a little blue coupe creeping along the highway. "He's here."

Eric studied the approaching vehicle. With the wind-shield reflecting the sun, he couldn't see how many people were inside, but no cars or trucks or sheriff's department SUVs followed. A good sign.

At least they had that much going for them.

He concentrated on breathing and composing his mind. He and Sarah would have time to work out whatever was bothering her. It would be fine. He had to believe that. Right now he had to focus on getting some answers from the reporter. And if he could win the guy's sympathies, all the better.

The car pulled in to the parking lot and a doughy-looking man wearing a blue polo shirt and khakis stepped out. He let himself in through the gate and walked around the trail, as Eric had instructed over the cell phone earlier.

Eric watched the car, but he detected no movement inside. From what he could tell, the reporter had indeed come alone.

Prohaska ambled down the trial with a shuffling, flat-footed gait. When he finally spotted Eric and Sarah, a smile played around the corners of his thin lips, not exactly happiness, but excitement. Chasing a story.

They made the introductions brief.

"Mind if I get this on tape?" the reporter asked.

"Go ahead." At least that way he'd have a record of

what they knew…in case they were arrested, or killed before they could tell the story themselves.

"So how did it happen? How did you become a murderer?" Prohaska asked straight off.

"I didn't do it."

He screwed his lips to the side and shook his head as if disappointed. "All murderers say they didn't do it. Try walking into the state pen in Rawlins sometime. That's what they'll all tell you."

Eric shook his head. They didn't have time for this.

"What do you know about Hodgeson?"

Prohaska's puffy smile faded. "I think he was murdered."

Eric nodded slowly, trying not to tip his hand, not until he learned more. "What makes you think that?"

"Like I said last night, I'm writing a book. I had one interview with the guy—kind of a dry one at that—and then he called me out of the blue." He paused, as if trying to lend dramatic import to his words.

"And said?" Sarah prodded.

Prohaska glanced from one to the other. "That he was planning to confess to a crime."

"A crime?" Sarah's eyes flew wide.

The wind was loud, swirling now. Maybe Eric hadn't heard him. He narrowed his eyes on the reporter. "What kind of crime?"

"Accepting bribes."

"From who?"

"You already know the who. You mentioned him last night. One of the biggest methamphetamine producers in the area. Walter Burne."

"So it was Burne's fingerprints in the meth lab?" Sarah asked. "And Hodgeson just lied?"

"Lied under oath. Add perjury to the list."

It didn't add up. Why take a bribe, lie on the witness stand and then confess for no reason? There had to be a reason. "Why would Hodgeson confess?"

"Because he was dying of emphysema. He was pretty far along. I guess he wanted to make sure his soul was prepared or something. I always wondered if I was jumping to conclusions about the murder, if he didn't decide to just kill himself instead."

Emphysema. Eric remembered an offhand comment Joy Hodgeson had made about her ex-husband being sick. And that he quit his job before his retirement benefits kicked in. But even though the circumstances seemed to suggest suicide, there was one detail that proved Hodgeson had been murdered more conclusively than the bullet hole in the back of his skull. "He didn't kill himself."

"You know that for a fact?"

"We found his body. Bullet hole in the skull."

"That doesn't rule out suicide."

"The place we found him does. At the base of Saddle Horn Ridge in the Absaroka Range. No way he could have gotten out there if he's in the later stages of emphysema."

The reporter nodded. "That sounds fairly solid."

"So Hodgeson threw Burne's case. Did he do that with any other cases?"

Prohaska shook his head. "Not that I could find. And I've looked, believe me. Ever since Hodgeson didn't show up at a meeting we were supposed to have, I've been trying to figure out what happened to him."

So he'd been working on the case for months and hadn't found anything. That didn't bode well for them.

Sarah tilted her head. "How about Danny Gillette? What can you tell us about him?"

"The Norris County Sheriff?" Prohaska's meaty brow creased. He lifted his shoulders in a jerky shrug. "Not much. Seems to do his job well, believes in America and apple pie and all that. Why do you ask?"

"So you don't know of any reason he has for wanting Larry Hodgeson dead?" Eric dropped the bombshell and watched for the reaction.

His eyes rounded. "You're saying Danny Gillette is responsible for killing Hodgeson?"

"And Randy Trask. And Glenn Freemont, too." added Sarah.

Prohaska lifted a hand, palm out. "Hold it right there. Can you prove any of this?"

A shot cracked through the canyon.

Eric's heart jumped to his throat. He stared at the reporter for a second as a red spot bloomed high on his shirt. Giving a low grunt, Prohaska flopped belly first into the dust.

Eric spun around, looking for where the bullet had come from. He hadn't seen anyone approach. Hadn't heard anyone.

Walter Burne stepped around the rock formation behind them, a handgun in his fist. "Hello, Sarah Trask. Where's my money?"

Eric's thoughts raced. This couldn't be happening. Where had Burne come from? How in the hell had he found them?

Sarah's eyes flared wide, her dark hair blowing in the wind. She glanced at Eric.

The drug dealer raised the gun and pointed the barrel straight at Sarah's face.

Pure, focused anger tightened Eric's muscles and hummed in his ears. Here he'd told Sarah that Burne wasn't a problem, nothing to worry about next to the sheriff. But he'd never expected this. How could he have been so wrong? He had to think. He had to stall. Scooping in a deep breath, Eric forced conviction past shaky lips. "Put the gun down. We have the money."

Burne lowered the gun a few inches, but still kept it pointed at Sarah. "You do, do you? Then give it to me. Now."

Eric had to do something. But what? He couldn't rush the scumbag. Burne wasn't standing that far away, but he could still get a shot off before Eric tackled him. A shot that would hurt Sarah…or kill her. He had to think of something else. Anything. And he needed to buy time until an idea came. "How did you find us?"

"I have my ways. I told you not to mess with me."

"The phone." Sarah's voice sounded choked. She wrapped her arms around her belly as if she could shield their baby from a bullet with flesh and bone.

"Very good. The lady wins a prize."

The phone. Of course. He knew police could find a cell phone by triangulating the signal between service towers. It had never occurred to him a guy like Burne could do the same, as long as he was willing to spread a little money around to the right people. Except for the time they'd spent waiting for Prohaska's call last night and the call to the reporter's cell phone today, he'd turned it off, for what good it had done. That last call had led Burne right to them.

Burne held out his hand, palm up. "Speaking of the phone, I'll take it back now."

Eric handed it over. If it wasn't their only link to the outside world, he'd be eager to be rid of the damn thing.

"How did you know to come around the other side of the badlands? Why not just take the road?"

Burne gave him a look that said he'd seen through Eric's stalling tack. "Because I'm not an idiot. You have about two seconds to give me my money."

"It's on the ATV."

"Nice try, but I checked when I parked my bike next to it. Which makes me think you don't have the money at all. Do you?"

Eric's throat felt drier than the badlands themselves.

"I'm tired of this. It'll be worth twenty Ks just to watch the two of you die." He raised the gun. A crack split the air.

Sarah jolted and fell.

Chapter Seventeen

Eric threw himself at Burne, the gunshot ringing in his ears. He hit the man full force. The two of them flew backward. Eric landed on top of him on the craggy ground.

The drug dealer gasped for breath.

The scum had shot Sarah. He'd shot Sarah. Eric pulled back a fist and let it go, smashing into the man's face. His nose popped under the blow. Blood gushed through his nostrils. Eric pulled his fist back to hit him again.

Burne lurched upward, slamming his forehead smack into Eric's nose.

Eric reeled backward, stunned for a second, pain clanging through his head.

Burne bucked his body, shoving Eric back and to the side. He brought something up. Something he held with both fists.

The gun.

Eric lashed out with his hands. His first thought was to block the bullet from crashing into him. But once his hands were moving, they seemed to take on an intention of their own. A will that moved faster than thought.

He grabbed the gun, the barrel hot against his fingers. He pulled, trying to wrest it from Burne's grip.

The scumbag's fingers clamped down on the weapon, his fists like iron. Strong for a weasel. But not as strong as Eric.

He grabbed Burne's wrist and twisted. Something popped. A grunt escaped Burne's clenched teeth. Still he didn't release the weapon.

Using all his strength, Eric twisted the gun around, still in the dealer's fist. He had shot Sarah. Eric would make him let go. He would make him pay.

The gun exploded between them.

At first, Eric wasn't sure what happened. Had the bullet gone wide? Had it hit him? He couldn't see anything but the man's shoulder. Couldn't feel anything but searing heat. Couldn't smell anything but burned gunpowder.

Then he smelled blood.

Burne gurgled deep in his throat. He stared at Eric with eyes that didn't see. Wetness oozed through a hole in the black leather duster. He shuddered and slumped to the ground. Limp fingers released the gun, leaving it in Eric's hands.

Dead? Hurt? Eric didn't know. Didn't care. All he could think about was getting back to Sarah. Making sure she was all right.

She *was* all right. She had to be.

He struggled to his feet and stumbled across the craggy ground, loose rock shifting under his feet. His heart thudded as if trying to break through his rib cage. She was lying fifteen feet from the reporter, crumpled in the place he'd seen her go down.

Please make her be alive. Please.

He fell to his knees beside her. She moved her head, meeting his eyes with a tight-lipped grimace.

Thank God.

"You're going to be okay. You're going to be okay." He didn't know if he kept repeating the words for her sake or his. Either way, he couldn't stop. "You're going to be okay."

A dark stain marred her jeans, the spot encompassing her whole thigh and growing. A tear marked the center of the indigo cotton.

"Burne?" Her voice was barely loud enough to hear over the wind.

"He's no longer a problem."

She nodded and asked nothing further.

"I'm going to look here. I'm going to see…" He fitted his fingers into the edges of the hole and pulled. The fabric gave, only a little, but it was enough to see blood pulsing from the puncture in her skin.

"How bad?"

"Not bad. It's going to be fine." A leg wound. It could be worse. She wouldn't die from that. Not, unless, she lost too much blood.

His throat felt tight. The thought of losing Sarah, of losing their baby…he could hardly breathe. He needed to think. He needed something to stop the bleeding. He fumbled with the buttons on his shirt. His fingers were thick, clumsy, trembling. Too big to fit buttons into holes. Grabbing each side of the fabric, he pulled, popping the buttons. He slipped the shirt off his back and wadded it into a ball, then pressed it against Sarah's leg. "I have to get you to a hospital."

"Hospital? No."

"I can't handle this on my own."

"You said it was fine."

"It is. It will be. If you get to a hospital, you'll be fine."

"But the sheriff…" A sob shook from her chest. "The sheriff. He'll find us."

She was right. The hospital would report a gunshot wound. The sheriff would find them.

He lifted the balled-up shirt from her thigh. Blood pulsed out of the wound, another wave seeping into her jeans. He clamped the cotton and fleece down tight. This couldn't be happening. He felt dizzy. Like he couldn't set his mind to reality. Like he was floating outside, somehow, watching events happening to other people. People he didn't know.

Sarah gritted her teeth. Her eyes looked shiny, glassy. The lines of her beautiful face contracted with pain. "A leg wound isn't going to kill me."

"It'll be…" He closed his mouth. Who was he trying to kid? It wasn't going to be fine. She wasn't going to be okay. Not unless he did something. Not unless he did something now.

Heat suffused his chest. Lose her. He could lose her. To blood loss. If not that, infection. Chaos spun through his mind, turning his stomach, making him want to double over in pain.

This was what had held him back four months ago. This. Not emotion or lack of control or anything else. If he never loved her, he would never lose her.

Problem was, he loved her with everything he was.

"I'm taking you to the hospital."

"Don't." She shook her head, several dark hairs sticking to the tears streaking down each cheek.

"There's no choice."

A groan came from behind him. Eric spun around.

The reporter moved his arm in the dust. Slowly, back and forth. He tried to lift his head but fell back against rock. He was alive.

With two people in need of medical care, two people he wasn't sure he could move, Eric knew he couldn't handle this on his own.

He grabbed Sarah's hand and pressed it to the shirt on her leg. The cotton was nearly saturated already and squished under her palm. "Hold this. Put as much pressure on it as you can stand."

She gritted her teeth and pressed down. "What are you going to do?"

"What I have to."

"Eric? What does that mean?"

He let out a long breath. Reaching out a hand, he brushed his fingers over her forehead, pushing back stray hair. "I've figured some things out, Sarah. About me. About what has been holding me back. I love you, Sarah. I love you, and I don't care if you believe it or not. And no matter what happens, I'm not going to let you die."

She made a small sound deep in her throat. A sigh, a whimper, he wasn't sure.

He leaned down and kissed her forehead. He'd been so stupid. He'd wasted so much time. Time he could have used making Sarah happy. Being happy himself. Time that could have meant something. Now he was nearly out.

He stood and stepped over the harsh terrain, making his way to where the meth dealer lay on his back. The man stared up into the wide Wyoming sky. Already his eyes looked opaque and dull, his complexion more like rubber than flesh.

Eric unzipped the man's coat. His whole chest was

soaked with blood, making it impossible to tell the true color of the shirt underneath. He ran his hands over the man's pants and inside the coat. Finding what he was looking for in a pocket in the lining, he pulled it out with a sticky hand.

He knew water would ruin a cell phone. He hoped the same wasn't true for blood.

SARAH STRUGGLED TO raise her head, to see what Eric was doing. Nausea claimed her stomach. She lowered her head back to the rocky ground and focused on breathing. In and out. In and out. Eric's words ran through her mind, over and over again, like an old compact disc stuck on Repeat.

He loved her. He loved her.

She'd wanted so badly to hear those words. Months ago, before he'd left and nearly every day since. But now that he'd finally said them, what did they mean? What did they matter?

A chill penetrated her skin, deepening until it worked into her bones. Her leg had stopped hurting. Really since that first cold, cutting sensation, the pain hadn't been as bad. Not as bad as her bloody jeans would suggest it should be. And that had her scared more than anything.

She heard a rustling from nearby. The shuffle of footsteps over rocky soil.

Eric loomed over her, his face cloaked in shadow, blocking the sun. He took the wadded-up shirt from her hands. She could feel the pressure increase on her leg. "How are you doing?" he asked.

She shivered. "Cold."

He gripped her hand, rubbing it between his palms.

"You're probably going into shock. Don't worry. Layton will be here soon."

"You called Layton?"

"I couldn't think of anyone who could do a better job of protecting you." He smiled, but his eyes didn't twinkle the way they did when he was teasing or wanted to kiss her or even the time she'd caught him watching her while she slept.

"What about you?"

He looked away, craning his neck to stare down the road as if willing Layton's truck to crest the hill.

"You're going to run, right?"

His chest rose and fell, sweat slicking his bare skin.

He didn't have to say it. She could tell from the weight of his silence that he'd made his decision. A decision he thought he had to make to protect her. "You can't be here when Layton arrives, Eric. He might bring the sheriff."

He pressed his lips into a bloodless line.

"Eric, the sheriff will kill you."

"Layton said he won't."

So he'd made a deal with Layton. If Layton took care of her, he'd turn himself in to the sheriff. She felt tired, so tired. As if getting each word out of her mouth was a desperate undertaking. "Please."

"I had to."

For her. He was doing this for her. Giving himself to the sheriff. Throwing his life away to make sure she was safe. "Eric." Her voice sounded dry in her throat, dryer than the land she was lying on.

He leaned close to her, his mouth only inches away, and suddenly all she could think about was kissing him. Pulling him down to her. Tasting his passion. Here she was hurt, Eric was going to die, and the only thing she could focus on was how much she wanted him. How much she needed him. And how she might never see him again. "I don't want to lose you, either, Eric."

Tears glistened in his eyes. "You have to trust me."

Trust him? Trust him to do what? Get himself killed? Throw his life away in exchange for hers? "You're not listening."

He leaned a little closer. "I'm listening now."

"Run."

He shook his head. "That won't work. They'll have you."

"But at least they won't have you, too."

"And when they threaten to hurt you, then what should I do, Sarah? Turn and walk away?"

"Yes. Pretend you don't care."

"And you think they'll believe that? You think they'll believe I would let you and our baby get hurt? Die? Because I'm not that good at pretending, Sarah."

A shiver shook her, one she would never be able to warm. "What did you tell Layton? What did you promise you'd do?"

"He's coming to take you to the hospital. The sheriff is with him. If I go without a fight, he'll say I kidnapped you. I made you go with me against your will. You won't be charged with anything. And you'll go to the hospital. They'll stop the bleeding. You'll be okay. Our baby will be okay."

So that was it. Just what she'd feared.

Tears streamed down her cheeks. Pain hollowed out her chest. Emptiness. She couldn't let Eric give his life, yet he was right about the baby. She had to think of their unborn child. "Layton will make sure I get to the hospital no matter what else happens. You don't have to make this bargain."

"Here he comes. Just hold on, Sarah. Everything is going to be okay. I promise."

Even without lifting her head, she could see the plume of dust rising from the road. "Eric."

"I'm not leaving you."

"Please, Eric."

He shook his head. "I told you I would never leave you, and I meant it. I love you, Sarah."

She'd yearned to believe those words. Prayed for it. Never thought she could really let herself. But she believed him now.

Only now it was too late.

Chapter Eighteen

The sheriff's white SUV followed Layton's pickup into the tiny parking area. Sarah watched it approach, her eye drawn to a black-and-white dot in the truck's bed just before the world smeared into a blurry mosaic of color.

She blinked back her tears but it was no good.

Layton climbed from the truck, a red box in his hand that Sarah identified as the first-aid kit he always kept in his truck for the horses and ranch hands. He ran along the trail, heading straight for them. The sheriff dismounted from his vehicle and followed in Layton's wake. As he drew closer, he pulled a gun from his holster and leveled it on Eric. "Stand back from her, son."

Eric gave her a long look, then slowly climbed to his feet and took several paces back.

The sheriff positioned himself between Eric and Sarah. He put his back to the edge of a small drop in the canyon. "That's fine. Stop right there."

Layton ducked to her side. He kneeled down and looked into her eyes. "Oh, Sarah." His voice ached with worry, with pain.

She had the urge to fold herself into his arms, to let him make things all better like he'd always tried to do when she was a kid and her parents had just had a knock-down-drag-out or Randy had just done something stupid and risky. "You can't let the sheriff take Eric, Layton. He'll kill him."

He lifted the saturated shirt from her thigh and replaced it with two layers of cotton quilting used under horses' leg wraps. "Ain't nothing I can do, honey."

She opened her mouth to correct him, to make him see, then closed it without speaking. It was no use. Layton had never believed Eric was innocent. He'd only gone along with it, because he'd been scared for her.

"Let me see your hands," the sheriff ordered.

Eric raised his hands, palms out. "Get Sarah to a hospital. Dennis Prohaska here, too. I think he's still alive."

The sheriff glanced down at the still bulk of the reporter, then back at Eric. "So you had to drag someone else into this mess?"

Eric raised his chin and met the sheriff's eyes straight on. "You'll find your boy Burne over there." He motioned to the other side of the rock formation with a nod of his head. "I hope he paid your bribe in full, because he's not going to be able to make good on any outstanding promises."

The sheriff frowned. He glanced at Layton. "Burne? Who the hell is Burne?"

"There's no reason to pretend." Sarah knew she should keep her mouth shut, but the words flowed out on a tide of anger and frustration, injustice and grief. "We know he paid you to kill Larry Hodgeson."

The sheriff swung his gaze to her. A chuckle broke from his lips. "Oh, you know that, do you? I guess you were right, Layton. We don't have to worry about this one."

Layton kept his eyes on Sarah's wound as if he hadn't heard the sheriff, even though they weren't that far apart. He wrapped a pressure bandage around her leg as tenderly as he could, securing the quilts over the wound.

"Hodgeson was paid, too, wasn't he, Sheriff?" Eric said. "Just like you. Paid to do whatever a drug dealer wanted. Even kill."

The sheriff shook his head. "Get down on the ground. On your belly."

"Get Sarah and Prohaska to the hospital. Then I'll do whatever you say, no fight. Just like we agreed."

"You won't fight me now. Not unless you want a bullet in your head."

"Some threat, Gillette. That's been your idea all along, hasn't it?"

The sheriff's shoulders seemed to slump, just a little, as if he was as bone tired as they were. "None of this has been my idea, son. Trust me on that."

None was his idea? Sarah wanted to scream. "Then why are you doing this? Money?"

The sheriff scoffed and shook his head. "I'm not for sale. Don't you forget it. I've never been for sale."

"Then why?" She didn't understand. Maybe she never would. He had men kill her brother. Same for Bracco and Glenn. Now he was going to kill Eric, and for what? "Why are you doing this?"

"Why?" He let out a long breath as if blowing smoke through tight lips. "Justice, that's why."

The most ridiculous answer Sarah had ever heard. "How does what you're doing have anything to do with justice?"

"We agreed. Sarah's out of this." Layton's voice rang vicious as a growl.

The sheriff shrugged a shoulder. "The lady asked."

Sarah looked from Layton to the sheriff. Something was going on between them. An argument unvoiced. "What does justice have to do with Randy's death? How about Glenn Freemont? And Eric? How can any of what you've done have to do with justice?"

Eric took a step forward.

The sheriff spun to face him. "On your belly, Lander. Now."

Eric didn't move.

Sheriff Gillette swung around and pointed the gun at Sarah.

Layton sucked in a breath. "Dan."

"Fine. Fine. I'm down." Eric lowered himself onto his stomach, hands and legs straight out from his body.

The sheriff swung his weapon back in Eric's direction. "Cross your ankles and place your hands behind your head."

This time, Eric followed instructions.

Tears clogged Sarah's throat. Her stomach swirled. Her leg started throbbing, making her wish with each beat of her pulse that she could go back to numbness. But no physical pain was as bad as what was unfolding in front of her. What she couldn't understand, let alone stop. "I don't think you know the meaning of the word *justice.*"

The sheriff grimaced. He shook his head. "It wasn't supposed to happen this way. It was never supposed to happen this way."

"Then why are you doing it?"

The sheriff didn't look at her. Instead, he stared at the rock formation beyond the spot where Eric lay, as if he was talking to a ghost. Or just muttering to himself. "It's not the way things should work. He's guilty. He was sentenced. He needs to pay."

Guilty? Sentenced? What was he talking about? Burne had been acquitted. Unless he wasn't talking about Burne. Unless he was talking about someone else.

She thought of the articles Eric had read in the library. The other cases in which Hodgeson had testified, and the very important one where he'd delivered the crucial piece of evidence to get a conviction. "You're talking about the drunk driver who killed your sister."

The sheriff spun around and stared at her as if he'd just discovered she was still there. "How do you know about that?"

"Sarah." Eric's voice was muffled, his face down in the dust, but she could still hear the warning tone in his voice, clear as if he'd shouted.

He wanted her to keep quiet. To not put the pieces together, to not push for the truth. He wanted her to let things just go on as they were. Where the sheriff put a bullet in his brain to keep him quiet, and she walked away, with Layton at her side protecting her.

But the problem with that was, if what she thought was right, the sheriff couldn't let her walk away, either. He would have to kill them all. At least if they acted now, if she made Eric and Layton understand, their odds would be three to one.

She knew Eric would believe her. He might have already added up all the pieces on his own. But Layton? If they were going to get out of this, she needed to convince Layton.

"Hodgeson was going to give himself up, wasn't he,

Sheriff? He was going to admit he took a bribe to lie about the fingerprints in the drug case against Walter Burne."

The sheriff glowered at her, but he didn't argue. He didn't say a word.

"The only problem with him confessing was that it would call all his fingerprint identifications into question, wouldn't it? All the fingerprint evidence Hodgeson analyzed in crimes across the whole state."

Her hands shook. Her back was slick with clammy sweat, but she forced herself to continue. She focused on Layton and willed him to understand. "And that means the drunk driver who killed the sheriff's sister would get a new trial. That is, if the state decided to spend the money trying him again at all. If they didn't just let him go with time served."

Layton closed his eyes. His shoulders slumped forward. He looked tired. Old. His face gaunt and mouth slack. "Oh, God, Sarah."

She reached out and gripped his shoulder. "It's true, Layton. It all adds up. You've got to believe me."

"Oh, he believes you," the sheriff said.

"Layton?" She looked from Layton to the sheriff and back again. A weight settled, sick in her stomach. It hadn't dawned on her. The entire time she'd been outlining the sheriff's situation, it hadn't dawned on her once.

The drunk who killed the sheriff's sister had been convicted on the strength of fingerprint evidence. It had happened only eight years ago. Recent enough to be in the newspaper's Internet archives.

But he wasn't the only one who'd had a loved one murdered.

A murder solved by fingerprint evidence. A murder

that could be tried anew or even overturned. Sheriff Danny Gillette wasn't the only one here willing to do anything to preserve justice.

She looked up at her mentor, her father in heart and word and deed. But he was the real father of another girl before he even knew her. A girl who was taken from him. A girl for whom he'd pledged his life to see justice was done.

And that it stayed done. "Layton, how could you have murdered my brother?"

EVEN FROM TWENTY feet away, lying facedown in the dirt, Eric could see Layton's face blanch. The older man opened his mouth, then shut it without saying a word. Tears wound down his worn cheeks.

"Your brother was a troublemaker, Ms. Trask. Always was," the sheriff said. Even he sounded tired, beaten down like Layton. "He was a loser out for an easy buck, whether he had to cheat, steal or cook drugs to get it."

Sarah raised her chin. Her eyes hardened. The breeze blew back her hair. "He didn't deserve to die." She looked like a warrior woman protecting her own. Breathtaking. Beautiful.

And if Eric had anything to say about it, she wasn't going to fight this war alone.

Slowly he moved his hands off the back of his head. He uncrossed his ankles. With Sarah commanding the sheriff's and Layton's attention, maybe he could get into a better position unseen, a position where he could attack the lawman and take his gun.

The sheriff tilted his hat back and wiped a hand across his forehead. "If you want to blame someone, blame Randy himself. He was the one who went looking for Hodgeson's body for his own gain. Or blame Hodgeson. He's the one who took the drug dealer's bribe. And then he had to ease his conscience, damn the consequences. Damn the whole system."

"They didn't kill anyone," she said.

"Really? Both of them would have brought down the whole justice system if we'd let them. You think flooding the courts with appeals for new trials isn't going to lead to some criminals being set free? Criminals who should rightly spend eternity behind bars? Criminals who will take more innocent lives as a result?"

She looked from the sheriff to Layton. "You took Randy's life."

The sheriff was the one who answered. "Your brother went looking for Hodgeson's body so he could black-mail us."

"I don't believe you," Sarah stammered.

"Believe it," the sheriff said. "He paid me a visit as soon as he was released from jail."

Sarah was silent for a long time. Finally she spoke. "How about Glenn? He was an innocent."

"Glenn Freemont? An innocent?" The sheriff barked out a smoker's laugh. "Not hardly. He was a coward with a weak stomach. He couldn't stick to the plan. He talked big about justice, but when it came to doing what was required, he couldn't hack it."

"Glenn? He was working with you?"

The sheriff didn't answer, but he didn't have to.

Eric tensed his arms, ready to raise himself in a push-up and from there, spring to his feet. He had to move slowly, carefully. One sound or sense of movement and it would be over.

"And Keith Sherwood? Is he working for you, too?"

"Keith Sherwood? He's a loser. Has an obsession with guns and no sense of responsibility to go with it. A loose cannon and a drunk, that's what he is. Do you think I'd take a chance on someone like that?"

Eric took his weight onto his arms and gathered his legs under him. So they'd been wrong about Keith Sherwood. It had been Glenn Freemont and Layton who had dressed as deputies and shot Randy.

"And this Bracco who died in jail. That wasn't suicide, was it? You killed him, too."

The sheriff continued. "You have no idea what a piece of scum Bracco was. If you want another one to blame, he's a good one. Him and his blabbing mouth. If he hadn't told Randy where to find Hodgeson's body, Randy wouldn't have been involved at all. I never should have trusted Bracco to help me take care of Hodgeson."

Sarah breathed hard, as if she couldn't quite catch her breath.

"We didn't mean to have any of this happen, Sarah." Layton's voice was so weak, Eric could barely hear it over the whistling wind. "We just couldn't…I couldn't let Allison's murderer get a new trial for something that had nothing to do with his case. Not when I could stop it. I couldn't risk that he'd go free on some technicality when he took my Allison away forever."

Sarah's face drew tight. "You killed Randy!"

"The blackmail…I couldn't risk… It couldn't be helped."

"And Eric?"

Eric held his breath, hoping Sarah's mention of his name wouldn't cause Layton to glance in his direction.

Sarah swiped at her eyes with the back of one hand. She

paused, her gaze landing on him for a split second, then she focused back on Layton. "You and Glenn dressed as deputies and shot at them. You killed Randy in cold blood."

"I'm sorry, Sarah."

"And me? Were you going to kill me?"

She was provoking now, giving him a chance to get in position, to make his move. But even though Eric was grateful for the chance, deep down he wished she would stop. He didn't like the way she was challenging them, making herself a threat.

He couldn't lose her.

"I know too much now, don't I? You're going to have to kill me."

Layton shook his head. "No, I'll always protect you, Sarah. You know that. I'll never hurt you."

"It's necessary, Layton."

Layton twisted around and stared a hole through the sheriff. "You gave me your word. If I brought you out here, you'd let me take Sarah to the hospital."

"That was before she added the whole thing up. Do you really think she is going to keep our secret? You shot her brother. We're about to shoot her lover. You really think she's as loyal to you as you are to her?" He swung the gun, pointing the barrel at Sarah.

Eric's breath froze in his chest. He crouched, hands and feet under him like a runner at the starting blocks, ready to charge, but he was too far away. The sheriff could pull the trigger, he could kill Sarah before Eric could reach him. He gasped in a breath, ready to shout, to focus the sheriff's gun back on him.

A growl ripped from the edge of the canyon.

The sheriff turned toward the sound.

A black-and-white form crouched among crags of

tan and red rock. Radar had jumped out of the truck bed, as if he'd sensed the threat to his mistress.

The sheriff leveled his gun on the dog.

Eric leaped forward. Head down like a football player, he ran for all he was worth. He smacked into the sheriff just as the gun went off.

Chapter Nineteen

A scream broke from Sarah's throat. She struggled to get up, to run to Eric and Radar, to help. Pain stabbed through her leg and it refused to move.

Straddling the sheriff, Eric slammed a fist into the man's face. Again. Again.

Another shot cracked through the air, shaking through Sarah's body, ringing in her ears.

Eric grabbed the hand with the gun and pounded it against the ground. The weapon skittered across red rock and slipped into a dip in the canyon. Another punch, and the sheriff's head lolled back against the ground, his face red with blood.

Still on top of him, Eric fumbled with the sheriff's belt. Handcuffs jingled, mixing with the constant howl of the wind.

Another jingle came from the canyon's edge. Radar rose from his crouch and slunk up through crags of rock. Head low, he wiggled to Eric's side. Submissive and afraid of the loud gunfire, but perfectly fine.

A breath shuddered through Sarah's chest. Eric. Radar. She focused on Layton, on the gun in the holster by his side.

He stared at Eric, watching him handcuff the sheriff as if in a trance. His jowls hung slack, his bushy brows sheltered low over moist eyes. His body slumped as if he was more than tired, as if he'd given up. A man beaten down by life.

She still couldn't wrap her mind around what he'd done. In her heart, she wanted him to always be the man she looked up to, relied on. But he wasn't that man. He was her brother's murderer.

Not only that, he'd shot at Eric before, tried to kill him. And he could do it again.

She reached for Layton's handgun. She didn't expect to get it so easily, and the roughness of the grip as her fingers closed around it came as a shock. She pulled it free of the holster. Fitting it into her palms, she slipped a finger into the trigger guard and pointed it at Layton. "It's all over."

He nodded but didn't look at her. Instead he focused on the dusty rock in front of him. "I'm sorry, Sarah. I'm so sorry."

"That's not enough."

"I know. When you lose someone you love, it's never enough. Allison's murderer was tried. He was locked away. Knowing he's locked away was the only thing I had to cling to. I couldn't risk that. But nothing makes up for what he's done."

No, she supposed it didn't. No matter what happened to Layton, Randy would never come back.

"Give me the gun, Sarah."

She narrowed his eyes. What, did he think she was out of her mind? "Not a chance."

"I'm not going to hurt you. Lander, either. But I don't want this to go on. I don't want you to suffer through a trial. And the fingerprints Hodgeson analyzed…it's all going to be called into question now, even the legitimate matches, even Allison's case. I don't want to see Allison's killer get another chance. Let me do the right thing. Let me save all of us a lot of pain."

He was talking about killing himself, and for a second, she thought about handing over the gun and letting him do it. The second passed. She shook her head. "I can't do that, Layton."

"It's the only thing that will make up for what I've done, Sarah. A life for a life. I would let you shoot me, but I know you'd never pull the trigger. So let me do it. Let me make things right."

"No, Layton. Things aren't that easy." A shadow fell over her. She looked up to see Eric eclipsing the sun. In his hands dangled a second set of handcuffs. Her eyes misted as he pulled Layton's hands behind his back and slipped the cuffs on his wrists. Eric pulled off Layton's boots next and secured his ankles just as he'd done to the sheriff.

She felt a nudge against her uninjured thigh. Glancing down, she watched Radar snuggle his nose into her, his tail wagging so hard his whole body vibrated.

She stroked her fingers over his black-and-white head. Her leg throbbed. The muscles in her back ached. But worst of all was the pain in her heart. Closing her eyes, she let the tears roll down her cheeks. It was amazing she could still cry, that she still had tears left, but she did. For Randy and Layton, for Glenn and the sheriff, for justice itself.

"It looks like the bleeding has slowed."

She opened her eyes to see Eric leaning over her,

checking the bandage on her leg. His chest was covered in dust, his face bloody. But here he was, alive. "A miracle."

"A miracle." Eric nodded. Shadows cupped around his eyes. "I used Burne's cell to call 911. Deputies should be here soon."

Sarah's stomach tightened. She couldn't quite trust it was all over. The whole thing seemed unreal. "Will they believe us?"

"They'll have to. Prohaska has the whole thing on tape. The wind might have drowned out a few things, but most of it near the end is clear as a bell."

The reporter. She'd all but forgotten about him. "How is Prohaska?"

"In pain, but alive. The bullet hit him in the shoulder. A few inches lower, and he'd be gone."

Another miracle. "Can he talk?"

Eric chuckled, low in his throat. "Well enough to tell me he has a bestseller on his hands."

Sarah couldn't help but smile at that, even though none of what had happened was remotely happy. Relieved. That's what she was. Tired and relieved. She'd come close as a whisper to losing everyone she loved, but she hadn't…she hadn't. Eric and Radar, they were okay. They were here. And no matter what had happened—with Randy, with Layton—she knew she had the strength to go on.

But there was one last thing. Before the deputies got there, before the EMS took her away, she needed to say something. She only hoped she could find the words. "Eric?"

He folded her hand in two of his. His touch was rough and warm and everything she needed. And for a moment she just sat there and soaked it in. And when she opened her mouth, the words were there, pouring out like a waterfall, clear and clean and sincere. "I believe in you, Eric. I believe in us. And from here on out, I always will."

His eyes took on a sheen that burrowed into her heart. "Does this mean you'll marry me?"

She nodded, warmth flooding through her. A giggle built in her throat and bubbled through her bloodstream, as intoxicating as champagne. She looked down at her leg. Red soaked through the pads and stained the pressure wrap. But none of it mattered. She'd live. She'd heal. And she and Eric had their second chance. "I'd love to marry you, Eric. As soon as I can walk down the aisle."

"Aisle? I was thinking we could say our vows in that little basin at the Buckrail, with the mountains as our church."

He remembered. Her stupid, offhand comment. Her childish dream. The thing she thought had destroyed their chances forever, and now it would cement their bond. "I'd like that. I'd like that a lot."

He moved close behind her. Careful not to disturb Radar or touch her injured thigh, he slipped a leg out on either side. She leaned back against his chest as if he was her easy chair. Her support. The muscles in her back eased, and for the first time in days, she let herself relax, just a little.

"I love you, Sarah." His voice tickled her ear and vibrated through her rib cage. "I want to hold you every day for the rest of my life. Not because I have to. Because I want to. More than anything."

He rested a gentle hand on her belly. And at that moment, she felt filled to the brim.

Epilogue

Eric hated being the bearer of bad news. Especially on a day like today. Sure, the air held a chill and the ground was dusted with enough snow that it really seemed winter had taken ahold of the Buckrail Ranch. But judging by a warm sun and cloudless sky that stretched on forever, neither of those things would hang into the afternoon.

Of course, weather wasn't the most glorious thing about this day.

He took a deep breath of the sweet scent of hay. The sound of grinding teeth hummed through the barn, comfortable, cozy, his morning chores already done.

Sarah would be awake soon. Sarah and Cody.

And that's what made today so special. It was the first day he, his wife and their sweet newborn son would enjoy breakfast together in their home.

If only he didn't have to ruin it.

He closed the barn door behind him and stepped out into the cold. A pickup rolled up the drive, gravel popping under tires. Eric tipped his hat to Keith at the wheel and the new hand, Steve, in the seat beside him, just arriving to start the day's work.

Eric had hated to quit the guide service at the beginning of the tourist season, but he hadn't had much choice. Getting through the summer and the fall roundup with only him, Keith and Steve had been rough, especially with Sarah laid up with her leg injury and her due date drawing near. But they'd made it.

As it turned out, Eric couldn't have done it without Keith. The kid had really cleaned up his act. Giving up booze had been tough for him, but it had really transformed his temperament and improved his work ethic. He and the new guy had more than pulled their weight. Selling off more cattle than usual had been a good move, too. And with the addition of guest cabins built over the summer, the Buckrail's transformation into a guest ranch would be complete by the time the next summer rolled around.

Eric would be back guiding tourists through the wilderness, and giving them a wild west style ranching experience at the same time.

Perfect.

And by the time that happened, he hoped much of the hurt Sarah had been through in the past months would be over. Or at least faded.

He passed the corral and stepped up onto the porch. For a second, he paused, hand on doorknob, but then forced himself to push the door open and step inside.

The house smelled like fried eggs and toast, and his stomach growled despite the fact that he didn't feel at all hungry. He shrugged off his coat and boots. Best to tell her right away and get it over with. He'd already held the news back for one day, not wanting to spoil the baby's homecoming. She wouldn't forgive him if he held it back any longer.

Radar trotted into the foyer, toenails clicking on the hardwood floor. Mouth open and tongue peeking out between lower canines, he looked like he was smiling. No doubt he was. He'd added another human to his pack last night, and all evening, he hadn't wanted to stop licking the baby's head.

"Radar, where's Cody?"

The dog tilted his head from one side to the other, as if trying his darnedest to decipher Eric's words. Turning, he trotted into the kitchen, as if he'd figured it all out.

Knowing Radar, he probably had.

Eric followed, his stocking feet whispering against the floor. When he reached the kitchen, Sarah was bent at the waist, hovering over the baby seat shaped a little like a bucket that sat on the table. Her hair draped around her face like a curtain. And in that curtain was tangled a pudgy little fist.

A chuckle bubbled from Eric's chest. "Good grip, huh?"

Sarah smiled up at him through her drape of hair. "I think he's going to be a roper. There's a lot of skill in these hands already. I can tell."

"Nah, he'll be climbing mountains by the time he's three."

Sarah laughed. "Maybe he'll do both."

Eric leaned down and kissed the soft fuzz on the newborn's head, then kissed Sarah. Warmth filled his chest as if the bright morning sun was shining from inside. He was so lucky. Sarah for his wife. A healthy baby boy. A future that was so bright it glowed. They just had to put away the past.

"What is it?" Having freed the baby's fingers from

her hair, Sarah narrowed her eyes on Eric. "Something's bothering you."

This was it. He had to tell her. He took a deep breath. "I got a call from the interim sheriff yesterday, before I picked you up at the hospital."

"And?"

"They found evidence that Randy was in Las Vegas around the time Burne gave him that money."

"So he gambled it away."

He nodded. "Probably thought he could pocket his winnings and still have the twenty thousand."

"Do they know what he was going to do with that money? Why Burne gave it to him in the first place?"

That was the question he'd been dreading. The truth they'd guessed at but hadn't wanted to face. The reason he'd wished he'd never gotten that call yesterday. "Yes, they know."

Sarah pressed her lips into a solid line and raised her chin. "What?"

Eric took a deep breath and pushed the words out. "He was setting up a meth lab for Burne."

Sarah's expression didn't change, but Eric could detect a slight droop to her posture, a slight sheen in her eyes. Her brother had let her down. Again. "I can't believe I didn't know about it. Setting up a meth lab, a gambling trip and trying to get the money back with a blackmail scheme. He lied about everything."

Eric took Sarah in his arms. He didn't know what to say. No words could make any of it better. All he could do was hold her and love her and keep working toward a future. Building their business. Building their family. And enjoying their love.

Sarah gave him a kiss and stepped back, wiping her

eyes. "So does this mean it's over? Finally? Or is someone else going to show up wanting money?"

"That's the good news." He let a smile break over his lips, more an expression of relief than happiness. But he'd come to appreciate relief in recent months.

"What good news?"

"There was big crackdown on Burne's organization. A state methamphetamine task force rounded up a bunch of producers and dealers with ties to Burne. The sheriff said we should have nothing more to worry about."

"Is he sure?"

"I asked the same thing."

"And?"

"He said to rest easy."

"And other scams? Was Randy into anything else we should know about?"

"According to the sheriff, they've turned his life upside down and that's all they've found that we don't already know."

"Good." She moved to the stove and lifted the lid off the sauté pan. A heavenly scent of eggs, ham, cheese and vegetables filled the kitchen. She folded the omelet onto a plate and handed it to Eric. "I got some news this morning, too."

Eric carried his plate to the table and sat down next to his son who was now starting to doze. He wasn't sure he could take any more news today. He'd like to ignore it all and just concentrate on his wife and son and how happy they made him.

But of course, that wasn't the way the world worked. "Good news, I hope."

"Sheriff Gillette confessed."

Eric looked up from his plate, his first forkful in mid air. "To all of it?"

"He's admitting to shooting Hodgeson and paying Bracco to dispose of the body. He's admitting to killing Glenn. And he's admitting to conspiring with Layton and Glenn to kill Randy and try to kill you. And me."

It all seemed so long ago now, even though it wasn't even half a year. Still, in that time so much had changed. Layton had pleaded guilty to Randy's murder immediately and was already sentenced. He'd apologized to Sarah in the courtroom, his only defense being Hodgeson's accepting a bribe in the Burne case would taint all of his other cases, even the legitimate ones, and that his daughter's killer would get a new trial.

Unfortunately, Layton had been right about that. The courts were flooded with petitions for new trials. And among the petitions scheduled to be heard were the drunk driver who'd killed the sheriff's sister and the slumber party killer, both convicted nearly solely on fingerprint evidence.

He dropped his fork and pushed up from his chair. He crossed the floor and took Sarah into a giant hug. She was soft and warm and smelled of eggs and shampoo and baby, and he pulled in a deep breath.

Life wasn't perfect. It never would be. Tragedies would happen. Injustices. Loss. But as long as he had these moments—moments spent with his wife and son, moments of joy like he'd never known—he knew he could get through. He knew every day would be a glorious adventure and love would flow like a virgin waterfall swollen by the melt of spring.

* * * * *

RAWHIDE RANGER

BY
RITA HERRON

All the characters in this book have no existence outside the imagination of the author, and have no relation whatsoever to anyone bearing the same name or names. They are not even distantly inspired by any individual known or unknown to the author, and all the incidents are pure invention.

First published in Great Britain 2011
by Mills & Boon, an imprint of Harlequin (UK) Limited,
Eton House, 18-24 Paradise Road, Richmond, Surrey TW9 1SR

© Rita B. Herron 2010

ISBN: 978 0 263 88542 2

46-0811

Harlequin (UK) policy is to use papers that are natural, renewable and recyclable products and made from wood grown in sustainable forests. The logging and manufacturing processes conform to the legal environmental regulations of the country of origin.

Printed and bound in Spain
by Blackprint CPI, Barcelona

Award-winning author **Rita Herron** wrote her first book when she was twelve, but didn't think real people grew up to be writers. Now she writes so she doesn't have to get a *real* job. A former kindergarten teacher and workshop leader, she traded her storytelling to kids for romance, and now she writes romantic comedies and romantic suspense. She lives in Georgia with her own romance hero and three kids. She loves to hear from readers so please write her at PO Box 921225, Norcross, GA 30092-1225, or visit her website at www.ritaherron.com.

To Sheila and Linda—friends, fans and cowboy lovers!

Prologue

"The case is not over," Ranger Lieutenant Wyatt Colter announced to the task force gathered in the courthouse in Comanche Creek. "We still have a murderer to catch."

Ranger Sergeant Cabe Navarro frowned. The last place in the world he wanted to be was back in his hometown. When he'd left it years ago, he'd sworn never to return.

But he couldn't disobey an order. And so far, the multiple murder case had been a mess. National media was starting to take interest, and if they didn't solve the case soon, the Rangers would be usurped by the FBI and look incompetent.

None of them wanted that.

Still, if they thought he could be a buffer between the Native Americans and Caucasians in town, they were sorely mistaken.

Cabe had never fit in either world.

Ranger Lieutenant Colter introduced the task force members. Forensic anthropologist Dr. Nina Jacobsen. Ranger Sergeant Livvy Hutton who absentmindedly rubbed her arm where she'd just recently been shot. And Reed Hardin, the sheriff of Comanche Creek.

Hardin cast a worried and protective look at Hutton, cementing the rumor that Cabe had heard that they had gotten involved on the case and now planned to marry.

"Okay," Wyatt said. "Let's recap the case so far. "First, two bodies were found on the Double B, Jonah Becker's ranch, property the Native Americans claim was stolen from them. The first body was Mason Lattimer, an antiquities dealer, the second, Ray Phillips, a Native American activist who claimed Becker stole the land from the Natives."

"They have proof?" Cabe asked.

"Supposedly there is evidence that suggests Billy Whitley forged paperwork to make it appear that the land originally belonged to Jonah Becker's great-great-grandfather. That paperwork overrode the Reston Act which had given the Natives ownership."

Cabe made a sound of disgust in his throat. "No wonder the Native Americans are up in arms."

Lieutenant Colter nodded, then continued, "Marcie James, who worked at the land office, had planned to testify against Jerry Collier, the lawyer who brokered the deal, but she went missing two years ago. Evidence indicated she was murdered and buried on the property and construction of the road going through was halted."

He paused. "But we now know Marcie faked her kidnapping and murder. She resurfaced though, but someone caught up with her, and killed her at a cabin on Becker's property."

Sheriff Hardin stood, a frown on his face. Cabe had

heard that Hardin was protective of his town and his job. "My deputy Shane Tolbert was found standing over Marcie's body holding a Ruger. He claimed he was knocked unconscious and someone put a gun in his hand. We arrested him, but forensics indicated that the blood spatter and fingerprints were consistent with his story, so he was released." Hardin rubbed a hand over the back of his neck. "But his father, Ben, was certain we were gunning to pin the crimes on his son, and tried to kill me and Sergeant Hutton."

"Ben Tolbert is in jail?" Cabe said.

"Yes. He copped to threatening us and destroying key evidence, as well as setting fire to the cabin where Marcie was murdered, but not to murder."

"Daniel Taabe, the leader of the Native American faction, was also murdered?" Cabe asked, knowing Taabe's death was the trigger for bringing him into the case. Everyone in town thought the Rangers were trying to cover up the crime.

"Right." Lieutenant Colter's eyes snapped with anger. "So far, our suspects include Jonah Becker, his son Trace, his lawyer Jerry Collier who brokered the land deal, the mayor Woody Sadler who could have been protecting Shane as Ben did, and possibly Charla Whitley, Billy Whitley's wife."

Holy hell. Half the town were suspects. Between that and the war raging between the Caucasian faction and Native American faction, he had his job cut out.

Especially since both sides detested him.

He'd get this case tied up as soon as possible, and leave town. And this time, nothing would bring him back.

Chapter One

Anxiety plucked at Cabe as he parked at the Double B where the murder victims' bodies had been found. He scanned the area, half expecting an ambush.

Someone had been sabotaging the investigation at every turn, and he had to be on guard every minute.

According to the lieutenant, Jonah Becker was furious at having the Rangers on his property. And he certainly wouldn't welcome Cabe in town or on his ranch.

Jonah had always made it clear that he thought the Comanches were beneath him.

Not that Cabe cared what the rich bastard thought. He'd dealt with prejudice all his life. Prejudice from both sides.

But his Native blood ran deep. So did his cop instincts.

And as he climbed from his SUV, the scent of death surrounded him.

According to Dr. Jacobsen, the forensic anthropologist brought in to study the bones of an unnamed cadaver that had also been found here, one grave held ancient bones belonging to a Native. That grave suggested that this land was a Native American sacred burial ground. Worse, the body had been *moved.*

Dr. Jacobsen was right.

The ancient war cries and whispers of the dead bombarded him as he walked across the dusty, rock-strewn rugged land. There were other graves here. Graves of Natives who'd been buried long ago. Spirits who were upset that their sacred grounds had been disturbed.

Noting the plywood platform the forensic anthropologist had built to excavate the first finds, he muttered a silent thanks that Dr. Jacobsen had respected the grounds.

The image of the most recent corpse in the morgue flashed back, jolting him to the past and the reason he'd left years ago. The way the legs had been bound with chord, the face painted red, the eyes glued shut with clay—all part of the Comanche burial ritual. Just the way Daniel Taabe's had been.

And exactly the way his little brother had been buried as well. Pain and grief suffused him. His little brother had died because his father had relied on the Big Medicine Ceremony to heal him instead of taking him to the hospital as Cabe had begged.

The moment they'd buried Simon, Cabe had left town, and he hadn't spoken to his father since.

Shaking off the bitter memories, he studied the area where the bodies of the antiquities dealer Mason Lattimer and Native American activist Ray Phillips had been discovered. Forensics had already combed the area and bagged everything they'd discovered. He didn't expect to find anything new, but took a few minutes to search himself. Yet as he touched his finger to the ground, a sense of violence and pain assaulted him full force.

He could always sense death. It was part of his Comanche heritage.

Now the stench, the anguish and suffering, the cries of the fallen Native Americans filled the air as if they still walked the land. He heard their footfalls, the stampeding horses, the screams of women and children and battle cries echoing from the ground. He saw their ghostly spirits gathering as one.

Their collective shouts that this land belonged to them.

With his gloved hand, he pushed aside a clump of thorny brush and pushed at the dirt below, then dug a sample of the clay from the ground. The lab could verify if it was the same clay used in the burial ritual.

"You're going to jail, Becker," he muttered. Tipping back his Stetson, he collected a sample and bagged it.

Horse hooves pounded against the ground, the sound coming closer. He glanced up, half expecting to see more spirits, but instead a woman wearing a black Stetson with silver trim approached, riding a palomino, her long curly red hair flowing in the wind.

Dammit. Jessie Becker, Jonah Becker's daughter. He'd heard about her, seen pictures of her. She was not only a knockout but supposedly the brains behind the ranch's recent rise in success.

And she hated the Rangers being on her land, had thwarted their attempts to interrogate her father, protecting him at every turn.

She galloped toward him, rage and anger spewing from her aura as she brought the horse to a halt barely inches from his side and glared down at him. The morning Texas sun was nearly blinding him, and he shifted his own Stetson to shade his eyes so he could see her more clearly.

God, she was a sight for sore eyes. Her nose was dainty, eyes a crystal shade of green like fresh spring grass, her body full of sexy curves. And those legs…

Her lean legs hugged the horse's flanks just the way they would a man.

His body tightened, his sex hardening against his fly.

Double damn. He didn't need or want to be attracted to the rancher, not when they were on opposite sides of the land issue—and perhaps the murders.

"What in the hell are you doing here?" she asked.

In spite of the anger in her voice, Cabe bit back a smile at her sassy tone. He hated pansy, whiny women and judging from her attitude—and the way she rode—she didn't fit that category.

But he had his priorities straight. His work as a Ranger. His people—the Comanches.

And women.

In that order.

The spitfire redhead giving him a go-to-hell look was a complication. But now the damn sex kitten—rather, tigress—was part of the job, part of the task force the Rangers had put together, and he had to deal with her.

He stood to his full six-four and pasted on his most intimidating stare. "Sergeant Cabe Navarro," he said. "I'm investigating the recent murders."

She slid one leg over the side of the palomino and dismounted as if she'd been born in the saddle, then planted her hands on her hips and squared her shoulders. Still, her head barely came to his chest, and he could pick her up with one hand tied behind his back.

"When are you Rangers going to stop harassing my family?" she barked.

His gaze settled over her, intense and suspicious. Since the Rangers had arrived, she'd been more or less the spokesperson for the Becker family. What was she hiding?

"When we find the evidence we need to put away your father for stealing Native American property." He paused for emphasis. "And for murder."

JESSIE BECKER GROUND HER teeth in frustration at the tall, dark-skinned Ranger's threat. She knew exactly why he was here, and she had about as much use for him as she had for the other Rangers and the sheriff who'd been traipsing all over her property the past few days.

No, she had *no* use for him. They'd brought out the big guns now. This one was Native American, a sexy broad-shouldered hunky one at that. But his heritage meant that he would definitely be out to slaughter her family.

And her as well.

She had to protect her family.

"My father didn't steal this land, and he certainly never killed anyone." Her tone matched his, and she dug the silver toe of her boot into the dirt.

"Are you sure about that, Miss Becker? Maybe you don't know your father as well as you think." He stepped closer, tilted his head sideways and pierced her with his laser eyes. "Or maybe you're covering for him."

Her stomach fluttered with awareness, but she steeled

herself against his accusations—and his sinful looks. The fringed rawhide jacket he wore gave him a rugged look that matched his brusque masculinity. Shoulder-length, thick black hair brushed his neck and his eyes were the darkest color of brown she'd ever seen. Brown and sultry and mysterious.

They were also as cold and intimidating as his thick, husky voice.

Both of which could melt the clothes right off a woman. Even *hers* and she was a hard sell when it came to men.

But she had to stay on her toes and couldn't let down her guard—or her bra straps—for a second.

"Or maybe you arranged to buy the land illegally," he said, "and you're responsible for murder."

"How dare you?" She raised her hand back, balled it into a fist, tempted to slug him, but his eyebrow went up in challenge, and her sanity returned. She had to get a grip. She couldn't attack the law or she'd end up in jail. Then what would her father do?

"How dare I what?" he asked. "Try to find out the truth? Try to solve the murders that occurred on your property?"

He inched closer, so close his breath brushed her cheek. A breath that hinted at coffee and intimacy and…sex.

She folded her arms, ignoring any temptation to take another whiff. "I thought Billy Whitley killed Marcie James, Daniel Taabe, and those others?"

He shrugged. "We have reason to believe that someone else might be responsible, that Billy Whitley's suicide note might have been forged."

"What makes you think that?"

"The handwriting analysis didn't pan out after all, and the blood used in the ritualistic burial doesn't match Billy's."

"What blood?" Jessie asked.

"The Comanches bury their dead in a ritualistic style. They bend the person's knees, bind them with a rope, then bathe them. Then they paint the deceased's face red, and seal the eyes with clay. The red face paint is made from powdered ochre mixed with fish oil or animal grease and blood." He paused again to make his point. "*Human* blood."

In spite of her bravado, Jessie shivered slightly.

"After that, they dress the deceased in the finest clothing, lay them on a blanket, then wrap the body in another blanket and tie them with buffalo-hide rope. The body is placed in a sitting position on a horse and taken to the burial place west of the Comanche settlement and buried."

"So you really think this land is sacred?"

He gave a clipped nod. "Yes. The cadaver found was definitely Native American, the bones years old."

Jessie rubbed her arms with her hands. "But why would Billy admit that he killed Marcie and Daniel if he didn't?"

Sergeant Navarro's eyes darkened. "Because someone forced him to write that confession, or forged it."

Tension stretched between them as she contemplated his suggestion. "If you think my father did all that, you're crazy."

His jaw tightened. "Your father had means, motive

and opportunity." He gestured toward the crime scenes where the bodies had been discovered, then to the latest grave where the Native American had been uncovered. "But if he's not guilty, then someone else is, and I intend to find them and make them pay."

His big body suddenly stilled, went rigid, his eyes sharp as he turned and scanned the grounds. She saw the animal prints in the soil just as he did. Coyote prints.

He moved forward stealthily like a hunter stalking his prey, tracking the prints. His thick thighs flexed as he climbed over scrub brush and rocks until he reached a copse of oaks and hackberries. Tilting his hat back slightly for a better view, he dropped to his haunches and pawed through the brush.

She hiked over to see what he was looking at. Hopefully not another body. "What is it?"

He held up a small leather pouch he'd hooked by a gloved thumb. "It looks like a woman's."

She knelt beside him to examine it closer, focusing on the beaded flowers on the leather.

"Have you seen it before?" he asked.

He turned it over, revealing the letters *LL* engraved on the other side, and perspiration dampened her breasts. "Yes."

"Whom does it belong to?"

She bit her lip, a memory suffusing her. "LL stands for Linda Lantz. She worked for us as a horse groom a couple of years ago."

He narrowed his eyes. "Where is she now?"

"I don't know. She left the ranch about the same time Marcie was killed."

The Ranger cleared his throat. "And you're just telling us about this now?"

She jutted up her chin defiantly. "I didn't think her leaving had anything to do with Marcie's disappearance and death. Linda had been talking about moving closer to her family in Wyoming so I assumed she left to go home."

"Without giving you notice?"

She shrugged. "It happens."

"Well, if she left that long ago, then this pouch has been here for two years. That makes her a possible suspect…" He let the sentence trail off and Jessie filled in the blanks.

A suspect or perhaps another victim.

Worried, she stood, massaging her temple as she tried to remember if Linda had acted oddly those last few weeks.

"Did she know Marcie?" Ranger Navarro asked.

"I don't think so, but they could have met in town."

He cleared his throat. "Maybe she disappeared because she knows something about the murders. What if she stumbled on the killer burying the bodies out here?"

"Oh, God…" Jessie sighed. "I hope that's not true. Linda was a nice girl."

A heartbeat of silence ticked between them. That knot of anxiety in her stomach gnawed deeper. What if Linda's body was buried here, too? What if it had been here for two years? Maybe she should have reported her missing.

The sound of animals scurrying in the distance reverberated through the hackberries and mesquites, then a menacing growl—a coyote?

Odd. Coyotes usually surfaced at night, not morning.

"They're watching," he said in a low tone.

"What?" Jessie searched the early morning shadows dancing through the trees. "Who's watching?"

"The spirits of the dead," he said in a quiet tone, as if he could see them. "Their sacred burial ground has been disturbed, one of their own moved, and they want the body returned."

Jessie tipped back the brim of her hat and studied him. "You really believe that?"

He nodded matter-of-factly. "See that tzensa on the ridge."

"That what?"

"Coyote."

"Yes." Intrigued that a man of the law believed in folk legends, she followed him as he walked over to a cluster of rocks, then peered up toward the ridge at the coyote as if he was silently communicating with it.

"The tzensa is an omen that something unpleasant is going to happen," he said in a deep, almost hypnotic tone. "He may even be a skin walker."

In spite of the warm spring sunshine, a chill skated up Jessie's arms. He'd followed the coyote's prints to the leather pouch. "What exactly is a skin walker?"

He gave her a questioning look as if he suspected her to make fun of him, then must have decided that either she wasn't, or that he didn't care and continued. "According to the Comanches, when an evil spirit is angered, it wants revenge and can sometimes possess the body of an animal."

Jessie shook her head. "That's a little far-fetched, isn't it?"

He gave a sardonic chuckle. "Some would say the same about religion."

Jessie mentally conceded the point. "You're a Ranger. I thought you believed in forensics and cold, hard evidence, not in superstitions."

He lifted his head as if he smelled something in the air, something unpleasant. Maybe dangerous. "A good cop uses both the physical evidence and his instincts."

She sighed, hands on her hips. "This is unreal. First you accuse my family of stealing land, then murder. And now you expect me to believe that evil spirits are here, wanting revenge."

His dark eyes fastened on her, unnerving and deadly serious. "Your father disturbed them when he bought the sacred land, and then that road crew stirred them up even more."

"If the land is indeed sacred, we had no idea when we closed the deal," Jessie argued. "And I sure as heck didn't expect anyone to be killed over it."

"But your father set the chain of events into motion," the Ranger said. "And now, if I'm right, you and your father may be in danger from the spirits."

"I'm not worried about spirits." Jessie waved her hand in a dismissive gesture. "But go ahead and do your job, Ranger. The sooner you arrest the real killer, the sooner you can leave us alone, and our lives can return to normal."

His gaze met hers, determination flashing in his steely gaze, but a warning also darkened the depths. She barely resisted another shiver. He really believed those legends.

But she was a by-the-book kind of girl. The danger lay in the Native American activists threatening her family, and the killer whom the Rangers obviously hadn't yet arrested.

Not some angered spirits.

Still, as if to defy her, the coyote suddenly howled from the top of the ridge and a gust of wind rustled the trees, the scent of the death on her land surrounding her.

CABE SILENTLY CURSED.

Hell, he knew how people in the town looked down upon the Native legends. But for a moment, something crazy had possessed him, and he'd spilled his guts to Jessie.

A mistake he wouldn't do again. She was the enemy. He was supposed to extract information from her, not the other way around.

But as much as he'd left the old ways and superstitions behind, he couldn't ignore his instincts. He felt the evil spirit lingering as he stared into the tzensa's eyes. The coyote was a great predator, a trickster.

And he was here for a reason. Cabe had felt the connection.

The animal angled its mangy head toward the ridge below as if silently passing on a message, and Cabe headed toward the spot where the tzensa had looked. Sun glinted off rocks and what looked like a bat cave below, and he skidded down the hill, climbing over shrubs and sagebrush, dirt and crumbled stones skidding beneath his rawhide boots.

Behind him, Jessie followed, her soft breaths puffing

out as she descended the hill. He spotted the dark entrance to the bat cave nearby. Weeds and brush shadowed the opening, and he frowned, grateful that bats were nocturnal and he didn't have to face them now. At night they'd be swarming.

He rounded a big boulder, and came to an abrupt halt. Owl feathers.

An owl was a sign of death.

The ground had been disturbed, clawed away, the earth upturned. He gritted his teeth, then dropped to his haunches and studied the claw marks. The tzensa's...

Bones poked through the soil, and a dirt-crusted silver headdress with emeralds embedded in the Native etchings shimmered in the sunlight.

"What did you find now?" Jessie asked behind him.

He shifted slightly as she approached so she could see for herself.

"Oh, my God," Jessie gasped as she spotted the skeleton.

A rustling sound followed, and Cabe jerked his head toward the woods, his heart pounding as he spotted a shadow floating between the oaks. Someone was there, watching them.

Someone who posed a danger.

A second later, a gunshot pinged off the boulder beside them. Jessie screamed.

He shoved her down to the ground, grabbed his gun and tried to shield her as another bullet flew toward them.

Chapter Two

Jessie's knees slammed into the ground as the Ranger threw her down and covered her with his body. Hard muscle pressed against her, his breath heaving into her ear, his shoulder pressing hers into the ground, his legs trapping her.

The scent of man and sweat assaulted her, then she tasted dirt. Pinned down by his big body, a panicky feeling seized her, and she pushed against him to escape. But another bullet zoomed within inches of them, bouncing off the boulder, and he rolled her sideways until they were near the bat cave, and hidden by the thorny brush.

"Stay down!" he growled in her ear.

Jessie heaved a breath, wishing she had the gun in her saddlebag. "Do you see the shooter?"

The Ranger lifted his head, bracing his Sig Sauer to fire as he scanned the horizon. She raised her head as well, searching and struggling to crawl out from under him. The big damn man was smothering her.

He jerked his head toward his SUV. "Get in my Land Rover, lock the doors and stay down. I'm going after him."

Without waiting on her reply, he jumped up, ducking behind brush and trees as he ran toward her horse, vaulted onto it and sent the palomino into a gallop toward the woods where the shots had come from.

"No!" She launched after him. No one rode Firebird but *her*. The nerve of the arrogant bastard. This was her land—she had to protect it.

But she wasn't a fool either. He had just ridden off with her weapon and she couldn't chase the shooter on foot.

Another shot skidded by her ear, nearly clipping her, and she realized she had no choice. It was the bat cave or his Land Rover, and she didn't intend to tangle with the bats.

She crouched low and sprinted toward his Land Rover, furious, and hoping he caught the man.

Firebird's hooves pounded the ground, and the shots faded as she climbed in the Land Rover, locked the doors and crouched on the seat. Tension thrummed through her body as she waited and listened. She felt like a sitting duck and lifted her head just enough to peer out the window to watch in case the shooter snuck up on her.

Her temper flaring, she checked for the keys to the vehicle. She'd drive it back to the house and leave the surly Ranger just as he had left her. But of course, the keys were missing.

Probably in his damn pocket.

Steaming with anger, she folded her arms and tapped her snakeskin boots on the floor while she waited.

Ever since her father had purchased that land, their lives had fallen apart.

When they'd first discussed the deal, he'd been

excited about the prospects of expanding his operations. She'd still been in college, but she'd grown tired of following her mother around from one man to another. So, she'd finished her degree and decided to come back to the ranch, reunite with her father and join his operation.

But when she'd returned, she'd immediately sensed something was wrong with him. Although the cattle operation was successful, her father had made some other poor investments. Odd, since he was usually such a shrewd businessman.

After reviewing the books, she'd realized they had to increase their cash flow, so she'd added boarding and training quarter horses to the cattle operation. With even bigger ranches than the Becker one around needing working horses, she'd struck a deal to train them and had increased their cash flow within months, enabling him to pay off the debts he'd accrued and steer the ranch back on track.

But her father's behavior had worried her.

At first, she couldn't pinpoint what was wrong, but little things had seemed out of sync, and she feared his memory had been slipping. He'd complained of seeing things on the land, of hearing voices and bad things happening. Lights flickering on and off. Shadows in the house. Cattle missing. A watering hole that had dried up when they had had torrential rains. Fences broken. A small barn fire that had nearly spread out of control which could have been dangerous for the livestock and ranch hands.

And now these murders.

Sergeant Navarro's warning about danger from the

spirits taunted her, but she blew it off. Spirits didn't fire guns or start fires.

Whoever had killed Marcie and the others was obviously still lurking around. And they didn't want her or the Rangers asking questions.

CABE KICKED THE PALOMINO'S sides and they galloped up the hill, scouring the wooded area where the shooter had disappeared. Another bullet soared near his head, and he ducked, then fired off a round with his Sig Sauer. The horse protested, whinnying and backing up, but he gave the animal a swift kick to urge him forward.

Another shot whizzed by his shoulder, and Cabe cursed and coaxed the horse around another bend of trees, but the shadow was gone, and the trees were too thick to maneuver the horse through, so he brought the animal to a stop, jumped off and ran into the copse of oaks.

He spotted a shadow moving ahead—the tzensa— then jogged to the east where the road lay, in case the shooter had a car ahead. Another bullet pinged off the oak beside him, the bushes to his right rustling as the man dashed through them. Cabe raced toward him, but a rattler suddenly lurched from the bushes in attack.

"Easy," he said in a low voice. Not wanting to kill the diamondback, he froze, aware any sudden movement would bring it hissing at him.

In the distance, an engine roared to life. He cursed. He was losing the shooter.

Furious, he grabbed a stick, picked the snake up and whirled it away, then jogged toward the sound of the car. The wind ruffled the mesquite as he made it to the clearing. The creek gurgled, water rippling over jagged rocks, and a vulture soared above, its squawk breaking the silence.

But the car disappeared into a cloud of dust so thick that Cabe couldn't detect the make of the vehicle or see a license plate. Dammit.

He'd never catch the car on foot, or horseback for that matter.

Stowing his gun in his holster, he turned and sprinted back to where he'd left the palomino, climbed on it, then rode back to the crime scene. He had to protect the evidence. Then there was the problem of Jessie Becker.

Mentally, he stewed over the identity of the shooter, considering their current suspects. Her father for one.

Jonah Becker was a ruthless businessman, but to chance hurting his own daughter—would he stoop that low?

The sun was rising higher in the midmorning sky and blazing hotter by the time he reached the crime scene, his senses honed. What if the shooter had been a distraction to mess with the crime scene? What if he'd had an accomplice and he'd gotten to Jessie Becker?

Slowing the palomino as he approached, he scanned the area. The original graves that had held the body of the antiquities broker and activist were still roped off with crime scene tape. Still keeping his gun at the ready, he dismounted, then checked the gravesites to verify that nothing had been disturbed. Everything appeared to be intact.

In two quick strides, he reached his crime kit, and examined it to verify that the evidence he'd collected was still inside. A lawyer could argue that it had been left, unguarded, and could have been compromised.

Hell. He didn't want to lose the case on a technicality.

Maybe Jessie could tell him if she'd seen anyone else around.

Sweat beaded on his neck as he strode over to his Land Rover. But when he reached for the door handle and looked inside, Jessie was gone.

His heart stuttered in his chest. God, he hoped there hadn't been another shooter.

He didn't want anyone dying on his watch. Even Jessie.

JESSE LAUNCHED HERSELF AT the Ranger and shoved him up against the Land Rover. "What in the hell were you were doing taking my horse and leaving me unarmed?"

A shocked look crossed his face, then fury flashed into his eyes, and he grabbed her arms to fend off her attack. "Trying to save your pretty little ass," he barked. "And why didn't you stay in the car like I ordered?"

"Because I don't take orders from anyone." Her pulse clamored, a mixture of anger at him mingling with relief that he'd returned and the shooter was gone. Although she'd never admit that to him. Then his comment registered, and she couldn't resist taunting him. "So you think my ass is pretty?"

His jaw tightened as if he was working to control his temper, and regretted any compliment, no matter how backhanded it was. "You have a gun?"

Good grief, he was going to turn the tables on her. "Of course. I live on a ranch, Sergeant. I have to protect myself from snakes and rustlers and whatever else." She gave him a challenging look. "And before you ask, yes, I know how to use it."

His eyebrow lift infuriated her more. "You're surprised? Don't tell me you were expecting some spoiled, rich girl with a dozen servants who lives off her daddy's dime."

His evil smile confirmed she'd hit the nail on the head.

She huffed in disgust. "For your information, I have a master's in business administration," she continued, squaring her shoulders. "I started the quarter horse training operation, and now we supply working horses to other ranchers. And I not only run the books, but work the ranch myself. I'm a damn good horse trainer, if I do say so myself."

"I bet you are," he said with a sultry smile that made her belly clench.

For a moment the air changed between them, their eyes locked, and she sensed she'd won his admiration.

Then his frown returned, and he gestured toward the spot where they'd found the bones. "Then you oversaw the purchase of this land?"

She stiffened, knowing he was backing her into a corner and yanked away from his grip. In spite of his razor-sharp voice, his touch had been protective and almost…tender.

She couldn't let him confuse her with those touches, or seduce her into incriminating her family. She was *not* her mother, a woman who fell into bed with every man who looked at her.

"No," she said cautiously, back in control. "Dad made the deal when I was away at school finishing my degree."

"How about your brother, Trace?"

She bit her lip. Things had been tense between her and Trace since she'd moved back. Because of Trace's animosity, she was staying in one of the small cabins on the property instead of the main house. "He put the deal together," she admitted.

"And your father's lawyer, Jerry Collier, handled the sale?"

She nodded.

"I'll need to question your father, brother and Collier."

That knot of worry in her stomach grew exponentially. She only prayed her father handled the interview without looking incompetent—or guilty. Between his ruthless business tactics, and his recent memory lapses, he might just hang himself.

"You're going to talk to them now?" she asked.

He regarded her with suspicion in his eyes. "No, but soon. First I have to take care of business, obtain that injunction against this land being used until the land issue is resolved and transport the evidence I collected to trace." He heaved a breath. "Did you see anyone else here after I rode off?"

"No."

"No one could have touched my crime kit?"

She narrowed her eyes as if she realized the direction of his thoughts. "No, there was no one else here. And I didn't touch your kit or the evidence."

"How do I know I can trust you? You and I don't exactly have the same agenda."

His husky voice skated over her with distrust…and sexual innuendo. Damn, the man was so seductive that for a moment, her chest pounded, and she wanted to win his trust. But she would not allow him to turn her into a pile of feminine mush.

"Yes, I want to clear my family's name," she said, "but I also know that the best way to do that is for you to find the truth."

Another long, intense look, and she barely resisted the urge to fidget—or turn tail and run. Normally his size and stare probably intimidated men and women, but she refused to allow him to rattle her. She lived in a man's world, did jobs men did on the ranch.

"You can take my prints if you want," she said with a saccharine smile.

A deep chuckle rumbled from within him. "If the lab turns up prints, I will."

She planted her hands on her hips. "So, what now, Sergeant?"

She intentionally made his title sound like a four-letter word, and was rewarded when a muscle ticked in his jaw.

"I'm going to look for the bullets and casings from the shooter, then make sure this crime scene and those burial sites are guarded around the clock."

She frowned, half wanting to stick around to see what else he discovered—and to watch him work. But she needed to check on her father and warn him about the Ranger. Hopefully her dad and Trace both had alibis for this morning. Her father had still been in bed when she'd stopped by for coffee, but Trace had already left the house. He was somewhere on the ranch.

He'd been adamant about getting rid of the Rangers. Would he have shot at this one to try to run him off?

Irritated, she turned and headed toward Firebird, but the Ranger called her name, his voice taunting.

"Where are you going, Jessie? Running to warn Daddy that I found more damning evidence against him? That I intend to take a sample of his blood to see if it matches the red paint used in the ritualistic burials so I can nail him for murder?"

She schooled her reaction, then offered him a sardonic look. "No, Sergeant. My father is innocent. Get a warrant and take your blood sample, and *you'll* prove it." She swung up into the saddle and glared down at him again. "And in spite of the fact that you're trying to take away our land and destroy our reputation, I have a ranch to run."

The challenge in his dark eyes sent her stomach fluttering again, then his look softened, turned almost concerned. "Be careful, Jessie," he finally said in a gruff voice. "Remember there's a shooter out there, and he may still be on your property."

She patted her saddlebag where she kept her pistol. "Don't worry. I can take care of myself." Settling her hat more firmly on her head, she clicked her heels against the mare's flanks, yanked the reins and sent Firebird galloping toward the main ranch house.

But his warning reverberated in her head, and she kept her eyes peeled as she crossed the distance in case the shooter was still lurking around. Not only were the Native Americans incensed about the land deal, but other locals were jealous of her father's success.

One of them had shot at the Ranger and her today.

She didn't intend to end up dead like the others.

A TIGHTNESS GRIPPED CABE'S chest as he watched Jessie disappear into the distance.

She was undeniably the most stubborn, independent, infuriating, spunky, sexy woman he'd ever met.

Even when she'd been hissing at him like a rattlesnake, his body had hummed to life with arousal. Unfortunately, the fact that she was so devoted to her family and defended her father to no end only stirred his admiration.

And she could tame a wild horse. Damn he was sure of that. In fact, he'd like to climb in the saddle with her and tangle a time or two.

He almost hated to take down her father and destroy her image of him. Or cause her any grief.

But the wind whispered with the scent of death, the murder victims' faces swam in his mind, the Native spirits screaming for justice.

He'd do whatever was necessary to ferret out the truth.

Jonah Becker and his son, Trace, had no scruples—that was the key to their success. Was it the key to Jessie's rise in the ranching business as well? Was she really going back to work, or running to help her father cover his crimes?

Remembering the hairs he'd found, the clay sample and the leather pouch, he punched in Lt. Wyatt Colter's number. Wyatt had been the first Ranger working the case and the lead. "Navarro."

Wyatt cleared his throat. "Yeah?"

Cabe explained about the evidence he'd collected and the attack.

"If someone forged Billy's suicide note or forced him to write it, then killed him," Wyatt said, "they obviously don't want us still poking around."

"Which means that Billy may not have killed the antiquities dealer, the activist, Marcie or Daniel Taabe. So the real killer is still at large and definitely wanted to scare me off."

"Maybe it was Jonah Becker or his son," Wyatt suggested. "We still believe he obtained that land illegally."

"Could have been one of them, I guess, but Jessie Becker was with me. She could have been hit as well."

"Dammit, this case has been nothing but trouble. Someone's been tampering with the evidence every step of the way." A long, tense moment passed. "Keep the scene secure and make sure you follow the chain of custody. When we catch this bastard, we don't want him to walk."

Cabe bit back a sarcastic remark. "I know how to do my job, Lieutenant. I'll take the evidence to the sheriff's office and have a Ranger courier pick it up to transport to the lab. But first, I'm going to search for the bullets and casings from the shooter." A noise in the brush drew his eyes, and he turned to study the woods again, wondering if the killer had returned.

"I also found a leather pouch with the initials *LL* on it. Jessie said it belonged to a horse groom named Linda Lantz who worked for her two years ago. Apparently Linda left the ranch about the same time Marcie faked her kidnapping and death."

"So she might have been involved?" Wyatt asked.

"Or she could be a witness. We need to find out if she's still alive. And if so, where she is now."

Wyatt mumbled agreement. "I'll see what I can dig up on her."

Cabe cleared his throat. "One more thing. I discovered another burial spot. I'm sure this one is an old grave, a Native American female, but I'll need the ME and Dr. Jacobsen for verification."

"We should excavate the entire area," Wyatt suggested.

"No," Cabe said emphatically. "These last two bodies suggest that this is definitely a sacred burial ground. We can't remove bodies or disturb the dead."

"But—"

"I'm telling you we can't," Cabe said sharply. "Besides the legal problems, it's too dangerous, Wyatt. The dead are already incensed over what's been done to them here. If we start digging up the bodies and moving them, the spirits will be even more angry and dangerous."

"You really believe in all this superstition?"

Cabe chewed the inside of his cheek. He'd hated the traditions, the way some of the Natives on the reservation refused to acclimate with the rest of the modern world. The animosity between the two sects in town and the old prejudices that refused to die.

But he couldn't deny some of the things he'd seen and experienced growing up. And again today.

"Yes," Cabe said. "And if you think the Native American faction in Comanche Creek is up in arms now, just try to dig up a sacred burial ground."

Wyatt sighed. "So what do you suggest we do?"

"Inform the forensic anthropologist that we have to do everything we can to preserve the burial grounds, any artifacts here, and identify the bones."

"Don't worry. Nina would do that anyway. She's very protective of her finds."

"Good." Cabe scrubbed his hand over the back of his neck. "I'm going to call a meeting of the Town Council and the leaders of the Native American faction. A court injunction should stop any more use of the land by the Beckers until the matter is resolved. Hopefully that will soothe ruffled feathers long enough for us to sort things out and find our murderer."

"I'll arrange for Deputy Spears and some floating deputies to guard the land twenty-four seven," Wyatt said. "Even though Deputy Shane Tolbert was cleared, I don't want him near our crime scene. His past relationship with Marcie still poses a conflict of interest."

"He strikes me as a hothead," Cabe said.

"He is," Wyatt agreed. "What about the Becker family?"

Cabe shifted and scrubbed dirt from his boots. "I'll question Jonah and his son and get a warrant for blood samples from both of them. If one of their blood matches the paint from Daniel Taabe's body, we'll know who's to blame."

"What about the daughter? Do you think she's covering for her father?"

Cabe hesitated. He wanted to believe that Jessie was innocent. But he'd hold off judgment until he fished around some more. "I don't know yet, but I'll keep an eye on her."

For some reason, the thought of spying on her disturbed him.

And she'd felt downright sinful when he'd covered her body with his. Of course, she'd shoved at him to get off her. She'd obviously hated him touching her.

Yep. Jessie Becker was a hands-off case.

He absolutely couldn't get involved with her. She and her family were his prime suspects.

And if she was covering for her father, he'd have to throw the book at her as an accessory.

Chapter Three

Jessie frowned as she rode back to the main house. If Billy Whitley hadn't killed Marcie and the others, then who had?

Deputy Shane Tolbert's father, Ben? He'd confessed to shooting at Sergeant Hutton and the sheriff, but he denied killing Billy, Marcie, Daniel Taabe, the antiquities broker and the Native American activist who first accused Jonah of the illegal land deal.

Instead of the investigation coming to an end, the situation was growing worse. The Rangers had only allowed her on their task force because she knew the lay of the land, and they trusted her more than they did her father or brother.

Then again, they had probably asked her to join them so they could watch her as a suspect.

Jessie tied the palomino to the hitching post, the sight of the Bluebonnets and Indian paintbrushes swaying in the breeze.

Spring was usually her favorite time of year, a time where life was renewed, the land blossomed with an array of colors, green leaves and flowers, and the beautiful blue of the Texas sky turned glorious shades as winter's gray faded and the sun glinted off the rugged land.

She paused to inhale the scent of fresh grass filling the air, but the memory of the brittle skeleton bones she'd seen haunted her—instead of life thriving now, there was too much death on their land. Violence and suspicion had invaded her home like a dark cloud.

She stomped up the steps to the porch, determined to protect her own. The ranch and her father were her life. And now that life and her family's future and good name were in jeopardy.

Her head ached from anxiety, and her shoulders were knotted and sore. She shoved open the door to the scent of freshly baked cinnamon bread, coffee and bacon, but her stomach churned. She couldn't eat a bite.

Lolita, the cook who had been with her father for years, loped in with a smile. "You hungry, Miss Jessie?"

She shook her head. "No, thanks. Is Dad downstairs yet?"

Lolita gave a short nod, but concern darkened her brown eyes. "In his private study. I took him coffee, and he's resting in his easy chair."

Good, at least he had an alibi. Not that Lolita wouldn't lie for him, but Jessie hoped to clear the family with the truth. "Did he have a hard night?"

Lolita nodded. "I heard him pacing the floor until near dawn."

"I'll check on him now." She swung around to the right, then knocked on her father's study door. He had insisted on maintaining a small private space for himself, so she and Trace shared a connecting office next door.

Expensive, dark leather furniture and a bulky credenza gave the room a masculine feel. An ornately carved wooden box sat on his desk where he kept his pipe tobacco, and built-in paneled bookcases held his collection of leather-bound historical journals and books.

A portrait of his father, William Becker, hung above the brick mantel, a testament to the man who'd bought the small parcel of land that had been the beginnings of the Becker ranch. He'd named it the Big B because of his drive to make it one of the biggest spreads in Texas, and first brought in the Santa Gertrudis which they still raised.

Her father didn't answer, so she knocked again, then cracked the door open. "Dad?"

He glanced up from his newspaper, took a sip of his coffee, his brows furrowed. "Jessie?"

She breathed a sigh of relief that he recognized her. Twice lately, he'd called her by her mother's name. She'd think he was still grieving for her, but they'd divorced years ago. "Yes. We need to talk."

He twisted the left side of his handlebar mustache, a familiar habit. "Come on in."

She moved into the room and settled on the leather love seat across from him. "Dad, another Ranger was here today, a Native American named Sergeant Cabe Navarro."

Worry knitted his brows together, and he tapped his pipe and lit it. "They brought in an Indian."

Jessie worked her mouth from side to side. "Yes, he's a Comanche, and you should show him some respect. Besides, this one is a Texas Ranger. He's sworn to uphold the law." And he'd probably had to overcome severe obstacles and prejudices to achieve his goals.

That realization roused admiration in her chest.

"Those Rangers need to leave us alone," her father spat.

"I know it upsets you, Dad, but they're not leaving until these murders have been solved and the issue of the land is resolved."

"Hell, I thought Billy Whitley admitted to the murders before he killed himself."

"The Rangers think the suicide/confession note might have been bogus, that someone might have forced Billy to write it, or that it was forged."

"Good God Almighty." Her father coughed and leaned back in his chair, looking pale and weak. "So what does that mean?"

"That Billy may have possessed evidence proving he doctored that paperwork on the land deal." Which meant the Native Americans were right. They deserved the land, and her father had made an illegal deal.

Protective instincts swelled inside her, and she clenched her teeth. He was a ruthless businessman, but he wouldn't have knowingly agreed to an illegal deal, would he?

No… He'd been acting oddly lately, not himself, his memory slipping. He'd undergone every test imaginable since her return, and the doctors could prove nothing. So why was her father's health deteriorating?

She might suspect guilt or grief was eating at him, but she didn't believe him capable of murder. And grief for strangers was not something he would feel. He'd hardened himself against loving anyone, had shut himself off from friendships and close relationships after her mother had run off with a ranch hand. Instead, he'd focused all his attention on building his business empire.

"Dad, there's more," Jessie said softly. "Ranger Navarro discovered another body today, a Native American he believes was buried years ago." She reached out and touched his hand. "Be honest with me, Dad. Did you know the property was a sacred burial ground when you bought it?"

"Don't be ridiculous," her father said, the strength in his voice reminding her of her old father, not the frail man he'd been lately, the man she'd feared might be suffering from early-onset Alzheimer's or dementia.

The man she tried to hide from the press and police.

If word leaked that Jonah Becker was seriously ill, especially mentally incapacitated, not only would the cops attack, so would the media and his competitors. Jonah's business investors might also lose faith in him and drop their support.

"They can't do that to us." Her father slapped a shaky hand on the arm of his chair.

"Dad, the land is the least of our worries," Jessie said. Not that she wanted her father arrested for a fraudulent deal, but murder was much more serious. "Daniel Taabe's body was buried in a Comanche ritualistic style just as those other two were. The face was painted with red paint, paint which has human blood in it. The blood didn't match Billy Whitley's, so now the Rangers believe that Billy didn't kill Marcie and Daniel, that someone forced him to confess to their murders, then killed him."

"I don't understand." That confused look she'd seen

the past weeks momentarily glazed his eyes. Releasing a weary sigh, he puffed on his pipe. A moment passed, then his lucidity returned.

"Someone else in this town killed them," her father snapped. "A lot of people in Comanche Creek are jealous of us, Jessie. Jealous of me and my success." He turned toward her, his eyes imploring. "Don't you see? Someone is trying to frame me."

Jessie squeezed her hand over her father's. "You're probably right," she said with an encouraging smile. "I'll find out who's doing this, I promise, Daddy."

Suddenly the door burst open, and her brother, Trace, stormed in. "What in the hell is going on, Jessie?"

She stiffened. "Calm down, Trace. What's wrong?"

"I heard you were hanging out with that Comanche Ranger. What were you doing, trying to help him hang us out to dry?"

Hurt mushroomed in Jessie's chest. Her brother had resented their mother for taking Jessie with her when she'd left and for leaving him behind. He also resented her return and any attention her father gave her now. He even hated the fact that the horse training she had arranged had garnered success.

And he looked sweaty and winded, panic in his eyes. Suspicions mounted in Jessie's mind. Trace had arranged the deal with Jerry Collier, and would do anything to win his father's favor and safeguard the family ranch.

She flinched, hating her own train of thought. Had Trace known the land was an ancient burial ground, that the papers giving ownership to their father had been doctored?

A sick feeling gnawed at her at the venom in his eyes. Had he killed Daniel or Marcie to keep his secrets and protect the business?

Was he the shooter who'd fired at her and the Ranger a few minutes ago and tried to kill them?

CABE PAWED THROUGH THE brush and dirt, examining trees and rocks for the bullets and casings. After several minutes, he finally located two bullets, one embedded in a shattered tree limb on the ground near where they'd crouched in hiding, the second a partial one that had hit the boulder, warped and landed on the ground a few feet from the grave he'd just discovered.

He searched for footprints, and noticed matted grass, but there were no definitive footprints, nothing clear enough to make a plaster cast.

A mud-splattered vehicle pulled up, gears grinding as it slowed to a stop. Dr. Nina Jacobsen, the forensic anthropologist who'd worked the original crime scene with Wyatt, threw her hand up in greeting as she climbed out.

He'd heard she and the lieutenant had hooked up during the investigation—like Sheriff Hardin and Livvy—and that they planned to marry.

"Wyatt said you found another body," Nina said as she approached.

"Yeah," Cabe said. "Evidence suggests it's a Native American female."

A smile of excitement tilted her mouth. "Then I was right. I thought this property was sacred."

The energy of the spirits and the sound of their cries reverberated through the air, and Cabe nodded, then led her down the embankment around the boulder to point out the latest find. "Wyatt is working on a court injunction to prevent the land from being touched and the bodies moved," Cabe said. "But we have to verify that the bones are not a recent murder, and if possible, identify who they belong to."

Nina squinted through the sunlight, excitement lighting her face as she skidded across the rocky terrain, and halted to hover over the bones. "Judging from that headdress, which looks like it might have been from the 1700s, you're probably right about it being a female. But I'll need to study the bones in detail to verify the age and sex."

"As long as you don't move the body," Cabe said.

"I understand." Nina's ponytail bobbed as she nodded. "Wyatt also mentioned that you found a leather pouch."

"Yeah, Jessie Becker identified it as belonging to one of her groomsmen who worked here two years ago, a woman named Linda Lantz. Let's just hope the girl it belonged to isn't dead and buried on the property as well."

Another vehicle rolled up the drive, this one a squad car.

"That's Deputy Spears," Nina said, shading her eyes with her hand. "He's been taking shifts guarding the site with the floating deputies Sheriff Hardin called in."

"Good. Once the Native Americans hear we found another Native buried here, some of them may be tempted to come out to pray for the dead."

"Or protest," Nina said. "That woman Ellie Penateka has been leading marches at the county office for months."

Ellie—a name blasted from the past. "I know. And I don't want trouble out here."

Nina adjusted her camera over her shoulder. "Don't worry. I'll alert you if there's a problem. I want to preserve and document this find myself."

A blond deputy climbed out and strode toward them, his stance wary as he studied Cabe. "Deputy Spears. Sheriff Hardin sent me."

Cabe shook his hand and introduced himself.

"I heard there was a shooting," Spears said. "Is Jessie all right?"

Something about his tone sounded personal. "She's fine," Cabe said. "Are you two…involved?"

A faint blush crept on the young man's face suggesting he wanted to be. "No. Not really. But I was worried about her."

Cabe clenched his jaw. What did it matter if the deputy and Jessie hooked up? Once this case was over, he'd be hauling ass out of Comanche Creek.

"I'm going to run some evidence by the sheriff's office, then call a meeting of the town and local Native American faction to update them on the investigation."

Spears nodded. "Don't worry. I'll guard the area."

Yeah, and he'd probably guard Jessie if the need arose.

But Cabe would handle Jessie himself. He didn't trust anyone else.

"Good luck," Nina said, as she headed back to her SUV to grab her equipment.

Cabe stowed the bagged bullets he'd recovered in his evidence kit, then started the engine, hit the gas and sped toward the road leading into town.

A few minutes later, he dropped the evidence at the sheriff's office, signed the chain of custody form for the courier, then phoned Mayor Sadler to request a town meeting. Sadler agreed to call the Town Council as well as the leaders of the Native American faction.

Cabe grabbed a quick bite at the diner, then headed back to the inn, showered and shaved. With an hour to kill before the meeting, he jotted down notes on the case and his discoveries.

At seven o'clock, he strode over to the town hall, his senses honed for trouble as he watched several people entering the building. Voices drifted to him from the meeting room, and when he went inside, the room was packed with a mixture of Native Americans, Hispanics and Caucasians.

A rugged-looking man with salt-and-pepper hair lumbered up to him and extended his hand. "I'm Mayor Woody Sadler."

So this was the man who'd raised Sheriff Reed Hardin. He'd also been spotted at the cabin where Marcie had been murdered, making him a suspect as well. Although Sheriff Hardin staunchly defended the man's innocence.

Cabe shook Sadler's hand. "Sergeant Navarro."

"Glad you're here," the mayor said. "Maybe you can calm these Indians down."

Anger churned in Cabe's gut. "There are two sides to every argument, Sadler, and I'm not here to play favorites, just to uncover the truth."

Sadler's bushy eyebrows rose with distress, sweat beading on his forehead. "Don't forget, Sergeant. This is my town, and if you make things worse, then you won't last long."

Cabe shot him a challenging look. "Is that a threat, Mayor?"

A smile suddenly stretched the man's weathered face. "Of course not, Sergeant. I'm sure you'll do the right thing."

"I'll do the *honest* thing," Cabe said in a calm but firm voice. "I'll find the killer and the truth about who that land belongs to." He took an intimidating step closer. "And no one will stop me or interfere."

The voices in the room grew heated, cutting into the tension vibrating between Cabe and the mayor. Anger from opposing sides charged the room as hushed mumbles and complaints echoed along the rows of people seated in metal folding chairs.

Cabe frowned at the mayor. "I requested a small meeting with just the leaders. You know this could get out of hand."

Mayor Sadler folded his beefy arms. "This matter concerns everyone in Comanche Creek. And I'm counting on you to keep the situation under control. That is why they sent a Native, isn't it?"

A muscle ticked in Cabe's jaw. "They sent me to bridge the gap." And maybe balance out the underdogs, the Comanches.

Out of the corner of his eye, Cabe spotted the sheriff scrutinizing him. Yes, Hardin definitely was protective of the mayor.

But Wyatt had assured him that Hardin was a professional and had done everything by the book.

Hardin stalked over to him. "I hope you're not going to stir up the town, Navarro."

Cabe's jaw tightened as he repeated his comment to the mayor. "I'm on the side of the law." He tapped the badge on his chest for emphasis.

Hardin gave a clipped nod. "Good. Then let's keep it orderly."

"I'll do my part, and you do yours," Cabe muttered.

The mayor loped over to the podium, and Cabe studied the room. Deputy Shane Tolbert stood leaning against the doorjamb in the back, his arms crossed, his posture antagonistic.

Tolbert had been cleared of Marcie's murder, but he still appeared on the defensive. That fact alone raised Cabe's suspicions. Evidence could be tampered with, doctored, especially by someone with the right knowledge. And Tolbert had taken classes in crime scene investigation.

Plastering on his stony face, he walked to the front to join the mayor, still skimming the crowd. Ellie Penateka waved two fingers at him from the front row. As always, she was dressed to seek attention in tight jeans and a bright red, hand-beaded he was sure, shirt that hugged her big breasts. Her long black hair gleamed beneath the fluorescent light, her brown eyes just as cunning as always. Ellie would use any asset she had to achieve her goal.

At one time, the two of them had been lovers, but she'd wanted, no demanded, more—a commitment. That and for him to join her as an activist for the Native American faction.

He'd said no to both and Ellie hadn't liked it.

Another young woman, this one with black hair tied in a scarf, sat in the second row, fidgeting with the scarf as if to hide her face. She looked nervous, frightened like a skittish colt. Senses alert for trouble, he studied her for a moment, wondering why she refused to make eye contact, and where she stood on the issues in town.

His old friend Rafe Running Horse gave him a friendly nod from a side row, but glares of contempt and distrust followed him as he stepped behind the podium. Jessie Becker's flaming red hair caught in the overhead light, and his gaze locked with hers for a moment, her body language defensive. But he also sensed that she wanted the truth and a peaceful resolution. Or could he be wrong?

Had her family solicited her to wield her feminine seductive powers on him to sidetrack him from arresting them? Hell, if that was the case, it wouldn't work.

Besides, he doubted Jonah Becker would encourage any kind of relationship between him and Jessie. Judging from everything he'd heard, Becker had made no bones about the fact that he believed the Native Americans were a class beneath him.

Defying Becker would be half the fun in proving him wrong. So much fun that for a brief moment, a fantasy flashed in his wicked head. Jessie Becker beneath him. But not in social class. Hell, race and class didn't matter to him.

But he would like the feel of her curves against him, her breasts in his hands, her naked body writhing as he thrust his hard length into her welcoming body.

He blinked, scrubbed his hand over his eyes, forcing the images away. He was at a damn town meeting, couldn't allow himself to be swayed by a pretty girl. Especially Jessie Becker.

When he focused again, Jessie's brother, Trace, stood with arms crossed beside her, his look filled with rage. Trace Becker was short and squatty and made up for his size with his pissy attitude. Cabe read him like a book. Trace wanted an end to this mess, too, and he didn't care if it was peaceful, as long as his family came out unscathed.

Cabe had expected animosity from the group, and it simmered in the air like a brush fire that had been lit and was ready to flame out of control.

Clenching the sides of the podium, he introduced himself, asked for everyone to listen. Intentionally using a calm voice to soothe the noise, he relayed the latest discoveries in the case.

Before he even finished, Ellie shot up from her seat with a clatter. "So that land definitely is a Native American burial ground?"

He slanted her a warning look not to stir trouble. "It appears that way. We'll release further information when our investigation is complete. Please bear with us though, that will take time. And for purposes of finding the truth, we can't reveal all the details until the investigation is concluded. That also means that the property is off-limits, so please don't show up to protest or gawk. If you do, you will be arrested for interfering with a criminal investigation and sent to jail."

Noises of protest rumbled through the room, but he held up a hand and explained about the injunction. "I need everyone to remain calm and trust us to do our jobs." He gestured toward the sheriff. "Sheriff Hardin, the Texas Rangers and our task force are doing everything possible to settle this matter in a speedy manner and to ensure your safety."

"What about our leader, Daniel Taabe?" a dark-skinned elderly woman with twin braids cried. "You're letting them cover up his murder."

"There is no cover-up," Cabe said staunchly. "We will find out who killed Daniel as well as the other victims in the town and see that they are punished. But we need your cooperation. If anyone has information regarding any of the murders, please inform the sheriff or me."

"I thought Billy Whitley killed Marcie, Daniel and those others," a middle-aged man in overalls shouted.

"The evidence is not supporting Billy's confession," Cabe explained.

"You mean Billy might have been framed?" someone else asked.

"Was he murdered?" a little old woman cried.

A teenage Comanche boy vaulted up from his seat, waving his fist. "He should have died if he faked those documents. That land belongs to us."

Cabe threw up his hands to calm the crowd. "As I stated before, everyone needs to be patient, and let us get to the truth."

Trace lurched toward him, shaking his finger. "Just whose side are you on, Ranger?"

"The side of the law and the truth," Cabe said through clenched teeth.

"You should be on our side," one of the Natives said, triggering agreement to rumble through the crowd from the Natives.

Trace turned to the crowd. "Navarro's not on the side

of the law. He's playing both sides." His voice grew louder, accusing. "He can't be trusted!"

Jessie grabbed her brother's arm in an attempt to pull him back to his seat, but Trace shook her off and charged forward. Others stood and began shouting and arguing, but the sheriff raised his pistol and fired at the ceiling.

"Stop it now," Sheriff Hardin shouted. "If anyone can't control themselves, I will arrest them and lock them up myself."

A newfound respect for Hardin filled Cabe, and he exchanged a silent moment of understanding, then two deputies Hardin must have brought in strode through the crowd restoring order and issuing warnings to those whose tempers were spiking out of control.

Finally the room settled down, and everyone slowly dispersed, the deputies corralling them outside and accompanying them to assure that the arguments from opposing sides didn't escalate into physical violence.

Rafe Running Horse wove through the crowd toward him, and Cabe breathed a sigh of relief that he had his old friend's support. Rafe was one of the few people he'd missed from Comanche Creek, a trusted childhood confidant who'd struggled with his own heritage and goals.

But Trace lunged toward Cabe and grabbed his shirt. "It's bad enough you're trying to take our land, but I know you were at the ranch today. Don't you dare use my sister to try to pin a murder rap on my father."

Cabe ripped Trace's hands off him. "Back off, Becker. If you touch me again, I'll arrest you for assaulting an officer."

Jessie raced up, and tugged at Trace's arm again, a

wariness in her eyes. "Come on, Trace. You're just making things worse."

Becker snarled at her, then pushed her out of the way.

Cabe clenched his jaw, then grabbed Trace's arm in a death grip. "Watch it, Becker."

"You're the one who should watch it, Indian."

Anger cut through him. "It's *Ranger* Sergeant Navarro."

Trace's eyes flashed with fury, then he jerked away and spit on Cabe's shoe.

Cabe fisted his hands beside him to keep from pounding the bastard senseless. But the entire town was watching, and he had asked them to show self-control. He had to provide a role model to them now.

"Get out of here, Trace," Sheriff Hardin growled.

Trace laughed bitterly, then spun around and stalked away.

Jessie shook her head. "I'm sorry, Ranger Navarro. He's just upset."

"He's an ass," Cabe said through gritted teeth.

And her brother's behavior only swayed suspicion toward him. But he didn't have to tell Jessie that—she was smart enough to figure it out. "Like I said earlier, Jessie, be careful."

She stared at him for a long moment, some emotion brimming in her translucent eyes, then spun around and walked away. He watched her leave in case Trace confronted her—or maybe he just liked watching that tumbling red hair shimmering down her back.

Ellie sidled up to him, and stroked a finger along his badge. "What was going on with you and Jessie Becker?"

He tensed, almost sympathizing with Jessie. He had the oddest sense that she carried the weight of the world—at least the weight of her family's problems—on her slender shoulders. "Nothing. Her brother is a jerk."

She lifted a dark brow, her tone suspicious. "How do you know her?"

"I don't," he said curtly, refusing to play Ellie's petty jealous games. "I met her today when I was on the property investigating the crime scenes."

She offered him a small smile, her eyelashes fluttering. "I'm glad you're back in town, Cabe. We need you here."

He braced himself for another Ellie confrontation. "I'm here to do a job, Ellie. I'm not staying long."

Her stifling perfume assailed him as she leaned closer to him. "Maybe I can change your mind this time. Why don't we grab a drink and catch up? I'll buy."

Yeah, but the cost would be too great. "That's not going to happen," he said matter-of-factly. "Nothing could keep me in Comanche Creek, Ellie. You understand. *Nothing.*"

Her lips thinned. "You don't know what you're missing. Cabe. We would be good together, and we could do so much for our people."

He ignored her barb. Ellie had her own political aspirations, and would achieve them. She didn't need him. It just griped her that he'd rejected her.

Anger radiated from her in waves as she stormed away, the scent of her jealousy lingering behind like poison.

Rafe whistled. "Damn, man, you're back in town for a day and you've already ruffled feathers. Plus you've got women chasing you left and right."

"Not women, Ellie." Cabe chuckled sardonically. "But we both know what she wants."

"Jessie Becker had her eyes on you, too," Rafe said with a toothy grin.

"Jessie just wants to protect her family and get me out of town. Period."

Rafe shrugged, then gestured toward Ellie. "I don't know about Jessie, but you're right about Ellie. She's always been strong-willed and obsessed with the activist faction. But lately…"

"Lately what?"

"I don't know. But I'd watch out for her." Rafe made a hissing sound between his teeth. "She seems…dangerous. Out of control."

Cabe watched Ellie disappear into the crowd, shaking hands and speaking to the Natives, his gaze latching on to her long black hair.

He'd collected two long black hairs today at the crime scene. Did they belong to Ellie?

Chapter Four

Could Ellie's obsession have festered out of control? Could she be a killer?

She was outspoken, opinionated, a voracious advocate for the Native American faction.

Except that she bordered on conniving and controlling, a lethal combination that could entice her to cross the line.

The activists sometimes forgot the bigger picture and became a negative force regarding their own people because their protests only roused anger and unrest instead of building peace and harmony between the two factions. Some even adhered to the old beliefs so strictly that they ignored the benefits of modern society.

It was the twenty-first century. Shouldn't these prejudices have died by now?

"Are you going to see your father while you're here?" Running Horse asked quietly.

Cabe met his gaze. No judgment there. Just an understanding that they were both straddling a fragile fence, especially in light of the recent revelations in Comanche Creek.

"I doubt he wants to see me."

"You might be surprised."

Cabe's wide jaw clamped. "What? Is something wrong with my father?"

Despite his resentment toward his father and the ugly conversation they'd had the last time he'd seen him, he didn't want to hear that his father was ill. He was…the only family Cabe had left.

At one time, he'd wanted nothing more than his respect. To make him proud. He'd thought becoming a Ranger might accomplish that, but the fantasy had died a sudden and fast death when he'd left the reservation.

"Rafe?"

"No," Rafe said. "It's just that you're here. And it might be time to mend broken fences."

Cabe shrugged, resorting as he always did, back to his job. "I have my hands full right now."

Besides, his father might be in cahoots with Ellie and the Natives who were ready to lynch Jonah Becker and Jerry Collier for cheating them out of their land.

A noise behind them snagged his attention, and he spotted Charla Whitley making a beeline toward him, her makeup stark beneath the lights of the room, a half-dozen silver bracelets jangling on her arm.

She offered him a conspiratorial smile but he detected a secret agenda. Part Native American, he'd heard she collected cultural artifacts and sold them on the side. She had also worked with her husband, Billy, as his administrative assistant, and might have been involved in the illegal land deal.

"Watch out for that one, too," Running Horse muttered. "Charla had a breakdown after Billy died and threatened to kill herself. She was admitted to the psych hospital for a while, and was just released."

Cabe gave a clipped nod. He didn't know whom he could trust in this town.

Her ruby red lips curved into a smile. "Cabe Navarro, I'm glad those Rangers finally brought in one of our own. We need someone working for us."

Once again, he felt compelled to reiterate his neutral position. "I'm a Sergeant, a Texas Ranger, Charla. I'm here to uncover the truth, and get justice for all the murder victims, not take sides."

"Of course you are, Cabe." Charla raked her blood-red fingernails across his arm. "I'm relieved you'll be investigating Billy's death. I know he didn't kill himself or commit those murders."

"You and Billy were married a long time, weren't you?" Cabe asked.

"It seems like forever." Tears pooled in her eyes. "And I miss him so badly I can't sleep at night. I…just can't believe he's gone."

"You said you didn't believe he killed himself. Why?"

She twisted her mouth in thought, dabbing at her eyes with a tissue. "Because he wanted to know who killed Marcie as bad as the rest of us. She was smearing his name with those allegations about the land deal."

"But the papers are convincing," Cabe said. "It looks like Billy faked the documents to make it appear that Jonah's ancestors owned the land."

"Billy wouldn't cheat anyone, much less the Comanches," Charla said firmly. "He knew I was faithful to our people."

Cabe made a grunting sound. He wasn't falling for Charla's innocent act. "But I'm sure Jonah paid Billy well for his help. Money can drive people to do things they might not normally do."

Irritation made the lines around her eyes stretch thin. "You sound like you think Billy was guilty, Cabe. Maybe Trace Becker is right. You're playing both sides."

"I already explained my position, Charla. As a matter of fact, I need to ask you about those artifacts in question. The ones you confiscated from Becker's land and sold."

Charla's cheeks turned a ruddy red. "Don't tell me you think I had something to do with all this."

Cabe narrowed his eyes. "Why would you steal from your own people, Charla? Those artifacts should have been left with the dead, or returned to the Comanche Nation."

"I only sold two items and they went to a true collector of Native American artifacts," she said haughtily. "And at the time, I believed I'd made a legitimate deal."

She'd admitted to selling them. Maybe he could push her into confessing more… "So you sold them, then when the truth about their origin came to light, you killed that antiquities broker to keep him quiet. Then you killed Marcie—"

Charla lips twisted into a snarl. "How dare you accuse me of such a thing."

"As far as I'm concerned, everyone in this town is a suspect, Charla. Neither race nor sex is going to factor into the equation when I find the killer. Caucasian or

Comanche, they're going to pay." Cabe pinned her with his eyes. "Now, I'm going to need the name and contact information for the buyer of those artifacts, along with a description of the items."

Charla fidgeted. "I don't have that with me."

"Then get it together. I'll drop by your house tomorrow and pick it up."

She swung around to leave, but he grabbed her arm. "And, Charla, don't you dare warn that buyer I'm coming. If he's gotten rid of the artifacts when I arrive, I'm holding you responsible."

Charla clenched her beaded purse strap with a white-knuckled grip. "Just because you left Comanche Creek, you think you're better than us. But you're not, Cabe. You're worse because you have no loyalty to your family or friends, much less your heritage."

Spinning around on her high-heel boots, she stormed away, her heavy perfume wafting in a cloud behind her.

Cabe almost laughed at her audacity as he watched her meet up with Shane Tolbert at the door. Tolbert placed his hand on her back, and they bowed their heads in conversation as they walked outside.

Just how close were those two? Could they have conspired to carry out the murders?

And why would Shane's father risk jail by setting fire to that cabin on Dead Man's Road, and shoot at a Ranger and Sheriff Hardin if he believed his son was innocent?

NIGHT HAD SET IN, EVENING shadows cloaking the street outside the building as Jessie stepped outside the courthouse. She spotted Trace and Ellie Penateka talking near Ellie's Jeep Wrangler across the street and frowned. Their noses were almost touching. They almost looked…friendly.

Ellie was well-known for her strong opinions around Comanche Creek, and one of the last people she would expect to be friends with Trace. Then again, maybe Ellie thought that if she could convince Trace to side with the Comanches, then he could sway the opposing faction in town.

As if she suddenly sensed Jessie watching, Ellie tilted her head, pivoted and locked gazes with her. A nasty look of disdain curled her mouth, sending a chill up Jessie's spine. Then Trace said something to her, and Ellie jerked away and bolted for her car.

What exactly was going on between them?

Before she could go after Trace to ask him, Mayor Sadler lumbered up on her heels. "Jessie, wait."

She tensed, pasting on a smile when all she wanted to do was drive back to the ranch, take a hot shower and go to bed. But the mayor and her father were friends, and she appreciated his loyalty. Still, she wondered if Mayor Sadler had helped soothe the way for her father to make the land deal. He was popular and had connections in the town that ran deep.

He tugged up his pants, which were riding low below his belly. "How's your daddy doing? I thought he'd be here tonight."

Jessie's chest squeezed with pain. Everyone else was probably expecting him to appear as well, especially since her father's name and future were at stake. It wasn't like Jonah to back down from a fight or not solve a problem himself.

She hated to lie, but there was no other way. "Dad's fine, just tired tonight."

The mayor's brows furrowed. "I hope all this controversy isn't wearing on him."

More than you know, Jessie thought.

Sergeant Cabe Navarro stepped from the building then, his broad shoulders stretching across that white shirt as he stopped to survey the streets. His black Stetson shielded those dark enigmatic eyes, his shoulder-length hair held at the nape of his neck by a leather thong. With that rugged tough exterior, the feral power in his stance and his stark cheekbones, he looked like an ancient Native American warrior, as if he should be carrying a bow and arrow instead of a gun.

For a moment, an odd fluttering started in her belly, a feeling she hadn't experienced before.

Cabe Navarro was strong, masculine, tough as nails…and sexy as all get-out. Heaven help her, but she wanted to forget he was a Ranger, and give in to the attraction she felt stirring in her chest.

But that Silver Star of Texas badge he wore on his chest like a mantra gleamed in the moonlight, reminding her they were on opposite sides.

"No," Jessie said. "Although having those Rangers on the land is unsettling. I was hoping by now they would have arrested Marcie's killer and stop hassling us."

"It's hard to believe we have a killer running around Comanche Creek," the mayor muttered. "I don't like all this trouble in my town. And I don't like that Navarro guy. I think your brother may be right. He may be playing both sides."

"But I was with him today on the ranch when he found another body," Jessie said. "So he may be right about the burial grounds."

The mayor leaned closer and spoke in a conspiratorial whisper. "That may be true, but I'm afraid he's gunning for your daddy. You don't want to see Jonah go to jail, do you?"

Panic stabbed Jessie. "No, of course not."

The mayor's bushy eyebrows rose. "You're a pretty girl, Jessie. Maybe you can convince Navarro that your father is innocent, that Billy pulled the wool over his eyes when he forged those documents."

Jessie chewed her lip, uneasy at his tone. Was he suggesting she cozy up to the Ranger and sleep with him to alleviate suspicion from her father?

Did Mayor Sadler know something more about the deal than he'd let on?

CABE SPOTTED JESSIE talking to the mayor, and wished he could hear their conversation. Were they plotting how to cover for Jonah?

Tomorrow he'd speak to Becker himself. But first, he'd obtain that warrant for a sample of Jonah's blood and DNA. Hopefully the lab would have the results of the red clay on the Double B, and he would know if it matched the blood used in the ritualistic burials. If that blood matched Jonah Becker's, he'd throw the rich old man in jail.

And if Jessie had covered for him…

He'd have to arrest her, too.

That thought made his gut knot, but he pushed the disturbing feeling aside and strode toward Jessie and the mayor. He'd come to Comanche Creek to catch a killer, soothe ruffled feathers and right the land deal, and nothing could deter him from doing that job.

Not the mayor, or Ellie, who'd been staging protest marches in front of the county land office, or the sexy Jessie Becker, who could disarm a man with her sultry eyes.

Still, another problem nagged at him. When the killer was arrested and the town settled down, the spirits of the dead who'd been disturbed needed to be put back to rest.

How the hell could he do that?

Your father would know how.

No…the last thing his father wanted was to see him.

The mayor shot him an angry look, then turned and walked toward the parking lot.

Jessie folded her arms in a defensive gesture as he approached.

"That meeting went well," he said sarcastically.

Her small laugh of agreement rang with understanding. But that laugh made him wonder what she would sound like if she wasn't being sardonic.

"There hasn't been a murder around here in over a decade, so it's normal for people to be on edge."

"True. And it's worse knowing the killer might be their very own neighbor."

"I'm sorry about Trace," Jessie said.

Sympathy mixed with admiration for her. "You're not responsible for your brother's behavior, Jessie."

She relaxed slightly as if to thank him for not judging her based on Trace's rude actions.

His stomach growled, reminding him he hadn't eaten all day, and he gestured toward the diner. "Hungry?"

She shrugged. "Are you inviting me to join you for dinner?"

A small smile tilted the corner of his mouth. "Why not? Concerned that it's bad for your image to be seen with me?"

She made a dismissive sound. "Who the heck cares about image? Half the men in town believe I'm a daddy's girl, the other half think I'm a tomboy."

"Because you can ride and work a ranch?"

A breeze blew a strand of hair across her face, and she brushed in back. The gesture was so damn feminine that it made his groin ache.

"Yeah. That and the fact that I can shoot as well as they can."

"Those guys are blind *and* idiots," Cabe muttered. Hell, she was smart, tough and a marksman. He'd like to see her with a gun.

Or with a rope, maybe tying him down…

Sweat exploded on this brow. What the hell was he thinking?

Annoyed at himself for letting his thoughts stray to dangerous places, he clamped his jaw tight. "Only cowards are intimidated by strong women."

A teasing smile flickered in her eyes. "But you're not, Ranger?"

"No way." In fact, he was intrigued.

If a woman could ride a horse the way he knew she could, she sure as hell could ride a man to oblivion.

He quickly blinked away the images that thought triggered and opened the door to the diner. Dammit. He had to keep this conversation professional.

Voices and laughter from the inside dragged him back to reality, and he scanned the room. Judging from the packed booths and tables, half the town had joined here to eat and rehash the meeting. But he shook his head in disgust as he noticed the division in the room.

It was almost as if a visible line had been drawn down the center with the right side filled with the Caucasian faction, the left filled with the Natives.

Both groups glared at him as if they'd like to tar and feather him.

"Want to rethink eating with me?" he mumbled.

She jutted up her dainty chin. "No. As you recall, I'm part of this task force, too."

"Only because of your land," Cabe said stiffly. "So don't lie to me or keep anything from me, Jessie."

Any lightness between them evaporated like water on hot pavement. "And don't railroad my father for something he didn't do."

A tense silence stretched between them as they claimed bar stools at the counter. One of the waitresses, Sally Rainer, approached with a nervous smile, glancing between them curiously.

A hefty man wearing jeans, battered boots and black leather gloves took the bar seat on the other side of him. Behind him, voices of disgust rumbled, the discontent palpable.

"Hey there, Sergeant Navarro," Sally said. "Glad to have you back in town."

He grunted. "Not everybody feels that way."

She slid two glasses of sweet tea in front of them, then handed them menus. "Some of us know better," she said. "And I, for one, am relieved you're here. We need a neutral party who understands both sides, don't we, Jessie?"

"Yes, we do," Jessie said pointedly.

Cabe flattened his hands on the counter. "Why can't everyone see that it's not about sides? Comanche Creek should be working as one united community, especially right now."

Sally patted his hand. "Honey, you're right. It's about right and wrong. And I have faith you'll see that justice is served, and help piece this town back together. Now what will you two have for supper?"

Cabe ordered the cubed steak and gravy and Jessie surprised him by doing the same. So she didn't eat rabbit food like some women these days.

He swallowed a big swig of tea then wiped his mouth with the back of his hand. "Tell me what you know about Charla Whitley."

Jessie traced a water droplet on her glass with her finger. "Charla is like a chameleon. She changes color and personality to suit the mood."

"You don't trust her?"

"Not as far as I could throw her."

He liked the way she spoke her mind. "Did she and Billy get along?"

Jessie toyed with her napkin. "As far as I know, why?"

He shrugged. "If Billy didn't commit suicide, then someone killed him."

Her mouth opened in surprise. "You think Charla killed Billy?"

"I don't know," Cabe said. "I'm just asking the obvious questions."

Jessie took a sip of tea and seemed to consider his comment as Sally slid the steaming plates of food in front of them. He dug in, still waiting on Jessie's response.

Finally, she set down her tea. "They seemed well suited," she said. "I know she worked for him and denied knowing the artifacts were stolen."

"She could be lying. Maybe she killed that antiquities broker, Phillips, and Marcie. Billy could have found out, and threatened to turn her in."

She scooped up a bite of mashed potatoes. "I guess it's possible."

Voices stirred around them, the man wearing the gloves got up and left, and Cabe followed his gaze as he disappeared outside. He would have to question most of the locals in town, and he wouldn't be making friends. He'd be adding more enemies to his list.

And God knew, he had enough of those that the shooter today could have been someone from Comanche Creek, or someone else he'd crossed in the past.

Another reason he couldn't get involved with a woman or let one distract him. He had to stay on his toes.

Suddenly a disturbance sounded from outside. Loud voices, arguing, other voices cheering them on.

"Fight, fight, fight!" male voices shouted.

Several patrons in the restaurant jumped up and dove outside to watch.

Sally shot him a panicked look, and he threw down some cash, and rushed to the door. Jessie raced outside on his tail. "What's happening?"

"Stay back," he warned.

The moment he stepped onto the sidewalk, he knew the situation was volatile.

A mixture of older teens, Caucasian, Hispanic and Native, were squared off in the street, circling each other like bloodhounds out for fresh meat.

"You people are trying to cheat us just like you did hundreds of years ago!" a dark-skinned Native boy shouted.

"The land belongs to us now," a tall kid with pale skin snarled.

"Fight, fight, fight!" a group of onlookers shouted.

Cabe stalked to the middle of the group and threw up his hands. "Stop it now!"

"Get out of the way!" another boy shouted.

"Let them settle this," someone yelled.

"No." Cabe raised his gun to fire a warning shot in the air to stop the madness when suddenly a gunshot rang out. The bullet whizzed by Cabe, then Jessie screamed, and he turned to see if she'd been hit.

Chapter Five

Another bullet flew by Cabe's head, and he ran toward
Jessie and pushed her behind one of storefront posts.
"Are you all right?"

Her breathing sounded choppy, but she nodded.
"Where are the shots coming from?"

"I don't know." He quickly conducted a visual of the
boys who'd been fighting, but didn't spot a weapon in
their hands. In fact, they'd scattered in different directions, rushing to take cover, the fight forgotten. Locals
rushed into the diner and raced to their cars in terror. He
glanced around for the mayor, but he had disappeared.

Jerry Collier, Jonah Becker's lawyer, was ducking
around back to the parking lot behind the sheriff's office.

Where was Trace Becker?

Sheriff Hardin stepped from the city hall, assessing
the situation, his gun drawn. A quick glance at Cabe,
and Cabe shook his head indicating he hadn't spotted
the shooter.

Squinting through the glare of the streetlight, Cabe
scanned the storefronts, the nearby alley, then checked

the rooftops. A movement above the hardware store caught his attention, and he gestured toward Hardin with a crook of his finger.

Hardin gave a slow nod, and Cabe grabbed Jessie's arm. "Stay put and stay down. I'm going after him."

Jessie clutched the column. "Be careful."

He ducked and raced along the storefronts toward the hardware store while Hardin covered him. The shadow moved again, running toward the back of the building, and Cabe fired a shot. Hardin darted across the street, running toward him.

"He's going around the back." Cabe gestured to the right. "Let's split up and maybe we can corner him. I'll take that side."

Hardin waved his gun. "I'll go left."

They quickly split. Cabe saw a couple of teens huddled in the alley, as he circled to the right, and motioned for them to run toward the front of the building. A white pickup truck darted from the parking lot and raced away from town, tires screeching. The sound of a garbage can being knocked over echoed a few feet away, and he spotted someone dashing through the alley in the back.

Hardin met him behind the hardware store. "Someone just ran into the alley," Cabe said.

Hardin gave a clipped nod. "I called Deputy Tolbert to search inside the store. I'll check the roof."

Holding his gun beside him, Cabe jogged down the alley until it opened up to a side street that led to a cluster of dilapidated apartments. Sweat slid down his brow as he searched the dark shadows, the nooks and crannies between the apartment buildings.

Then he spotted the figure, and his pulse pounded. Trace Becker.

Had Trace been shooting at him?

Becker paused and leaned against the staircase railing of one of the units, panting and checking over his shoulder.

Inching toward the first building, Cabe held his gun at the ready, then closed the distance, making certain to keep his footfalls light to avoid detection. A dog appeared from the patio next door, and Cabe put out his hand, speaking softly to soothe the animal so it wouldn't bark or attack.

Becker started to move again, but Cabe vaulted from behind the apartment and pointed his gun at the man's chest.

Trace's eyes went wild with panic, and he threw up his hands in a defensive gesture. "Don't shoot," Trace screeched.

Cabe clenched his jaw. "Spread your legs and keep your hands above your head."

"Look, Ranger—"

"Do it," Cabe ordered.

Becker's brown eyes flicked with a nasty snarl, but he complied. Cabe quickly patted him down, searching for a weapon.

"I didn't do anything. I'm not armed," Becker growled.

Cabe removed handcuffs from his belt, jerked Becker's arms behind him and snapped the cuffs around his wrists.

"Dammit, take it easy, you son—"

"Shut up," Cabe said, practically daring him to mouth

off, "or I will slap a resisting arrest charge on you and throw your butt in a cell."

Trace stiffened. "You can't arrest me. I haven't done anything."

"I can and I will," Cabe said through gritted teeth. The guy needed to spend a night in jail just for being a smart-ass bastard. "What did you do with the gun, Becker?"

Trace grunted as Cabe spun him around and took him by the arm. "I told you I'm not armed," Trace shouted, "and I didn't fire those shots."

"Then why were you running?"

Becker hissed out a breath. "Because I figured you'd try to pin the shooting on me after what happened in the city hall."

Cabe narrowed his eyes, scrutinizing Trace's every movement. Funny how Trace and Jessie were siblings, but were nothing alike. She was strong and tough and attractive, where he just looked smarmy.

And dammit, if Becker hadn't fired at him, then Trace's dash to escape had sidetracked him from chasing after the real shooter.

Cabe shoved Becker in front of him, his gun still trained on the man's back. "Then you won't mind coming me with me and letting me process your hands for gunshot residue."

JESSIE'S HEART POUNDED when she spotted Ranger Navarro shoving her brother in front of him as they emerged from behind the hardware store.

The shooting had ceased, the streets had grown quiet as people dispersed, and Sheriff Hardin appeared from the opposite direction. Deputy Shane Tolbert exited the front of the hardware store, a pinched look on his face.

Dear God. Trace was handcuffed. Was her brother the shooter?

The men met in front of the courthouse, and she rushed to join them, frantic to hear what was going on.

"Did you see anyone?" Ranger Navarro asked the sheriff.

"No." Sheriff Hardin arched a questioning brow at Trace but turned to Deputy Tolbert first.

"Shane, what about inside the building?"

Deputy Tolbert shook his head. "I checked the store, the offices, the storage room and the back staircase. "Nobody was inside but the owner, Henry. When he heard the gunfire, he locked himself in his office."

The sheriff cocked his head toward Trace. "What happened?"

Jessie held her breath. She knew Trace would go to great lengths to protect their father, but would he actually resort to murder?

"I caught him running away in the alley," Ranger Navarro said.

"Was he armed?" Sheriff Hardin asked.

The Ranger shook his head. "No. But he could have stashed the gun someplace. Maybe the alley, a garbage can. Somewhere inside the hardware store."

Hardin nodded. "If he did, we'll find it."

"Good," Cabe mumbled. "I'm going to take him and process his hands for GSR."

"You're wasting your time." Trace glared at the Ranger, then at Jessie. "I didn't do anything."

"Why were you running then?" Sheriff Hardin asked.

A belligerent look darkened Trace's beady eyes as he flicked his hand toward Cabe. "Because I knew *he* would try to pin the blame on me."

"Stop whining," Ranger Navarro said coldly. "You asked for it. And if you weren't the shooter, then your running caused me to chase you and miss the real perp. I should lock you up for interfering with an investigation."

"That's preposterous," Trace growled.

Jessie crossed her arms. "Where are you taking him?"

"To the jail to process his hands."

"Call Jerry Collier and tell him to meet me at the sheriff's office," Trace said to Jessie. "This guy is not going to railroad me into a cell for something I didn't do."

"Yes, Jessie, call Collier," Cabe said. "I want to question him, too." He turned to the sheriff. "Hardin, escort Becker to a holding cell while I retrieve my crime scene kit from the SUV. I want to search for those bullets before the scene gets any more contaminated than it already has been."

Hardin nodded. "I've decided to ask the mayor to issue a curfew for the residents until this whole mess is cleared up. A shooting in a public place, those boys nearly fighting—this situation is way out of hand."

"Good idea," the Ranger agreed. "We don't want any more casualties just because tempers are running high."

"Meanwhile Deputy Tolbert can start searching for a weapon," Sheriff Hardin said.

The fact that the deputy had been a suspect himself must have troubled Cabe because he cleared his throat and addressed Tolbert. "Do you mind if I see your hands and weapon?"

Tolbert cursed, but extended his hands and flexed his fingers. The Ranger leaned over and examined them, then asked to see his gun. Tolbert removed his Smith and Wesson, checked the safety, then handed it to the Ranger.

Jessie dug in her purse for her cell phone to call Jerry Collier while Navarro examined Tolbert's weapon.

Tolbert glared at Cabe. "See, it hasn't been fired recently."

Cabe checked the magazine clip, then, reloaded it, and handed the weapon back to the deputy.

Tolbert gave a smug grin as he stowed it back in his holster.

"All right," the Ranger said. "Go back to the hardware store and search for a weapon. Check everywhere, including the vents, and the Dumpster outside."

Tolbert scowled as if he disliked taking orders, but must have decided not to push the Ranger's buttons by arguing. Jessie watched the power struggle between the men with trepidation.

Shane Tolbert had always struck her as a hothead. He liked women. Had a quick temper. And he had been infatuated with Marcie. Jessie still wondered about his innocence.

Trace grunted as the sheriff hauled him next door to his office. Even she had to admit that Trace looked suspicious.

She had to protect her family. Not that Trace didn't deserve to be taken down a notch, but it would kill her father if Trace went to jail for murder.

CABE HALFWAY HOPED Trace did turn out to be the shooter, and he could lock the little SOB up. But the look of distress on Jessie's face gnawed at him.

She and Trace might not get along, but arresting Trace—or her father—would definitely upset her world.

Too bad, he thought.

A sliver of guilt wormed its way inside him. Jessie was…innocent.

Either that or she was a damn good actress.

Focus, Cabe. Lives depend on you keeping a clear head. You don't want the body count rising on your watch.

He kept his senses honed for trouble as he rushed to his SUV for his crime kit. The parking lot was near empty now, the town quiet as the shooting had driven most citizens home.

A storm cloud rumbled, making him hurry his footsteps, and he grabbed the kit from his SUV and rushed back to the front of the diner. He pulled on gloves, retrieved a flashlight from the kit and began to scour the street, the sidewalk, the front wall of the diner and storefronts for the bullets and casings. But after half an hour, he came up with nothing.

He closed his eyes, mentally reliving the moment when he'd stepped outside to stop the fight. Jessie had been right behind him, the boys arguing. He'd stepped into the middle of the circle of the boys, then the shot had rung out.

He turned in a wide arc, analyzing their positions, where he'd been standing, how close the bullet had come to his head, then studied the top of the hardware store building. Judging from the angle of the shooter, the distance the bullet had traveled, the line of fire…

His stomach knotted.

Had the shooter been firing at him or Jessie?

The realization that he might not have been the target presented momentary relief as well as surprise, but the fact that Jessie might have been the perp's target disturbed him even more.

Why would someone want to kill Jessie Becker?

Because she had secrets? Because she was protecting her father?

And who wanted her dead?

Trace?

He hissed a breath between clenched teeth, then pivoted, this time focusing on where Jessie had stood, and strode over to the diner's front wall again. He was about six-four, Jessie probably five-five, so this time he skimmed his hand down the wall again, considered the angle of the shot and distance, and shone the flashlight on the surface. About an inch above where Jessie's head would have been, he spotted a break in the plaster.

Muttering a curse, he removed his pocketknife from his jeans pocket, flipped it open and dug the bullet from the wall. Using tweezers, he examined the bullet.

It was warped, but the lab could do wonders these days. He retrieved a bag from his kit, dropped the bullet inside, sealed it and placed it in the kit. Sweat trickled down his neck as he waved the flashlight across the wall again, looking for the second bullet. Nothing.

Rethinking the scene, he remembered he and Jessie

had ducked behind the column for cover. The shooter had obviously tracked their movements. He knelt, spied the broken plaster in the crevice of the wall behind a fake rosebush in front of the diner, and dug it out as well.

After securing it in his crime kit, he headed to the sheriff's office and jail. Jessie Becker sat in a straight chair tapping her foot while she waited.

He gave her a perfunctory look, the camaraderie they'd shared during their meal together lost as business took center stage.

Sheriff Hardin emerged from the back. "Did you find the bullets?"

"Yeah." He removed them from the kit, and signed transfer papers for the courier for chain of evidence to be sent to the lab in Austin.

The sight of Jessie sitting all alone stirred some primal protective instinct inside him that he had to ignore. She had removed her hat and was running her fingers through those red tresses. The movement made his fingers itch to feel the silky strands.

But he couldn't touch her now.

If Trace had shot at them, or at *her*, then he had to be stopped.

He adjusted his hat as he walked past her, then down the short hall connecting the jail cells. He'd let Trace stew a while and talk to Ben Tolbert first.

Cabe found the tired-looking man in the first cell, pacing. "Ben Tolbert?"

Tolbert stopped pacing and glared up at him. "Who are you?"

"Ranger Sergeant Cabe Navarro."

"Another damn outsider," Ben grunted. "I've already given my confession. What do you want?"

"To know why you shot at a Ranger and a cop if your son was innocent."

Tolbert rubbed his bloodshot eyes. "My boy *is* innocent," he said firmly. "But I've been around long enough to know that the law doesn't always work."

"So you risked your own future by trying to kill a cop?"

"I'm Shane's father. I'd do anything for my boy."

Cabe studied him intently. The man seemed sincere, at least sincere in that he believed in his son's innocence.

Animosity flattened Tolbert's eyes. "Now, unless you came to release me, leave me the hell alone."

Cabe silently cursed. He recognized a dead lead, and Tolbert was one.

Leaving the old man, he walked back to the interrogation room. Trace sat at the table with his arms folded, hatred spewing from his eyes.

"Where's my lawyer?" Trace grumbled.

"You don't need one if you're innocent," Cabe said sharply.

"That's a load of crap," Trace muttered. "I don't trust you or the law in this town. For all I know you volunteered to come here so you could throw your badge around and make life hell for those of us who weren't your buddies when you lived in Comanche Creek before."

Cabe slanted him a steely look. "If you think I give a damn about high school and you idiots, you're a bigger fool than I thought." He gestured at the table. "Now let me see your hands."

The door screeched open, and the sheriff escorted Jerry Collier inside. Collier was a weasel of a guy with dusty gray eyes and sandy hair. His pinched face made him look untrustworthy like the sack of garbage Cabe had expected him to be.

Collier planted his briefcase on the table beside Becker. "What's going on here?"

"I'm Ranger Sergeant Cabe Navarro. Gunshots were fired tonight near the diner. Your client was running from the scene."

Collier's eyes flickered toward Trace, then back to Cabe. "Did he have a weapon on him?"

"No, but we're searching the hardware store, streets and alley now."

"Is he under arrest?"

Cabe swallowed back irritation. "Not officially. He's here for questioning."

Collier nodded. "All right, let's get this over with so he can go home."

"First, I need to process his hands."

Trace twisted his mouth into a grimace, but complied. Cabe studied Becker's palms and fingers, but didn't spot GSR on his skin. Still, he removed a swab from the kit, dabbed it in the chemicals the lab had issued, and brushed it across Trace's hands and fingers. Then he took a DNA swab from Becker's mouth, and bagged and labeled both of them.

Cabe leveled his most intimidating stare at Trace. "Now, tell me again, why you were running down that alley."

Trace shoved his hands down into his lap. "Because I heard the shots, saw you coming and figured you'd blame me."

"Why were you behind the hardware store anyway?" Cabe asked.

"When I heard the commotion in the street, I decided to take a shortcut to my car."

"Sounds logical to me," Collier said. "Now, unless you have enough evidence to arrest him, which you don't, Sergeant, we're done here."

Trace stood, and Collier reached for his briefcase.

Cabe slid a hand to his weapon. "Don't leave town, Becker. And if I find that gun and it has your DNA on it, I will come after you. And this time, no lawyer is going to get you off."

"I should file harassment charges against you," Trace snapped.

Collier herded Trace toward the door. "Let's go, Trace."

Cabe stepped in front of the door and folded his arms. "Just a second, Collier. Where were you when the shooting took place?"

Collier's eyes bulged with outrage. "After your little impromptu meeting, I hid out in my office to escape the mob of activists. I was afraid there might be a riot."

Shooting Cabe a defiant look, Collier shouldered his way past Cabe, and he and Trace rushed down the hall to the front office.

Cabe followed, and saw Jessie jump up to speak to Trace. "I'm going home," Trace said to her. "And if you know what's good for you, Jessie, you'll leave that Comanche alone."

Collier shoved Trace outside, and Jessie glanced up at him just as he walked back into the room.

The wary look she gave him knotted his insides, and he strode toward her and stroked her arm. A tingle shot through him, the need to pull her against him and ease her burdens nearly overwhelming him.

"Be careful, Jessie," he warned in a gruff voice.

A mixture of emotions flickered in her eyes. "I appreciate your concern, Ranger, but I can take care of myself," she said softly.

Her gaze met his, something passing between them, an attraction that completely caught him off guard.

What the hell was wrong with him? He never got tied in knots over a woman.

An almost panicked expression lit her eyes as if she'd read his mind. "I have to go." Then she eased her arm from his hand, and darted out the door.

Anxiety filled him as he spotted Trace standing outside watching through the window. "She can't save you or your daddy if you're guilty," Cabe muttered. "And she can't save your daddy if his blood matches the victims' either."

He just hoped to hell that Jessie wasn't covering for them.

He didn't want to have to arrest her.

TRACE STORMED TOWARD Jessie as soon as she exited the sheriff's office.

"If you aren't going to stay away from the Ranger, at least you could try to sway suspicion from me and Daddy."

Jessie glared at him, tired of his bully ways. "You

need to behave, Trace. If you hadn't practically attacked Cabe at the meeting, he might not be suspicious of you. If he arrests you, it'll be your own damn fault."

"So now you're taking up for him?" Trace said in a nasty tone.

Instead of acknowledging his comment, she rolled her eyes in disgust, then turned and stalked down the sidewalk toward the parking lot and her Jeep. She wouldn't have blamed the Ranger if he'd thrown Trace's butt in jail for the night. Her brother's hotheaded ways would land him in real trouble someday.

If it hadn't already…

A light breeze stirred the trees as she drove back to the ranch, but the Santa Gertrudis roaming the land and horses galloping in the pastures were a comforting sight. Concern for her father overrode her exhaustion, and she stopped by the main house to check on him. But when she entered the house, it was dark.

A note on the kitchen counter from Lolita explained that her father was already in bed. Maybe it was better they talk in the morning anyway. She didn't want to upset him by having to relay that Trace had nearly been arrested.

She gathered the other messages and flipped through them. One of her grooms had reported that a second creek bed in the north end of the ranch was dried up. Odd. What had caused that? A second message asked her to check on one of the quarter horses. The vet had already treated his injured foot, but Jessie had requested that she be informed any time there was a problem.

Wanting to check on him herself, she walked back out to her Jeep and drove over the graveled road to the stables where they housed the quarter horses. She left her hat in the car, jammed her phone in the pocket of her jeans and hiked over to the barn.

The smell of hay and horses soothed her frayed nerves as she entered, the horses whinnying and kicking the walls in greeting. Brown Sugar jammed his nose through the grate of the stall, wanting her attention, and she paused to pet him. "Hey there, sugar. I missed you, too."

She moved down the row of stalls, petting Honey and Pepper as well, then stopped at the last stall to check on Buttercup. She was lying on her side, but lifted her head and looked alert. Jessie unlatched the stall door and slipped inside, then stooped and stroked her back. "How are you feeling, Buttercup? Is that foot getting better?"

Buttercup nudged her head, and Jessie lifted the bandage edge and checked the wound. Already the redness was dissipating, the swelling going down. Relieved, she started to stand but the floor creaked behind her, and the lights went out.

Panic slammed into her, and she scanned the darkness, but suddenly the floor creaked again and a hulking figure lunged toward her. She threw up her hands to ward off the blow, but his hand came down and something sharp and hard slammed into her head.

Pain knifed through her skull, the barn spun in a dizzying circle, then she collapsed into the darkness.

Chapter Six

Cabe was still stewing over Trace's threatening tone with Jessie when the sheriff's cell phone trilled.

Reed snapped it open. "Sheriff Hardin." Pause. "Jesus. All right. I'll send Sergeant Navarro out there now."

Cabe frowned. "What's wrong?"

"That was one of the ranch hands at the Becker place. He found Jessie unconscious in the barn."

Cabe's pulse spiked. Dammit, maybe he'd been right about the shooter targeting her tonight. Had he followed her home, then attacked her?

Or had Trace come after her?

"The ranch hand called an ambulance," Reed said. "You want to check it out while I help Deputy Tolbert search for the gun used in the shooting tonight?"

Cabe was already heading toward the door. "I'm on my way." Perspiration beaded on his neck as he jogged to his Land Rover, jumped in and sped from town. Traffic had definitely died down since the earlier shooting. The quiet of the countryside should have been soothing, but knowing Jessie was hurt fueled his anger.

Why would someone want to kill her? Because of her father's enemies?

Or had she and Trace fought over him?

If that was the case, he'd kill the SOB.

The rumblings in the diner when the two of them had walked in echoed in his head. What if someone in town was riled because they thought she was siding with him?

Miles of scrub brush, mesquites and oaks dotted the landscape as he ate the distance between the town and ranch. The ranch hand who'd found Jessie must have already opened the gate for the ambulance, so he zoomed up to the drive, then veered off onto the dirt road leading to the horse barns.

His headlights flickered up ahead, and he spotted Jessie's Jeep and an old pick-up truck to the side. He raced to a halt, jumped out and hurried into the barn. The smell of hay and horse assaulted him, the sound of the horses' whinnying filling the air.

A craggy-looking man wearing jeans and weathered boots limped toward him, favoring his right foot. "I'm Wilbur. You the law?"

"Ranger Sergeant Navarro. How badly is she hurt?"

"Looks like she took a blow to the head. She's startin' to stir, but I didn't want to move her till the paramedics said it was okay." The old man gestured toward the back stall just as the sound of a siren rent the air. "I'll meet the medics and send them in."

Cabe gave a clipped nod, then strode toward the back stall. His heart pounded as he pushed open the stall door, and saw Jessie lying on her side in the bed of straw. The horse lay beside her, nudging her face with his nose.

Her brilliant red hair was tangled around her, and her face was pale and chalky. He spotted a few droplets of blood in her hair, and knelt to examine her. Gently, he lifted strands of hair away from the wound to judge the depth and severity.

A gash about an inch long marred her scalp, but thankfully the cut didn't look too deep.

"Jessie," he said softly, "can you hear me?"

A low moan sounded, and he gritted his teeth. "It's all right, Jessie," he whispered. "The medics are here now."

Voices rumbled from outside, then closer as the medics hurried into the barn. Cabe stood and moved outside the stall, allowing them access.

One medic checked her pulse while the second one examined her wound. He glanced up with a frown. "Looks like she needs a couple of stitches."

"Her vitals are stable." The second medic glanced up at Cabe. "We'll get the stretcher and transport her to the hospital for X-rays. It's possible she has a concussion."

Cabe nodded. "I'll meet you there. I want to search the barn for the weapon her attacker used."

Maybe he'd get lucky this time and find some other forensics as well.

But his anger mounted as he studied Jessie's pale face and closed eyes, and protective instincts surged to the surface.

From now on, he'd make sure she was safe. No one would ever hurt her again.

JESSIE BLURRED IN AND OUT of consciousness, her head aching as if a jackhammer was pounding her skull. Perspiration trickled down her neck and into her shirt, and she pawed her way through the darkness, struggling to grasp on to something to help her up.

But her body felt weighted and heavy, the air humid, the rumble of a car engine whining in her head.

Where was she? What was going on?

She blinked against the dizziness, pinpoints of light pricking her eyes.

"Just relax, Miss Becker," a strange male voice murmured. "You have a head injury, and you're in an ambulance. We'll be at the hospital soon."

Head injury? Hospital? What happened?

As the ambulance raced along, slowly the events of the night returned. The trip into town. The shooting. The Ranger questioning her brother. Her confrontation with Trace. The attack in the horse stall.

Someone had struck her over the head. But why? Who would want to hurt her?

Trace?

Good God, surely not.

Thoughts of her troubled family taunted her. Did her father know she'd been assaulted?

She prayed he didn't. Bad news would only agitate his condition.

And Trace...he had no reason to be jealous of her.

Her father didn't love her, at least not the way Trace thought. If he had, he never would have allowed her mother to take her away when she was a little girl. He would have insisted on visitation, holidays, but he hadn't, not once.

And her mother—at first, she'd lived in a fantasy

world, believing that her mother had wanted custody because she couldn't live without her. But then she'd jumped from man to man, from city to city, and Jessie had realized that the only reason she'd taken her was to hurt Jonah, and to get the money he regularly sent.

A soul-deep ache rolled through her. No matter what she'd done to impress her parents, she'd never been close to either one of them. Moving back to the ranch had been her attempt to win her father's love.

But then his mind had started slipping away.

And she'd felt more alone than ever.

Ranger Cabe Navarro's strong, chiseled face flashed into her mind. She'd heard his voice in the barn, soothing, husky, sultry, like a hot summer's night washing over her. She closed her eyes and, for just a moment, allowed herself to think that he really cared about her, that he was sliding those muscular arms around her and pulling her to his broad chest.

That his mission might not destroy her family.

That she was lying in his arms, safe and loved, and that someone hadn't just tried to kill her.

THE ODDEST FEELING pressed against Cabe's chest as the ambulance drove away with Jessie. Something akin to fear that he might lose her.

Which was ridiculous. Jessie didn't belong to him, and she never would.

But the night his brother died rose to haunt him, and he couldn't shake the worry that he needed to be by her side.

"Reckon I'll go tell the family about Miss Jessie," Wilbur said.

Cabe nodded. "Did you see anybody when you first got out here?"

Wilbur scratched his chin. "Naw. Weren't no cars here, and it was pitch-dark."

"Did you hear anything? Maybe a car nearby or a horse galloping away?"

Wilbur angled his head in thought. "Not that I recall. Don't know how long Miss Jessie had been out, but I saw her Jeep and went inside. It was quiet, that kind of spooky quiet where you know something is wrong." He worked his mouth side to side as if he had a wad of tobacco in his cheek. "You know what I mean?"

He knew exactly what he meant. Instincts. "Yes, sir. Then what happened?"

"Then I checked to see if she was breathing. Thank God she was." He raked a hand over his scraggly hair. "So I called for an ambulance."

"How long have you worked for the Beckers?" Cabe asked.

"Half my life. Mr. Jonah's been good to me. He's not as tough as everyone thinks." The old man shifted and rubbed at his leg as if it was aching. "So if you think I'd hurt Miss Jessie, you're wrong. I love that little girl like she was my own. Her coming home was the best thing ever happened to her daddy."

Sincerity rang in the old man's voice, the affection he felt for the family obvious. "All right, Wilbur. Let me know if you think of anything else."

"Sure thing. Now you find the creep that hurt Miss Jessie. That little lady don't deserve this."

No, she didn't.

Wilbur flicked his hand in a wave, then limped toward his truck.

Dragging his mind back to the task at hand, Cabe retrieved his flashlight and kit from his SUV, then paused to pat the palomino in the stall.

The animal rolled its head sideways, pawing with his uninjured foot as if to say he was upset about Jessie as well. "Don't worry. I'll find out who hurt her, fella."

Cabe pulled on latex gloves, then swept his flashlight across the barn, digging through the straw and wood shavings scattered on the floor. He spent the next half an hour searching the barn, the garbage, the storage room. He methodically examined the grooming tools, searching for blood on the brushes and hoof picks, then searched the neighboring box stalls.

Finally he discovered a hammer that had been dropped down into the stall next to the one where Jessie had been attacked. Blood dotted the hammerhead, so he bagged it to send to the lab. Another sweep-through of the stall, and he spotted a bracelet wedged between the cracks of the wooden slats.

A Native American gold bracelet with garnets embedded in a pattern symbolizing the Morning Star.

The Morning Star was the brightest on the horizon at dawn. Natives revered it as a spirit and most Pueblos honored it as a kachina. The star also symbolized courage and purity of spirit. According to the Ghost Dance Religion, it represented the coming renewal of tradition and resurrection of heroes of the past.

Unease tightened Cabe's chest. He'd seen this bracelet before.

It belonged to Ellie Penateka.

Good God. Had Ellie attacked Jessie?

JESSIE ROUSED IN AND OUT of consciousness as the doctor examined her head. "Miss Becker, you're going to need a couple of stitches. Then we're going to do X-rays and a CAT scan."

She nodded miserably. All she wanted to do was go home.

Or talk to Ranger Navarro and see if he'd found out who had assaulted her.

Her head was throbbing, so she closed her eyes while the doctor cleaned the wound and stitched her. The ride down the elevator for the X-ray and CAT scan was bumpy and made her nauseated. A claustrophobic feeling engulfed her in the cylinder, and she clenched her hands by her sides, willing herself to remain calm. She was strong and tough. She would not fall apart in the hospital.

Finally the lab technicians rolled her from the machine. Perspiration coated her skin, and she gasped for fresh air.

"We'll take you to a room now to rest," the tech assured her.

Jessie clenched the handrail. "I want to go home."

He gave her a sympathetic smile. "The doctor will have to read your tests first."

Frustrated, she massaged her temple while they helped her into a wheelchair and an orderly rolled her back to the elevator. The scents of antiseptic and alcohol flowed through the halls, the droning sound of machinery grating on her nerves.

The orderly dropped her at the nurses' station on the

second floor, and a plump nurse with white hair pushed her toward a room. "Come on, honey, let's settle you in bed so you can rest."

"I hate hospitals." Jessie tried to stand, but a dizzy spell sent the room swirling, and she had to reach out for help to steady herself.

The nurse caught her arm and helped her to the bed. "Take it easy."

Jessie slid beneath the covers, still struggling for control. She was accustomed to taking care of everyone else, not being vulnerable and needy. "I've been stitched up, X-rayed and had a CAT scan, so why can't I go home now?"

"Honey, nobody likes hospitals," the nurse murmured as she adjusted the pillows. "But the doctor insists that you stay under observation for the night."

"But I would rest better at home," Jessie argued.

"Listen, Miss Becker." The nurse's voice grew firm. "It's already midnight. Just go to sleep, and in the morning you can go home."

Jessie clutched the sheets to her, feeling guilty for being a problem, but still anxious. The last thing she wanted was for her father to find out that she'd been attacked on the ranch.

He was in bed when she'd stopped by earlier. Surely Ranger Navarro wouldn't disturb him in the middle of the night…

CABE DIDN'T CARE IF IT WAS the middle of the night. He was going to talk to Ellie and find out what the hell was going on.

The land grew more barren as he left the town and drove to Ellie's pueblo-style house bordering on the edge of the reservation. Apache oaks flanked her property, and bluebonnets swayed from her flower bed. Ellie's place had always boasted of their culture, but her obsession with her cause had colored her tolerance of others who weren't so strong-minded.

Essentially, she liked to stir trouble for trouble's sake. And she had a political agenda.

He had zero tolerance for that kind of behavior— the reason he'd walked away from her and never looked back.

Her small gold sedan was parked in the drive, and a faint light glowed from the bedroom. He rolled his shoulders as he climbed from his SUV and walked up the limestone path to her house. If she hadn't attacked Jessie tonight and was sleeping, she was going to be pissed that he'd disturbed her. And even more so that he considered her a suspect.

But her anger was something he'd live with.

He raised his fist and knocked twice, a light breeze rustling the trees as he waited. A minute later, he knocked again, then saw the kitchen light flicker on, and heard shuffling inside.

"It's Cabe, Ellie, open up."

The peephole opened, and Ellie's eyes widened as she recognized him. "Cabe, what are you doing here?"

"We need to talk," Cabe said.

The click of the lock turning sounded in the quiet of the night, then the door swung open. Ellie tucked a strand of her hair behind her ear, then tied the belt to her satin robe. Her eyes looked blurry, as though she might have been sleeping.

"Cabe, it's late. What's going on?"

"Where were you tonight?"

An instant spark of anger darkened her brown eyes. "You saw me at the meeting, Cabe."

"What did you do after you left?"

She pursed her lips. "I met with some of the supporters of our faction at the barbecue place down the street, then came home."

"What time was that?"

She shrugged and glanced at the clock on her wall. "About nine, I guess. Why are you asking all these questions?"

"You heard the shooting in town. Do you own a gun, Ellie?"

She stiffened. "No. And I was with my friends when that fight broke out. We stayed inside until it was over."

That fact could easily be checked out. "Let me see your hands."

Her eyebrow rose. "What?"

"Just let me see your hands."

She gave him a withering look. "You've got to be kidding, Cabe. I knew you'd crossed the line, but now you're actually turning against us. Against me." She shook her head. "And here I thought we were friends."

"I'm not turning against anyone," Cabe spoke through gritted teeth. "I'm just doing my job."

He lifted her hands and examined them for GSR, but detected no visible signs.

"Satisfied?" she asked bitterly.

"Not yet," he said, ignoring her condemning glare. "You didn't happen to drive out to the Becker ranch, did you?"

"Cabe, why are you asking me these questions?" she asked in a testy voice. "What happened?"

"Jessie Becker was attacked tonight in the barn."

Ellie gasped. "And you think I attacked her?" Hurt crossed her face. "Why in the world would I attack Jessie Becker?"

He steeled himself against her. "Because of her father."

Ellie waved a dismissive hand. "That's ridiculous. I may be an activist but you know I'm not violent." Her lips thinned into a pouty frown. "I can't believe you'd even suggest such a thing, not after the past we shared."

A past that he couldn't allow to interfere with the case.

Pinning her with a stony expression that had intimidated men twice his size, he removed the bagged bracelet he'd found in the barn stall and held it up. "Then why did I find your bracelet in the stall where Jessie was attacked?"

Chapter Seven

Cabe watched Ellie fidget. "It is your bracelet, isn't it, Ellie?"

She chewed her bottom lip, but her gaze lifted to him, a pleading look in her eyes. "You know it is, Cabe. My grandmother gave it to me."

He nodded. "Then why was it in the stall where Jessie was attacked?"

Ellie's face paled slightly, then she gulped and seemed to recover. "There is a logical explanation."

He arched a brow, waiting, his jaw tight. "I'm listening."

"I said I could explain. But I'd rather not." She pressed a hand to the side of her cheek. "It's... personal."

Impatience made him hiss. "Listen, Ellie, I don't give a damn how personal it is. I'm investigating an assault and attempted murder. So if you have a good explanation, you'd better cough it up."

Ellie clamped her teeth over her lip and glanced around nervously. "I *was* out at the Becker place, but not tonight."

"Then when?"

She shrugged. "A couple of evenings ago."

Cabe crossed his arms, suspicious. "What were you doing there?"

Again she glanced over her shoulder, and it struck him that she might not be alone. Was someone in her bedroom?

"Ellie?"

"I went to see Trace."

"Trace? Why? Did you think you could convince him to incriminate his father and turn over the land?"

A slight hesitation. "Not exactly."

"Stop stalling, Ellie, and spit it out."

A long-suffering sigh escaped her. "I've been having an affair with Trace."

Shock bolted through him, ending in a chuckle of disbelief. "Try again."

She raked her gaze over him, angry, defiant, challenging. "Don't act so surprised, Cabe. Do you really think I've been sitting around pining for you?"

"No," he said dryly. "I thought you and Daniel Taabe had a thing."

She shrugged. "Sometimes opposites attract."

"Right. Or maybe you have another agenda. Maybe you're trying to seduce him into helping your cause." That sounded more likely.

"I resent your implication," Ellie said.

"And so do I." The male voice came from behind her, at the door to Ellie's bedroom.

Cabe muttered a curse as Trace Becker sauntered toward Ellie. "You've been listening?" Cabe said.

Becker swung an arm around Ellie. "Damn right I

have. And Ellie was with me tonight, so there's no way she attacked Jessie."

Cabe narrowed his eyes. The two of them were providing each other with alibis—he didn't like it. "Some brother you are. You aren't even going to ask if your sister is all right?"

Trace's bony shoulders lifted. "I figure she is or you would have said she was dead."

Cabe fisted his hands by his side. Trace's tone suggested it wouldn't have bothered him if his sister had died.

"I also found two long black hairs out at the site where that Native body was buried. They look like yours, Ellie."

Ellie huffed. "I was not at the burial site."

"Then let me take a sample of your hair for comparison, to eliminate you as a suspect of course."

Ellie muttered a sound of disbelief, then reached up and yanked out a strand of hair. "Go to hell, Cabe."

She dropped the black strand into his palm, then slammed the door in his face.

Cabe carried the hair to his SUV, bagged and labeled it to send to the lab. The lights flicked off inside, and he imagined Trace and Ellie sliding back in bed together.

Not that he cared who Ellie slept with.

But the fact that they'd hooked up raised questions in his mind.

Was Trace the one playing both sides, maybe to get back at his father for something?

Would Ellie and Trace lie to protect each other? And if they had been in cahoots, what exactly was their agenda?

JESSIE DRIFTED IN AND OUT of a fitful sleep, but the sound of the door squeaking open made her jerk awake, and she blinked trying to distinguish the shadow in the doorway.

Had the person who'd attacked her come here to hurt her again?

Fear clogged her throat, and she threw the covers off her, ready to run.

"It's okay, Jessie. It's me."

The voice—deep, throaty, unerringly male, as potently enticing as his big body. And his scent…like musk and man and sex.

She remembered him soothing her as the ambulance had arrived and had clung to that voice.

"Jessie?" He moved toward her, with silent steps that emanated an air of power and strength.

She exhaled shakily and reached for the covers with a trembling hand, once again feeling naked and exposed.

And more vulnerable than she had in her entire life.

Because she was attracted to this dark-skinned Ranger. More attracted than she'd been to a man in years.

That thought terrified her the most.

She could not fall prey to every sexy man's charms like her mother. And she especially couldn't hop into bed with a man who was determined to destroy her father and the last chance she had of becoming a part of his life.

But as Cabe grew nearer, and she inhaled his scent again, her chest clenched with the need to whisper his name and beg him to stay with her. To confess that she didn't want to be alone.

Not in the dark in this hospital bed knowing that someone had tried to kill her.

He stopped beside her bed, towering over and looking down at her with those brooding, deep brown eyes. Eyes that had seen more than his share of pain and sorrow.

Eyes that had detected spirits on the land in question.

Eyes that could steal her soul—and her heart if she wasn't careful.

"I didn't mean to frighten you," he said gruffly. "How are you feeling?"

Sweet, tender, erotic sensations momentarily numbed the pain in her head at the sound of his concerned tone. She had to clear her throat to speak.

"I'm all right."

He traced a gentle finger into her hair toward the wound. "Headache?"

"A little," she said quietly.

For a moment, it felt as if the two of them were cocooned into the room, as if nothing could touch them or come between them. As if the world and all its problems had faded away.

She wanted the moment to last. To be real.

For the world to disappear. For the murders to be solved. And for Cabe Navarro to stand before her just as a man. Not a Ranger in charge of the case in a town where their two worlds divided them.

"I'm sorry, Jessie." Sincerity laced his voice. "You don't deserve to be in the middle of this mess."

For some reason she didn't understand, tears burned her eyes. Embarrassed, she tried to blink them away, but he must have noticed because he dragged the corner chair over beside the bed, then sat down.

"This is ridiculous," she said, hating her weakness. "I'm not usually so emotional."

"It's natural," Cabe murmured. "You were attacked tonight."

She twisted her hands in the sheets. "You didn't talk to my father, did you?"

"No. Wilbur was going to stop by your house."

"Oh, gosh. I don't want to upset my father."

"Ahh, Jessie." He brushed a strand of hair from her forehead. "Always protecting others, aren't you?"

"That's what families do," she said softly.

"Not always." His expression grew hard. "Do you want me to go?"

A pang of panic went through her chest. "No. I…don't like hospitals. When I was little I got pneumonia, and my mother left me alone for days."

His angular jaw tightened. "She didn't stay with you or visit?"

"No. Her social life was more important." She shook her head, battling bitterness at the memory. God, why was she being such a baby? She'd never told anyone how much that experience had hurt.

He dropped his gaze to her hands, where she'd knotted them in the sheets, then pulled one hand into his big palm. "I'll stay right here and hold your hand all night if you want."

A tingle of awareness ripped through her. "You don't have to do that, Cabe."

Suddenly he stood, walked to the window and looked

out as if he needed to put distance between them. Immediately she missed his closeness. His touch. The connection she'd felt.

"I'm in charge of this case. The person who attacked you might return any time."

A shiver rippled through her, disappointment on its heels. So he wasn't staying out of concern, but because of his job.

She had to remember that.

"Did you get a look at your assailant?" he asked.

"No, the lights went out and he hit me from behind."

He scrubbed a hand through his hair. "Your ranch hand claimed he didn't see anyone either. Do you trust him?"

"Wilbur?" Jessie gave a soft laugh. "With my life. He's like a second father to me." Or maybe a real one.

"I found a hammer that appears to have been the weapon the attacker used. It had blood on it, so I dropped it at the sheriff's office to be couriered to the lab for analysis. Maybe this perp messed up and left a print."

Jessie considered that. "Maybe."

His tone grew darker. "There's something else."

Cold dread filled her. Did he think Trace had attacked her? "What?"

"I found a bracelet in the stall that belonged to Ellie Penateka."

"Ellie? I don't understand. When was she at the barn?"

A sliver of moonlight playing through the window glinted off his strong jaw. "I went to her house and asked her that myself. She claims she and your brother are having an affair."

Shock momentarily robbed Jessie's breath. "Ellie and Trace? You've got to be kidding."

"I didn't believe it either," Cabe said. "But Trace was there. He came out of Ellie's bedroom, and they gave each other alibis for tonight."

Jessie frowned. "I saw them talking after the meeting, but it looked as if they were arguing."

He chuckled sarcastically. "They obviously made up."

Jessie contemplated the implications of Ellie and Trace being together. Trace had been furious when Jessie had showed up at the ranch and announced she was moving back in. He and her father had also argued about the land deal. But Trace had arranged it.

And Trace was worried about losing the ranch to *her*.

Would he team up with Ellie to sabotage her father? No, that didn't make sense…

Unless Trace wanted to hurt their father. Unless he thought that if Jonah went to jail, he would inherit the ranch…

CABE'S GUT PINCHED at the worry on Jessie's face. Maybe he should have waited until she'd recovered before he revealed Trace and Ellie's affair.

But if either of them had tried to hurt Jessie, he needed to push for answers.

She rubbed her temple with her fingers, and he choked back any more questions. She had had a rough night. She needed rest, not pressure.

"You need to get some sleep."

"I can't sleep yet," she whispered. "Will you sit and talk to me for a minute?"

Her eyes looked so soft, her body small and vulnerable, her voice beckoning him by her side. And he knew that she was independent and didn't ask for help often.

Unable to resist, he gave a short nod, and reclaimed the chair, bracing his legs apart. He ached to pull her hands into his again.

To connect with her and hold her and kiss her pain away.

"Tell me about your family," she said. "You grew up on the reservation?"

The last topic he wanted to discuss was his past. "Yes. My father still lives there."

"How about your mother?"

He chewed the inside of his cheek, then removed his Stetson and set it on the bedside table. "My mother committed suicide when I was a teenager after my younger brother's death."

Jessie's eyes filled with sympathy. Sympathy he didn't want.

Still, when she reached for his hand, he relented, clung to the scent of her skin.

"What happened?" she whispered.

A long-suffering sigh escaped him. "My mother was white, my father Comanche. People around town gave them a hard time, then my little brother became ill. My mother begged my father to take him to the hospital, but my father believes only in the old ways. He insisted on using the Big Medicine Ceremony to heal him instead."

"Oh, God," Jessie whispered. "I'm so sorry, Cabe."

Cabe shrugged. "So, you see, I think hospitals are good places to be when you're ill." This time he did reach up and touch her, just a gentle sweep of his fingers across her brow. "Or when you're injured."

"Do you still see your father?"

He shook his head. "We had a falling out when I decided to leave the reservation and Comanche Creek. Like some of the other Natives, he felt I was turning my back on him and the old ways."

"Were you?"

Her directness surprised him. "In a way, I guess I was," he admitted. "But my culture is still a part of me. I'm just not married to it to the point that I refute the advantages of modern ways."

"Your Native blood allowed you to sense the spirits on the land?"

A small smile curved his mouth. "Yeah."

"And the other Rangers brought you here because they thought you could bridge the gap between the two factions in town?"

He chuckled sarcastically. "I told them it was a mistake. I never fit into either group. In time, I thought things would change, but apparently they haven't."

"Not everyone shares those prejudices, Ranger." She reached up and pressed her hand against his cheek. A tingle ripped through him as her soft skin brushed his rough jaw. He'd seen so much violence on the job, so much hatred between the people, so much cruelty that her tenderness tripped emotions in his chest.

The sudden urge to hear her say his name slammed into him. The need to kiss her followed. "It's Cabe," he said in a low voice. "Call me Cabe."

A tiny smile curved her mouth, making her look

more beautiful than he could have imagined. "All right, Cabe. And just so you know, I think you *can* bridge the gap here, that you're exactly what this town needs."

He didn't believe her. But her voice sounded like an angel's.

Yet angelic thoughts fled when her damp tongue slipped out to trace her lips. He wanted his mouth there, wanted to taste her. Her breath hitched as if she recognized the hunger in his eyes.

He expected her to drop her hand, to tell him it was time for him to leave. Instead, she traced her fingers down to his mouth, scraping beard stubble in her path. She was so soft next to his rough exterior. So gentle, while he dealt with hard-core criminals and violence.

Even injured and weak, he'd never seen anything so beautiful.

"Cabe…"

"Tell me to go," he said, already bracing himself for her to utter the words.

"Please don't." Her breath whispered against his cheek as she gently coaxed his face toward her.

His body hardened, need firing through his sex, and he finally gave in to his need and claimed her mouth with his.

Chapter Eight

Cabe had never tasted anything as deliciously sweet as Jessie's kiss. Hungry for more, he traced the seam of her mouth with his tongue, probing her lips apart so he could delve inside. She moaned his name, and arousal splintered through him in shocking waves that threatened to destroy his sanity.

Sliding his hands through the silky tresses of her hair, he pulled her closer, angling her head so he could deepen the kiss. Heat flared between them as she flicked out her tongue to meet his. Their lips and tongues danced in a lover's dance, sweet, tender, erotic, passionate.

He wanted more. Wanted to touch her, trace her entire body with his fingers and his tongue. Wanted to strip her and climb in that bed and plant himself on top of her, inside her, wrap her up in his body. A body that was raging out of control with hunger and desire.

A knock sounded on the door, then the door squeaked open. "Um, excuse me."

Cabe tore himself away, then whirled his head around

to see the doctor standing in the doorway. He glanced back at Jessie, and saw her dazed look. She looked well-kissed, her hair tousled, her chest rising and falling with a labored breath.

A blush crept up her face, and even though he knew it was wrong, a smile of pleasure ripped through him.

"Miss Becker, I just came to check on you," the doctor said.

The realization that he'd crossed the line hit Cabe with gut-wrenching force, and he walked to the window, putting his back to Jessie while the doctor approached her bed.

Dammit, he was a Texas Ranger. A professional.

But he'd been kissing Jessie senseless, fantasizing about climbing in bed with her and making love to her when she was injured and in a damn hospital room. He'd really screwed up this time.

Jessie was a part of the task force, her family murder suspects, his ability to maintain control and objectivity vital to doing his job.

Sleeping with Jessie Becker could destroy that objectivity. Could mess with his head.

Distrust rose like a fireball in his belly. And what if she was just using him, seducing him so he wouldn't arrest her father?

JESSIE'S BODY TINGLED with need, the desires Cabe had stirred with that kiss making her ache for another round.

For more of his mouth on her. His lips touching hers.

But Cabe turned his back to her as the doctor approached, and she had to pull herself together.

"Hello, Miss. Becker. I'm Dr. Finwick. How are you doing?"

"I'm ready to go home."

The older man chuckled. "Tomorrow will be soon enough. You do have a minor concussion, but your X-rays and the CAT scan look good. You need to take it easy for a couple of days."

Jessie sighed. "All right, Doctor."

"Any nausea?"

Jessie shook her head. "No. I'm just tired."

"Then rest. But the nurse will come in to check on you periodically during the night."

The doctor glanced at Cabe, then her. "I'll see you in the morning, Miss Becker." The door closed behind him, and Jessie sighed.

"Cabe?"

His shoulders stiffened, but he refused to face her. "You heard the doctor. Get some sleep."

She lifted her fingers to her lips, aching for him again, missing the closeness. "Don't you want to talk about what happened?"

Finally he turned toward her, but the hunger and desire in his eyes had faded. Instead the brooding cop had resurfaced and distrust colored his expression. "It was just a kiss, a mistake," he said matter-of-factly. "Forget about it, Jessie. Nothing can happen between us."

His words were like a slap in the face.

He was here to investigate her family, and when the case ended, he would leave Comanche Creek. He'd already made it clear that he didn't belong here, and that he hadn't wanted to come back.

And after hopping from one town to another all her life, she wanted and *needed* a home, a life and a family here in Comanche Creek.

CABE WAITED UNTIL JESSIE finally fell asleep, then settled in the chair to grab some shut-eye himself. He didn't trust that whoever had attacked her might not return to finish the job.

His mind ticked over the suspects. Trace topped the list. And then there was Ellie, her anger about the land deal, her political aspirations and her relationship with Trace.

She stirred in her sleep and whispered his name, and he had to clench the chair edge with his hands to keep from going to her.

She was growing more and more intriguing, more and more appealing.

More and more of a threat to his control and sanity.

But haunting memories of losing his mother and brother taunted him, and he forced any emotions aside.

He was a loner, and he liked it that way. No entanglements, no commitments.

Except to his badge.

Besides, Jonah Becker would probably kill him if he touched his daughter's lily-white skin with his dark hands.

Muttering a curse, he leaned back in the chair and closed his eyes. He'd grab a few winks before morning. Then he'd drive Jessie home, confront Jonah and take his blood and a DNA sample.

He also needed to visit Charla and get that list of artifacts and the buyers. Maybe the lab would have some results for him on the evidence he'd processed so far.

Finally sleep claimed him, but it was fitful. Every time Jessie moved or moaned, he woke and checked to make sure she was all right. And when she whispered his name in the middle of the night, he almost succumbed to temptation and crawled in bed with her.

They both might have slept better if he'd held her.

But he'd already traveled into dangerous territory with that heated kiss, and his willpower couldn't endure any more tests. At least not tonight.

The night dragged by, but as morning light cracked the sky, the nurses brought breakfast. He stepped outside for coffee and to call the lab. "Did you find out anything on the bullets I sent yesterday morning?"

"Yes, Sergeant, they came from a .38. Find the gun, and we can make a match."

"Right." Easier said than done, but he refused to give up. "I collected bullets from a shooting in town last night and they're being couriered over, along with two black hairs I found at the scene of an attack on Jessie Becker. Compare them to the strands found at the gravesite, and see if they match."

"I'll let you know as soon as I have time to process them."

"What about that clay sample used to glue the victims' eyes shut in the ritualistic burial? Did it match the clay from Jonah Becker's property?"

"Yes, sir. It's a match."

Cabe's lungs tightened. That wasn't good for Jessie's father.

Of course, he could argue that any number of people, including his hands, had access to the land.

"Thanks." He jammed some coins into the vending machine and watched as coffee spewed into a foam cup. Needing the caffeine buzz, he blew on the black coffee and took a sip. Steering his mind back to the case, he phoned Hardin and asked for a warrant to search the Becker house for a weapon.

"I'll have it when you stop by the office," Reed said. "The one for Becker's DNA sample and blood is on my desk."

"Thanks. I appreciate your assistance, Sheriff."

By the time he disconnected and reached Jessie's room, Jessie was signing release papers. "Now remember, take it easy," the doctor ordered. "Do you need me to call someone to drive you home?"

Cabe cleared his throat. "That's not necessary. I've got it covered."

Jessie shot him an almost panicked look. She knew he was going to interrogate her father. She'd been protective of him ever since the investigation started. Wyatt had speculated that she'd appointed herself Jonah's spokesperson to cover for him.

The doctor left the room, and Jessie pushed away the covers. "I need my clothes."

"Where are they?"

"In the cabinet." She swayed slightly, and he reached for her, but she threw up a warning hand. "I'm fine. I just stood up too quickly."

A stubborn look tightened her mouth as she shuffled over to the closet and dug out a plastic bag which held the clothes she'd been wearing when the medics brought her in.

"Do you need help?" he asked, then immediately regretted the question when she glared at him.

"No."

He offered her a clipped nod. "Fine. I'll wait outside." More for his own sanity than for her. If he saw her naked, he'd definitely lose his grip.

A minute later, the nurse appeared with a wheelchair, and he went to pull the SUV up to the hospital pick-up area.

"I could have called someone," Jessie said when he climbed out to help her into his vehicle.

Cabe cut her off. "Don't sweat it, Jessie. We're working together on this task force, and you've nearly been shot twice and then attacked. I don't intend to let you out of my sight until this case is over."

Shock strained her face. "What?"

He chuckled at the horror in her voice. "You heard me. I'm your bodyguard."

Even as he said the words, worry knotted his gut along with protective instincts—and arousal.

He sure as hell didn't want anything bad happening to her body. In fact, his hands and tongue itched to give her pleasure.

Jessie fastened her seat belt. "I can't believe this is happening."

Her sour tone reminded him that he'd hurt her by dismissing the kiss the night before. "I know you don't like it," he said. "All the more reason we figure out who attacked you, and who killed all these people and lock them up. Then you can go back to your life and your daddy."

"Like he really cares if I'm here," she muttered.

He turned to stare at her, confused by her statement. "I thought you and your father were close."

"And I thought you were tough and strong, not a coward, Cabe."

He gritted his teeth. "What the hell do you mean by that?"

"One hot, explosive kiss between us, and you run from me just like you ran from the town and your family."

A fireball of anger erupted in his gut. "You don't know what you're talking about."

"Don't I?" She crossed her arms and turned to look out the window. "But don't worry, I'd never beg a man for his affection."

He frowned, disturbed by her statement. Was she talking about him or her father?

It's none of your business, he reminded himself.

Jessie lapsed into silence as he swung by the sheriff's office to retrieve the warrants, and her mood grew more anxious as they approached the Double B.

The sight of the cattle grazing in the fields and the horses roaming in the pens stirred his baser love of the wild rugged land of Texas. He'd been so busy chasing his career and criminals the past few years that he'd forgotten how much he missed it.

Becker might be unscrupulous in his business tactics, but he ran a first-class operation, had always raised prime stock and was rumored to have incorporated the latest techniques to create leaner beef and treat his animals humanely.

Was he capable of murder?

JESSIE STRUGGLED TO ADOPT a congenial face as Cabe parked in front of the main house. The damn man was infuriating.

His dismissal the night before roused her insecurities. Her father had let her go with her mother because he hadn't loved her enough to fight for her. And since then, every relationship she'd had had failed. She knew that was her fault—she'd closed herself off from others, had guarded her heart.

So why was Cabe Navarro getting to her?

Reminding herself that she didn't *need* a man, or Cabe's affections, she forced her personal feelings aside. She had bigger problems to worry about.

So far, she'd been able to protect her father from the Rangers' interrogation tactics. But Cabe was persistent, and wouldn't give up.

What if he detected her father's mental capacity had diminished? Would Cabe take advantage of his condition? Make it public knowledge?

"Jessie, you know I have to get to the truth," Cabe said as they climbed out and walked up to the front entrance. "This is not personal."

Was he apologizing before the storm? "It is personal to me," she said quietly as she opened the door.

Lolita rushed toward her, her hands plastered to her cheeks, her eyes filled with concern. "Oh, my goodness, Miss Jessie, we have been so worried. Wilbur told us you were attacked. Your daddy is frantic."

Jessie's heart clenched. "I'm fine, Lolita." She gestured toward Cabe. "This is Ranger Sergeant Cabe Navarro. Where's Dad?"

Lolita's once-over was filled with disdain. "In his study. I tried to convince him to go back to bed, but he insisted he couldn't rest until he saw you."

"Thanks, Lolita. I'll go and assure him I'm fine."

Inhaling a deep breath, Jessie silently prayed her father was coherent as she crossed the foyer to his study. She felt Cabe's eyes boring into her back, and hoped she could pull off this meeting without any trouble.

Palms sweaty, she rapped on the door, then pushed it open. "Dad, it's me. And Ranger Sergeant Navarro is with me."

Her father pivoted his office chair toward her, then stood. Exhaustion lined his face along with worry. "My God, Jessie, Wilbur said you were attacked, that you were in the hospital."

"I'm sorry, Dad. I should have called, but it happened late last night and you were in bed. I'm fine, really."

He swept her into a hug, which made fresh tears swell in Jessie's eyes. It was the first time he'd shown affection toward her since she'd returned.

"I was so worried about you, baby." He pulled back to examine her. "What happened?"

Cabe cleared his throat. "Someone assaulted Jessie in the barn, sir. I recovered a hammer I believe her assailant used. Hopefully we can lift some trace from it and nail whoever did it."

Her father's gaze darted to Cabe and he released her. Deep groove lines fanned besides his mouth as he scowled. "I don't believe we've met."

Cabe extended his hand. "Ranger Navarro. I'm here investigating the recent murders."

Her father's forehead creased with a scowl. "And what exactly are you doing with my daughter?"

Jessie pressed a soothing hand to her father and urged him back to his chair. "Sergeant Navarro came out to the barn to investigate my attack last night, Dad. And he drove me home from the hospital."

"Why would someone want to hurt my daughter?" Jonah asked.

The tension thrumming through the room made Jessie's head throb again.

"I don't know, sir. Perhaps someone in town thinks she's covering for your crimes."

Jessie gasped at his bluntness. "Cabe—"

"We all know that the land you purchased was made through an illegal deal, Mr. Becker," Cabe continued. "And the most recent cadaver I found proves that that land is a Native American burial ground."

"I had no knowledge of a burial ground when I purchased that property. Billy Whitley faked those papers." Jonah rubbed a hand over his chin. "Why can't you let it go? That damn Whitley man wrote a confession before he killed himself."

Cabe cleared his throat. "We now believe that note was forged, Mr. Becker. That Billy didn't commit suicide, that he was murdered. And—" he paused, his gaze meeting Jessie's "—forensics proves that the clay used to glue the murder victims who were buried in the ritualistic style came from your property."

Jessie's arm tightened around her father's shoulders. "Anybody could have sneaked onto the ranch, dug up the soil and buried those bodies while we were all asleep. Someone is framing my father."

"Maybe," Cabe admitted. "All the more reason for me to continue this investigation." He removed the warrant from his rawhide jacket. "Sir, I have a warrant requesting a sample of your DNA and blood."

"Why my blood?" Jonah asked.

"Because the killer's blood was mixed in the face paint used on the bodies. If you are innocent, then letting me test your blood can eliminate you as a suspect."

Her father's strained expression sent alarm through Jessie. She hadn't been around her father in years. How well did she know him?

If he was innocent, why did he look so nervous?

Chapter Nine

Cabe took the DNA and blood sample and locked them in his crime kit. Then he left a disgruntled Jessie with her equally hostile father while he searched Trace's room for the .38. As he expected though, Trace's suite was clean.

The house furnishings had a country feel. Paintings of horses and the rugged land decorated the walls, antiques, oak and pine furniture filled the rooms, and handmade quilts covered the beds.

A room with a four-poster bed draped in pink satin drew his eye, the rosebud wallpaper suggesting it was Jessie's room. Or it had been in the past. The closet was bare of a woman's clothes, and there were no personal photos on the dresser or walls. He made a mental note to ask Jessie where she was sleeping. If not in the main house, she could be staying in one of the smaller cabins on the Double B.

On the chance that Trace had hidden the gun somewhere else in the house, he searched the upstairs quarters, the closets, drawers, then the downstairs suite which belonged to Jonah.

Inside Jonah's bathroom, he found several bottles of prescription pills, an array of vitamins, medication for high blood pressure, cholesterol, arthritis… Was the old man's health failing?

No gun anywhere in his room though, so he headed to the kitchen. The cook glared at him, and he asked her to step out of the room while he searched. The pantry was stocked with food, liquor and a variety of teas. He pushed the cans and boxes around, even checked the canister set in case Trace had ditched the gun inside, but found nothing. The drawers held cooking supplies but no gun either.

Frustrated, he moved to the outside of the house, checked the garage, the gardening shed, the trash. But his search yielded nothing.

By the time he returned to Jonah's study, Trace had joined Jessie and her father.

Animosity radiated from Trace. "Dad called and said you were searching for a gun."

Suspicion mounted in Cabe's chest. "You own a .38? Where is it, Trace?"

Trace gave him a smug smile. "I did. But I loaned it to Ellie a few months ago."

Ellie? Evidence was stacking up against her. "I guess I'll have to talk to her again then."

"It won't do you any good," Trace said snidely. "Ellie said the gun went missing over a month ago."

Cabe clamped his mouth tight. "Did she file a report?"

"Yeah, with the sheriff's office. You can check."

"I will," Cabe said. Then he directed his gaze to

Jessie. "I'm going to check out the burial sites and see if Dr. Jacobsen has made any new discoveries."

"I'll go with you," Jessie said.

Cabe frowned. "Are you sure you're up to that? The doctor ordered you to rest."

She folded her arms, her jaw set stubbornly. "I'll rest once I prove that you're wrong about my father, Ranger. I want my family's name cleared and you off the land as soon as possible."

Cabe gritted his teeth. So, it was back to calling him Ranger instead of Cabe. Damn.

Not that he could blame her. She probably felt violated now he'd searched her family home.

Still, his job demanded he explore every lead and suspect. Even if he had to hurt Jessie in the process.

"I'd like to stop by my cabin, shower and change clothes before we go to the site," Jessie said as they stepped back outside. "I can meet you out there."

Cabe grunted. "No. I told you, you're in my protective custody now. I'll make a call to the sheriff and verify that Ellie filed that report on the gun while I wait."

Anything to distract himself from the fact that Jessie would be stripping naked in the bathroom, and that he had to keep his hands off.

"YOU'RE NOT GOING to spend the night at my house," Jessie argued as Cabe drove her to the cabin she kept on the ranch.

Cabe shot her an impatient look. "Jessie, someone tried to kill you last night in the barn, and before that we were both shot at in town. I am staying with you, so get used to it."

She'd like to get used to it. That was the problem.

But having him in her home, near her things, leaving his scent and the imprint of his body behind would be pure torture.

Still, she refused to give him the satisfaction of revealing how much he rattled her. And how much she wanted a repeat of that kiss.

Instead, she muttered a sound of disgust and stared out the window, the sight of the horses running freely in the pasture a reminder that she was no longer free.

"Sounds more like prison," Jessie muttered.

"I'm sorry you feel that way," he said in a low voice. "But it's better than being dead."

Of course he was right. But she didn't have to like it.

A minute later, he parked at her cabin, then she jumped from his SUV and hurried to the door. She needed to escape Cabe's presence. He was confusing the hell out of her. Last night when she'd been injured, he'd been protective and tender. And when he'd shared the story about his family and his brother's death, she'd felt a connection, an intimacy that had roused deep feelings for the man.

He had obviously been caught between two worlds, two cultures, his entire life. And now to return and face the same issues and prejudices had to be difficult.

And that kiss…that kiss had been erotic and sensual and had incited a hunger in her body that only he could sate.

Damn the man.

But today he'd acted as if that kiss had never

happened. As if it had meant nothing. As if they were complete strangers.

He was back to professional cop mode—cold, distant, brooding. He could arrest her father and throw him in jail without hesitation—or concern for her.

Irritated with herself for wanting him anyway, she left him standing in her den, looking out of place next to her feminine décor and antiques.

Seething, she rushed to her bedroom and bath, then stripped her clothes, tossed them in the laundry basket, and climbed in the shower beneath the warm spray of water. The sharp pain in her temple had subsided into a dull ache, and exhaustion pulled at her. All she wanted to do was crawl in bed and sleep the day, and her worries, away.

Except she didn't want to crawl in bed alone. She wanted Cabe tucked in beside her, holding her, caressing her, running his fingers over her bare skin and making her body hum.

Closing her eyes, she imagined him opening the bathroom door, stripping and standing in the midst of the steamy small room. She could see his powerful muscles bunch on his arms, his broad chest rising and falling as he stared at her, his thick long length hardening and throbbing to be inside her.

Stop it, Jessie. You're not going to throw yourself at a man like your mother.

Especially not Cabe Navarro, the Texas Ranger who wants to put your father in jail.

Darn it. She rinsed, climbed out and dried off. While she'd been fantasizing about the man, he was probably snooping around her cabin looking for evidence to incriminate her family.

It was up to her to save her father.

And the only way she knew to do that was to help Cabe find out the truth about the murders.

Then he could leave town, and she could forget that she'd ever wanted him.

CABE PUNCHED IN the sheriff's number while he studied Jessie's house. Light pine furniture and earth tones dominated the connecting den and kitchen. An afghan embroidered with horses draped the top of a crème sofa, and candlewick throw pillows were scattered across the back. Splashes of soft green in the two wing-backed chairs and matted photos added color.

Interesting that she'd chosen to stay in this small place when the main house had enough room to accommodate her.

But she and Trace obviously didn't get along, so she probably needed the distance between them. God knew he couldn't stand the bastard.

Sheriff Hardin's voice came over the line, yanking him back to the case.

"Hardin, it's Navarro. Listen, I searched the Becker ranch house for that .38 but didn't find it. Trace admitted he owned one, but said he gave it to Ellie."

"Trace gave Ellie a gun?"

"Yeah. Apparently they've been having an affair."

"Geesh. That's news," Hardin muttered.

"Shocked me, too. And Jessie had no idea." The shower water kicked off, and Cabe inhaled a deep breath, forcing his mind off an image of Jessie's naked body. "Anyway, Trace claims that Ellie told him the gun went missing about a month ago. Did she file a report?"

"Not with me, but she might have filed it with one of my deputies. Let me check."

Papers rustled in the background, and Cabe walked over to the fireplace and studied the collection of iron horses Jessie had lined up on the mantel. Odd, but there were no family photos, no cozy shots of her and Jonah here either.

"Here it is," Hardin said, interrupting his thoughts. "It was dated six weeks ago. Shane Tolbert took the report."

"Tolbert. Funny how his name keeps cropping up."

Hardin made a clicking sound with his teeth. "I know, it is disturbing."

"So what was Ellie's story?" Cabe asked.

"According to the report, Ellie insisted the .38 was in her purse at one of the rallies. A fight broke out, and later she discovered it was missing."

"So any number of people could have stolen it."

"Yeah. Looks that way."

Another dead end. "I have the DNA and blood sample from Jonah Becker. I'm going to run by the burial sites and see if Dr. Jacobsen has found anything else, then talk to Charla Whitley and meet up with you later."

Jessie appeared in the doorway just as he ended the call. She'd swept her long curls into a ponytail, pulled on a hot-pink T-shirt and jeans, all of which should have made her look like a tomboy. But the pink shirt highlighted the natural rosy glow of her lips and cheeks. And the way the thin fabric hugged her breasts made his mouth water. Dragging his gaze from her chest, he forced his eyes south. But that proved no better. Those tight jeans showcased hips and lean muscular legs that he wanted wrapped around him.

Damn.

She jammed her Stetson on her head. "Ready?"

Cabe nodded, and they walked silently to his SUV, the midday sun heating his back and neck. Five minutes later, he parked at the site where they'd discovered the bodies. Crime scene tape still roped off the various areas, and Dr. Jacobsen had built a platform over the excavation site of the Native American graves to protect the grounds and bones.

A slight rumbling beneath Cabe alerted him to the disgruntled spirits below, the whisper of the spirits rising up to him from their graves and pleading for justice. War drums pounded, the screams of the dead piercing and painful.

A small handful of students had gathered to assist Dr. Jacobsen, who was running some kind of machine over the grounds. When she looked up and spotted him, she stopped, leaned it against an oak and approached them.

"What are you doing?" Cabe asked.

Nina tilted the brim of her cap, squinting through the sun. "Using ground penetrating radar—it's called GSSI, Subsurface Interface Radar—to search for other graves. The equipment can detect coffins as well as bones buried beneath the ground."

Cabe scoured the land visually, wondering how many bodies might actually be buried here. "Have you found any other burial spots?"

An excited smile spread over her face. "I sure have. Two so far, but there are more, I just know it."

Jessie's brow furrowed. "You found two more. My God."

Nina motioned for them to follow her. "I also unearthed two more artifacts which confirm our theory about the bodies being Natives. Come and see."

Cabe and Jessie trailed her to a workstation she'd created beneath a tarp, and she indicated two items bagged and lying on the folding table.

Cabe's breath stilled in his chest. A gold armband adorned with garnets and Native American etchings—rare and probably priceless. And a pacho, a prayer stick, notched out of painted cottonwood.

"Those are beautiful," Jessie whispered.

"And extremely valuable," Nina added. "I also researched that headdress you found, Cabe, and confirmed that it was dated back to the 1700s."

Cabe whistled. "You're right. Collectors would pay a fortune for these as well as that headdress."

"My father didn't know anything about this," Jessie said defensively. "He wanted ranch land, not Native American artifacts."

But that antiquities broker, and Billy and Charla Whitley, had known, and they'd probably realized they had a treasure chest at their fingertips.

And if someone intended to expose the truth and stop their treasure hunting, any one of them might have killed to protect their secret fortune.

As Cabe drove toward Charla Whitley's house, Jessie twisted her hands in her lap.

She had to accept that the land her father purchased was a Native American burial site, and that it rightfully belonged to the Comanche people. Perspiration beaded on her neck, making her hair stick to her skin.

The only question in her mind was if her father had known that he'd bought it illegally. She wanted to protect him, but if he had knowingly cheated and robbed the Natives, her respect for him would be crushed.

Her cell phone jangled from her purse, and she grabbed it and connected the call. "Hello."

"This is Dr. Taber. May I speak to Miss Becker?"

Jessie's heart thumped. "This is Jessie."

"Miss Becker. I'm sorry to disturb you, but I wanted to touch base. I examined your father yesterday, and I hate to say it, but his mental capacity and coherency seems to be declining even more."

Worry knotted Jessie's stomach. She wanted good news. "What do you think is going on, Doctor?"

"I'm not sure. We'll probably need to run another battery of tests. I've consulted a specialist, and I'll be back in touch to schedule them. Meanwhile, maintain his medicine regime."

"Thanks, I will." Jessie hung up, feeling defeated, her heart heavy. She'd come home to reconnect with her father and now might lose him to prison, or possibly some physical disease. Life so wasn't fair.

Cabe pulled in front of Charla's sprawling ranch house, and she frowned as they made their way up the limestone walkway. Had Charla and Billy both known the truth about the burial grounds and tricked her father?

It was common knowledge that Charla collected Native American artifacts—had she sold them knowing they belonged to the Comanche Nation?

If so, she understood why the Comanche faction was so upset.

"What will happen to the artifacts you recover?" Jessie asked.

Cabe cleared his throat, then pressed the doorbell. "They'll be returned to the Comanche Nation."

Dark storm clouds hovered above, casting a gray to the sky, and the wind sent the mesquite beside the house bristling. A second later, Charla opened the door, clad in a bright purple gauzy blouse with Indian beading, a denim skirt and dozens of silver bracelets.

"We need to talk," Cabe said without preamble.

Charla's laser-sharp eyes cut over them, but she stepped sideways and gestured for them to enter. Jessie had never been in Charla's house and was surprised to find eclectic furnishings mixed with Native American blankets, leather containers and conches. Several shadowboxes contained handmade Native American jewelry, arrowheads, and one held an elaborate feather chest plate.

"I need those documents that we discussed and the name of the person or persons who bought the artifacts from you," Cabe said.

Charla sauntered over to an oak desk, removed a folder and handed it to Cabe. "As you requested, Ranger Navarro."

Cabe accepted the folder with a scrutinizing look. "We found more artifacts and bodies on the land," Cabe said. "Did you know about them, Charla?"

For a brief second, interest flickered in her eyes, before she masked it. "No."

"You're lying. I think you and Billy both knew," Cabe said. "And when Marcie realized what you planned to do, that you'd found a gold mine, you killed her and that broker to keep the artifacts to yourself. And everyone knows you hated Daniel Taabe." His voice hardened in disgust. "I just can't believe that you let Billy take the fall."

"You're wrong," Charla screeched. "And unless you have proof, which you obviously don't," Charla snapped, "get out."

"I'll get proof," Cabe warned. "And when I do, Charla, you're going to jail."

Fear flashed in Charla's eyes along with hatred. Cabe ignored her mutinous expression, then pivoted to leave.

Jessie followed, her heart thumping wildly. She'd never cared for Charla, but she'd also never thought her capable of murder. But today she'd witnessed a different side of the woman.

A dangerous side that made her wonder if Cabe was right. If Charla was a killer.

CABE REVIEWED THE documents Charla had given him, then the address for the buyer of the artifacts.

"What does it say?" Jessie asked.

"Charla sold them to a man named Mauri Mc-Landon. He lives in Austin." He started the engine and veered onto the highway. "We'll pay him a visit, then I'll drop the evidence in my crime kit at the lab."

Jessie's expression grew pinched, and he knew she was worried about the blood and DNA from her father. The urge to soothe her hit him, but he kept his hands firmly clamped around the steering wheel.

Still, for her sake, he hoped that the evidence exonerated the man.

Forty minutes later, he steered the SUV onto a sprawling piece of property outside of Austin, not a working ranch but a mansion set on fifty acres of prime real estate. Cabe made a quick mental assessment.

McLandon must have a fortune, and was a perfect buyer for Charla. She'd probably expected a hefty cash flow rolling in from the man.

Did McLandon know the artifacts belonged to the Comanches? Did he know about the murders, and if so, had he taken part?

He stopped at the security gate, and punched the button. "Ranger Sergeant Cabe Navarro," he said into the speaker. "I'm here to see Mr. McLandon."

A male voice answered. "Mr. McLandon isn't here right now."

Cabe hissed in frustration. "Can you tell me where he is? It's important I speak with him."

"He left a while ago."

"Does he have an office?"

"Yes, but he's not at the office. I believe he had a business lunch meeting."

"Then give me his cell phone number."

"I'm sorry, sir, but I'm not at liberty—"

"This is a police matter, sir," Cabe cut in bluntly. "Either give it to me, or I'll park myself in the house until he returns."

The security guard sighed loudly, then recited the number. Cabe punched it into his cell phone, but the phone clicked over to voice mail, so he left a message.

"Let's drop by the crime lab, then grab something to eat," Cabe suggested. "Maybe by then, McLandon will have returned my call."

Jessie nodded, and he swung the SUV around and headed back toward Austin. The land was isolated, flat, prime pastureland. In the distance, he spotted some wild mustangs racing across the prairie.

They were beautiful. Big, black horses galloping across the land—free.

He understood that need for freedom.

So why was the woman sitting next to him tempting him to throw aside his own freedom, drag her in his arms and bond with her?

Dark clouds opened up to dump rain on them, and he turned on the wipers and defroster and slowed.

But a truck raced up on his tail, forcing him to speed up. He squinted through the rain to discern the make and color, but only a small swatch of white flashed through the downpour.

Suddenly the trucker behind him gunned the engine, sped up and rammed into him.

Jessie screamed, her hand hitting the dashboard as the impact bounced her forward.

"Son of a bitch." Cabe clenched the steering wheel

in a white-knuckled grip in an attempt to keep the SUV on the road.

But a gunshot pinged the back windshield, then the truck slammed into his bumper again, and sent them careening off the embankment into the ditch.

Chapter Ten

Jessie screamed as the SUV bounced over the ruts and nosedived into a ditch. Tires screeched, metal crunched, and glass shattered.

She covered her head with her arms as the air bag exploded.

Cabe cursed, slashed his air bag, then hers, deflating them. "Are you okay, Jessie?"

"Yes…I think so."

A gunshot pinged off the vehicle from the bank above, and Cabe shoved his door open. "Stay down!"

He vaulted from the driver's seat, crouched down and circled behind the vehicle heading up the rugged slope. Jessie's pulse raced. Once again, she felt like a sitting duck with her life in Cabe's hands.

But another shot shattered the front windshield, and Jessie plastered herself on the seat face down.

Good heavens. Who was shooting at them?

Not her father—he'd never do anything to endanger her life. Besides, since his illness, he'd barely left the house.

But Charla had been irate and belligerent when they'd left her place. Had she followed them and tried to kill them?

CABE WAS SICK OF THIS cat-and-mouse game. He yanked his gun from inside his jacket, jogged up the hill and spotted the tail of a white truck roaring away. He fired at the tires, but the truck was too fast. It disappeared around the curve and into the distance spewing dust and rocks.

Dammit.

His mind ticked back to the details Wyatt and Reed and Livvy had gathered so far. Three people in Comanche Creek owned white pickups. Jonah, Ellie and Charla.

Considering the fact that they'd just left Charla's, she jumped to the top of his suspect list.

Remembering Jessie and the evidence he'd stored in his SUV, he jogged back down the hill. Rocks skidded beneath his rawhide boots as he approached the vehicle. If Charla had fired at them and run them off the road, she wouldn't get away with it.

His front bumper was jammed into the ditch, the rear end crunched from the impact of the truck. A small streak of white paint marred the back bumper.

Relief surged through him.

He'd have forensics process the paint sample—then he'd know who'd been driving that damn truck.

Heaving a breath, he spotted Jessie hunched over in the front seat. The air bag lay in shambles, glass littering the seat and floor. Jessie must have heard him because she jerked up her head.

Her beautiful eyes were wide and frightened, and a sliver of glass had caught in her hair.

Furious that she might have been injured, he stowed his weapon in his holster, then opened the door, knelt and plucked the glass fragment from her hair.

"Are you okay?" he asked gruffly.

She nodded. "Yes."

In spite of her reply, her voice quivered, and she was trembling. Needing to know she was safe as badly as she needed comfort, he pulled her into his arms. A sigh of relief gushed from her, and she fell against him. Breathing in the scent of her hair calmed him slightly, and she clung to him and buried her head against his chest as he stroked her back.

They held each other for what seemed like hours, him simply drinking in her sweetness. When she finally lifted her chin and looked into his eyes, the fear and vulnerability in her expression twisted his stomach into a fisted knot.

Adrenaline still churned through him, but hunger for her erupted like a flame that had just been lit.

To hell with keeping his distance. They'd damn near been killed. His control snapped, and he lowered his mouth and fused his lips with hers.

The low throaty moan she emitted sent a surge of raw need through him, and he deepened the kiss. She tasted delicious, like sweet tenderness and tenacity and a breath of sensuality. Her tongue reached out to tease him, and his chest heaved as he plunged into her mouth and made love to her with his tongue.

His hands dove into her hair, her hands clawing at his arms, and his jacket as if she wanted to strip him. He'd known she'd be a tigress in bed, and the thought of taking her right here in the car made his sex throb and harden.

But the sound of traffic above echoed. For God's sake, he was a law officer, and anyone who noticed that they'd crashed might see them. He couldn't do that to Jessie.

Forcing himself to end the kiss, he pulled away slightly and cupped her face between his hands. They were both breathing raggedly. "We need to go."

She nodded against him. "I know." Yet she didn't release him. Instead she tightened her hands on his chest. "Cabe, my father didn't run us off the road."

His dark eyes studied her. "How can you be sure?"

"Because he wouldn't shoot at me or a cop. He's too smart for that."

"Trace could have taken his truck," Cabe suggested.

"That's possible, but we just left Charla's. She probably called McLandon and warned him we were coming, then she chased us down."

"That's logical," Cabe said. "The truck left paint on my bumper. The lab should be able to identify the make and model. Then we'll pinpoint exactly whose truck hit us."

She slowly dropped her hands from his shirt, although an instant of regret flickered in her eyes. That made him want her even more.

"Then let's go," Jessie said, her voice stronger now. "Whoever murdered those people and cheated my father needs to pay."

CABE RAKED GLASS from his seat, then started the engine. It took several tries before he managed to extract the SUV from the ditch, but finally they bounced back onto the road. While he headed toward Austin, he phoned the sheriff and relayed the situation. "A white pickup truck slammed into us, ran us off the road and shot at us," he told Hardin. "We had just left Charla's. Check and see if she's home. If she is, look for evidence on her truck, maybe a dent or paint scratches."

Hardin mumbled agreement. "I'll drive to her place right now."

"Thanks." Cabe snapped his phone closed and glanced at Jessie. She sat huddled in the seat, her hair blowing from the wind flowing through the shattered window. Still, she didn't complain.

"What are you going to do about your SUV?" Jessie asked.

"While the lab processes it, I'll arrange for a rental."

She shivered and picked another piece of glass from the seat. "I still can't believe Charla tried to kill us."

Cabe had seen worse, but refrained from sharing. "Greed drives people to do unspeakable things."

Jessie lapsed into silence again, and when they arrived at the crime lab, he left her in the front office while he carried the evidence inside.

Gary Levinson, one of the CSI techs, took Jonah Becker's blood and DNA sample, while another tech rushed outside to the SUV to collect the paint sample.

Levinson led Cabe back to his workstation. "I analyzed those two black hairs you brought in from the burial sites."

"Did they match Ellie Penateka's?"

"No. As a matter of fact, the hair was naturally blond, but had been dyed."

Cabe considered that information, but no one specific came to mind.

"The DNA will take time to run, but the preliminary blood test will only take a few minutes."

"Good," Cabe said. Then he'd know if the blood used in the ritual burials matched Jonah's.

"I'm going to arrange for a rental truck while you run the test."

Levinson agreed, and Cabe stepped back into the front lobby and phoned Wyatt to give him an update. "The hairs I found at the burial site don't match Ellie Penateka's. In fact, the strands were naturally blond."

"Hmm, that could be helpful."

"Maybe. See what you can dig up on a man named Mauri McLandon," Cabe said. "According to the papers Charla gave me, he purchased the illegal artifacts from her."

"Hang on and I'll run him through the system," Wyatt said.

Cabe glanced around for Jessie and noticed her deep in conversation on the phone, her brows furrowed with worry.

"Listen, Dad, we'll talk about it when I get home," she said softly. "Please don't upset yourself."

She cast Cabe a wary look, then walked to the corner to speak in private.

"Navarro," Wyatt said, jerking him back to the conversation. "I found McLandon. He's five-eleven, has short brown hair, hazel eyes, weighs about 180. He's an independent dealer with a long line of family money, and lives in Austin."

"Yeah, I know. I went to his house but he wasn't home, and I've left a message on his cell. Does he have a record?"

"He was arrested a couple of years ago for selling a fake painting, but he beat the charges. Claimed he had no idea the painting was a forgery, that someone must have replaced the one he bought with a forged one."

"Call the Austin police and see if they can pick him up for questioning. We need to get the artifacts he bought from Charla back."

"Will do." He ended the call and approached Jessie. She looked exhausted, her hair disheveled, her face showing signs of strain. Judging from the fact that she'd been attacked the night before, suffered a head injury and had nearly died today, she had a right to look frayed.

But he sensed something else was bothering her. Something to do with her father. What was she hiding?

She ran a hand through her hair, then tucked a strand behind her ear. She looked so damn vulnerable that he wanted to drag her in his arms and comfort her again.

Considering they were in the lab and the CSI was processing her father's blood, though, he resisted.

"What's happening?" she asked.

"Let's pick up the rental and grab something to eat while CSI processes my truck and the evidence I brought in."

"They're testing my father's blood?"

He met her gaze, his chest tightening slightly at the apprehension in her eyes. "Yes."

Her face paled slightly, but she pasted on a forced smile of bravado, then followed him outside. They took a cab to the rental agency, rented a Jeep, then found a Mexican cantina in downtown Austin. Jessie nibbled at her burrito while he inhaled a platter of fajitas. He knew she was worried about the test results and couldn't blame her.

If the blood matched Jonah's, he'd have proof that her father was a cold-blooded killer. And he'd have to arrest him.

JESSIE PUSHED AWAY from the table, unable to eat for her churning stomach. Her father had been irate about undergoing more tests.

There had also been trouble on the ranch. Some fencing had been intentionally cut, allowing several head of cattle to escape. The stream in the north pasture had completely dried up, so they needed to move the cattle to another pasture, or reroute water, which would be costly.

The waitress brought the bill, and she reached for it, but Cabe snatched it. "I'll pay."

"We can split it," Jessie offered.

Cabe glared at her. "I said I'd take care of it."

"Fine." Needing a reprieve from him before she broke down, she excused herself and went to the ladies' room while he paid the bill. Nerves knotted her muscles as they drove back to the crime lab.

The CSI tech Cabe introduced as Levinson met them in the front office.

"What are the results?" Cabe asked.

The CSI tech flipped open the folder in his hands. "The blood type did not match Jonah Becker's. He's O negative, the blood from the clay is A positive."

Jessie nearly staggered with relief. "I knew it wouldn't."

"How about the paint sample?" Cabe asked.

"My guy is still working on that. He's running a program to trace the type of paint with the make and model of the vehicle now. I'll call you when he pinpoints the information."

Cabe thanked him, then they walked back outside to the Jeep. The earlier downpour had dwindled to a light rain, the sound almost calming as it drummed on the roof of the car.

"Have you checked Charla's blood?" Jessie asked.

"Not yet, but I intend to." Cabe gave her a sideways glance as he shifted gears and wove into traffic. "What's wrong with your father, Jessie?"

"I don't want to discuss my father with you." Night had fallen, the storm clouds obliterating the moon and casting a grayness across the rugged land as they left the city.

"I'm not the enemy," Cabe said gruffly. "And for what it's worth, I'm glad the blood didn't match your father's. I don't want to see you hurt."

Jessie rubbed her arms with her hands to ward off a sudden chill. "Come on, Cabe. You don't like my father. You wanted him to be guilty."

Cabe's hands tightened around the steering wheel. "That's not true, Jessie. All I want is to find the person or persons responsible for these murders."

Regret slammed into Jessie for her accusation. Cabe had faced prejudices his entire life, and had good reason to have been suspicious of her father.

She wanted to reach out and soothe his jaw, apologize, confess that she admired his dedication to his job. That she actually liked and admired *him*.

And that she yearned for him to kiss her again. Spend the night in his arms. And maybe longer.

But he would be leaving soon, and if she allowed herself to succumb to her feelings, she was terrified she'd lose her heart to him.

And Jessie Becker didn't give her heart to anyone.

JESSIE SHOULD HAVE been relieved her father's blood hadn't matched the killer's, but the fact that she still seemed agitated worried Cabe. There was obviously more to the problems with her father than she wanted to admit.

He remembered the number of pill bottles in Jonah's medicine cabinet and frowned. Just how sick was the man? Was that the real reason Jessie had moved back to the ranch? To take care of Jonah?

His cell phone trilled, and he grabbed it. "Navarro."

"It's Hardin. I went by Charla's house, but she wasn't home so I posted a deputy to watch the house in case she returns."

"Good. I need a warrant for a sample of her blood. Jonah Becker's was not a match. CSI is still working on the paint sample they extracted from my SUV." He glanced at Jessie, and saw her rub her temple. "And Lieutenant Colter is calling the Austin police to pick up McLandon, the man who purchased the artifacts from Charla."

"Thanks for the update," Hardin said. "I'll let you know if Charla turns up."

Cabe snapped his phone closed and glanced at Jessie again. "You look exhausted," he said as they neared the Becker property. "I'll drive you straight to your cabin."

"No, I want to stop by the main house and check on my father."

The rain had died as he pulled through the turnstile gate, drove up the winding drive and parked in front of the main ranch house. Cabe climbed out and followed Jessie inside. Lolita greeted her and asked if she wanted dinner.

"No, thanks, I ate," Jessie said. "I just want to check on Dad."

"He's in the study," Lolita said, then clucked her mouth sadly. "But I'm afraid he's had a bad day."

Jessie thanked the woman, then crossed the foyer to the study, rolling her shoulders as if to prepare for trouble.

As soon as she opened the door, Jonah's ranting echoed from within. Cabe stopped at the doorway to give her privacy, but the man's chalky pallor and wild-eyed look shocked him. Jonah seemed disoriented and confused, a different man from the one he'd spoken with earlier.

"Rachael, don't leave me again," Jonah cried. "Please don't go."

"It's Jessie, Daddy," she said softly. "Calm down. Everything's going to be all right. I promise."

Sympathy for Jessie shot through Cabe. Jonah must be suffering from dementia or some other mental incapacity. That was the reason Jessie had been covering for him. It also meant that someone could have duped him into the illegal land deal without him being aware the documents were forged.

Cabe had the sudden urge to shoulder her burdens. But he didn't want to violate her privacy. Still, standing outside the door and listening as the man continued to rant incoherently and she attempted to calm him took every ounce of his willpower.

Meanwhile Lolita walked in with tea and a tray with pills on it.

Cabe's impatience mounted as the minutes ticked by, but finally Lolita and Jessie came through the door, flanking Jonah on both sides as they coaxed him upstairs to bed.

"I want my nightcap," Jonah mumbled.

"Daddy, you don't need alcohol on top of your medication," Jessie said.

"But Trace always gives it to me," Jonah said in a petulant voice.

"Miss Jessie's right," Lolita agreed. "Mr. Jonah, you need to go to sleep."

Cabe turned away, then paced the foyer, anxious for Jessie to return. When she finally reappeared, fatigue lined her face and her eyes looked bloodshot from crying.

Dammit, he wanted to pull her in his arms and hold her. "Come on," he said softly. "You're going home and to bed yourself."

The fact that she didn't argue indicated the depth of her turmoil, and they rode to her cabin in silence.

Her shoulders sagged as they walked up to the cabin, and she unlocked the door. But she turned to him and stopped him from entering. "Cabe, you can go now. I'm home. I'll be fine."

He stepped inside and flipped on the light. "We've discussed this, and I'm not leaving." He gently took her shoulders. "I'm sorry about your father, Jessie. What do the doctors say?"

Her lip quivered. "They've run tests but haven't found anything definitive. And he seems to be getting worse." Her voice trailed off, and a tear rolled down her cheek.

Cabe clenched his jaw, but his heart ached for her and he pulled her into his arms. She collapsed against him, her body trembling as she struggled to suppress her tears.

Hating to see her suffer, he stroked her hair. "It's all right, Jessie. Just let it all out."

"No," she said, shaking her head. "I can't. I have to be strong for Dad's sake. He's counting on me."

A low chuckle rumbled from him. "You are strong, but you've been injured, shot at and nearly killed. All that and your father's illness, and I'm amazed you haven't fallen apart sooner."

"I don't want to fall apart."

"I know. But you can lean on me, and I won't tell anyone," he said in a teasing tone.

"No, I have to stand on my own." She clutched his arms. "And I have to protect Daddy. If word leaks that he's ill, business investors may refuse to work with us. And even you thought he was guilty of murder."

"Maybe if you'd confided to me about his condition, I would have dismissed him as a suspect earlier."

Her labored breath rattled in the air between them. "I know. But I wanted to protect him. To make him proud… I wanted him to love me."

Her last words wrenched his heart. Emotions churning in his throat, he swallowed to make his voice work. "How could he not love you, Jessie? You're beautiful, strong, smart, you take care of everyone, and you've helped make the ranch a success."

"Then why didn't he want me enough to fight for me years ago?" she whispered. "Why didn't he ever send for me or plan visits?"

Her anguish tore at him, and he had to alleviate her pain. So he lifted her chin, and forced her to look at him. "Ahh, Jessie…"

She tried to look away, seemed embarrassed that she'd admitted a weakness, which only fueled his admiration, and his need to assure her that she was loveable.

And that he wanted her.

Heat speared his body as her gaze met his and passion flared between them. Her feminine scent enveloped him, her eyes implored him to touch her, her lips begged for a kiss.

The pull of passion overcame him, and he succumbed to the need, lowered his head and claimed her mouth with his. She leaned into him, pressed her palm against his cheek, and met his kiss with a moan of desire.

Their tongues teased, danced together in a sensual rhythm that made hunger drive him to slide his hands down her shoulders, then to yank her up against him. She threaded her fingers into his hair, deepening the kiss and stroking his calf with her foot.

A groan of excitement erupted from deep in his chest, driving him to trail kisses along her jaw down to her neck. Hungry for more, he nibbled the sensitive flesh of her ear, then slipped open the buttons of her blouse to reveal luscious breasts encased in red lace.

God, she was sexy. All feminine and needy and whispering erotic sounds that made his sex throb.

With a flick of his fingers, he opened the front clasp of her bra, then hissed a breath of appreciation as her gorgeous breasts spilled from the restraints into his waiting hands.

She threw her head back in abandon, and he accepted her offering, and lowered his mouth to one ripe, bronzed nipple. She groaned and whispered his name, and he licked the tip of the turgid peak, teasing one breast then the other, until her breathing grew raspy.

His heart pounded with the need to take her, fast and furious, but he forced himself to slow down. He wanted to pleasure her, to alleviate her pain for the night.

Dammit, he wanted to forget the case existed, and show her that she could be loved.

That he wasn't the enemy, but a man who craved her body. One who'd wanted her from the moment he'd laid eyes on that fiery red hair and those killer legs.

He sucked her nipple between his lips, and her legs buckled. She clung to him as he lifted her and carried her to her bedroom. With one quick swipe, he tossed the homemade quilt back and laid her on the covers.

His body was wired, tense, his sex hard and aching, about to explode.

But just as he reached for the zipper to her jeans, a boom exploded in the distance.

Jessie stared at him in fear and horror. "That's in the north pasture," she whispered.

Cabe choked back a command to urge her to forget the noise, that he had to have her now, that he wanted to taste the sweet heart of her between her thighs and pound himself inside her until she cried out his name in ecstasy.

But the ground was rumbling, the echo of the explosion reverberating through the room.

They had to go.

PANIC SPURNED JESSIE into action. An explosion had occurred on her ranch. Were animals hurt? Work hands?

Cabe adjusted his jeans, and she realized his erection was still straining against his fly. For a brief second, she allowed herself to revel in the fact that he'd wanted her, and regretted the intrusion.

But the echo of that explosion haunted her. They had to find out what had happened.

"Ready?" Cabe asked.

She nodded, and they rushed outside to the Jeep. Her pulse raced as he sped over the ruts in the dirt road toward the northern end of the land. In the distance, she spotted smoke and dust curling into the darkness, and she prayed none of their hands had been injured.

"What the hell?" Cabe muttered as he threw the Jeep into Park.

Dirt and rock had been disturbed, bushes and small brush uprooted, a mound of broken rock blocking the creek. He removed his weapon and forced Jessie behind him as they climbed out and slowly searched the area.

"The creek in the upper part of north pasture has dried up," Jessie said. "Someone has been sabotaging us."

"No one is here," Cabe said as he swept a flashlight

across the terrain. "The explosion must have been set on a timer." He hissed, then swung around to Jessie. "The burial site. Whoever set this knew we'd come here to check it out. It was a diversion."

Jessie's pulse clamored with the realization that he was probably right, and they raced back to the Jeep, jumped in and flew to the site. As soon as they arrived, they leaped from the vehicle.

"Oh, my God," Jessie gasped, then pointed to a jagged rock. "There's Deputy Spears. He's been hurt."

Cabe pulled his gun again, his gaze skimming the perimeter as he crept toward the deputy, then knelt and checked for a pulse.

"Is he still alive?" Jessie whispered.

"Yes. Go back to the Jeep, call an ambulance and the sheriff."

Jessie's heart pounded as she raced to do as he said. But when she reached for the Jeep door, footsteps crackled behind her.

Then the cock of a gun echoed in the eerie silence.

Fear crawled up her spine, and she started to scream, but the sharp jab of a gun stabbing her back forced her into silence.

Chapter Eleven

Deputy Spears was still alive, but Cabe spotted another man lying on the ground beside the platform Nina had built, and cursed.

Blood oozed from his chest, and his eyes stared blankly into the night, wide with the shock of death. Judging from the description he'd been given of McLandon, he guessed this was the collector who'd bought the artifacts from Charla.

A shuffling noise behind him made him twist around and swing his Sig up, ready to fire. But the blood rushed to his head when he spotted Charla pointing a gun at Jessie's head. Charla looked panicked, wild-eyed. Dangerous.

"Charla," he said between clenched teeth, "what are you doing?"

Her hand shook as she waved the .38 at Jessie's temple. "Make a move and I'll kill her."

"Charla, please don't do this," Jessie whispered. "No one else needs to die."

Charla shoved Jessie down onto her knees in the dirt.

"You should have left things alone," Charla cried. "None of this would have happened if you Rangers hadn't shown up. You've ruined everything."

"McLandon is dead," Cabe said. "Why did you kill him, Charla? Was he getting greedy?"

"Yes, the stupid jerk," she screeched. "He found out there were other artifacts here and got impatient."

"So he set that explosion to draw us away long enough for him to steal some of them," Jessie said.

"Yes," Charla wailed. "I tried to convince him it was too risky, to wait until things died down. But he wouldn't listen."

"So you shot him," Cabe said matter-of-factly.

Charla's face crumpled, tears blurring her eyes. "We fought and the gun went off. It was an accident." She snatched a hank of Jessie's hair and Jessie winced in pain.

"But it won't be an accident if you kill Jessie and me," Cabe said.

"Please, Charla," Jessie said. "We'll tell everyone you didn't mean to kill him."

"Was Billy's death an accident, too, Charla?" Cabe said harshly. "Or did you kill him because he threatened to expose you?"

"I didn't kill Billy," Charla shouted. "I would never have hurt him."

"But you doctored the papers for the land deal, then arranged the deal with Jonah."

A brittle laugh resounded from Charla. "Yes, and we made a good deal. He got the land and I got the artifacts."

"You took advantage of my father," Jessie shouted.

"Do you know how valuable those artifacts are?" Charla screamed. "They're worth a fortune."

"Yes, they're invaluable," Cabe said between gritted teeth. "But those artifacts belong to the Comanche Nation."

Charla shook her head madly. "Why? So they can sit in some stupid museum?"

"Is that why you killed that antiquities broker, Mason Lattimer?" Cabe asked. "And Ray Phillips? They discovered you didn't rightfully own those artifacts, and threatened to overturn the deal."

"Those stupid men panicked," Charla snapped. "They claimed there were spirits on the land, that they had been haunting them, that we had to return the artifacts."

"So you lured them out here, then murdered them and buried them in a ritualistic style to throw off the police and make them think that Daniel Taabe had killed them," Cabe said. "That's cold, premeditated murder, Charla."

Jessie twisted her head around to glare at Charla. "My father was sick, and you made the Rangers suspect him. How could you put him through that, Charla?"

"Shut up!" Perspiration trickled down Charla's face, and she raised the hand holding the gun and swiped her hair back from her face. "You should have stayed out of it, Jessie."

"And you shouldn't have murdered those innocent people!" Jessie snapped.

Cabe's finger tightened on his trigger, ready to fire, but Jessie swung her body around and jabbed her elbow into Charla's knee.

Charla yelped in pain, her leg buckling. She grappled

for control, but her gun fired into the air, and she fell backward and dropped the gun.

Cabe lunged forward in attack, and kicked the weapon out of reach. Charla struggled to push herself up, but Jessie punched her in the face, and she cried out as blood spurted from her nose.

Screeching like a crazed person, Charla launched up to attack Jessie, but Cabe aimed his gun at her chest. "It's over, Charla. Touch her and I'll shoot."

Charla froze, and he helped Jessie stand, keeping his Sig trained on Charla. The realization that she'd been caught registered in her defeated look, then she began to sob pathetically.

CHARLA LOOKED SO pathetic that Jessie almost felt sorry for her. But she had almost killed her, and she had committed multiple murders.

Sheriff Hardin roared up with Dr. McGrath, the coroner, on his tail, and an ambulance.

Cabe pushed Charla toward the sheriff's car while the paramedics rushed to take care of Deputy Spears.

"Charla tried to kill Jessie, and she confessed to murdering Lattimer, Phillips and McLandon," Cabe said.

Charla balked against the handcuffs, but Cabe squeezed her arm tightly. "There's no use fighting it, Charla. We caught you red-handed. You're going to jail for a long time."

"What about Marcie and Daniel Taabe?" the sheriff asked. "Did you kill them, too?"

"No," Charla cried. "I swear I didn't."

Jessie frowned. Why would she deny murdering two

other people when she was already going to jail for four counts of murder?

"Get in the car." Cabe shoved Charla's head down until she relented and collapsed in the backseat of the squad car. When the door slammed shut, pinning her in, she started to cry hysterically again.

Cabe shook his head in disgust, then turned to the sheriff. "McLandon, the man who bought the artifacts from Charla, is over there. He was shot in the chest. Charla claims it was an accident, that they fought for the gun and it went off."

The coroner nodded. "I'll do an autopsy." He headed over to examine the body. Cabe bagged Charla's gun and handed it to the sheriff. "Courier this over to the lab. It's probably the gun that was used in the other shootings."

"Good work," Sheriff Hardin said. "I'll drive Charla to the jail and let Dr. McGrath take care of moving McLandon's body to the morgue."

"Make sure he goes by the book. We want every piece of evidence possible to make sure Charla's arrest and confession sticks."

Hardin made a low sound in his throat. "Don't worry. I want this over with just the same as you do so peace can be restored in Comanche Creek."

One of the medics approached. "How is the deputy?" Cabe asked.

"He took a hard blow to the head, but he should be all right. We're transporting him to the hospital now."

"I'll check on him later," the sheriff said.

The medics went back to Spears and loaded him in

the ambulance, and Jessie trembled. God, the past few days had been a nightmare.

"I'm going to drive Jessie back to the house, Hardin," Cabe said. "Call me if you need anything."

Jessie tore her gaze away from Charla locked in the police car. Still, the sight of the dead body on her father's land sent a shiver through her.

Cabe took her elbow and guided her to the rental Jeep. By the time they reached her cabin and went inside, a tremble had started deep inside her that made her legs wobble.

Cabe caught her arm. "You're shaking, Jessie."

"I don't know why," she said, hating the quiver to her voice. "It's over now."

Cabe turned her to face him and stroked her arms. "You did great back there, but now the adrenaline is wearing off. It's a natural reaction." He pulled her toward the bathroom. "Come on, a hot shower will do wonders."

She nodded numbly, the sound of his strong masculine voice so hypnotic that the images of the dead man faded, and memories of what they'd been doing before the explosion returned.

She welcomed the reprieve from the horror and embraced the hunger that ripped through her. Cabe was here now. He had saved her life.

He would leave once Charla confessed to the other two murders.

She couldn't let him walk away without being with him.

"Come with me, Cabe," she whispered.

His dark brown eyes skated over her, searching. Desire flashed in the depths but also caution.

"You've had a rough night, Jessie. You need rest."

Her heart swelled at the concern in his gruff voice. "No, I need you, Cabe."

Raw need darkened his eyes, and his breath hissed out. Still, for a moment, he stood stock still, and she thought he was going to turn her down and leave.

But emotions replaced the mask of control in his eyes, and he pressed a hand to her cheek. "If anything had happened to you," he murmured gruffly, "I couldn't have stood it."

"Nothing happened," she said softly.

A muscle ticked in his jaw. "But I let Charla get to you."

She pressed a kiss to his palm. "You saved my life, Cabe."

A heartbeat of silence stretched between them, then hunger flared in his expression, and she saw him relent to the heat between them.

With a sultry smile, she led him to the shower. Muttering her name in a throaty whisper, he reached for her shirt, and slowly unfastened the buttons, then eased the garment off her shoulders.

His gaze greedily raked over her chest.

A slow smile twitched at her lips, just before he tilted his head and claimed her mouth with his. Erotic sensations pummeled her as he probed her mouth apart with his tongue and trailed his fingers over her shoulders.

There were too many clothes between them.

Heat enflamed her as their movements became more frenzied. Their clothes fell to the floor in a mad rush, but she paused to drink in his heavenly body. Big muscles that bunched in his arms and chest, a smooth, corded torso that tapered to a trim waist and thick thighs. And his sex, huge and hard, jutted toward her in invitation.

She trembled again, the chill inside her earlier turning into a minefield of hot, explosive aching.

He paused to stare at her, too, his dark gaze roving from her breasts to her hips and then her heat. A feral gleam lit his eyes, and he made a guttural sound of need that brought erotic sensations cascading across her body.

"You are so damn beautiful, Jessie." He trailed his hands over her bare shoulders, then flipped on the warm water and urged her beneath the spray. He reached for the sponge and soaked it, then traced it down her body, pausing to watch her skin bead with the soap bubbles.

She moaned as her nipples hardened, turning to turgid peaks, then he dropped the soapy sponge and used his hands to tease and explore her. She did the same, her fingers gliding over firm taut muscles, diving into his hair and pulling him close for another kiss. Tongues danced and mated, their bodies slid against one another, and he flipped off the water, grabbed a towel and hastily dried them.

"I can't wait any longer," he said in a passion-glazed voice, then scooped her into his arms.

Jessie feathered her fingers through his hair, brushing it from his forehead. "Then don't."

In three quick strides, he crossed the room and eased her onto the bed. Desperate to feel him inside her, she reached for him, clawing at his shoulders as he knelt above her and cupped her face between his hands.

She wanted the moment to last forever. To know that he wouldn't leave after they made love.

But Cabe and her long-term was impossible. Men always left. Nothing good ever lasted.

So she closed her eyes and savored the moment.

CABE'S HEART POUNDED as he rose above Jessie. She was so damn beautiful and wonderful that he felt humbled that she wanted him.

Her red hair fanned across the pillow, and her rosy lips were parted in invitation. He drank in the image of her opening to him, of her nipples pink-tipped and pebbled, waiting for his mouth. Her sweet feminine scent sent shards of need through him. And her slick heat lay at the center of her creamy thighs, a home waiting for him.

Hungry to taste her, he kissed her lips first, deeply, plunging his tongue inside her mouth in a teasing dance. His breath caught at the sound of her excited moan, and he dragged his lips down to her throat, gliding his tongue along the sensitive skin of her earlobe, then paving a delicious path to her breasts.

One hand twisted her left nipple between his fingers while his lips sucked her other one into his mouth. She bucked, rubbing her foot along his calf, her body quivering as he suckled her. He laved both breasts, his hunger mounting at the feel of her soft skin brushing his, her hips undulating beneath him.

She threaded her fingers into his hair, then clutched his shoulders, urging him to enter her. But he wanted to prolong her pleasure, so he dove south toward the heart of her femininity, licking her belly, then he parted her legs and swept his tongue over the sensitive flesh of her inner thighs.

"Cabe…"

A smile curved his mouth at her breathy sound, and he licked his way toward her heat, then over her swollen nub, teasing her until her body began to convulse with her orgasm. The taste of her honeyed release sent erotic sensations assaulting him.

He had to have her.

Groaning her name, he rose above her again, then guided his erection toward her damp chamber. She lifted her hips, her body trembling, begging for him to fill her.

Enflamed by her hunger, he reached for his pants on the floor, grabbed a condom, ripped it open and sheathed himself.

She was fumbling to help him, stroking his shaft, urging him to hurry. Heaving a breath to control himself before he burst, he kissed her again, then thrust inside her.

She was so small, tight, her insides clenching as he pounded inside her. Panting, she wrapped her legs around his waist, allowing him even deeper access. Excited by her throaty moans, he stroked her over and over, cupping her hips in his hands and building a frantic rhythm until her body quivered, and she climaxed again. Her cries of pleasure triggered his own release, and his own orgasm built, powerful and intense.

His chest clenched and spasms rocked his body. He'd made love to a lot of women, but never had he felt so connected, as if he'd lost his heart and soul in the moment.

The thought sent a lightninglike bolt of fear through him. No, he couldn't fall for Jessie. Couldn't allow himself to feel anything but the pleasure of the moment.

They belonged to two different worlds. She was a Becker. And he was a Texas Ranger, not a man with a woman in his future.

Chapter Twelve

Jessie curled into Cabe's arms, her body still humming from the aftermath of their lovemaking.

Lord help her, but she didn't want him to ever leave. She wanted to have him in her bed every night, holding her, making love to her, groaning her name as he came inside her.

The fear that she'd fallen in love with the Ranger gnawed at her, threatening to ruin the moment, but she pushed it away.

Nothing mattered now except that she was safe, that Cabe was holding her, that they'd finally found the killer tormenting Comanche Creek.

Content with his big body beside her, she fell into a deep sleep. Dreams of Cabe filled the night.

The two of them were riding across the pasture on horseback with the wind whipping through her hair. His Stetson was cocked to the side, giving her a glimpse of the sexy smile that he saved only for her. The grass was green, wildflowers dotted the hill, and the air smelled of honeysuckle and spring.

They galloped over to the pond, then climbed down, and Cabe suddenly knelt in front of her and took her hand. Tears pooled in her eyes as he removed a velvet ring box from his pocket and opened it. A stunning engagement ring glittered up at her.

"Oh, my God, that's beautiful."

Moonlight highlighted his bronzed skin, and he suddenly looked nervous. "Will you marry me, Jessie?"

Pure joy flooded her chest. "Yes, of course, I will. I love you, Cabe."

His hand shook as he slid the ring on her hand, then swept her into his arms and kissed her. "I love you, too."

Suddenly the shrill ringing of her cell phone jarred her from the blissful dream. Jessie sat up, searching the bed for Cabe, but he stood at the window, his back to her.

"Cabe."

He slowly turned toward her, and her heart clenched at the turmoil in his eyes. He'd tugged on his jeans, but hadn't buttoned the top button and they hung low on his hips, making him look sinfully sexy. Her gaze was drawn to his bare chest, then the bulge in his fly, and she ached to beg him to come back to bed.

But her phone trilled again, and the hunger in his eyes faded as his look turned brooding and dark.

"Your phone is ringing." His hooded gaze raked over her breasts where the sheet had fallen down, and her body tingled. She wanted him, needed him. But he didn't make a move to come back to her.

Feeling vulnerable, she jerked up the sheet, then scrambled to reach her phone on the nightstand. "Hello."

"It's Lolita, Miss Jessie. Your father…he had a rough night. I think you should come. I've called the doctor."

Worry immediately knotted her shoulders. "I'll be right there."

Cabe's eyes narrowed. "What's wrong?"

"My father had a bad night," Jessie said, reaching for her shirt. "I…want to talk, Cabe, but—"

"You have to go," he said matter-of-factly. "And so do I."

She tugged on her shirt and pulled it together, then walked over to him. The remnants of her dream taunted her. "Cabe, about last night—"

He pressed a finger to her lips. "We both know I'm leaving Comanche Creek, Jessie." He gestured outside. "This ranch is your home. I don't belong here."

Hurt knifed through Jessie. The scent of his skin, of their sex, clung to him, making her belly clench. She finally understood how her mother could become so enamored with a man that she'd throw herself at him. The thought of never seeing Cabe again terrified her even more than the thought of getting hurt.

Had she become like her father over the years, closing herself off to relationships because she couldn't face rejection?

Maybe it was time she stopped allowing fear to rule her life.

Inhaling a deep breath for courage, she decided to be honest with herself and with him. "I…love you, Cabe. We could make it work if you wanted."

He shut his eyes for a moment, but his posture stiffened, and he clenched his jaw.

When he finally looked at her again, regret shone in his eyes. "I'm sorry, Jessie. You want this ranch, a family, Comanche Creek as a home. Things I can't give you."

Pain rocked through her. She'd given him her heart, yet he didn't love her.

"Now, go to your father. I need to interrogate Charla, and tie up the loose ends to the investigation."

Without another word, he grabbed his shirt, his gun and jacket, then pulled on his boots, and walked out the door.

Jessie waited, hoped, prayed he'd look back, but he didn't.

WALKING OUT OF JESSIE'S bedroom was one of the hardest things Cabe had ever done.

Last night had been so damn…erotic.

Emotions he'd never thought he'd feel had crowded his chest while he'd watched Jessie sleep. Curled in his arms, she looked like an angel. He'd felt himself sinking into fantasies, falling for her, *needing* her.

He didn't want to need anyone.

Yet, for a brief moment he'd imagined sleeping with her every night. Making love to her every day.

Sharing a life with her that would last forever…

But that was impossible. Their two worlds divided them.

Loving someone meant risking losing them just as he'd lost his mother and brother years ago.

He never wanted to endure that kind of pain again.

Still, part of him wanted to go with her to see her

father, wanted to help shoulder the burden of his illness and any other problem she encountered.

Dammit. He had to go. Finish tying up the case.

Jessie was tough and strong and would survive just fine without him.

I love you, Cabe...

No, she didn't love him. She couldn't. She'd just been through a terrifying ordeal, and he had been close by to comfort her. She would forget him after he left, find another man to hold her, comfort her, make love to her.

Anger shot through him at the thought, protective and possessive instincts surfacing.

Dammit. He had to let her go.

Daylight shimmered off the drive as he slid into the Jeep, jammed the key into the ignition and peeled from the drive. He forced thoughts of Jessie from his mind as he left the ranch and drove to the jail.

Sheriff Hardin was already in his office, and gestured to the coffeepot so Cabe helped himself to a cup. "Have you been here all night?" Cabe asked.

Hardin shook his head. "No, I left one of the deputies here to guard Charla."

"Did you get Charla's official statement?"

"No, she was so hysterical I had to call the shrink who worked with her at the pysch ward when she was admitted before. He came over and gave her a sleeping pill to calm her."

"You think she'll try to plea out on an insanity charge?"

Hardin shrugged. "Either way, we have to make sure she stays locked up. She might have killed the first victim out of panic, but the others were premeditated. And using that clay to glue the victims' eyes shut to imitate a ritualistic burial, that was damn near cunning."

"I agree. Call her doctor back and tell them we need a blood sample to confirm that it was her blood in the paint used on the victims' faces."

Hardin nodded. "I'll take care of it."

Cabe adjusted his Stetson. "I'd like to question her again. I want her confession in writing."

Hardin glanced outside. "Jerry Collier is on his way. He's representing Charla."

Cabe shook his head. He still didn't like the sleazy lawyer. He could have his own agenda—he probably wanted to make sure Charla didn't implicate him in the phony land deal.

Hardin strode down the hall to escort Charla to the interrogation room. Just as he'd said, Collier arrived, clutching a briefcase in his hand, a pompous look on his face.

"Ranger Navarro, have you questioned my client without me?"

Cabe silently cursed. "Isn't this a conflict of interest for you, Collier?"

"Absolutely not. Now take me to Charla."

Cabe retrieved the tape recorder from his crime kit along with the case folder, and he and Collier met Hardin and Charla in the interrogation room.

The normally flamboyant woman looked disheveled and withered as she sank into the straight, hard chair. Her face was pale, makeup smudged, and purple bruises darkened the skin beneath her bloodshot eyes.

Cabe pulled out a chair and faced her. "Charla, let's start from the beginning."

She stared up at him with glassy eyes. "I told you everything last night."

Cabe removed a picture of Lattimer and Phillips, pointing out the way their eyes were glued shut. "You lured these men out to the Becker land and killed them, then used clay from Jonah Becker's land to make the ochre to glue their eyes shut."

Her mouth tightened as she studied the grotesque photos of the men. "Yes, I told you I did. They wanted to expose me and the deal I made with Jonah."

"Did Jonah know the land belonged to the Native Americans?" Cabe asked.

She ran a trembling hand through her hair, and sighed wearily. Her normally manicured fingernails were jagged and chipped from where she'd chewed on them during the night.

"No. Jonah hasn't been well," Charla said in a tired voice. "Billy and I doctored the paperwork to make it look as if the land originally belonged to Jonah's great-great-grandfather."

Cabe nodded. "And Marcie knew all this, so you killed her?"

Charla jerked her head up, shaking her head wildly. "I told you I didn't kill Marcie or Daniel Taabe. And I certainly didn't kill my husband."

Cabe and Hardin exchanged frustrated looks. Why would she deny killing them when she already had four murders on her head?

"But you killed McLandon?" Cabe pressed.

"Yes," she cried. "Yes, I did because he was going to ruin me forever."

"That's enough," Collier interjected. "My client has a diminished mental capacity."

Hardin glared at Collier. "Your client is ruthless, and confessed to premeditated murder."

"You mean McLandon was going to expose you, don't you, Charla?" Cabe snarled.

Charla broke down and began to sob again, muttering incoherently.

Cabe and Hardin spent twenty more minutes reviewing the case details, but she still refused to admit that she'd killed Marcie, Daniel or Billy.

Cabe's cell phone vibrated and he checked the number. Wyatt.

"Excuse me. I need to take this." He gestured to the sheriff. "Get Charla's confession typed up and make sure she signs it."

Hardin agreed, and Cabe stepped from the room. "Sergeant Navarro."

"Cabe, it's Wyatt. The Captain is satisfied that you've solved this case and is ready to disband the task force. He's already spoken to the press and announced that Charla Whitley was responsible for all the murders and is in custody."

Cabe cursed. Charla's confession—or lack of one regarding Marcie's, Billy's and Daniel's deaths—troubled him. "We can't do that just yet. Hardin and I just interrogated Charla again, and she insists she didn't kill Marcie, Daniel or Billy."

Wyatt made a frustrated sound. "Hell. Then keep

pushing, Cabe. I'll stall for time, but I want every detail to fit before you pull out."

Cabe agreed, then snapped his phone shut. If Charla hadn't killed Marcie, Billy and Daniel, then their killer was still at large.

His stomach knotted.

And Jessie might still be in danger.

"DADDY, PLEASE CALM DOWN," Jessie cried. "I hate to see you so agitated."

Her father had been pacing the study, pulling at his hair, and making a ticking sound with his teeth. "It's the ghosts, those damn Indian spirits," he ranted. "They're haunting me, Jessie. They beat their war drums all night long. They're coming for me."

Jessie twisted her hands together. Cabe claimed he felt and heard the spirits on the land, but now her father heard them, too? Was it possible? Or was her dad hallucinating?

"Daddy, Dr. Pickford is on his way." She reached for her father to urge him into a chair, but he shoved her hands away and continued pacing.

"I don't need a doctor. I need someone to get rid of these damn ghosts. Give them back the land if that'll satisfy them."

A knock sounded at the door, and Lolita poked her head in. "Dr. Pickford's here."

Jessie sighed, feeling helpless. Her father needed medical treatment, maybe even hospitalization. "Thanks, Lolita. Please send him in."

Her father swirled around, walked to his cabinet, removed a bottle of Scotch and poured himself a glass.

"I know you think I'm crazy, Jessie, but I'm not. There's something awful going on here at the ranch. I wish to hell I'd never bought that land."

"So do I, Daddy," Jessie said as the doctor entered the room. That sale had caused so many deaths so far. Maybe he was right. Maybe the land was cursed.

"Just let Dr. Pickford take care of you, Dad."

He grabbed her hands in a death-grip. "And you take care of the ranch, Jessie. Promise me you'll do that, and that you'll get rid of that Ranger."

Except she didn't want Cabe to leave Comanche Creek. "Dad, Ranger Navarro will be gone soon. He arrested Charla Whitley last night for those murders, so hopefully soon things will settle down."

Her phone buzzed in her purse, and she gave her father a quick kiss on the cheek. "I'll be back in a little while." She spoke to the doctor, then left the room, dug her phone from her purse, and flipped it open. "Hello."

"Jessie, listen to me. Charla Whitley didn't kill Marcie. I know it."

The woman's voice sounded strained. Frightened. Familiar. "Who is this?"

"Linda Lantz." Her breathing rattled between them as if she might be running. "Oh, God, Jessie. I know I should have come forward, but I was afraid I'd end up dead like the others."

Jessie's lungs constricted. "Linda? I was afraid you were dead. Where are you?"

Linda started to cry. "I'm scared, Jessie."

"I know," Jessie said softly. "But the Rangers will protect you. Cabe Navarro is here. You can trust him."

Linda sighed shakily. "All right, I'm at the Bluebonnet Inn under the name of Megan Burgess."

"I'll be right there." Jessie snapped her phone closed.

Dear God, Linda knew who had killed Marcie. And the killer was after her.

She had to hurry.

Chapter Thirteen

An uneasy feeling stabbed at Cabe as he and the sheriff retreated to Hardin's office.

"Charla signed the confession," Hardin said. "But Collier will try to convince the judge to commit her to a mental institution instead of serving time in prison."

"You think the judge will agree?" Cabe asked.

Hardin shrugged. "I don't know. But as long as she can't hurt anyone else, I don't see as it matters. And with her confession about the illegal land deal, the land can be returned to the Comanche Nation so you can soothe those ruffled feathers."

"True." Although Jonah and Trace Becker wouldn't be pleased.

Cabe leaned against the doorjamb. "Lieutneant Colter called, and the Ranger Captain wanted to pull us from the case."

"So you'll be leaving town?" Hardin asked.

Cabe huffed. "Not yet. It still bothers me that Charla insists she didn't kill Marcie, Billy and Daniel."

Hardin scrubbed his hand through his hair. "Yeah,

that doesn't make sense. She's already confessed to multiple murders. What's two or three more?"

Cabe grabbed a chair and parked himself in it. "Maybe we should review our suspect list."

Hardin nodded. "First, Deputy Shane Tolbert, who was found holding the Ruger that murdered Marcie. Then Jerry Collier, who handled the land deal and works for Becker. Then Jonah Becker."

"We can rule out Jonah."

Hardin slanted him a sideways grin. "Why? Because you have the hots for Jessie?"

Cabe gritted his teeth. "No. Because he's ill and having memory problems. That's the reason Jessie has been handling things in town and with the task force. They didn't want anyone to know he was sick."

"You're sure this illness is for real?"

"Yeah. I saw him myself. He's not strong enough physically or mentally to have pulled off those murders. In his confused state, he could easily have been duped into the land deal." Cabe paused. "Of course, Trace is still on the list. He's conniving, spoiled and jealous of Jessie."

"What about Ellie?"

"The hair fibers I found at the original cadaver site didn't belong to her. But she and Trace are having an affair, so I suppose they could have conspired. Although I can't imagine Ellie allowing any artifacts to be removed from the land. And if she'd known it was a sacred burial ground, she would have moved hell or high water to keep the property in the custody of the Comanches."

"Maybe Trace lied to Ellie."

Cabe nodded, following his train of thought. "And he wanted to protect his daddy's investment."

"He could have killed Daniel because Daniel was onto the truth. And if Trace is in love with Ellie, getting Daniel out of the way paved the road for Ellie to move up the political chain."

"Ellie does have high political aspirations," Cabe admitted. The uneasy feeling he'd had earlier escalated. "I'm going to phone Jessie and warn her to stay put, that another killer may still be at large. Then let's plan some kind of trap to draw the second killer out of hiding."

He punched in Jessie's number, but the phone rang and rang and no one answered. Finally the voice mail kicked on.

"Jessie, this is Cabe. A killer still may be out there, so stay with your father." He snapped his phone shut. He didn't like the fact that she hadn't answered.

He never should have left her at her house. What if the killer had already gotten to her?

JESSIE'S CELL PHONE BUZZED in her purse as she parked on Main Street, but it rolled over to voice mail before she could dig it out. She cut the engine, then checked the message box in case Linda had changed her mind. But the message was from Cabe.

He had called to warn her that another killer was still at large. She started to return his call, but Linda had sounded spooked, and Jessie was afraid that she'd run again if she didn't hurry to her.

Throwing the car door open, she slung her purse over

her shoulder, checking around her for strangers as she walked up to the porch to the Bluebonnet Inn. Praying Linda hadn't already bolted, she opened the front door. The owner, Betty Alice, was carrying a tray of tea and shortbread to the buffet in the dining room.

"Why, Jessie Becker, what are you doing here?" Betty Alice said with a grin.

"I came to meet one of your guests, Betty."

The plump woman's eyebrows shot up. "Really? A young man?"

Jessie's cheeks stained pink as she remembered her lovemaking with Cabe. She wished she was here to meet him for another romantic rendezvous.

"No, Betty. A woman named Megan Burgess."

"Oh, yes, that sweet girl. She's in the pink room. Do you want me to ring her and tell her you're here?"

"No, thanks. I'll just go straight to the room. She's expecting me."

Betty Alice threw her fingers up in a wave, and Jessie rushed up the staircase, then down the hall to the pink room, the room where Betty housed most of her female guests. It was decorated with antique furniture and a balcony opened to the second-floor porch.

The door was closed, so Jessie knocked. "Linda... Megan?"

Her pulse raced as she waited, and she thought she heard movement inside, so she knocked again. When Linda didn't answer, she jiggled the doorknob and the door swung open. She made a quick scan of the room and bath, but they were empty.

The door to the porch was open, so she crossed the

room and stepped onto the porch, hoping to find Linda outside. But the porch was empty, too.

Frantic, she glanced down at the gardens, and saw a few people on the sidewalk on Main Street, but no Linda. A movement caught her eyes, and she noted a tall woman with black hair wearing a scarf weaving through the crowd. She'd seen the same woman at the town meeting.

Linda had been blonde, but she was using a fake name. What if she'd dyed her hair?

Something must have spooked her, but what? Had the killer found her?

Deciding she'd walk to the jail from the inn, meet Cabe and explain about Linda's call, she left the room, hurried down the stairs and rushed out the front door.

But just as she stepped from the porch, Deputy Shane Tolbert appeared. "Jessie?"

"Yes?"

"I was just at the jail. That Ranger asked me to escort you home."

Anger slammed into Jessie. Was Cabe going to avoid her now they'd made love? Pawn her off on another cop? And Shane Tolbert? She didn't even like the man. "Why didn't he come himself?"

Deputy Tolbert shrugged. "I don't know. I'm just following orders." He gestured toward his squad car, which was parked behind her Jeep. "Get in and I'll drive you."

"I can drive myself," Jessie said emphatically. "Besides I want to go to the jail and talk to Cabe. I have some information about the killer."

Shane's brow shot up. "Tell me and I'll pass it on."

So Cabe was avoiding her. "I spoke with a woman who claims she knows who killed Marcie and Daniel Taabe. I was supposed to meet her here, but when I went to her room, she'd disappeared."

"I see." His eyes turned cold, his voice hard. "Get in the car, Jessie."

He reached for her arm, but she jerked away. She refused to let Cabe dismiss her. "No. I told you I'm going to the jail."

Shane grabbed her arm again so tightly this time she winced. Then he pulled his gun from his holster and pointed it at her waist. "I said get in the car."

Fear rolled through Jessie as he shoved her into the backseat of his car, forced her to lie down, then slammed the butt of the gun against her head. Pain ricocheted through her temple, and the world spun as he jumped in the driver's seat and raced off.

Dear God, he had killed Marcie and Daniel.

And now he was going to kill her, too.

CABE HAD TO FIND JESSIE. While Sheriff Hardin phoned Livvy to check on her, Cabe called Jessie's house, desperate to hear her voice, and hating that he was desperate. But if anything had happened to her...

"Becker residence. Lolita speaking."

"This is Ranger Navarro. Is Jessie there?"

"No, sir," Lolita said. "She left a while back."

"Do you know where she was going?"

"No, she didn't say." The woman's voice dropped a decibel. "Why, Ranger Navarro? Is something wrong? Has something happened to Miss Jessie?"

Cabe gritted his teeth. "Not that I know of. I'm just trying to reach her. If she phones you or comes back to the house, please have her call me."

Cabe thanked her, hung up, then phoned her brother. "Trace, this is Ranger Navarro. Where are you?"

"Why do you want to know? So you can harass me again?"

"I'm looking for your sister, Trace. Is she with you?"

"Hell, no. I thought you were glued to her."

Cabe silently cursed. Trace could be lying. "I asked you where you are."

"I'd rather not say."

"Listen to me, Trace, if you have your sister or have hurt her, you'll answer to me."

"I told you my sister isn't with me," Trace bellowed. "I'm in Austin. I came over here to talk to one of my father's doctors about more tests."

Cabe clenched the phone. Dammit. Trace's heated response had the ring of truth to it. "If you hear from her, tell her to call me."

Snapping his phone shut, he headed out the door of the jail. Maybe Jessie had ridden back to the burial sites on her property. But a young woman with shoulder-length black hair barreled into him. He threw up his hands and caught her by the shoulders.

"Help, you have to help me!" she cried.

"Whoa." Cabe pulled her into the front office and shut the door. "Calm down and tell me what's going on."

"My name is Megan Burgess…" She paused to take a breath. She was trembling, her green eyes flashing with fear. "I mean Linda Lantz."

"Linda Lantz? You worked for Jessie and disappeared two years ago?"

She bobbed her head up and down, then pressed her hand to her chest to catch her breath. "Yes, but I left town because I was afraid someone would try to kill me."

He noticed her black hair, remembered the photo he'd seen of the blonde Jessie had identified as Linda Lantz, and realized that the two dyed strands he'd found at the burial site belonged to her.

"Come on and sit down," he said, coaxing her to a chair. "Tell me everything."

She twisted her hands in her lap. "I was working on the Becker ranch two years ago when I saw Marcie fake her kidnapping and death. But then I noticed a man in the shadows and he saw me, so I ran." She lifted a hand to her cheek. "I left town, had plastic surgery and dyed my hair so he couldn't find me."

Cabe's chest tightened. "Did you recognize the man?"

She shivered. "Yes."

"But you didn't come forward?" Cabe asked angrily.

"No," she whispered raggedly. "I told you I was scared. But then when I heard about those bodies being found, and that Marcie was really murdered, I came back to town. I knew I had to do something, but I didn't know whom to trust. Then I saw you were with Jessie, and I was afraid you'd blame me, that you would arrest me for not coming forward sooner. I thought…I hoped you'd find out the truth before anyone else got hurt."

Cabe gripped her arms. "Linda, who killed Marcie?"

Her lower lip quivered, and she sucked air through her teeth. "Deputy Tolbert."

Cabe's heart pounded.

"I called Jessie to tell her," she rushed on, "and she came to meet me at the Bluebonnet Inn. But then he showed up."

"Deputy Tolbert showed up?"

She nodded miserably.

Cabe's blood ran cold. "Then what happened?"

Panic and fear strained her features as a sob escaped her. "He took Jessie."

Chapter Fourteen

Cabe's heart lurched to his throat. The mere idea that Jessie's life hung in the hands of a ruthless killer made him furious.

"Listen to me, Linda, where was Deputy Tolbert taking Jessie?"

"I don't know," Linda whispered. "I really don't know. He just shoved her in the back of his car and hit her with the butt of his gun."

Cabe sucked in a sharp breath. "Was she all right?"

"I don't know." She swiped at more tears. "He must have knocked her unconscious, because she didn't get up. Then he jumped in the front seat and sped off."

Cabe stood. He had to take action. Every second that passed meant Tolbert was getting farther and father away with Jessie.

JESSIE SLOWLY ROUSED back to consciousness, but her head throbbed and nausea clogged her throat. She wiggled, determined to escape, but her hands were tied behind her back, and she was gagged.

The police car hit a bump, and pain ricocheted through her skull as the car rumbled across a road that had to be dirt and gravel. How long had he been driving? How far were they from Comanche Creek?

How would Cabe ever find her?

Despair clawed at her chest, and tears pooled in her eyes. Cabe had no idea Shane had killed Marcie, much less kidnapped her. He didn't even know Linda was still alive.

Had Shane killed her, too? If so, where was her body?

Feeling panicky, the urge to sit up and scream at him, to beg and plead with him to let her go, drummed through her. Yet what good would that do?

She blinked back tears, frantically struggling for control. She had to stay calm, try to talk to Shane, stall.

Wait for an opportune moment so she could escape.

The past few years of her life flashed back in vivid clarity. Her college years where she'd held herself back from relationships. Her pride in earning her degree.

The fights with her mother.

Her vow to be different, not to be led around by a man, or to lose her heart. But it was too late for that.

She had lost her heart to Cabe.

But he had rebuked her. Didn't love her.

Her chest clenched as her dreams died. Secretly she had wanted stability. Her mother's love. Her father's. The family that had been broken years ago.

And she wanted it with Cabe.

But that would never happen.

Still, she would survive. She had to.

Her father needed her.

The car swerved, then spun right, the terrain growing even more rocky and uneven. Gravel crunched beneath the tires, and she focused on the sounds outside, hoping for a clue as to where Shane was taking her.

The river…she heard the river raging over rocks. It had to be the Colorado River, which wasn't too far from Comanche Creek. Shane slowed slightly, and her heart raced as she glanced up at the hulking trees and realized the place was secluded.

Suddenly the car bounced over another rut, gravel spewed, and he screeched to a stop. The movement jarred her, and she almost rolled off the seat and onto the floor, but caught herself with her foot.

Shane climbed out, then jerked the back door open, and grabbed her arm. She tried to remain limp, pretended to be unconscious, but he shook her as he dragged her from the car.

"Come on, Jessie, you should be awake by now."

His icy, harsh voice sent a shiver up her spine, and she opened her eyes and gave him a hate-filled look.

With a vicious yank, he dragged her across the rocky terrain. "You know too much now."

Jessie gulped back fear, visually assessing her surroundings. They were in a secluded spot by the river, and an old log cabin sat near the bank, shrouded by bushes and trees. The place looked run-down, and weeds choked the front porch as if no one had been here in years.

The isolation of it made her tremble in blinding panic. Even if Linda had survived and mustered up enough courage to go to the police, Cabe would never know to look for her out here.

She tried to speak to him, but the gag caught the sound. Shane cursed, then pulled it from her mouth and threw her up against a tree.

"Where are we?" Jessie asked in a ragged whisper. The rough bark bit into her back and arms, the vile stench of a dead animal wafted around them.

"My father's cabin," Shane growled. "But don't get your hopes up. No one knows this place even exists."

"Your father does," Jessie cried. "Do you think he'd want you to do this? To kill me?"

"My father loved me. He'll do anything to protect me."

"That's right, Ben is in jail now, isn't he?" Jessie snarled. "All because you're a murderer."

Shane raised his hand and slapped her hard across the cheek. Perspiration trickled down Jessie's back, the sting of the blow making her ears ring. "You're good at beating women, aren't you, Shane?"

"Shut up, Jessie. You should have stayed out of this." Shane pressed the gun to her temple. "Now tell me where Linda is."

Hope budded in Jessie's chest. If Shane wanted to know Linda's whereabouts, she must still be alive. Determined not to reveal how terrified she really was, Jessie jutted up her chin. "I don't know."

"She called you?"

"Yes," Jessie said. "She told me what you'd done, that you killed Marcie." Jessie sucked in a sharp breath. "Why, Shane? Because she broke up with you?"

"She loved me," Shane said in a sharp tone. "She loved me and we should have been together."

"But she discovered that you're a brute," Jessie said.

"That's why she left you. But you couldn't stand that, could you? You were a bully, and she was so scared of you that she faked her own kidnapping and death."

His hand connected with her face again, this time even harder. Despite her bravado, tears stung her eyes and escaped. She clenched her jaw to keep from screaming.

Shane pressed the gun to her temple. "Tell me, Jessie. If you don't, I'm going to kill you."

"You don't have to do that," Jessie whispered.

A leering, evil look flickered in his eyes, a maddening look that made her heart thunder.

"I have nothing left to lose, Jessie," Shane bit out. "So either tell me where to find her, or you're a dead woman."

CABE CALLED HARDIN IN TO the front office, introduced him to Linda, and explained what had happened.

"You saw Marcie fake her kidnapping and death?" Sheriff Hardin asked.

Linda nodded miserably. "But Shane came after me and I ran. I was…so scared." She swiped at tears rolling down her cheeks. "Maybe if I'd come forward then, these other murders wouldn't have happened."

Cabe almost felt sorry for her. *Almost.*

But Jessie was in the hands of a madman now, a dangerous cold-blooded killer.

Hardin propped his hip on the edge of the desk. "Hell, Livvy's going to have a fit. She was the one who figured out that Shane's prints had been planted on that gun."

"It's not her fault. Shane intentionally cleaned the gun, then planted just enough prints to confuse us and force you to release him," Cabe said in disgust.

Hardin pulled at his chin. "I hope she sees it that way." He turned to Linda. "Did you see Shane kill Marcie?"

A pained look crossed her face. "Yes. After she disappeared the first time, we connected. We came back here to make things right, but Shane found Marcie in the cabin. I ran outside and hid in the woods, but then he shot her."

Cabe scrubbed his hand over the back of his neck. "We have to find Shane before he hurts Jessie." He turned to the sheriff. "You know Shane better than anyone, Hardin. Do you have any idea where he'd take Jessie?"

"To his place maybe?"

"I doubt he'd be foolish enough to do that, but why don't you check?" Cabe suggested. "I'll call Lieutenant Colter and brief him, then question Shane's father and see if he might know."

"I'll put out an APB for Shane on my way to Tolbert's place and alert the county deputies to watch out for his car."

"Check out Ben's place as well as Charla's," Cabe said. "He might hide out in one of those."

"Right." Hardin gestured to Linda. "Come on, Linda. I'll drop you with Ranger Hutton, so I can make sure you're safe."

Cabe punched in Wyatt's number and gave him a quick update.

"Son of a bitch," Wyatt muttered. "I never did trust Tolbert."

"We have to find him fast," Cabe said. "He's already killed. He won't hesitate to take another life."

"I'll see what I can dig up on him. Maybe he owns some other property where he might take Jessie."

A place where Shane might dump her body. The

unspoken words hung between them, making Cabe's pulse pound.

"Let me know if you find anything," Cabe said, already heading to the back of the building toward Tolbert's cell. "Ben's still here. I'll see what he knows."

"I doubt he'll cooperate," Wyatt said. "He's protected Shane at every turn."

"He'll talk," Cabe said through clenched teeth.

Wyatt started to say something, but Cabe cut him off and disconnected the call. He didn't give a damn right now about protocol or Tolbert's rights or his job.

Jessie's life was all that mattered.

He grabbed the keys to the jail cells, praying it wasn't already too late.

Rolling his hands into fists, he stalked down the row of cells. Charla was hunched on the cot, her eyes glazed as she stared at her hands. She looked pitiful, dazed, in shock, as if she'd slipped into a catatonic state.

She and Shane were friends. If Ben didn't cough up something useful, he'd question Charla.

Ben sat up from his cot when Cabe approached, his face haggard, his hair disheveled, his eyes filled with anger.

Cabe unlocked the cell and stepped inside. "I need to talk to you, Tolbert."

"What the hell do you want?"

"We have a witness who says that Shane killed Marcie. Now your son has kidnapped Jessie Becker at gunpoint."

Ben lowered his head into his hands and muttered a curse. "Dear God…"

"You'd better be praying," Cabe said sharply. "And

you'd better be talking. Because if Shane kills Jessie, I'm holding you responsible, too."

"I don't care about myself," Ben muttered. "All I care about is my son."

"What about Jessie Becker?" Cabe growled. "She's an innocent woman, Ben. How can you not help us?"

"I can't believe this is happening," Ben said in a brittle tone. "He won't hurt Jessie. He won't."

Cabe jerked him by the collar. "He killed Marcie, and maybe Daniel and Billy. What's one more death to him?"

Ben snapped his head up, his expression pained. "No…Shane is not a killer."

"Shane *is* a murderer. And if he kills Jessie, I'll make sure he receives the death sentence."

"No, you can't do that," Ben hissed.

"I can and I will," Cabe ground out. "Murder during a kidnapping is a capital offense. And Texas has the highest rate of executions in the nation."

"You son of a bitch—"

"Where would Shane take Jessie, Ben?"

Ben's eyes bulged with fear. "I don't know."

"Come on, Ben." Cabe tightened his grip on the man's collar, choking Ben. "Do either of you own a cabin or property other than your houses in Comanche Creek?"

Ben's weathered face reddened as he struggled to breathe. "I can't let you hurt my son."

"But you'll let him kill an innocent woman and go to death row," Cabe said. "What kind of man are you?"

Cabe's cell phone trilled, and he reluctantly released Ben, and checked the caller ID. Lieutenant Colter.

He punched the connect button, one eye trained on Ben in case he tried to escape. "Navarro."

"Cabe, Ben owns an old fishing cabin on the Colorado River. It's about a half-hour drive from Comanche Creek."

Cabe gritted his teeth. A half an hour? It might as well be days away.

"I would send a chopper to see if his car is there," Wyatt continued, "but it's too remote and there's no place for it to land."

"I'm on my way." Cabe jotted down the GPS coordinates, then turned to Tolbert. "I know about your cabin," he said in a lethally calm tone. "And if I'm too late, then you and your son are going to pay."

He slammed the jail cell door shut, and jogged outside. He had to hurry.

Jessie's life hung in the balance.

Chapter Fifteen

"Shane, please don't do this," Jessie cried. "You need help."

"What I need is to know where Linda is." He jammed the gun at her back and shoved her toward the porch. She stumbled over loose rock, and nearly tripped as she climbed the steps, but he caught her arm with clawlike fingers, yanked open the screened door, and pushed her inside.

Muttering a curse, he threw her down on the floor. Jessie's knees slammed into the wood floor, pain rocketing through her bones as she struggled to catch herself. But with her hands tied behind her, it was impossible, and her shoulder slammed into the corner of the rickety pine coffee table.

She frantically glanced around the cabin for an escape route, a weapon, anything to use to defend herself. But the room was bare except for the worn plaid sofa, the stuffed trout on the wall, the photos of Shane and his father when he was younger on a fishing trip.

"Think about your dad, Shane," Jessie pleaded. "Would he want you to do this?"

Anguish darkened Shane's eyes. "My father is in jail because he was trying to protect me from going to prison. Getting arrested would kill him now."

"You think he wants you to murder again?"

"I think he wants me to stay free, and that's what I'm going to do." He grabbed her arm and yanked her up, then shoved her into one of the kitchen chairs. She stiffened as he retrieved a piece of rope dangling from his pocket, and began to tie her to the chair.

She kicked at him, but he slapped her across the face again, and she tasted blood.

"This is what we're going to do," Shane said with a mad look in his eyes. "You're going to tell me how to contact Linda, then she'll come here and we'll all have a big party."

"I don't know how to contact her," Jessie said. "She called me."

He ran to the car, then returned a minute later with her cell phone, and Jessie gritted her teeth as he scrolled through her phone log.

"Dammit, I thought you said she called you."

"She did," Jessie said. "But I don't know where she was when she called."

Shane paced, waving his gun and scraping his hand through his hair, obviously desperate.

Jessie's phone buzzed, and her stomach clenched. What if it was Linda or Cabe calling?

Shane grabbed the phone and glanced at the caller ID. A menacing smile curved his mouth as he punched the connect button.

"Hello, Ranger Navarro."

Jessie's heart raced.

"Yes, Jessie is here with me. Why don't you join us?"

Cold fear slid along Jessie's spine. If Cabe showed up, he'd kill them all.

She loved Cabe too much to let him die.

"And if you want to see Jessie alive," Shane said in a sinister tone, "then bring Linda with you."

"No," Jessie cried. "It's a trap, Cabe. Stay away!"

Shane slammed her phone shut, then stalked over and whacked the gun against her temple. The impact sent her head flying backward, and stars danced in front of her eyes.

She tried to fight it, but once again the darkness swallowed her.

CABE CURSED A BLUE streak at Tolbert's demands.

He had no intention of going back for Linda. He'd been in law enforcement long enough to know that Shane was out of control, desperate, and that he wouldn't let Jessie, Linda or him go.

Not alive.

Better he protect Linda and save Jessie.

If he had to kill Shane to do it—hell, he would have no qualms. The man deserved to die.

The Jeep ate the miles to the cabin, the sun fading and night creeping on the rugged terrain. Limestone bluffs and scrub brush dotted the horizon, the more populated area disintegrating into isolated dirt roads and cabins scattered occasionally along the Colorado River. He checked the coordinates and turned onto a side road that had never been paved, sweat beading on his forehead as the Jeep bounced over the ruts and ridges.

The quiet normally would seem peaceful, but tonight it only served to remind him that Jessie was out here alone in the hands of a killer with no way to call for help.

And no one to hear her if she did.

Before he left the vehicle, he called Hardin in for backup and gave him the coordinates. But he couldn't wait. Every minute that passed gave Tolbert time to kill Jessie.

Needing the element of surprise on his side, he crept down the dirt road, weaving around the curves and through the tangled trees, slowing a half of a mile from the place where the cabin should be. He pulled to the side of the one-way stretch, cut the engine, then slipped from the Jeep, making sure he eased the car door closed so as not to make a sound.

Images of Jessie tormented him as he slowly crept along the edge of the woods toward the cabin. Jessie riding up to him on that horse wearing her Stetson with her gorgeous red hair flying in the breeze. Jessie scrunching her nose when she'd argued with her brother at the town meeting. Jessie shivering after she'd nearly been shot and killed.

Her rosy lips parted and inviting, plump and sensual, so ripe he'd had to have a taste. Her fingers diving into his hair as she dragged his mouth closer for a kiss. Her tongue flickering out to meet his, her body quivering beneath his touch. Her skin glistening with the moisture from his tongue. Her nipples hard and thrusting upward in need of his mouth.

But another image replaced those sensual ones—
Jessie tied and bound, Shane Tolbert's gun pressed to
her head. Shane pulling the trigger and killing her just
as he had Marcie, Daniel and Billy.

Panic threatened to immobilize him, but he inhaled
sharply and wrestled with his temper. He had to shut out
the images. Stay sharp and focused.

Save Jessie, or he wouldn't care if he lived to see
another day himself.

Shadows flickered off the giant oaks as he scanned
the riverbank in case Tolbert had decided to lay a trap.

Or in case he'd already killed Jessie and planned to
dump her body into the Colorado River.

Fear and fury raged through him at the thought. If he
had killed Jessie, he'd not only arrest the bastard, he'd
make him suffer first.

He finally spotted the cabin through the thicket of
mesquites and oaks, and saw Tolbert's car parked at an
angle in the overgrown weed-choked yard. A quick
visual of the perimeter, but he saw no one outside.

Mentally he debated his tactics. Sneak up on the
house and look inside, or call out to Tolbert and lure him
outdoors in the open away from Jessie?

He didn't have time to second-guess himself. He
inched through the woods toward the house, but the
front door opened, and Tolbert appeared in the doorway.

The deputy stood ramrod straight, his brows furrowed as he searched the yard and riverbank. Cabe
ducked behind a tree, holding his gun at the ready, then
peered around the massive tree trunk. His lungs constricted as Tolbert dragged a burlap bag from the

inside and hauled it across the yard toward the river a few feet away.

God, no… He was too late.

Tolbert had already killed Jessie.

A soul-deep ache gripped his chest in a vise. No…he couldn't be too late. Jessie had to be alive.

He needed her. Wanted her.

Loved her.

Grief clogged his throat, threatening to spill over. But Tolbert shoved the bag into the river, jerking him back to reality.

Dammit, he couldn't let Tolbert escape. Wielding his gun, he ran through the woods until he reached the clearing near the river.

"Stop!" he shouted. "Don't move, Tolbert."

Tolbert swung around and fired his weapon. Cabe felt the bullet skim his left arm, and cursed, then jumped behind an oak to dodge the next shot.

"Dammit, Tolbert, you aren't going to get away with this," he growled. "The sheriff knows you killed Marcie. Even your father knows the truth."

"You stupid Indian," Shane yelled. "I'll kill you and then I'll leave this godforsaken town, and no one will ever find me."

"The Rangers will track you down," Cabe shouted as he wove through the trees to close the distance between them.

Adrenaline pumped his blood, and he launched forward and fired at Tolbert.

Tolbert cursed and fired again, but Cabe released another round, this time hitting Tolbert in the shoulder and the knee. Tolbert went down in pain and dropped the gun as he grabbed his chest.

Cabe threw himself at Tolbert, knocking him backward. But Tolbert was strong and fought back, and managed to land a blow to Cabe's belly.

The punch only riled his anger, and his need to make Tolbert suffer, and Cabe hit Tolbert dead-on in his injured shoulder. Tolbert shouted an obscenity, and Cabe slammed his foot into the man's bleeding kneecap. Tolbert buckled with a moan, and Cabe pinned him with his body.

Out of the corner of his eye, he saw Jessie's body begin to float, then sink into the raging river, slamming against the jagged rocks with the force of the current.

Dammit, he had to hurry.

Every second that passed meant Jessie was sinking deeper into the icy water. If she was alive, she wouldn't be for long.

He grabbed his gun from the dirt, and pointed it in Tolbert's face. "Move again and I'll blow your damn head off."

Shane stilled, his eyes feral and dawning with the recognition that he had been caught.

Cabe straddled him, the gun still firmly jammed into the bastard's face as he yanked his handcuffs from his back pocket. Then he forced Tolbert to roll over facedown, and clicked the handcuffs around his wrists. Determined to make sure Tolbert didn't escape, he dragged him over to the porch edge, found some rope on the porch and tied his arms and feet to the wood posts.

"You son of a bitch," Tolbert spat. "You can't send me to jail."

"You're not just going to jail," Cabe growled. "You're going to be sitting on death row."

"It's too late to save your girlfriend," Tolbert muttered.

Hating the man with every fiber of his being, Cabe rolled his hands into a fist and punched Shane in the face again, this time so hard the sound of bones crunching rent the air.

Blood oozed from his shoulder wound and knee, and Shane's eyes turned buggy as he faded into unconsciousness. The urge to finish him off clawed at Cabe.

But fear for Jessie rattled him into action.

Sweat poured down his neck as he sprinted toward the riverbank. He scanned the surface, but he didn't see her.

Stowing his weapon beneath a jagged rock at the river's edge, he threw off his jacket and boots, then scanned the river again. He finally spotted the top of the burlap bag floating downstream, but most of her body was submerged.

Praying Shane had lied, that Jessie wasn't dead, he dove into the water. The current swept him toward some jutting rocks, but he put his head down and swam with all his might, heading downstream toward Jessie. One stroke, two, a rock jabbed his thigh, others battered his body as the current raged on.

Ignoring the pain, he increased his speed, channeling all his energy into reaching Jessie. Precious seconds passed, but he forced himself to believe that she was still alive.

Driving himself harder, he finally reached her. Diving

beneath the water, he pushed her body above the surface. Panting for air, he secured her under his arm and swam toward the riverbank.

Rocks pounded them, and the current was relentless, but a minute later he managed to reach the riverbank. He rolled her to the edge, then climbed out and hauled her body to a clearing. His chest ached for air, his body thrumming from exertion as he ripped open the top of the bag and tore it down the center.

Jessie lay inside, bound and gagged, her eyes closed.

God, no…

She wasn't breathing.

Chapter Sixteen

Cabe's life flashed before his eyes as he stared at Jessie's lifeless body.

You have your job, Cabe.

That was all that had ever mattered before. But suddenly that job meant nothing without Jessie to share his life with.

If only he hadn't left her alone. If he'd made her go with him...

No, he couldn't give up now.

He punched in Hardin's number, at the same time retrieving a knife from his pocket and slicing Jessie's bindings. Then he jerked the gag from her mouth, hoping that would allow her oxygen. "I'm almost there," Cabe said. "I've got Tolbert, but Jessie's in trouble," he shouted to Hardin. "Get an ambulance up to Tolbert's place ASAP."

He didn't wait on a response. He tilted Jessie's head back, checked her air passageway, then leaned over and began CPR. Sweat trickled down his neck as he blew air into her lungs and pumped her heart.

Agonizing seconds crawled by as he counted compressions. "Come on, Jessie, you can't die on me. I love you, dammit."

One, two, three, another breath, over and over and over. "Jessie, sweetheart, I need you. Come back to me."

The breeze picked up, rattling the trees and tossing leaves across the ground. The sound of the river slapping the embankment echoed around him, a reminder that Jessie had been lost to it moments before.

He lowered his head, blew another breath into her mouth, then stroked her cheek. But she lay limp, her body cold, stiff, unmoving, and terror clogged his throat. Had he fallen for Jessie only to lose her?

JESSIE FELT COLD. She was drowning. Her head ached, her body hurt, she couldn't move. And it was dark…so dark.

She hated the darkness.

But slowly a light invaded that darkness. The sound of a gruff voice echoed in the distance. Strong hands were beating on her chest, and a warm mouth closed over hers, blowing air into her lungs. Air she needed desperately to claw her way from the endless sea of darkness.

She had to fight her way back. Cabe was calling her. And her father needed her…

A sharp burning sensation climbed from her stomach to her throat, and her belly clenched and spasmed.

He pounded her chest again, and suddenly she felt the surge of water coming back up. Choking and coughing, she slowly opened her eyes, and Cabe angled her head sideways while she purged the water from her lungs.

She lifted her hand and clutched at him, and he

patted her back. "That's good, Jessie, that's good, baby. Let it out."

She spat out the water, dragging in a breath, trembling and shivering.

Cabe slid his arms around her, then pulled her to him, rocking her back and forth. The ambulance wailed in the distance, and he tried to warm her until the medics arrived. Then the ambulance screeched up, the medics raced toward them with a stretcher.

She hated hospitals.

She wanted Cabe to go with her. But his hand slipped away from her as the medics carried her to the ambulance.

TWO DAYS LATER, Cabe, Wyatt, Livvy and Reed met to tie up the details of the case.

Cabe requested a meeting of the townspeople, and once again, the room was packed, the room divided with the Caucasian and Native American factions.

Mayor Sadler called the meeting to order, and demanded that the two groups be quiet, then turned the meeting over to Cabe.

"Deputy Tolbert has been arrested for multiple counts of murder," Cabe said. "He confessed to killing Marcie, Daniel Taabe and Billy Whitley and will be going to prison for the rest of his life. Charla is being moved to a psychiatric unit and will spend the rest of her life locked up as well."

"What about our land?" Ellie Penateka asked.

"With Charla's testimony regarding the illegal land deal, the land will be returned to the Native American faction."

Trace Becker remained quiet, almost contrite as he sat beside Collier.

"Will charges be filed against Jonah?" Ellie pressed.

"No. Evidence suggests that Jonah did not know about the impropriety. Also, on his behalf, Jessie made arrangements to allow the Native American factions access to much-needed water on the Becker land."

Rumbles of questions began, but he quickly silenced them. "It's a win-win situation for everyone, Ellie. This town needs to work together, and the Beckers have taken the first step. Hopefully, others will follow their example, and today will mark the beginning of peace in Comanche Creek."

Clapping and shouts of agreement echoed through the room, and Cabe felt a sense of relief that he had managed to do the impossible—solve the case and bridge the gap between the two factions in his hometown.

But he couldn't have done it without Jessie. He wove through the crowd toward her, his chest swelling with love and admiration for her. But he still hadn't been able to confess his feelings. Still wasn't sure how he could handle a relationship, or if he'd be any good at it.

And Jessie deserved the best of everything.

She smiled at him, and his heart melted. "Everyone seems pleased, Cabe. And you deserve the credit here, not me."

"You played a big part by meeting with the Natives, Jessie. I meant what I said. You are an excellent role model."

A blush stained her cheeks, but an underlying

sadness still lay in her eyes. "I'm just glad they don't hate my father anymore. Now, if he'd only get better."

He wanted to promise her that Jonah would recover, but he wasn't certain about the man's condition. Still, he wanted to try something. "I'm going to visit my father, Jessie." He paused, a tightening in his belly.

"Oh, Cabe," Jessie said softly. "I'm glad you're going to reconcile with him."

He nodded. "We'll see."

Pleasure lit her eyes but a wariness remained also. He'd hurt her when she'd confessed that she loved him and he hadn't reciprocated.

He wanted to. In fact, he itched to take her back to her place and make love to her, but he had to speak with his father first.

"I'll see you again before you leave town?" Jessie asked.

He cleared his throat, then gave a clipped nod, but didn't trust his voice to speak, so simply walked outside to his car.

Memories of his family and his cultural teachings suffused him as he drove to the reservation. Pleasant memories mixed with others that troubled him, but the values and traditions he'd been taught as a child had shaped him into the man he'd become.

So had the hard lessons.

He parked the SUV, and walked across the limestone rocks, solemn and respectful as he approached his father, Quannah Navarro. His father had been named in honor of a great chief.

His hair had grayed and lay in a long braid down his

back, his sun-bronzed weathered skin looked leathery and wrinkled, but deep spiritual beliefs and strength still emanated from him.

Quannah didn't bother to look up. He had probably known Cabe was coming. He seemed to posses a sixth sense that had been almost eerie.

Except he'd believed the Big Medicine Ceremony would save Simon, and it had failed.

"Cabe, my son, I've been expecting you."

Cabe dropped to the ground, then sat cross-legged beside his father and the fire. He addressed him with the Comanche word for *father*. "Ap. You heard what happened in town?"

"Yes." Folding his gnarled hands, his father turned toward Cabe, his gaze intent as he studied Cabe. "You bridged the gap between our people and the others. Comanche Creek will change because of you, my son. For that, I am proud."

Emotions threatened to choke Cabe. His father had never praised him before.

"I knew that you would do great things, Cabe," his father said. "You are strong, brave and understand the old ways and the new."

Cabe nodded. Maybe he'd had to leave and then return to Comanche Creek to appreciate his heritage. "There is one more problem," Cabe said. "The land has been returned to the Comanche Nation, but there were angry spirits on the burial grounds."

"Yes."

"Jonah Becker has been ill lately," Cabe said. "Jessie

said he insisted that he was hearing ghosts, that the spirits were tormenting him."

"His actions disturbed the spirits, so they have been haunting him."

Cabe nodded. He'd never thought he'd ask his father for help, but Jonah's illness was tormenting Jessie. "Is there any way to put the spirits to rest and free Jonah?"

A smile curved his father's mouth, and he pushed his frail body to his feet. "Yes, my son. We will use meditation and perform the ancient ritual. Then there will be peace."

Cabe nodded. Then Jessie would be happy.

And her happiness was the most important thing in the world to Cabe.

ANXIETY NEEDLED JESSIE as she rode out to the sacred burial land.

Linda, who'd come back to work for her, had phoned to say that Cabe and an older Native American man were performing some kind of Native ceremony on the property.

Firebird cantered up to the site, and she slid from her palomino, but kept her distance and she watched from the shadows as they lit a fire and chanted to the heavens. Cabe had dressed in Native attire, the feather headdress accentuating his strong cheekbones and bronzed coloring.

She watched, mesmerized by the beauty of their movements, intrigued by the sound of their ancient language.

And Cabe… He was so damn sexy she wanted to eat him alive.

Yet she understood the spiritual significance as well as the importance of this shared moment with his father and dared not interrupt. More than anything, she wanted Cabe to make peace with his past, to reconcile with his father.

And she wanted him to know that she respected his culture and would support his choices. Even if it meant leaving her forever.

Although she'd doubted Cabe's ability to sense the spirits when she'd first met him, she believed now that he had actually heard and felt them.

Suddenly a shimmering glow radiated over the land like some kind of magic dust had been sprinkled over the terrain, and the whisper of the breeze—or ancient voices—rose in the wind.

Jessie stilled, mesmerized by the beautiful picture and the rhythm of Cabe's and his father's voices mingling with the spirits.

A heartbeat later, the earth quieted, the glow settled like a blanket over the land, and Cabe paused, opened his eyes and looked up at her.

Jessie's heart swelled with longing and with love. She'd never thought she could care so much about another person. But it wasn't the infatuation that her mother harbored over man after man. Jessie's love was unselfish and would last forever.

In fact, she loved Cabe enough to let him go if that was what he wanted. He was like a wild untamed mustang who needed to run free.

And she would not take away that freedom.

CABE SENSED THE UNCERTAINTY in Jessie's reaction as she watched him and his father. He'd known the moment she'd arrived, had intentionally not spoken to her, gauging her reaction to his customs and his father.

Now that he'd reconnected with Quannah and the Comanches, he regretted the time he'd lost. He wanted his father and the Comanche beliefs to be a part of his life, a part of his family's life.

If Jessie would have him and make that family with him.

But would her father accept him?

Quannah looked drained, and Cabe silently vowed to return to speak to Jessie, then drove his father back to the reservation, thanked him and gave him a hug.

"It will work out with your woman," his father said, as if he'd read Cabe's mind. "You have my blessings, son."

Cabe shook his hand. "Thank you for putting the souls to peace, Ap." He only hoped that doing so had healed Jessie's father.

"Before you go, I have something to give you." Cabe followed his father to his hogan, where he handed him a beaded pouch.

"This belonged to your grandmother. It is yours now."

Cabe's chest clenched as he removed the silver-and-garnet ring. It was decades old, handcrafted by his ancestors. It might be considered an artifact, was priceless, a part of his family's heritage.

"Give it to your wife-to-be," Quannah said. "Then she will be one with us."

Cabe nodded. He only hoped Jessie would accept it, and that Jonah didn't cause problems. Jessie's family was too important to her for him to come between them.

He carefully stowed it back in the pouch and headed to the Jeep.

His pulse raced as he drove to the Becker land. As he expected, he found Jessie at the main house. When he entered, sounds of joy echoed from Jonah's study.

Lolita bustled out with a smile and welcomed him. "*Sí,* Ranger Navarro. It is a blessed day. Mr. Becker has come back to us. He is his old self again." She suddenly reached up, cupped his face in her hands and kissed both his cheeks. "Miss Jessie told me what you did. You have cured him. It's a miracle! I get champagne for us to celebrate!"

Cabe grinned at her excitement, and hoped that Jessie and her father would both welcome him. Perspiration dotted his hands as he knocked on the study door and pushed the door open. "Jessie?"

Her beaming smile greeted him. "Cabe, come in. My father has had a radical recovery."

He entered, filled with trepidation over Jonah Becker's reaction to him. The man he'd met before had been ill, disoriented, but the real Jonah was an unscrupulous businessman.

"Jessie, Mr. Becker."

Jonah gave him a wary look, but waved him in. Jessie introduced him, and he extended his hand. "Mr. Becker, we met once, but it's nice to see that you're feeling better."

"My daughter tells me that I owe my recovery to you. That you solved the murders around here, saved her life, and that you and your father exorcised the spirits from my land."

He gritted his teeth. "We didn't exorcise them," Cabe

said, protective of his cultural beliefs. "We helped the spirits find peace. And you aided in doing that by returning the land to them."

Jonah shrugged. "Yes, you're right. It did belong to them." He slid a protective arm around Jessie. "I want to thank you for protecting and saving my daughter. You did a good job, Ranger Navarro."

Cabe glanced at Jessie. Love for him shone in her eyes, but there was an acceptance there as well. She would not beg him to love her or guilt him into being with her.

Her unselfishness only made his love grow stronger. And it gave him courage. She'd been right when she'd accused him of running before.

He didn't intend to run now.

"I did do my job," he admitted, then squared his shoulders. He faced hardened criminals every day. Why was it so damn difficult to confess that he loved someone, to open up his heart? "But, sir, it wasn't just my job. I care for your daughter."

It was an old-fashioned thing to do, to ask for Jonah's permission. Perhaps even lame. But tradition and family ties mattered, and he would never forget it again.

Sweat beaded on his neck, but he told himself Jessie was important enough for him to take a chance. Although if her father answered no, then he had no idea what he'd do.

"I see." Jonah pinned him with his eyes. "And your intentions, Sergeant Navarro?"

Cabe flexed his hands, trying to shake off his nerves. "I love your daughter, Mr. Becker. And I'd very much like to ask you for her hand in marriage."

Shock flashed across Jessie's face, then a brilliant smile that made his heart pound. She was just as uncertain about her father's reaction as he was, but she took a step toward him, offering hope.

Jonah gave him a long assessing look, then turned to Jessie. "I believe that decision is up to my daughter. Jessie?"

"Dad, I love Cabe," Jessie said softly. "And I would like your blessing."

Emotions glittered in Jonah's eyes. "I love you, too, Jessie. I always have." He pulled her into a hug, and tears trickled down Jessie's face.

"Thank you, Dad."

Jonah wiped at his own eyes, then cut his gaze toward Cabe. "But if you hurt her, Navarro, you'll deal with me."

"Yes, sir." Cabe finally breathed. "You have my word, sir, that I will love her with all my heart and protect her with my life."

He reached for Jessie's hand, pulled the beaded leather pouch from his pocket, then dropped to his knee. "Jessie, I love you. And if you'll do me the honor of marrying me, I will respect you, cherish you and love you for the rest of my life."

More tears filled Jessie's eyes, tears of joy. "Cabe, oh, yes. Of course, I'll marry you."

His hand shook as he slipped the ring from the pouch, then held it out to her. "It isn't a diamond, but it belonged to my grandmother and has been passed down through my family for generations." He hesitated. "My father said it will symbolize us and the joining of our families and cultures."

"It's beautiful," Jessie whispered. "Absolutely perfect."

His heart swelled as he slipped it on her finger.

An excited laugh came from her, then she launched herself into his arms. Her lips met his, and he kissed her tenderly, passionately, the pent-up need over the past two days rising to taunt him.

Lolita bobbed in with a bottle of champagne, and they pulled apart long enough to toast Jonah and their upcoming marriage. But one toast, and the secret, sultry smile Jessie graced him with indicated she was ready to be alone.

His sex hardened, the need to make love to her overpowering as they rushed back to her cabin and fell into bed.

They made love like teenagers, like lovers, like newlyweds, like a couple who had been destined to be together forever.

And he promised her that they would.

* * * * *

INTRIGUE...

BREATHTAKING ROMANTIC SUSPENSE

My wish list for next month's titles...

In stores from 19th August 2011:

❏ Magnum Force Man – Amanda Stevens

& Powerhouse – Rebecca York

❏ Shadow Protector – Jenna Ryan

& His Case, Her Baby – Carla Cassidy

❏ A Soldier's Redemption – Rachel Lee

& Secret Agent Sheikh – Linda Conrad

❏ Deadlier Than the Male – Sharon Sala &
    Colleen Thompson

Available at WHSmith, Tesco, Asda, Eason, Amazon and Apple

Just can't wait?

Visit us Online

You can buy our books online a month before
they hit the shops! **www.millsandboon.co.uk**